THE POWER OF
ONE TO ONE

THE POWER OF
ONE TO ONE

IAN KENNEDY

BRYCE COURTENAY

MARGARET
GEE

Published by
Margaret Gee Publishing
an imprint of
Margaret Gee Holdings
P.O. Box 221, Double Bay NSW 2028
A.C.N. 005 604 464
Telephone (02) 363 5191

First published in 1995

Distributed by Gary Allen
9 Cooper Street, Smithfield NSW 2164

National Library of Australia
Cataloguing-in-Publication entry

Kennedy, Ian.
    The Power of One to One

    ISBN 1 885574 30 1.

    1. Direct marketing. I. Courtenay, Bryce, 1933–
    II. Title.

381.1

Jacket design by Reno Design Group, Sydney
Typeset by Midland Typesetters, Victoria
Printed by Australian Print Group, Victoria
Production by Vantage Graphics, Sydney

WRITERS' BLOC

THE READER IS ALWAYS RIGHT

Contents

Chapter 9.

'How I learned to bring dead money back to life with a label
attached to my big toe.'

Mail and how to make it work

The paradox of Telecommunications

Anti-attrition and root cause analysis

TV the most powerful media of all

The environment is the most important factor affecting
response

The do's and don't of the Print Media

Public relations, a powerful response technique

The importance of testing

Chapter 10.

'Jesus don't make a souffle rise any higher but He can sure
curdle the sauce on top.'

The genius of the Galloping Gourmet

The psychology of the offer

Prospecting

How to increase response with FREE

The positioning of the premium

How to create a sense of urgency

Twelve different offers

Chapter 11.

'The Manager's row and pulling live lobsters out of Jane
Mansfields bum.'

The talent of Pete and Dud

The worst job I ever had

The importance of headlines

Catalogues—Problems and opportunity

How people read letters

How to turn features into benefits

Words that motivate

How to create effective copy

The Polo Ralph Lauren Australia story

How to create brochures that sell

Coupon check list

Acknowledgements

My life has been enriched by interaction with some remarkable people. The sum total of my experience has as its most vital component, the knowledge, wisdom, compassion, understanding, wit and love of those people whose influence changed my life.

The words of most of the relevant books on direct marketing really come to life when you are debating some of the issues with the author. Being the only Australian for many years on the International Speaking Marketing circuit, gave me the opportunity to meet these authors, and in some cases, develop life-long friendships with the people who have shaped our industry.

To the wisdom of my friend and mentor for over 40 years, Tamp Lynam. To my 'partner' and friend of 25 years, Michael Harrison, who started me down this very exciting road in 1969. To David Ashley-Wilson for the disciplines, both in numbers and in words—a true professional. And to Barbie Davis, the best numbers practitioner in the Australian industry for nearly 25 years.

To my dear friend Eddy Boas, one of the pioneers of the Australian Direct Marketing industry, who gave me my first chance to speak in Australia in the early Pan Pacific days and says he hasn't been able to shut me up since. To Murray Raphel, one of the most loving, caring people I know, and the greatest Direct Marketing speakers in the U.S. today. To Herschell Gordon Lewis, the master wordsmith whose work and books comprise one of the best teaching basis for direct copywriting in the world. To Walter Schmidt, founder of the great Montreaux Direct Marketing Symposium, who made me the first Australian to speak at the Symposium in the 80s and invited me back, and back and back.

And Jerry Reitman, recently retired Vice President of Leo Burnett, the best intellect in the Direct Marketing industry today. Jerry and I have worked, spoken, written, laughed and cried, together all over the world for more than ten years.

To Judy Casey who gave 12 years to working with me on sourcing merchandise.

Finally, after fighting advertising agencies all my life in the battle for Measurable Marketing, I discovered at George Patterson's one of the most remarkable cultures I have ever known in business. Their integrity and loyalty and professionalism is something I never expected to find in the advertising industry. From the indefatigable ex-Chairman Geoffrey Cousins, to the remarkable Alex Hamill their current Chairman. All the extraordinary individuals at Patt's embrace integrity as part of their lives. More than 95% of buy-outs disfranchise the vendor within two or three years. Eight years later, George Patterson's and I are still together working towards many exciting new horizons and my ultimate dream—the true integration of Advertising and Direct Marketing.

My commercial life, and this book, could not have matured without the unflagging help and dedication of Karen Stroud, my assistant for eight years, and before her Karen Spratt, and Marcelle Grolman the talented, wise, creative gold mine who worked on and off with me for nearly 20 years.

This book is the work of all these people and their contribution has, in many ways, been greater than Bryce's or mine. This book belongs to them.

Ian Kennedy

Introduction

The trouble with most marketing text books is that they are dreary. Generally, they are too long and written with a ponderous pen. They are seldom a pleasure to read and more often an onerous duty—something we **have** to do to pass an exam, to get a raise or to become a 'smart-arse' in the boardroom.

When you think about it, the writer of a text book ought to be someone who has gone out and done all the things he or she writes about: men and women who have taken the risks involved in running their own businesses, who have dared their genius to walk the wildest unknown way and who have experienced the disaster of losing, and the thrill of winning, and have survived.

Now, this is not always the case. Business text books are often the stuff from which academic careers and reputations are built. Thus, they are wise in hindsight, hollow in tone and perfect in theory. Boring books that weigh down student's rucksacks and look impressive behind the diamond shaped, lead-light glass book case in the managing director's office. Books to be seen and not heard about again.

So, when Ian Kennedy, one of the world's top direct marketing experts, invited me to co-write this book, I agreed on the basis that it should be a book about a man's life and not simply one filled with the usual diet of business babble.

I also appreciated why he asked me. While he was the perfect man to supply the stuff of which good business text books are made—he has practical experience, commonsense and a willingness to take risks—he was not a writer. I am. We agreed that I would accept the task of writing about the life, times and the wisdom acquired in the course of Ian Kennedy's life and business career.

If there is such a thing as a biographical text book, the story of one man's adventures in the business of life and in the life of business, then this is it. It is a book intended to be a useful, practical, working text book, as well as an interesting story. It is a business reference book which will, hopefully, become dog-eared from use by anyone wishing to venture into the truly exciting business of direct marketing.

I think of The Power of One to One as a simple, accessible reference book overlaid with the humour, wisdom and intelligence of Ian Kennedy, a quietly spoken Australian who has done an awful lot of wise and foolish things in a life which has made him one of the world's most successful direct-marketing people.

My part in this book is a purely practical one. Though I know something of the direct marketing business, I am as a babe in arms compared with my co-author, who brings to my pen all his considerable knowledge and wisdom. Why he should do this, I can't imagine. He doesn't need the money and if I knew this much about anything, I'd keep the knowledge very close to my chest. There is enough original information in this book to make you very rich indeed.

You will gain a great deal from The Power of One to One. Just remember not to falter when you get to the part about crunching numbers. Numbers and direct marketing can't be separated, and the successful use of the numbers is where wealth is created. Numbers can be boring, but it is better to be a little bored before becoming a lot richer!

Direct marketing is essentially a business of people, of their good parts and bad, their greed and anxiety. It is the stuff of gamblers and dreamers, as well as the hard-nosed money men. It will put you into bed with the good, the bad and the beautiful, and it often requires the patience of Job and the optimism of Don Quixote. It is a business skill which can touch human emotions like no other. And when it works well, it is matched by only a few businesses on earth. Indeed, few are more compulsive, or make a man or a woman take greater pride in their work. Enjoy, with our compliments!

Bryce Courtenay

This book is for Alex Hamill,
a friend indeed.

This book is for my son Sam

Ian Kennedy

**Don't even think
about buying this book
until you've read this page.**

Do you honestly need another book on direct marketing?

How many have you already got? Quite possibly a small library full? Many of them say about the same thing don't they? Corny cartoons, mystifying graphs, headlines with dollar signs everywhere, cute slogans in boxes, lists of handy hints to tick and, of course, the promise of your ultimate success on every other page.

And then there are the case histories. No direct marketing book is complete without half a dozen case histories, each of which, you are assured, made the author so much money he never again had cause to design another coupon or reserve a toll-free response number.

Well, if this was true, then what insanity made him or her sit down and write a book spilling the beans? If you had the secret of making big money, retirement-in-the-Bahamas-type-money, and you could reduce your knowledge into a simple set of sure-fire rules, why in God's name would you publish them and sell them for a few lousy bucks? Plainly, you'd clasp them so close to your chest your lungs would collapse.

So, if you think this book is going to save the company, turn your losses into profits overnight, parlay your takings from the family garage sale into a fortune in less than twelve months, or get your foot out of a 'meadow cake' and on to clean green grass, then put your money back under the mattress. Or use it to buy a lottery ticket or a candle, and light it for your favourite saint or some such, but, whatever else you do, *don't* buy this book!

This book is about people. People on a one-to-one-basis. And people are difficult creatures to understand and seldom react predictably. If you are prepared to work harder than most, think more deeply, exercise a fair amount of commonsense, **test everything you do**, subdue your ego, **test everything you do**, listen to what people are saying, **test everything you do**, stop being a smart-arse, **test everything you do**, don't think you know better, **test everything you do**, don't use the argument that your circumstances are unique, **test everything you do**, don't cut corners, **test everything you do**, have the courage to learn from your failures, **test everything you do**, be prepared to spend money on quality merchandise or make an offer that is perceived as valuable, **test it**, make a promise you know you can keep, **test it** … then, and only then, will **The Power of One to One** help you to build a career, run a successful business and allow you to ultimately live in a manner to which you have absolutely no right to become accustomed.

Now, that's a real promise, nay, an unconditional guarantee!

—Ian Kennedy   *—Bryce Courtenay*

P.S. Test everything you do!

Chapter One

People are people through other people

The Xhosa people are the largest African tribe south of the Zambesi river and they have a saying: 'People are people, through other people.'

What the hell does that mean? Well, it means that we only exist because all of us know we exist. A cow doesn't know it's a cow, or a rabbit doesn't try to influence another rabbit to do what rabbits do best after munching lettuce. They are simply programmed to do what cows and rabbits do naturally. Only people know they're people, because without each other we fail to have meaning, or, if you like, we become cow-like or rabbit-like, mooing and screwing.

The gift of speech is only possible because we have been given the gift of imagination. Imagination is one factor which makes us human. It's what makes us afraid or brave, lovers or villains, clever or dumb, good people or bastards. It is also what makes us want things. Imagination gives us choices: we can see things as they are and try to maintain the status quo, or we can *imagine* them as they could be and then work to change them.

Imagination allows us to alter the circumstances around us, that is, to manipulate the environment in which we live and alter the state of all the creatures within it, including ourselves. And the way we manipulate things, change them, is through people. This happens either through consensus, or by force, or by manipulation. It happens through desire, power or greed or the promise of eternal life. This is also what is meant by the term, 'people are people through people.' And people come in all shades and dispositions—saints and sinners, dull and clever, timid and extroverted, good people and, of course absolute shits.

Let me tell you about a real bastard I once knew. A 100-per cent, dyed-in-the-wool, unmitigated bastard!

I was 18 and crazy about cars, so I got myself a job as a junior in a rather upmarket car dealership. Junior salesman was simply a euphemism for the kid who cleaned the cars, learned all the specs off by heart, made the coffee, ran messages and manned the salesroom when everyone else went out to lunch.

I would dream of some rich bloke coming in when I was alone eating my mum's sandwiches. I'd jump up, straighten my tie and with a bit of mercurial salesmanship, I would cover every selling point from chassis to duco and trim, even mentioning the light in the glove box. I'd then take my prospect for a quick drive around the block and have him signed up for a brand new De Soto before the boss had time to properly unfold his napkin at Nick the Greek's before his daily meal of lamb on the bone with rice.

Well, one day it happened. I had a mouth full of peanut butter sandwich, which was giving me a mild dose of lock-jaw, and in walked this guy. Funny how you can smell money. He walked over to a De Soto, a gleaming black bullet of a car, the chrome work adding half a tonne of extra weight for the big six-cylinder engine to cart around. But in those days chrome meant prestige and petrol was practically for nothing, so cars had chrome added like a fat person ladles cream on a bun.

'Get the keys, kid!' The big man jerked his thumb in the direction of the De Soto, 'Let's take this heap of shit for a ride.'

My mouth came unstuck with a loud smacking noise. 'Yessir!'

I was back in a flash with the auto and showroom keys, opened the double doors of the showroom, ushered my client behind the wheel and closed the driver's door for this big fat guy, who was already over-revving the engine. I excused myself to him, rushed into the boss's office and dialled Nick at the restaurant to ask him to tell the boss the showroom was temporarily closed as I was on a demo!

'Wait, I go get him,' Nick had said. 'No, ferchrissake! Just bloody tell him!' I whispered urgently, afraid the boss would walk the five minutes back to the showroom and heist my very first sale.

With my client behind the wheel, we drove out of the showroom. Then, with the horn blasting, and tyres squealing he shoved aside the on-coming traffic and we zoomed away.

He was the world's worst driver and we managed not to get killed about eight times. Eventually we arrived back to find the boss standing on the pavement outside the showroom, with his arms across his chest and steaming from the nostrils like Puff, the magic dragon.

'You're fired, son!' he said out of the corner of a mouth thin as a razor slit. I slid the key into the showroom door to open it. 'Wait till I close the sale,' I thought. Then the boss smiled his big salesman smile as my client lurched the big De Soto into the showroom, stopping only inches short of the door to the customers' lounge. My boss opened the door for the big man to get out.

'Jesus! The bastard's going to pinch my sale!' I thought.

The big man got out from behind the wheel and pulled at the lapels of his coat. 'Naw! Just what I thought. It's a heap of crap!' Without a further glance at me or the boss he walked out of the showroom, each cheek of his big fat arse massaging the other.

The boss indicated in a few carefully selected words that it was appropriate for me to see him in his office. 'Okay, son, you copped a bastard! But we don't sell cars to nice guys, we sell cars to *people* and some of them are bastards and some of them are suckers and some of them are just people looking for a good motor, but *all* of them are customers and *all* of them can be sold, all you've got to do is find out what *they need!*'

He leaned back in his chair and tapped the side of his desk with a pencil, 'As far as I'm concerned you screwed up that sale! You owe me the commission on one black six-cylinder De Soto!'

'Yessir,' I said shamefaced and then asked, 'Am I still fired, sir?'

'What? And lose my commission! Forget it, son, from tomorrow you're a full salesman, but right now get your arse into gear and detail that car so it's ready for the next bastard who comes in!'

I'd learned the first lesson in the Power of One to One: people are only concerned with their own needs. I'd sold every feature of the car perfectly, but for one thing, the emotional reason why that De Soto, with a six-cylinder engine and fluid drive, was the kind of car a person as successful as the rich fatso should be seen driving.

I had forgotten, or rather, I didn't know at the time, that very few decisions humans make are made by logic alone, that emotion is the driving force behind us all. Most of the decisions we make in life are essentially emotional with perhaps a hint of logic added to satisfy the dubious demands of our intelligence. It's a bit like eating two peanuts with 18 beers to convince yourself you're not drinking on an empty stomach. Humans are human all over.

For instance, when you met your partner, the man (or woman) you felt certain had been tailor-made in heaven just for you, did you make an immediate appointment with your doctor for him or her to have a blood test to see if any nasty ergy-burgies were lurking in the shadows to stop your future offspring from being perfect? Did you then check his/her family history to find out whether there were any nasty surprises, like congenital heart disease or a few whacko cousins quietly incarcerated in a home behind a high wall? Did you have your family dentist examine the longevity potential of his/her teeth, or ask for the name of his/her bank manager, or the number of his/her old man's account, to see if there was the prospect of a big fat inheritance, or at least sufficient for the initial deposit on the two-storey waterfront house you have your eye on?

Of course, you did no such thing! You lit up like a sunburst every time you saw him/her and you couldn't wait to jump into bed together to make the 2.3 children, who will be the millstone around your neck for the next 20 years.

But to do any or all of the things described above would have been perfectly logical. Yet, the most important decision you'll possibly ever make was almost certainly made entirely on an emotional basis.

Selling is all about people and their emotions. People don't buy a drill because it has 10 speeds and can drill through eight kinds of concrete. They buy the drill so they can hang a picture. In other words, they don't buy the drill, they buy the hole it can make to hang the picture their genius three year old finger-painted at kindergarten.

You probably know all this stuff anyway, so let me get back to the De Soto.

I got the polish and the chamois and the vacuum cleaner out and, much saddened and somewhat confused by my recent experience, started to clean the car that was going to cost me three-months' salary if ever I sold it. I opened the driver's door to vacuum the floor and there on the seat was a wallet, which in wallet terms could only be described as so over-weight as to be obese!

It's funny how, when you pick up someone else's wallet, or look into a lady's handbag, you immediately feel guilty. It's a bit like walking in on two people making love, a feeling that you're invading their personal space, intruding upon their privacy, about to find out things about them you really would prefer not to know. Wallets are similarly tricky 'critters' to handle, full of dark corners.

I opened his wallet. It was stacked with big denomination notes of the kind you only see on the movies, neatly stacked in a brief-case and usually lying next to a violin case. I searched for his driver's licence and found his address. Fatso lived in a posh suburb on the same bus route as I took home. I would do a kind deed and deliver it back to him. You never know, there could be a fiver in it for me, and it was that time of the month when my resources were down to small denomination silver coins and my mum's peanut butter sandwiches.

The house with a lush tropical garden and lots of lawn, was set back from the road. The wind swished and tore high up in the papery palm fronds, sounding like far-away waves coming into shore, and a sprinkler hose was going 'chit-chit-chit', as it spat water in a circle somewhere behind a brilliantly flowering azalea bush.

The front door was studded with heavy metal bolts pretending to be a medieval castle portcullis. On either side of it was a stained glass window, into each of which was set a different lead-light coat-of-arms.

I pressed the bell and heard it donging, louder than St Mary's calling the faithful to Sunday Mass, as it echoed through half an acre of pretentious real estate.

I can smell rich, but I can also smell bog Irish. My name is not Kennedy for nothing. If Fatso was a knight of the realm, then I was King Arthur!

To my surprise he came to the door himself. I stammered: 'You, er, left this in the De Soto, sir … you know, when we went for a demo?'

His expression showed no surprise, not even a lifted eyebrow or the slightest delight at having recovered his wallet. He simply accepted it from me with a grunt. 'Wait here!' he commanded.

I figured he was tough, probably a crim of some sort, but he'd be back with a fiver and a second grunt (I doubted he was capable of a thank you). Probably hadn't said the word'thank you' since he'd beat his daddy up and left the bog to see the world. Several minutes passed and, eventually, I heard his heavy footsteps echoing down the polished hallway. The door swung open.

'It's all there, you can go,' he said.

The castle door banged in my face. I was too surprised and perhaps too young to react or even to tell him to go forth and multiply. I had met the definitive bastard and as I stood at the bus stop waiting for the next bus I felt very sorry for myself.

But there you go, another lesson. People almost never react the way you expect them to. If you're looking for grateful in your life from a Jimmy Cagney, you get a grapefruit in your face. This is particularly true in the direct response business. The reason for this is usually quite easy to understand. The offer you are making is based on self-interest, *your self-interest,* you have bought something fairly cheap and in bulk and evolved a proposition which, if *they* buy it, will end up making *you* richer. But, what *they* are looking for, and what you have forgotten, is that what *they* are looking for is a product or service which will make *them* richer, or more rewarded, or satisfied, when they buy it. They couldn't give a continental sausage about your needs, or your desired status in life.

The fat bastard who didn't buy the De Soto felt no obligation to be grateful. He'd left his wallet in a car at an upmarket car dealership and he expected it to be promptly returned. Returning it was nothing less than businesslike, and I was simply the messenger boy who had been given the task of doing so.

The annals of direct response marketing are strewn with the bodies of marketers who carried only their self-interest into the marketplace, who thought only of themselves and not of the customer's needs.

After I'd calmed down and stopped feeling badly done by, I decided I needed to know more about Mr Fat, the big Irish knight of the realm. It wasn't too hard, he was pretty well known. He was a big investor who was involved with mining. A bit more digging found out that the reason he was such a lousy driver was that he had a chauffeur. After loitering on the pavement outside his house on my way back from work, eventually I saw the chauffeur washing a big blue Packard, though I was delighted to observe, not a new one. I introduced myself, gave him my new salesman's card, and invited him to come in for a demonstration drive of the new De Soto.

To my surprise he came in the very next day. He even said he liked the car a lot. I learned that his boss was afraid of flying and they drove all over Australia to visit the various mine sites. Gasoline consumption was important to Mr Fat who, it turned out, was as mean as cats' piss. But, most important, was the *back* seat of the car. A big man travelling for long stretches, who works in the back of the car, needs lots of leg room and a good wide seat for his bum. He wants to step out of the car at the end of a trip feeling roughly like a human being. Comfort, comfort and more comfort! I had located Mr Fat's achilles bum!

So I wrote to him and got the boss's secretary to type the letter on our General Motors stationary. I can't remember exactly what the letter said, and it was probably pretty crude and naive by today's slick copywriting standards, but it went somewhat like this:

Dear Mr Fitzsimmons,

        I don't suppose you remember me, but you took a test drive in one of our De Soto cars, a black one. I thought you liked it, but it turned out you didn't. I think that was my fault. I talked about engines and gear ratios and stuff like that.

    Did you know that your chauffeur thinks its a terrific car? I don't suppose you care, but he says you travel a lot all over Australia. So I measured the width of the back seat of your Packard and it turns out the back seat in our new De Soto is four inches wider and has an extra five inches of leg room. Also, with fluid drive, which it also has, you save half a gallon of petrol for every three gallons you use. For someone who drives a lot, like you do, that's a big saving. At 10,000 miles per year, you would save more than £100.

    Anyway, I just thought you ought to know how I stuffed you up with the wrong information when you came in. Your chauffeur says you don't like people who stuff up. Lucky I returned your wallet, eh?

Yours faithfully,

Ian Kennedy
Salesman.

It seems almost too corny to tell you, but I sold him the De Soto. He came into the showroom a few days later shouting: 'Where's the cheeky little bastard who works here, I want to buy a car from him!'

    The real bastard turned out to be my boss who still took half the commission. *Bastard*!

    So there you are, Lesson One again: people are people through people ... and most bosses are bastards!

    So now you know why a statement such as:

'Buy one, get one free!
works twice as well as one which says
50% off!'

Chapter Two

Fourteen-year-old schoolboys make lousy lovers.

★ ★ ★

I lost my virginity so soon after puberty that I hadn't yet learned to spell the word. I was 14 and I was seduced by the 22-year-old daughter of my father's best friend.

I was sent on an errand to her house after school and she was home on her own.

'Like a drink?' she asked.

I nodded, expecting her to go to the fridge and hand me a Coke. Instead she poured me a scotch and, moments later, undid the two top buttons of her blouse so that her breasts practically tumbled out.

'You could stay a while,' she said, 'I'm here alone.'

I sipped at the scotch and tried not to pull too much of a face, and then she took it out of my hand and placed it on the coffee table and unzipped my fly.

Of course I was terrified. But not terrified enough to run for my life. Perhaps I was paralysed. But after a while I started to get the idea and thought to myself: 'Jesus, I'm going to get *it!*'

I was flushed, hot and excited and afraid I wasn't going to know what to do when the time came, you know, how to get it in. But I hung in, not that that's the right word, and she seemed to know what to do and the next thing you know I'm in schoolboy heaven.

I walked home feeling about nine foot tall. I could still count each of my pubic hairs and suddenly I was no longer a virgin! However you spelled puberty it was the best thing that had ever happened to me before or since.

'I'll have some more of that!' I thought to myself, feeling smug as all get-out. But when I returned the next day she said: 'Run along you silly little boy!'

I was devastated, hurt, humiliated, depressed, you name it. I couldn't look another woman in the eye until I was 17. But I will never forget that first seduction. The weird taste of scotch in my mouth gone dry, the heat and the wonderful culmination. I had made love to a woman, a beautiful woman. I was a man!

Well, I suppose I'm labouring the point a bit, but direct response is a bit the same. You set out to seduce your prospect, to make love to her and when it works, it's marvellous and you think you're a hot shot. So you try to do the same thing again, but this time you expect it to be easy. You take it for granted. You don't put in the work. You lucked in the first time, why not again? After all, you're clever, a positive genius, the mail is coming in by the bag full.

But the second time around, your prospect rejects you. Throws you out on your neck. You have taken the offer for granted, you are thinking *only* of yourself, your gain, your own gratification and so your prospect, quite naturally, throws you out on your ear.

The analogy is not a silly one. Every direct response offer should have all the elements of a fresh seduction. You may not get lucky again, but if you've done your homework, tested your offer and know your prospect's needs, then the hit-or-miss element is largely eliminated. In short, your chances increase in direct proportion to the work and thought you've put into the conquest.

The best thing you can have in the direct marketing business is an ongoing relationship. But if you treat your prospect like a partner in a dull marriage and not like a lover, you will most certainly lose him or her and you won't win them back in a hurry. Every offer you make is a fresh seduction, a new surprise, and it is always made in the terms of your prospect's needs.

The most important thing you will ever own in direct marketing is your prospect list, your database, the names and histories of your past lovers. This is more important than the real estate you occupy or your warehouse inventory. It is your very life as a direct marketer.

Satisfied lovers make love over and over again if you prove you're not a silly schoolboy. A direct marketing seduction should always end in friendship and trust. So don't forget to say: 'Thank you, I think I love you, may I come back again?'

I want to talk a little more about Emotion-versus-Reason in direct marketing.

There is a second direct marketing scenario to my loss of virginity. While being seduced was a highly emotional conquest of me, one I shall remember all my life, it was a discretionary action for the lady who was kind enough to seduce me. Certainly, she had been overcome by a sudden emotional need and I came along and nicely filled it. But it was not one of life's major decisions on her part, simply an immediate reaction to a stimulus unexpectedly made available to her.

So, don't make the mistake of thinking that if you get the emotional appeal right the sale is a certainty. Emotion remains the primary element in the sale, but it also often comes with an after-factor-rejection!

If you're selling a product which will be paid for mostly from discretionary income, in other words, you are not selling something someone needs in a practical sense, the more emotional the appeal, the better chance you have of getting your prospect to buy. But equally, the more chance you also have of having the goods *returned!*

Remember, in the direct marketing industry everything is sold with a money-back guarantee and you had better take this very seriously. If the results of your seduction are not *emotionally on-going,* your prospect will exercise the money-back guarantee.

At the time, my sexual benefactor thought she wanted the schoolboy. But, remember, the next day she sent him home with his tail between his legs. Her emotions made her indulge in the first instance, but the 'after-factor' sent him away, unwanted, rejected just one day after the ultimate teenage conquest.

Jewellery, glamourous electronics and fashion have the three highest return rates in mail order because, essentially, they are highly emotional decisions. Now, I'm not saying women are more vain then men, because I cannot prove such a statement. But several mail order clothing companies, with which I have been dealing in Europe, have substantially reduced their returns on women's clothing by making the garments slightly oversize because they have found that woman usually lie to themselves about their own size. People are people through other people!

So, where does that leave you?

Well, sometimes you need two peanuts to justify an evening on the grog, and sometimes you need a good steak without the fat trimmed. A little logic should exist in every proposition. This is called, 'The Justifying Factor.'

People will often buy something for purely emotional reasons but they'll often require a *justifying factor* to explain their purchase in semi-logical terms to wife or husband, girlfriend or boyfriend, or peers in general.

So if you can add a tincture of logic, (the splash of tonic with the gin, the two peanuts to justify a night of drinking), it helps when you're dealing with a discretionary purchase. But logic will not work alone. The mix will always be very much in favour of emotion.

This is because people, while they may like to think of themselves as sensible, nevertheless all have aspirations and dreams. Direct marketing of discretionary income items is tapping the dream.

If I buy a 7-piece cooking set, or respond to the knife commercial with so many add-ons that I can equip the entire crew of a pirate ship with fierce blades between their teeth, I am not buying a knife or a pot, I am becoming in my mind a great chef. If I wear a $99.00 cubic zirconia nobody can tell from a diamond, it will enhance my life, impress my friends. I'll have something of the aura of a celebrity, because my ring finger will do the speaking for me. If I buy this luggage set, I will instantly become a world traveller. I will be sophisticated, world-weary: 'Ho-hum, been there, done that!' Direct marking is about selling dreams, about meeting aspirations.

An almost perfect example of this is the Ralph Lauren fashion label. He puts a little bloke riding a pony and carrying a polo stick on his shirts and stuff. This doesn't simply say to his customers that Polo is an upmarket sport only played by squillionaires. That is, if you want people to think you're loaded, wear this shirt. It does much, much more. The jock on the pony with a stick in his hand creates an atmosphere, an environment of *old* money, old conservative money. What this silly piece of stitching on your chest is saying is: 'When I wear this I'm conservative and respectable and I feel like old money. Talk about Emotion! But then he adds something else; superb quality, *the justifying factor*, it is built into the garment you are wearing.

In direct marketing you use the same set of rules, the premium, the *aspirational* premium, *must* be one which reaches the needs and expectations not only of the dream, but in fact.

Any way you want to look at it, 14-year-old schoolboys make lousy lovers, the immediate post-pubic quality of the merchandise is in serious doubt, and there is no justifying factor present in making love to a minor. And, of course, the dreams and apirations of the relationship are non-existent. Life can be real tough sometimes, but there you go.

'The product that most immediately springs into her head is the one which begins in her heart.
Very few things are wrought by logic alone.'

Chapter Three

It's not compulsory to like your Dad, but it helps.

★ ★ ★

A good reputation. Love, trust and respect. These things are essential qualities in a direct marketer. But the path to these qualities is sometimes strewn with contradictory experiences. My path certainly was.

I guess I was not the first kid to crash headlong into his father. Now that I look back, there are some things he did to me which I didn't understand at the time and do today. Though I'm not entirely sure this statement is strictly true. Because, if I'm being perfectly honest, even now in my mid-'50s, I still occasionally feel a clutch at my stomach when I think of him.

My father's father was an Irish-American, a Baptist preacher who had been sent to Australia to preach the gospel by his childhood congregation. He seemed somehow to have lost the support of his American church and, while remaining a preacher, fell upon hard times.

My father was born into desperately poor circumstances in an Irish Catholic neighbourhood in Sydney and, the way he told it, had to start fighting for the right to breathe the air around him almost from the moment he could climb unaided from the cradle.

He grew up street smart, a bare-foot slum kid who learned how to beat his opponents or, in turn, be beaten. Then, when he was old enough to pit his wit and considerable intelligence against the world, the Great Depression struck and any chance he may have had of acquiring a trade or skill (he'd even hoped at one time to enter the ministry), was blown for the duration.

I guess it is harder for a preacher's son. He lost his faith and with it his sense of trust in others and, as a consequence, he became pretty cynical and very tough. Although he prospered in his later life, I don't think the little Irish Protestant street kid inside him ever quite went away.

Like a lot of men of his time he was a heavy drinker, at least a bottle of whisky a day, though if he was an alcoholic he certainly never went on binges or beat up my mother or was violent around the house.

Even though I thought of him as a violent man, it wasn't a physical thing but something inside of him. I think he must have been angry inside and his dominating manner with me made me think of him as violent. He beat me quite often, but, there were other kids at school who got no better treatment at home and I was certainly far from being an abused child. But I think I was a frightened one.

I was always afraid of him and like most kids who are afraid of their father, I tried desperately to please him. I sometimes think I am still trying. And, of course, the harder I tried the more I was rejected by him. I was later told that it was the only way he knew, that he was terrified that I would grow up to be a sissy. To a man of his background, gentleness was not a characteristic to be admired in a man and any signs of it in a male child was to be stamped out ruthlessly.

You will find as you read further into this book that what we perceive is the truth is usually truth enough for most of us. We believe what we want to believe.

My perception was that my dad wanted me to be tough and talk dirty and command physical respect. The sort of young guy who sows his wild oats, becomes a hero among his peers when he contracts one of the more benign social diseases and is not in any sense thought of as a fool.

Respect was an important word to him, and it had both a physical and an intellectual meaning. Respect was something you
demanded and, if necessary, enforced. It was a bare knuckle word
but could also be earned with wit and intelligence. This was my
perception of him and so, for me, it was the complete truth about
my father.

I recall how he would show me how to short-change someone,
a piece of sleight of hand of which he was very proud. Though I
hasten to say it was a talent he'd once practised as a young adult
straight off the street and not one he applied to his later business
life. Nor did he, I feel sure, expect me to attempt to emulate him
in my own life. He simply wanted me to know how tough things
could get and how, if you knew the ways of the street, you
wouldn't grow up a fool with no respect.

The point I am trying to make is that he didn't show me the
sleight of hand required to short-change someone as a trick you
might play with a child, but did so as a serious lesson. He'd crack
me over the head until I could manipulate the coins in my hands
to his satisfaction.

'If you know the way it's done then no one can do it to you!'
he'd explain with each whack.

For the same reason he'd play cards with me, always for money,
and he'd cheat and then get furious with me because I could
never spot his deception even when he went over the way he'd
tricked me in slow motion. What's more he never gave back the
money he'd cheated from me.

He was a man who had an almost pathological fear of being
thought of a fool or as someone who didn't command respect
among his peers. I guess he was determined to put his somewhat
naive and, to him, over-trusting male child onto the positive side
of a world in which he believed there are only two kinds of people,
winners and losers, those who are *not* fooled and those who are.

He may even have been right about me. I was an enthusiastic,
trusting, reasonably bright child and did as my sweet, gentle,
English mother suggested and tried not to tell lies or to be decep-
tive and so wasn't in the least bit street smart.

I don't think I improved greatly in this last respect as an adult, so that I've had one or two bumpy rides to freedom, been made a fool of more than once, had more than my fair share of business disasters and, in the process, had an awful lot of laughs I would have loved to have shared with my father.

If he's looking up or down at me now, he's probably shaking his head at this very minute and wondering if I'm ever going to be worthy of his Irish name.

It's funny how these early things affect you, how children can be the victims of their parents perceptions and spend the remainder of their lives trying to do the right thing and never quite succeeding, even in their own eyes, corrupted forever by someone else's expectations of them.

I had some pretty miserable experiences with my old man and he, I now understand, must have had a few with me. He desperately wanted me to grow up and be someone. Someone who had gone to university, made money and commanded *real* respect in the community.

Instead, I dropped out of university after the first year, did not contract a social disease, became a car salesman and never made any real money while he was alive.

I guess we ended up just about quits.

But this didn't stop me trying very hard to impress him. I wanted him to love me, to admire me, to show him I was worthy. I really wanted him to be proud of me, but I couldn't emulate him. It meant I was destined to be a loner. I never stopped trying to earn his approval, you never do; kids never get over their parents and I've tried very hard not to put this kind of pressure on my own son. I guess I learned from my experience.

So, love, trust, respect and your good name are paramount in direct marketing. Your reputation is everything and without trust you're soon out of business.

But a great many direct marketers are very cynical about their database, about the people who buy their products or services, and sooner than later the cynicism shows. You have to learn to respect your customers, to understand their differences. You must earn their trust, even learn to love them. And you *never* give up trying to earn their approval.

You may think loving them may be going too far. Why? After all, they pay your salary, they listen to you when you talk to them, they trust you with their money, they respond to your needs by buying from you and by doing so they materially benefit you and emotionally stimulate you. A great many relationships conducted in the name of true love do far less for the people involved in them.

In return for their love, you also have very real obligations. You don't lie or cheat your customers or clients: we listen very carefully to them, you pay attention to their needs and you treat them like the heroes they are. Sometimes they may not appear to be as sophisticated as you imagine yourself to be, or as smart, but they are the means of your livelihood and success and without them you're history. Love them, respect them and trust them. And, most of all, *get to know them.*

The problem I had with my relationship with my father was that neither of us knew the other very well. I called him 'Sir' until I was 23-years-old and that was his wish. He never wanted me to show any affection to him. I can't remember him ever holding me or kissing me. In other words, we made judgements about each other without understanding, demands without consideration, we required respect without earning it, made decisions without consultation, and we didn't trust or consider, each other's opinions. Nor were we very interested in each other's needs or achievements. We may have tried to please each other, attempted to earn approval from each other, but we were trying to earn the approval on our own terms and, in each instance, from someone who amounted to a comparative stranger.

Now, it's simple enough when you think about it. You can't really trust, respect, love or earn the approval of someone without trusting them and knowing them on a fairly intimate basis. Knowing their weaknesses and their strengths, their likes and dislikes, what makes them laugh and what makes them cry, their likely responses to various stimuli and all the things that go into the human condition. Love, understanding, trust, respect are all built from a basis of knowledge and mutual trust.

It may be crazy to think that parents don't know their children, nor children their parents. But it is, nonetheless, largely true. This is more particularly so of males than of females, but the gap is rapidly narrowing.

I read recently that the average male middle-executive spends only 4½ minutes alone with his children a week! He pays more personal attention to a golf ball or the TV set than he does to the one-to-one relationship he has with his kids.

With female executives, in homes with both parents working, the time mum spends alone with each of her children is steadily decreasing each year. It's not entirely unfair to say that, increasingly, we don't know our parents very well nor do they know enough about us. We are often strangers sharing a roof , the odd meal and the occasional outing together.

If I appear to be belabouring the point it is only to emphasise that without knowing a great deal about the person who responds to your offer of goods or services you are going to be in a lot of trouble. In direct marketing terms, you are flying blind.

In the good old days, when the world was a much more simple place, the relationship with your customer was a lot more direct. There were only five elements in making the marketing task. There was a *buyer,* a *seller,* a *place,* a *product* and a *price.*

Street markets still work on the same basis and that's why they generally work so well. In Europe and Asia there are street markets which have being going virtually uninterrupted for a thousand years. Typically in the Western world the market assembles on a Saturday morning at a *place* which is known to the *buyer* who comes to meet the *seller* and haggle or bargain over a *price* of a *product* which usually ends up with a sale.

Put into simple terms, Farmer Brown comes to an established and familiar market to sell his apples, soon he knows his regular customers by name or he may always have known them. If his apples are too sour one week, or over-ripe the next, he's going to hear about it. If he doesn't listen to his customers, and continues selling bad or sour apples, his regulars will go elsewhere. His relationship is based on the quality and price of his merchandise, his knowledge of his customers, their trust and respect for him and his for them. He can make immediate adjustments to meet his customer's demands based on their direct feedback.

'Harry, your bloody apples are lousy!'

'Sure, for eating maybe, but for strudel, perfect!'

He even knows which of his customers like red apples, which yellow and which green. He knows who wants apples to munch and who uses them for making apple pie or dumplings. He chats with them, knows the names of their kids, has a drink with their husbands in the pub and his children play with their children in the local football or basketball team. His daughters will marry one of their sons and their sons one of his daughters. The love, trust, respect and knowledge of the selling circle is complete.

Today's apple growers are several times removed from their customers. In fact they don't know who they are. Their apples go from grower to wholesaler, and from wholesaler to retailer before eventually reaching the eater, who is no longer *his* customer at *his* local Saturday market, but someone else's customer at an anonymous and very impersonal supermarket.

Nor can today's apple grower control his own destiny by making adjustments to meet his customer's demands. Government boards may regulate his price, the same for unripe as for over-ripe or perfect, crisp or floury, big or small, eating apples or pie apples. He may be forced, for mass marketing reasons, to become a member of a co-operative who may regulate production or size or even quality. His apples may be bulk shipped overseas to satisfy macro-economic policy, or his traditional overseas markets may be taken away from him for political reasons. The point being that Farmer Brown is no longer in control of his apples. He doesn't know who buys them so he cannot hope to establish a basis of customer knowledge, or one of trust, respect and loyalty. In terms of knowing and servicing his customers, this simply leads to chaos in the marketplace.

In recent years there has been a quiet revolution in sales technique, known as *Direct Marketing.* Order and *orders* out of chaos. Direct marketing is getting back to the old relationship between the seller and the buyer, it is allowing big companies to get to know their customers in almost the same old-fashioned and intimate way as Farmer Brown once knew his.

Because everything has to have a name, this is called *relationship marketing*, but it is simply getting back to the Saturday market and back to Farmer Brown knowing you and responding to your pie baking, strudel making or apple munching needs. Though perhaps it is now done in a somewhat more technically sophisticated way.

Not that direct marketing is a new way of doing business. Catalogues and coupons have been around a long time. Even the database concept is really not new: the Reader's Digest was using it 30 years ago as a marketing tool. But what it does is allow the mass marketer, people such as Proctor & Gamble and General Foods, big banks, insurance companies, travel organisations and a host of smaller goods and services businesses, to get very close to their customers and to service them effectively.

The paradox is, that this is being brought about by using the very technology sociologists have, for years, been lamenting would cause an end to the personal touch in business.

The impersonal, uncaring, anonymous '70s and '80s are largely over, and the caring '90s are beginning. The love you receive may well be for the dollar in your pocket, and not because of the colour of your eyes, but it's a lot better than having the money ripped out of your hand, without so much as a 'please' or 'thank you.'

This is how it works.

Your local supermarket will invite you to receive and use a *Loyalty Card*, in appearance much like a credit card. This card is swiped through a character reader at the check-out counter and the retailer's computer system records every item you've purchased—its size, price and any other details—against your name and address. You will receive prizes and discounts when you reach certain *dollar milestones* (The Yanks have a name for everything). And, logically, like an airline frequent flyer system, the more you buy, the more you get: or the more you fly, the more you fly free. Greed is a very powerful motivating force in most humans. The idea is, of course, to encourage regular purchase and to reward loyalty.

You can't win by cheating or cutting corners or trying to exploit the gullibility of your end-users. When you think your customers are stupid, that's an almost certain sign that the stupidity factor is originating from your own office!

There is nothing wrong with running sales promotion and incentive programs that appear to appeal to the greed factor in your potential users, as long as you understand quite clearly that there is a big difference between an *incentive program and a loyalty program.*

If you cease an incentive program, you stop the sale. The 'what's in it for me?' aspect of an incentive program eliminates all other reasons for buying. Frequent Flyer programs fall into this category. You may well like one airline better than another, but if the one you least prefer adds an incentive which is not present in your preferred airline you are likely to change airlines.

So important has the frequent flyer concept become to airlines, that British Airways, the world's largest carrier, now spends more of its total revenue on its frequent flyer service, than it does on advertising.

The loyalty program is an entirely different promotional concept to the incentive program. The loyalty program is based on a feeling of trust in the company with which you are dealing or doing business. When it is working properly, it manifests itself in a feeling of surprise and disbelief when something appears to have gone wrong between the customer and the company. So much so that instead of curtailing the relationship on the spot, the customer will try to patch it up, to have the complaint rectified. Research shows quite clearly that customers are less price sensitive to a company to whom they feel themselves loyal.

More about the loyalty cards: they are getting smarter. Just think what's happening—an immensely valuable database is in the making! Down there among the microchips is all your weekly shopping information, which is being analysed every which-way you care to think. You are being identified by the products you buy and the brands to which you have shown a loyalty. Or maybe by your lack of brand loyalty, the ones you switch to, like a flighty teenager, changing every time you are made a better offer. Your price sensitivity and reactions to a special promotion are being carefully plotted—how often you buy, on what day of the week you buy, what seasonal changes you make, when you went on a diet, a health kick or on vacation, and what the product preferences of your kids, or your husband or wife.

In the old days all this stuff would go onto a huge list and clever people with rimless glasses would spend their highly-paid careers analysing and forecasting and playing God with things called *consumer profiles*, or some other computerspeak or market analyst language.

These days you will find yourself on a hundred or more separate short lists, which go like this:

—*you* buy shampoo once every four weeks, you bought your last bottle three weeks ago and you generally respond to special offers.

—*you* made your very first recorded purchase of Nutri-Grain breakfast cereal last Thursday. Is there a health kick coming up?

—*you* regularly buy three or more Heinz products.

—*you* often buy convenience foods yet, strangely you don't own a microwave oven.

—*you* only buy dry pet food and not wet.

What a surprise to open your mail one bright Thursday morning (Thursday: Public Service pay day, late-shopping day), to find a letter suggesting that you're probably short on shampoo (How the hell did they know that?). So when you do your shopping tonight, why not try 'Breeze,' the new, 'body 'n shine' shampoo from the same range you prefer but at a price discounted *especially* for you.

This discount is *personal* and just to make sure you don't buy something you won't end up liking, a small, free sample of the new shampoo is enclosed with the compliments of the manufacturer and as a 'thank you' for your brand loyalty.

One of the action devices is known sometimes as *electronic couponing.* You simply present your loyalty card, which has been activated for this special shampoo offer, and when you buy the new 'Breeze' shampoo the saving is automatically deducted from the shelf price at the cash register. Another example might be if you were to purchase pre-packaged bacon, you could receive a coupon giving you a discount at the supermarket's delicatessen in an attempt to get you to use it more frequently. Again, if you are new in the neighbourhood, or new to the supermarket, your arrival on their data-base should trigger a 'welcome pack' with all kinds of tempting offers to encourage you to make a return visit. Supermarkets have learned the same lesson as mail order companies and credit card providers: if you can get a customer or user to complete a second-time transaction, they are 10 times more likely to convert to a third. And a third purchase is getting close to becoming a habit as people are far more likely to defect early in the relationship.

The latest relationship device at the check-out counter is a TV monitor triggered by the bar code, which flashes up the picture and price of your purchase together with a promotional message.

The great difficulty in the increasingly anonymous environment of the supermarket is that the only real chance you have of establishing some sort of rapport with the customer is at the check-out. The quality of staff, admittedly, varies, but the average supermarket check-out person is hardly charismatic and is often too busy to scratch.

Murry Raphel, an internationally known speaker, author and direct marketing man from Atlantic City in the U.S. tells the story of how he purchased $174 worth of grocery items from a Sydney supermarket in order to photograph them for a talk he was giving at the Food Marketing Institute conference at Darling Harbour. The check-out lady was particularly surly and so, as he paid her, he said: 'Look, m'am, I've just bought around $170 worth of groceries, it would be real nice if you could say, thank you.'

Without moving a muscle she fixed her gaze on him and replied: 'It's printed on the receipt.'

There are, of course, people who may well think that all this is going a bit far. What about personal privacy? You've heard about 'the thought police' and bar codes on people's foreheads and computers that think and people who manipulate people for their own ends.

I don't suppose there is any point in lamenting this state of affairs, but computer technology is now available for making live creatures respond. For instance, many dairies now have tiny microchips planted in the foreheads of milk cows and as they enter the stalls to feed, the computer scanner reads the information on the micro-chip. It then dispenses the current fodder required for the cow to produce the requisite milk, while at the same time improving the cow's overall health. Pets are now linked to the same system, which activates a 'finding bleeper' so that they can never be lost. The French are experimenting with plans to put micro-chips into the engine blocks of cars so they can be traced when stolen. Bridges and overpasses have been fitted with scanners so that a stolen car activates the scanner and is immediately tracked. It sounds like a good idea, but to date progress in France has been muted because of the Invasion of Personal Privacy Act. The French are fanatical about it.

This is not an essay on morality and every advance ever made in the communications business is in some ways manipulative. Also, it's perfectly true that the more you know about someone, the more likely you are to know how to respond to their needs—both physical and psychological. To some people this is manipulation: in the minds of others, it's called personal service.

The point is that using a loyalty card, as in the 'Breeze' shampoo example, is not all that far removed from Farmer Brown's apples. Nor from the old-fashioned corner grocer, who knew you got paid on a Thursday, what brand of shampoo you used, how often you bought shampoo. When you came in, he took the trouble to courteously remind you that you probably needed shampoo and that you may like to try this new brand being put out by the same manufacturer?

'By the way, Mrs Thompkins, why don't you take this free sample and try this new Breeze? There's enough shampoo in it for a week. It's made by the same people who make the brand you usually buy, but if you like it, then next week we have a special

20% discount offer going. If you don't think it works for you , well you've lost nothing have you? You can go back to your old favourite again?'

Now *that's* what you would call old-fashioned, personal service of the kind which traditionally builds customer trust and loyalty. When you think about it, in outcome, the loyalty card is not very different from the personal service you received from old Mr Perkins and the added attraction is that you don't have the doubtful pleasure of hearing all about his wife's arthritis or his son's pop singer girlfriend.

In four million homes in America, where the loyalty card has been tested, the vast consensus among users is that the system is miles better than the old mass-market approach, which treated them like cash-paying robots.

Direct marketing is helping to create orders out of chaos, and the customer, manufacturer and the retailer is benefiting from the result.

> *Remember the song from, The King and I.*
> *'Getting to know you ...*
> *getting to know how to love you!'*

Chapter Four

The man who drives the nappy van is always in the poo!

As I grew to be a young man, my relationship with my father went from bad to worse. I'd dropped out of University at the end of first year Economics, and while I was doing very well selling De Sotos, I had to get away from him. Away forever. The never-coming-back kind of away.

So I decided to emigrate to Canada. I was ambitious and confident and admired America and the American way of doing things. And as Australians couldn't emigrate directly to America, I figured I'd go to Canada and, well, hop over the border when no one was looking.

Curiously, my father agreed and gave his written permission. I was only 19 and in those days you needed the approval of your male parent if you wanted a passport.

In fact, I got off to a flying start in terms of the things to come. I sailed away in the Orsova in the cheapest berth they had, F-Deck, directly opposite the laundry and well below the portholes. Home was an 8-berth cabin. The smell was terrible. We couldn't afford the laundry directly opposite, and our damp washing steamed all day on makeshift lines strung across the cabin. By nightfall, the air smelled like an over-ripe cheese.

I recall standing on the deck of the Orsova as she sailed out of Sydney Harbour, right past our house in Rose Bay, where I knew my mother would be standing bawling her eyes out. I had carefully explained to her that I was departing forever and it must have come close to breaking her heart. She knew why I was leaving and, I think, hated my father for it. But there was nothing she could do. She was losing the son she loved.

My father had come down to see me off, but was unable to come on board. He stood in a crowd below, under a softly raining day, looking up at me. I found myself crying, I'm still not sure why, I was leaving forever; he could never get at me again, yet I have never felt quite as alone.

I could never have been called an abused child, my father, despite his drinking and his own broken soul, was a man who took care of his family. I lacked for nothing except his inability to show me the love he had for me.

The voyage was a little strange. One of my cabin mates was a guy named Laurie, who was a boy scout returning to Canada from a scout jamboree in Australia. He was sick five minutes after we'd left the Heads in Sydney and, while the ship's doctor visited him every day, he did not leave his bunk except to go to the toilet. He was quite unable to hold anything down except water and after each meal we'd bring him a dry bread roll. He looked terrible and by the time we got to Honolulu he was skeletal in appearance and still very sick. They took him ashore in a stretcher. We then realised that a good part of the smell in the cabin came from Laurie's bunk. We tossed up to see who would clean it up. I lost and with a handkerchief tied around my nose I climbed into it and there among the filthy sheets were 132 breadrolls, some green and mouldy, and some as hard as bullets.

I cleaned the bunk with some disinfectant from the laundry opposite. But the smell lingered. It was a combination of vomit and disinfectant, enough to cause anyone entering to gasp and leave in a few moments with their eyes streaming.

One of my cabin mates was a strange guy from Sydney called Clive, who had come aboard with a suitcase packed with green weeds. The leaves were somewhat spikey and formed in a cluster, shaped somewhat like a hand. To add to the general confusion and the smell, he hung these green weeds in the cabin to dry out. When they were completely dry, he crushed them into the consistency of fine tea leaves, which gave off a distinctly acrid sort of smell. He then rolled the leaves into cigarettes with a little machine which took cigarette papers and rolled almost perfect cigarettes. When I asked him what they were, he said they were medicinal cigarettes much sought after in Los Angeles. He expected to make a fortune selling them to the Yanks. I must admit I was pretty doubtful. He smoked one once, and his eyes got very red and it smelled bloody terrible. When he suggested I take a puff, I politely refused.

Anyway, in Honolulu I heard one of the crew mention that they always kept one or two cabins empty in case someone became infectious and had to be quarantined during the voyage.

I dreamed of getting one of these cabins to myself. That night, I pinched Clive's lighter fluid and rubbed it vigourously under my arms right down to the waist repeating this several times during the night. By morning, I had a lulu of a rash which stretched from under both armpits to my waist. I was sitting in the doctor's cabin at 10 a.m. sharp when the surgery opened.

It was as simple as that, the doctor examined me and appeared mystified as to what the rash might be, the words that came from his mouth were music to my ears. 'I'm afraid we're going to have to quarantine you, young man.'

I told Clive what had happened and he dropped his cigarette rolling machine in astonishment at my good fortune.

'There's still plenty of your lighter fluid left?' I volunteered as I packed my things to repair to my cosy two berth cabin on C-Deck, complete with two portholes through which a gentle Pacific breeze would continue to blow all day and night.

The last six days of my voyage were heaven. Clive tried the same stunt and the doctor diagnosed it as a common rash and gave him some sticky sulphurous smelling ointment to apply, another potent mixture to add to the aerified stew that concocted itself in his cabin. By the time we stepped off the ship in Los Angeles, the doctor pronounced me cured and I landed on American soil a free man.

In L.A. I bought a Greyhound bus ticket to Detroit, the nearest I could get in one hit to Toronto. I recall it cost me $28.00 for three days and two nights on the bus. The bus was a marvel. While it had no toilet, it had two decks at the back and was air-conditioned. It made the hot, fart-infested buses at home seem like primitive inventions indeed. Every four hours we'd make a 20-minute toilet and refreshment stop and every morning we'd stop for an hour at a bus station, where you could shower and shave for a nickel and breakfast for a dollar. I guess it was pretty rough, but I thought I was in five-star heaven.

At a small town along the way we took in a group of university students in wonderful lumber jackets, with huge letters on them, as well as long football scarves. They were on their way to a football game. A pretty girl in bobby socks sat next to me and I couldn't believe my luck. She was friendly and chatted along as though she'd known me for ages. When I asked her where they were going, she said to Indianapolis. When I asked why, she said: 'Why, to root for my team!'

She looked just like the girl next door, all-American apple pie.

'What, the whole team?' I asked, atonished.

She looked at me as though I was mad or something, 'Well, for my boyfriend as well?'

Boy, I sure was in the Land of the Free.

However, later she mentioned that she was a part-time secretary to the sales manager of a Chevrolet franchise and I felt immediately comfortable. I knew about cars. I could chat up a girl endlessly if I could talk about selling cars. Then she mentioned that she was learning how to sell and that her boss gave her a part of his commission if a contact she had made led to a sale.

'You must get a good screw,' I responded.

She gave me this really filthy look and excused herself and went to sit in the front of the bus. Strange people these Americans: very loose in the morals department, but obviously very uptight about money.

I arrived in Toronto in the fall and the little money I had brought with me was soon spent. Autumn turned into winter and my life fell apart. Toronto in 1955 was an awful place. I lived in the Italian district, off West Bloor Street, in a succession of boarding houses, each one cheaper and colder than the last. I shared a bed with a friend, Max White: Max worked nights and I worked days and as I got out of bed to go to work, Max got into it coming home from work.

Coming from Australia, I knew nothing of the mental hibernation which takes place in people who live in cold climates. There were simply no jobs available in the winter and I couldn't believe the cold! On several occasions I honestly thought I was going to die, just slowly freeze to death. I imagined that one day Max would come home from work in the morning and find me in bed, stiff as a board, with icicles stuck onto the end of my nose and my hair so brittle it would break in your hand if you tried to bend it.

We were both stony broke and used to eat Cream of Wheat. A four day supply was always plopping away softly on the stove downstairs. I am a world authority on Cream of Wheat. You can eat it for four days before you got diarrhoea. Then, you had to keep moving your cheeks for fear that your bum would freeze and stick to the dunny seat.

I can remember only one night when I was warm. The landlady was a fat woman who claimed she was half Indian and half Eskimo. One night, she fell into a drunken sleep on an old couch she kept in the kitchen and her cigarette set it alight. Max arrived in the morning to find the place filled with smoke and me, smilingly asleep, warm at last, in a state of near asphyxiation.

In an effort to put out the fire, and because the pipes were all frozen, Max had grabbed the pot of Cream of Wheat on the stove and used it to douse the couch, which had disappeared in a billow of smoke. The scalding Cream of Wheat brought the unseen and unconscious landlady alive and she came steaming through the smoke covered in Cream of Wheat shouting: 'Fire! Porridge! Shit!'

I soon developed a toilet fixation, starting with trying to stay alive on a diet of Cream of Wheat. When at last I got a job, it seemed only natural that it should be as the off-sider on a nappy van for Ontario Towel and Linen Supply.

They gave me two smart grey uniforms with 'Ian' embroidered on the shirt above my heart. Because of the nature of the job, I needed to wash one shirt each night and hang it in the kitchen to dry. The pants and shirt also came with a wonderful cap, with gold braid like a general's embroidered on its peak, and a bag which I carried about my neck with the word 'SOAP', also in gold, lettered on its side. Because of the cold, when I put my spare uniform on in the morning, it was usually still damp and always smelled of Cream of Wheat and the landlady's cabbage stew.

It was about as shitty as a job can get, but it was winter and your nostrils froze so you could get through a shift picking up diapers from private houses, nursery schools and hospitals without passing out.

Half-way through winter I got a promotion from diapers to doing towels for women's wash rooms, though still as an off-sider. Washroom towels were a definite step up in the world, though I now found myself tied to the tampax end of the labour force.

I'd go into toilets to replace the towel rolls, empty the tampax bin, fill up the tampax machine and replace the soap in the basins. After nappies, it was good clean work and I was grateful to be eating.

There was one aspect of that particular job which left me curiously bemused, unable to understand why it happened. You'd bang on the door of the washroom and shout, 'Towel Supply! I'm coming in, okay ladies?'

Nothing. So you'd repeat the process.

Bang, bang, bang! 'I'm the towel man, can I come in, please?'

Nothing.

So you'd just walk in and see all these feet behind the doors with knickers around their ankles and nobody is making a sound. No scrunch of paper, no chain pulling nor hiss of flushing. Everything is held in suspense, frozen in time, not a word, not a sound, not a cough, nor sneeze, nor rustle, nor squeak.

So you do the job as quickly as possible and whistle as you work, so that they know you're still around.

'All clear!' you'd shout as you left and as you walked out of the door you'd hear a sudden flurry of activity—paper tearing, toilets flushing, chains clinking, shoes scraping, elastic step-ins snapping, doors banging and women coughing.

Not once in all the time I did ladies' toilets did any one ever say: 'Wait!' or 'Stop!' or 'Just a moment' or even, 'Come in!''

Every day I hated Toronto more. Though I was making some sort of progress. After six months, the towel company gave me my own truck and, of course, as the lowliest truck driver, I got the dog and cat run which, in turn, was known as 'doing B&P'—'Bark and Pussy.'

I used to do the veterinary hospitals between Toronto and London. The truck carried no off-sider so I had to handle the dirty towels myself. It was summer by this time, stinking hot and the towels were used in operations on animals, mostly dogs and cats. With a couple of thousand post-operative towels in the back of a metal truck without air conditioning, the smell was unbelievable. You were forced to leave the driver's window open and when you'd pull up at a red light, people would faint within a radius of a hundred yards of the truck. Well, almost!

And then I got ring worm. I guess it was inevitable working with veterinary towels. I'd never seen a ringworm, didn't know what one looked like. I thought it was just something you got from eating too much Cream of Wheat, or from a generally rotten diet, like scurvy. Not that I knew what that looked like, either.

Soon my body was covered in ringworm and I couldn't bare the pain and the itch any longer. So I asked a lady vet to look at them and she nearly fainted when she saw under my arms, across my chest and in my scalp. She called a specialist and made an appointment for me right away, telling the nurse it was urgent. I drove the truck back into the depot and then took a bus into town and sat in the specialist's waiting room for a couple of hours.

You know how it is when you know something is going to be done about something painful you've been carrying around, you give in to the pain. Suddenly I couldn't cope. By the time it was my turn to see the specialist, I was blubbing like a baby. But all I could think to say between the sobs was: 'I'm sorry, doctor, I can't pay. I've got no money!'

'Don't worry about it, ' he said, 'let's take a look.'

And he looked at my problem. I had ringworm everywhere I had them, under my arms, in my head, between my legs, up my bum. It was horrific.

'You're in a lot of trouble, son,' he said, finally, then added: You're out of work and out of money. But don't worry about the money, let's fix you first.'

I've never forgotten his kindness and it turned out he paid for my medication himself. He never did send me a bill for treatment though finally I did pay him back. I'd been, practically, a basket case, but I didn't intend to be a charity case as well.

The first day I was in bed, someone from the towel company came to visit me and gave me a pay envelope with the three days due to me. He then demanded my uniform and soap bag back. The doctor's staff had burned it in their incinerator, so he took back my pay envelope and told me I was fired.

I remember his exact words, pedantic and formal as though he had done this particular job a great many times before: ' Mr Kennedy, Mr Ian Kennedy, you are forthwith fired!' Every time I receive a letter, usually a legal one, with the word *forthwith* in it, I chuckle. *Forthwith* means ringworm and Cream of Wheat and cold beds and shitty towels and nappies and a damp uniform that smelled of boiled cabbage.

It is little wonder I have almost no regard for the legal profession! I also kept the spare uniform for years and when I was going through a bad patch I'd put it on and go out to a dinner party with friends. It gave me a bit of a laugh. You can't help laughing, can you?

The Canadians have an old expression: 'Some days you eat the bear, and some days the bear eats you!' I suppose that's the world for all of us—some good patches, some bad. But in my opinion, Cream of Wheat and lawyers add up to about the same thing: too much of either soon gives you the screaming shits.

At 19, I was growing up fast. I had come to understand one of the fundamental lessons in life—that there is a bottom rung and a top rung and the man who drives the night cart is always going to be in the shit because it's no rung on the ladder at all! It's both feet planted firmly in the poo! I was learning that if you wanted to climb any sort of ladder, you needed to use the part from the head up and not the bit from the shoulders down. If anyone was going to survive another winter in the crappiest town on earth, it wasn't going to be as the bloke who drove the poo-cart for the Ontario Towel and Linen Company.

I am aware that I may be stretching the analogy a fair bit, but in direct marketing there is a concept which explains the process of *relationship marketing.* and which is usually called, *The Ladder of Loyalty.*

The *Ladder of Loyalty* was either invented or popularized by the previously mentioned Murray Raphel. It is probably the single most important model in direct response, the very foundation of *Relationship Marketing.*

The theory is not a lot so different to life itself and states that all potential customers start on the bottom rung of the *Ladder of Loyalty* and may, or may not, progress to the top.

At the bottom they are no more than drivers and off-siders for the Ontario Towel and Linen Company. In other words people without a specific purpose in the eyes of the marketer. But if you can get them to the top rung of the ladder, they become both your best customers and your best salespeople or advocates. You've taken them out of obscurity into a place on your database where anything is possible.

Your job as a direct marketer is to help them move upwards if they come to a halt, or look like falling off. The loyalty ladder, of course, gets narrower as it gets higher and you can never hope to keep everyone on it. It's a bit like the skin specialist who helped me by responding to my ringworm problem. You work to fix the problem and, eventually, it pays off in good faith and loyalty— with a dollar or two earned for your efforts.

The *Ladder of Loyalty* works like this: You begin at the bottom rung with a target audience. These are the people who you think are *most likely* to respond to your offer. That is, you've figured out the *probables* from the *possibles.* Be a little careful though, and afford some research if you can. It's a good idea not to make assumptions about target audiences. There are traps for the unwary in this area and people are not as predictable as they may seem.

For instance, you may be a large insurance or banking organisation selling financial services to women. (That's a nice switch, a service which isolates the particular needs of women in an overall package!) Theoretically, your target audience is *all* working women from the age of 19 to 60. But you know some of this very wide target audience range will be potentially more interested than others. Narrowing down, finding the most likely user, your *probables,* is going to be paramount to your success.

If you're too small to employ a research organisation, it is still not a good idea to guess. Keep your eyes open, ask questions, make notes of what people are doing, get to know the typical prospect by working together with your sales people. The information you can gather with your own eyes and ears is significant. For instance, you may be selling a collectable, say a commemorative plate or a porcelain figurine. So every time you enter a home, look into the china cabinet or on the walls. If there is evidence of a collector ask questions, get to know why this person likes to collect, what they expect to pay, how they go about paying, what their priorities are? Soon you will begin to get a good feel for your prospect, your most likely customer. Research is, after all, only a question of asking the right questions to find out who your *probables* are.

Anyway, the *probables* also are referred to by the not very welcoming name of *suspects*—the people you believe might be most interested in your offer. They are the target audience, though not all of them will end up buying from you.

When you know more or less who your *suspects* are, you enter the most difficult and expensive stage in the marketing process. Again, if you are large enough, this is where the integration of advertising and direct marketing is at its most effective.

People don't like buying from a stranger or from an unknown source. They feel much happier if something comes recommended by a friend, or someone they know and have reason to trust. So advertising is often the way to soften the direct marketing environment. Naturally, the *suspect* is more likely to respond sight unseen to a direct marketing offer if the product is 'a product friend.'

Advertising has the job of making friends for the product (brand or service) by creating an impression, and even presenting its superior emotional and physical qualities. It softens the selling environment and creates a predisposition.

Direct marketing fine-tunes the offer. It gives the *suspect* the right mix of emotional and logical reasons to indicate interest in purchasing or seeking further information. Your *suspect* has come *alive* for you by indicating a willingness to act. The moment they put up their hands and respond to an offer—such as: A free gift; further important information; the willingness to enter into a contest—they *qualify* themselves.

When this happens, *suspects* becomes *prospects*. They have taken the first important step up the ladder of loyalty, they have stepped onto the *prospect* rung.

It is at this rather exciting point that a lot of marketing organisations make the first really bad mistake, failing to strike while the iron is hot. This is the first time they have a relationship with you. Think about it in human terms, perhaps even in terms of ringworm versus a mild itch. The latter requires a simple pharmaceutical remedy and it's over. The former requires intensive medical treatment prior to a cure.

The point is that when a suspect becomes a prospect, they are not captive, they are not desperate. At best they have a mild itch and if you don't attend to it very quickly, you've got a very good chance of losing them.

That's why instant response is critical in direct marketing. Instant response is no later than 48 hours. The speed with which you respond to your prospect has a very significant effect on your conversion rate and dramatically affects the quality of the relationship from then on. Simple, really: emotional responses cool down, life goes on.

People are people through people. It's no different to being introduced. You walk into a room and are introduced to someone who wants something from you. But instead of making a fuss over you he shakes you lightly by the hand and then, with a hasty excuse, turns away and attends to something else. You are left standing and waiting. The chances are that you're going to respond negatively when eventually he gets around to asking you to respond to him. Once you've got the attention of your suspect, you must show just how keen you are to turn him or her into a trusted friend.

Now obviously you need to move your new found *prospect* up the ladder of loyalty to become a *customer*, an actual user of your product or service. You want the *suspect* to share an experience with you. When two people do something enjoyable together, they bond more closely.

Though the analogy is more like a blind date than an appointment with a skin specialist, you are now at the stage when you have to start finding things out. The blind date has progressed to sitting at a table in a restaurant with a bottle of wine. Now you need real information if you are going to be successful in your later conquest. But let me continue for a moment with the same ringworm metaphor, repulsive as it is. The first thing the specialist does is seek information. The where, how, what and when of the horrible itching circles on my skin. In other words, he starts a *database.*

This is a pretty important thing to do. For instance, he now knows that I hate Cream of Wheat and am living on an inadequate diet, come from a hot climate and am not Canadian, have a menial job, which exposes me to infection, suffer terribly from the cold, need building up, have lost confidence in myself, a single, 19, poor, honest and not afraid to do a day's work.

Not a bad start for a database. A whole heap of conclusions can begin to be made from just this information. It seems almost redundant to say: '*The more you know about your customers the more likely you are to find ways to please them.* Your database is *everything!'* Information is the key to all your future success.

Okay, so you got back to your prospect by mail in less than 48 hours. She likes her free gift, or the information you sent, and decides to ignore all the warnings she's heard about shonky direct mail operators. Besides, she's seen your company or brand advertising for years, so she sends for your product or service. Hooray! She becomes a *customer.* You've taken her from *suspect* to *prospect* to *customer* and she is travelling nicely up the ladder of loyalty, with you, pushing from behind.

Now, if you're like most Australian or New Zealand businesses you bank the cheque she sent you and promptly forget about your hard-won, enthusiastic, prepared-to-become-loyal-to-you customer. You leave her sitting like a shag on a rock.

The easiest time and place to gather information about your customer is immediately after the sale, and at the point of sale. If they had to come into your shop or office, it's easy. If you can telephone them as a follow-up, and ask them if they are happy with the purchase, you have an ideal opportunity to get information. If you use a follow-up letter, with a self-addressed envelope and a few easy boxes to tick on an enclosed card, you'll be surprised at the willingness of your customer to respond. An ideal way to start an on-going relationship is a guarantee card, on which your customer is required to register several details you will later find useful.

When they respond, you are about to push them up onto the second top rung of the loyalty ladder. This is the beginning of the *Power of a One to One* relationship. You are about to start a commercial friendship, to develop a belonging process, to create reasons for your *customer-friend* to stay in touch. Without your customer's particulars, not just name and address but all the things you know about him or her, there is no further step up the *Ladder of Loyalty.*

For instance, if you're a retailer or a business who wants to strengthen your relationships with your customer-friend, you may choose to introduce your *private label card* (PLC.)

A PLC is simply a credit card. It often carries the label or logo of one of the major credit card organisations, eg. VISA, but it works exclusively for *your* organisation. Or it can simply be a card which, even without the credit facility, works to establish the customer's importance, or gives an automatic discount on presentation. The PLC is not all that different from a loyalty card, but it can be used to entitle your customer to a number of other corporate privileges.

For example, you may be an airline with a lot of competing airlines fighting for your customer's travel miles. Your PLC may entitle your customer to book a seat on a special, no-delay toll-free number, give them credit, earn them extra bonus miles, give them the use of a business lounge with free fax, telephone, conference room, toilet, shower, snack and cocktail facilities. It may even earn frequent flyer points every time you the customer shops with the card.

Or you may be a dress shop which extends credit to a PLC holder. The card also allows your customer to come in the day before your summer or winter sale and get first choice of the merchandise. It might also give the customer-friend an extra 10% off the marked-down sale price, special invitations to fashion shows and free subscriptions to fashion magazines.

The possibilities for making customer friends are, of course, endless, but they must all begin with a good database. *Without information there can be no inspiration and no innovation.*

In the United Kingdom, where private label cards were first developed, research shows that people leaving home to shop are *five times* as likely to visit their PLC store than some other outlet selling the same type of merchandise.

It is a direct marketing truth that you *never* buy a sale as cost-effectively in the open-marketplace as you can from your own customer database.

People will always buy Farmer Brown's apples first, because they know him, trust him and have tasted his apples on a previous occasion. They *know* that they are excellent for making strudel, pies or simply for munching.

But now, if Farmer Brown sends his slightly hail-marked apples free to the local pony club, and Mrs Brown gives her husband's regular customers the· recipe for her famous apple dumplings, and is a willing contributor of nice-apple-things-to-eat to the local church fetes, then the Browns have their customer relationship firmly cemented.

But, we're not yet on the top rung of the *Ladder of Loyalty*. The final step, like most climbing in an upward direction, is perhaps the hardest. But, it is also the most rewarding.

The top rung on the ladder is the most profitable for the marketer. This is when the customer is converted into an active salesperson and begins to bring in new prospects. This is no different in essence to the recommendation of a friend in a normal relationship. But it is the most powerful sales stimulus of all because it is customer-generated. The most common name for this process is *lead-generation, though customer recommendation* is an equally good name for the process which brings the rewards when your customer reaches the top rung of the loyalty ladder. The credit card people call it, literally, *member get member*.

There is simply no better relationship for a direct marketer. There is no more cost effective way of buying business than by directing your promotions to your loyal customers and rewarding them for bringing in new prospects. The direct marketing term for this process is called *customer-based advocacy*.

What must have become pretty apparent by now is that direct marketing is not mass marketing. More and more, we are beginning to understand how to use the power, the awesome power, of one-to-one marketing relationships.

'Your own customer's recommendation of your services to someone else is the biggest untapped source of business any direct marketer can possibly have.'

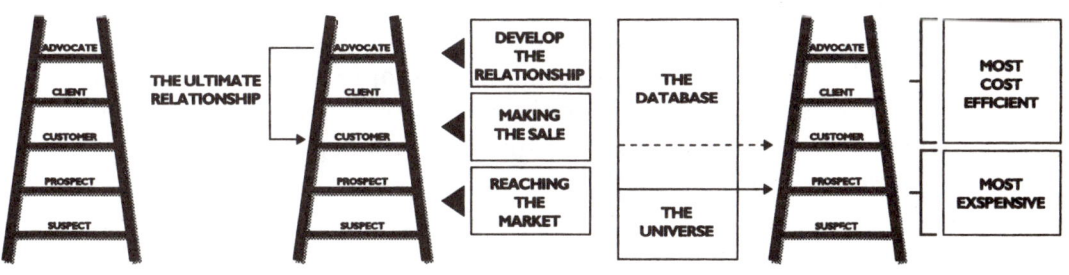

1. Best schematic representation of relationship marketing.

2. The three stages of relationship marketing and the ultimate relationship when the advocates bring you new customers.

3. The database functions to ensure that the marketing relationships above the customer rung are the most cost effective.

Chapter Five

He who wears the dunce cap doesn't get to see Lottie the Body drop her knickers.

Spring came to Canada at last. The sun shone, trees turned from witches' broomsticks into wild hairdos of green and brilliant flowers. My skin was repaired and I had a new, clean job, pricking eggs.

I was selling egg prickers, a little spring-loaded plastic device which you held firmly at the end of an egg and let go and it put a microscopic hole in the bottom of the egg that let the air out. With the air escaped from the egg, it didn't expand as it heated and so the shell remained intact. Such a simple little thing. I soon convinced myself every household in the world ought to have one. Belief in your product is a very important aspect of salesmanship.

So egg pricking I do go! With a microphone around my neck, I was selling off a small table set up inside a large department store. I was pretty good at it too and soon I'd added Wonder Knife-O-Clean, guaranteed to make old knives look like new! (Well, almost). I loved the work. People thought I was funny and liked my accent and, after nappies and pussy-cat shit, I thought I was in egg-and-knife heaven.

Unfortunately, I was too good at what I was doing and I sold the entire stock of egg prickers and Wonder Knife-O-Clean. The wholesaler couldn't resupply in time and so I was out of a job.

The department store must have been somewhat impressed with my efforts, because they offered me a job in their electrical department selling TV sets on commission only. I guess people think about buying a TV set much harder than they do about an egg pricker, but with my De Soto experience I didn't do too badly all that summer.

Nevertheless, Canada wasn't growing on me and the leaves were beginning to fall—great big yellow and orange ones, falling like fat spiders onto wet pavements. The sun was growing more tepid by the day and the mornings were distinctly chilly. I decided, with Max White, my mate of the Cream of Wheat experience and another Australian, with the unpromising name combination of Clive Cuthbert, the son of a Presbyterian Minister from St Kilda, Melbourne, that it was time to fly South, to immigrate illegally to the U.S.

We were all pretty broke but we'd heard of a driving scheme from Detroit, delivering new cars to the West Coast of America. They gave you a car to deliver and you got a trip across the States for the price of the petrol, or gas, as they call it. Between us we had enough money for hamburgers and petrol and we didn't need accommodation as we'd sleep in the car.

The trick was to get over the border without a working permit. A bloke I'd met at the Towel and Linen Company had first told me about the scam. He was from Liverpool in the U.K. and advised me to take the five-past-midnight bus to the Buffalo border and to learn to say in a perfect Canadian accent: 'Ian Kennedy, I was born in Toronto, Ontario.'

The point was, that every day, thousands of Canadians cross the border into America to shop and work. It simply isn't possible to process all the passports, so the Customs officials come onto the buses and walk down the aisles and ask each passenger two questions: Name? Where were you born? If you had an accent or looked strange, they would haul you off the bus for a more thorough examination.

It seemed that the post-midnight bus arrived at the Buffalo border in the early hours of the morning when the Customs people had been sleeping. Bleary-eyed officers would climb aboard the bus with a torch and shine it on each customer's face and ask the dreaded questions, 'Name? Where were you born?'

Max and I practised our accents for several weeks until we had it down perfect, the slightly softer roll of the Canadian inflection. But Clive was a different matter. I'm sure the names our parents give us influence the way we turn out in life. Clive Cuthbert has to be a distinct disadvantage in the great roll-call of life. He was just like his name sounded. He was a bit naive and he claimed he had a 'lousy ear' for accents. This was undoubtedly true as his St Kilda accent rasped like sandpaper on sheet metal. He'd only tagged along a week before we were due to leave and was as nervous as hell. But he was the most cashed-up of the three of us, and we figured we'd eat a lot better if he came along to share the driving.

At the border all went to plan and the immigration officer moved quickly from one passenger to the next asking the same two questions in a demanding, irritable voice, 'Name? Where were you born?' Max answered like a native Canadian and I followed suit. The torch passed onto Clive, shining into his wildly panicking eyes. He must have forgotten his lines, because he answered in a broad Australian accent: 'Same as me mates!' That was the last we saw of a rueful Clive as they hauled him off the bus.

In Detroit, we were given a Pontiac to deliver to Freedom Pontiac in Los Angeles and off we went. Without Clive, we'd have to eat a few less hamburgers, but we had sufficient money for gasoline.

In L.A. we delivered the car and I talked fast to the guy who ran Freedom Pontiac. Told him I was a car salesman. Car salesmen are like Irish priests, when you've known one you know them all. He was impressed enough with my De Soto experience to give me a job as a junior on the sales lot and in a short time, I did a lot of growing up.

In those pre-Ralph-Nader days, consumer protection meant carrying an umbrella above the head of a prospect on a rainy day on the way to the demo car in the yard. You could and would do *anything* to sell a motor car. The tricks and deceits were so frequent that I am ashamed to say I simply accepted them without ever thinking about whether they were honest. They were just what you were instructed to do to sell a car.

For instance, as a matter of standard procedure, all the selling booths had one-way listening devices installed. They were *wired*. I think it would have come as somewhat of a surprise to any of the salesmen if you'd pointed out to them that bugging a customer wasn't exactly *kosher*. It was simply part of the sales process—listening covertly to your customer to prepare him to spend bigger bucks. This was known as *closing the sale*. In fact, the booth was often referred to as a closing room.

The salesman would show the car to his potential buyer, take them for a demonstration drive and then move them into a booth to show them the specs, the brochure and the extremely easy 24-month repayment terms. Halfway through the talk, when there was a bit of a pause usually engineered by the salesman himself, he'd break into the silence to excuse himself for a few minutes.

Of course the prospect and his wife, a couple of simple souls from the Salinas Valley, are only too pleased about the unexpected respite from the slick sales approach which has been putting them under every kind of nod-your-head-and-say-yes' pressure.

The salesmen then goes into a glass office and picks up a telephone where his prospects can actually see him, but sufficiently far away so that he can't be heard. The phone is, in fact, connected one way to the booth where the couple are busy arguing with each other.

'No, it's too damned expensive! He'll need to come down at least $200 if I'm going to talk turkey and I want a black one. He don't believe I want black, he's pushing the red one, I hate red! C'mon, honey, we'll tell him we'll come back some other time. Let's get the hell out of this turkey yard.'

The salesman puts down the phone and on his way back to the booth stops for a few moments to talk with the sales manager.

'They want a black, we haven't got a black. The duco?'

The sales manager nods, not even looking up from his paperwork

He returns to the booth, whistling so the couple can hear him approach and so quit arguing. The salesman apologises again for being on the telephone for so long, shrugs and smiles his explanation disarmingly; 'You know, mothers?'

'Is she all right, honey?' the wife asks, concerned.

He looks at her and grins bravely, 'Thank you ma'm, she's fine, a large ovarian cyst removed which happily turned out to be benign.'

Both prospects smile, he's won the wife hands down. Then the salesman claps his hands, changing the subject, 'Let's celebrate! I guess it's my lucky day, yours too!' he explains, 'My boss just took a call from Detroit while I was on the telephone to my mama, they've told us to discount your model Ponti, *two hundred and ten bucks!* But only on black cars.'

The couple shoot a knowing glance at each other. The salesman lowers his voice, ''Something to do with the duco. The guys in the paint shop got the damned duco mix wrong again!' He laughs and thinks for a moment, then seems to decide.

'Tell you what I'm gonna do for you! We is gonna write your *red* Pontiac down as *black*, a gift from my mama. Shucks, Detroit ain't gonna know if we don't tell 'em, now are they? We'll give you the full $210 discount. You're real nice folks and you deserve it. What do you say, have we got a deal going here?'

Despite themselves the couple both nod. They've outsmarted the salesman and a red car ain't so bad, what with the black paint job being suspect.

Now you may be thinking that the customer has just saved $210 dollars on the retail price so, despite the immorality involved in bugging a booth, the customer has benefited. But, sadly, this is not the case.

There is in fact no fixed retail price. It simply isn't possible for the customer to work out the price of a car as there are too many options. Each salesman has a base price for a car. This goes directly to the company and the salesman's personal commission is based on how much he can get for it over this basic unit price.

With over $200 now saved, the customer is strongly urged to include a few options: white wall tyres, chrome side mirrors, pigskin seat trim—three add-ons that gobble up his $210 discount as quickly as it takes to mention them. They are not genuine discounts in the first place, because you always added $250 to the base price when the potential buyer first inquired about the price of the auto. This is known as 'The Fat' and is the amount the salesman has to work with to drive the price up.

It isn't over yet. Not by a long shot. The salesman does the paperwork for the sale and carefully fills in the add-ons, writing the word 'Black' in the box denoting colour, even saying the word out loud so that his customer is immediately included in the conspiracy. Then he asks the husband to sign on the dotted line. At the same time, he points out that it is routine to take the signed contract to the Vice President Sales for approval, and for his personal signature.

The proud owners of a new red Pontiac follow the salesman into the Vice President's office. Let's say the salesman in this instance was me. I introduce the couple, Mr and Mrs Roberts. He stands up as we enter and makes a big fuss of them and asks me what automobile they've purchased.

'The red Chieftan,' I say proudly.

'Best auto on the lot! 'Could just be the best G.M. ever made!' Almost absently, he takes the contract from me and sits down again and puts it on the desk and with only a cursory glance at it he brings his pen over to sign it. His pen is poised, about to scrawl his signature, when somehow his eye is drawn to something on the page and his head jerks back in some surprise.

'What's this?' he asks and picks up the contract and examines it more closely. Then he stands up suddenly, his swivel chair rolling back and hitting the wall behind him.

'Jesus, Kennedy, what have you done!' He looks up at the couple who have just moments before signed to buy the car.

'I'm sorry, sir … madam … but I think there's been a mistake!' He waves the contract in the air. 'I can't possibly let you have the car for this price!' Then, in front of their eyes, he tears up the contract. 'No way!' he says, shaking his head and throwing the scraps of paper on the floor as he retrieves his chair and sits down again. 'No way! No can do … Jesus!'

Now he slumps over his desk with his head in his hands thinking. Finally he looks up at the shocked couple and then at me: 'You're fired, son! Pack your bags and pick up your pay, you're through at Freedom Pontiac!'

I turn to leave. 'Stay! Let's see what other screw-ups you've made!'

He turns to the embarrassed couple and shrugs, 'He's Australian!' He says this, as though it explains everything. Then he searches about among the paper on his untidy desk and grabs at a sheet of General Motors stationary and pushes it over to the couple.

'Look, Mr and Mrs ....'

'Roberts,' I add quickly.

'Mr and Mrs Roberts, take a look for yourself, here's the cost price from G.M., the price *we* paid for this car. It's on General Motors' letterhead and dated yesterday. Can you see the terrible mistake this stupid young man has made?'

Of course the phoney price list he is showing them has been typed by his secretary daily and it clearly shows the wholesale price of the tomato red Pontiac is quite a bit higher than the price agreed to on the now torn-up contract. He sighs again, shaking his head, 'Look it's a disaster, but it's not your fault, we feel we owe you a favour, how about meeting us halfway? We've got a special discount on black cars which came through this afternoon, your car is red, but we'll call it black ...'

'Excuse me, sir, but I already did that,' I pipe up fearfully.

'You did what?' he asks in an incredulous voice.

'Allowed them the $210 discount, sir.'

'But that was *only* for black, the duco thing?' he looks at me and shakes his head in disgust: 'It'll have to come out of your commission, son!'

'He's a nice boy, his mama's sick!' The wife protests.

The sales manager ignores this: 'I'm going to have to give you folks this car for the factory price. The price *we* paid for it!'

Greed wins over any further thought of commiseration and they both smile, but the husband pushes it further: 'What about the whitewalls and the side mirrors and pigskin trimming on the front seat,' the customer asks tentatively, 'We took them instead of the $210 discount.'

'I'm sorry Mr Roberts, but you can't get blood out of a stone. It isn't black, your Pontiac is red!'

'But you just said..?'

'No sir! You're getting the car at a stupid price already!' the V. P has his head in his hands again.

'It don't seem fair to take the money out of the young man's commission,' the wife protests.

Her husband gives her a dirty look.

The sales manager looks up at her in surprise.

'Why, that's nice! That was real nice of you to say that, ma'm!' He frowns at me and then smiles again at the wife. 'The kid don't deserve it but I won't take it out of his commission. I can see you people are real nice folk, generous minded.' He leans back into his swivel chair and folds his hands over his stomach, ' Okay, I know it's crazy, it must be the approaching silly season,' he moves forward smiles and sticks his hand out over the desk, 'Happy Christmas in September, Mr and Mrs Roberts. You can have *all* the add-ons the kid promised you, pigskin, mirrors and whites, for $150 added to the factory price of the Chieftan!' He smiles expansively, rises from his chair and, clasping the husband's hand in both of his own, shakes him warmly by the hand to consumate the deal and does the same to his wife. Then he looks around as though afraid he might be overheard and speaks in a slightly lower voice, ' But *only* if you promise not to speak to anyone about this? We have a reputation for giving our customers the best deal in town, but we don't want to be known around L.A. as the bunch who break the G.M., wholesale price maintenance agreement!'

The ordeal is over and he smacks his forehead with the butt of his hand, he can't believe he's been forced into such a compromise by this stupid kid from Australia.

The sales manager was called the 'Turnover man.' A good turnover man could put another $500 on the selling price of a car before a client finally left his office. Moreover, the buyer, in this case, the couple, would depart convinced that they'd still gotten the bargain of a lifetime, the best Pontiac ever made by G.M., for which they had paid the cheapest price in L.A. What's more, they'd secretly preferred tomato red as a colour all along.

I am not proud of my time as an auto salesman in L.A. It reminded me too often of my father and his sleight of hand when he taught me how to short-change people and cheat at cards. Selling in America in the fifties was all about high pressure, fast talking, sly moves and mental sleight-of-hand.

If you didn't sell a car for a week at Freedom Pontiac, you came under pressure. You were made to feel inadequate, not good enough, a 'real goose'.

Lunch was at noon when it was our team's rostered day in the showroom. This meant the salesmen would be back on the floor for any lunchtime prospects. All but one salesman would repair to an Irish Pub named Kitty O'Gorman's. Here, a very large Black lady named Lottie the Body would do a strip show to Cole Porter's immortal song, 'Love for Sale!' The show ended in her dropping her knickers and doing unspeakable tricks with a champagne glass, using the anatomical part her enormous *dainties* usually concealed.

For a junior salesman, the reward for selling an auto was an invitation to lunch at Kitty O' Gorman's with Lottie the Body in attendance. Despite her performance, and the offer she made in the song, the large, lascivious Lottie could not manage to sell her body to any of the salesmen present.

However, if you went for a week without selling a car, you were required to spend your lunch hour standing on the pavement directly outside the dealership wearing a large silver dunce cap with a red 'D' painted on it. You would stand there every lunch hour until you sold your next car or you were fired for incompetence. I confess, I spent quite a lot of time out on the street.

Now, obviously, this sort of tactic encouraged salesmen to go to any length to sell a car. As a breed, salesmen are a thick-skinned lot; they can take almost anything but humiliation. Sales is an area where personal ego is of the utmost importance and cheating the public was a very small price to pay to avoid this kind of humiliation.

The problem with business organisations which are not on the level is that everything you do eventually gets bent. Being dishonest becomes the natural state of affairs and you spend your life looking for an angle, working a scam. You become corrupted, not a very nice person. You lose sight of the most precious commodity a business and a salesman can have—honesty and a reputation for fairness. This is the quality that wins customer-friends and makes them come back, knowing they can trust you to take care of their interests.

Between them, the owners and salesmen in Freedom Pontiac, in fact, the entire car industry at that time, shared a culture of greed. They thought only of themselves and their own immediate gain, and paid little or no attention to customer satisfaction and even less to their long-term corporate image. They bonded with each other by being collectively dishonest, and in so doing they created a corporate culture that was basically unsound. The result was a sale made, a commission paid, but never a repeat sale. They had forgotten to leave a little salt on the bread for the customer. Customers eventually got to understand that they'd been ripped off and, of course, they never came back. It got so bad that the media stepped in and the public became aware of the rip-off practices. Consumer bodies went beserk and demanded a clamp-down. In the late '50s, legislation was introduced which required each car to have a Government-approved sticker, which showed the list price of the car and nominated the price of all the extras.

Bloody good thing, too! Apart from the immorality, conning the buyer is simply bad business. Very few businesses will grow or even remain open on the basis of a single sale, even a large single sale, such as an automobile. Furthermore, a reputation for putting a bunch of sharks on a sales lot soon gets around and you're out of contention as a competitor. Never under-estimate the intelligence of a customer; on a great many occasions in your daily life you are one yourself.

A lot of quite big businesses forget to *put a price* on good customer relations, image and reputation. Yet these are the most important assets your business can own. They are money in the bank. This is especially true when times get tough and the company needs to review its overall expenses.

If you've ever worked for a large company you'll know that the first item on the agenda to be slashed is usually the *training budget*. In many organisations, training the work force is still regarded as a bit of a luxury, a fine thing to do when times are good but expendable when they're bad. I have always thought this a very strange way of thinking.

Commonsense tells you that trained people, good salesmen and women, sell more goods and services than poor sales people, who will eventually cost you far more than the training budget. But, then, in my experience, commonsense is not a common commodity in most board rooms and is even harder to find on a Budget Committee.

But before we bemoan the shortcomings of a management panicked into budget slashing, we should look at some of the reasons why short term expedience is so endemic in many otherwise quite soundly-run businesses.

Now, suppose you are the marketing manager of a fairly large company. You are senior, but not senior enough to sit on the board. You will be heard, your opinion is even respected, but your recommendations are not always accepted. Times are tough, something's got to give. It's slash-the-budget time.

The financial controller (he's always on the main board), a bald guy with a long nose and rimless spectacles, fixes you with a steely glare. (The training budget has gone already and now it's your turn). He has his eye on your promotions and advertising expenditure. You argue hard and finish with a flourish, appealing directly to the good sense of the chairman.

'If we cut our promotional budget by 80 per cent, we risk …'

'Yes?' the finance controller asks, anticipating the statement to come.

'We risk damaging our image, losing share of mind in the marketplace and dropping sales!'

The bald head glistens, the nose sharpens and the steely eyes pinpoint you behind their rimless frames and cut through you like a laser beam. A small, cruel smile flickers at the corner of his cruel mouth.

'Can you measure it? Can you put a return figure on our

investment in advertising? What percentage of sales can be directly attributed to our advertising? How many units of product will we lose if we slash the budget by 50%?'

At this point you realise that you are skating on thin ice. You know, he knows, the whole bloody committee knows, that you can't measure mass consumer advertising in terms of extra dollars returned or sales made. Advertising is an investment in share of mind. You can't measure increased or decreased sales on a dollar spent, or withdrawn, from promotion and advertising. Advertising is only one of many variables in making a sale and it's the one which *can't* be measured in dollar returns.

But you also know that these guys on the Budget Committee only respond to red or black figures in a ledger and all you've got to prove your advertising is working is a research report, which says 40% of the general public, both sexes, aged between 15 and 55, know roughly who you are and the name of your product.

At this stage the chairman comes to life. There's not much he understands but he is delighted with the opening you've just presented to him.

He clears his throat, a signal to all, particularly you, to shut up and pay attention. You've been here before; you know what's coming. In the early '60s, he attended a three-month Harvard Business School Course, where he acquired absolutely no skills of consequence, except a liking for fat Cuban cigars that stink the boardroom out.

'Well, now ...' he spreads his hands expansively, 'we should all know *the first principle of business*, should we not, eh?' He eyes each member of the committee in turn, though his hooded gaze lingers momentarily longer on you, his young marketing manager, the kid with a future if only he would learn not to be so defensive.

'Oh, God, here it comes, Harvard class of '64!'

'If you can *measure* it, you can *manage* it!' he pronounces smugly and looks around for the congratulatory smiles he knows will be forthcoming. Then he takes a deep, self-satisfied pontifical puff at his cigar and smirks through a haze of expensive blue smoke, 'Not good enough, young Kennedy, you'll have to do better than that!'

The chairman hath spoken, your budget is history. It's game, set and match to the bloody bean counter whose scalp is flashing like a traffic beacon as he grins at you like the organ grinder's monkey he is.

Unfortunately, as an aphorism, it's true—it may be not the whole truth, but it is a significant amount of the truth. If you can measure a customer's responses, you can manage them. If you can't, be prepared to see your advertising and promotional budget slashed.

Bugging the booths at Freedom Pontiac was a way of measuring the customer's response, admittedly a dishonest one. But, nevertheless, it gave an exact measurement of the customers needs and responses. Once you knew he wanted a $200 discount and a black automobile, you could manage the information in a highly profitable and advantageous way.

The hard answer as to why organisations get away with mutilating the training and the advertising budget when things get tough is that, more often than not, they are not doing a great deal of harm to the company in the process. In many cases, the elimination of the training budget and a 50% cut in advertising expenditure, really *doesn't* matter.

Training is often so bad and advertising so misguided and haphazard and self-indulgent that slashing it by 50 per cent or more, seems to make little difference. Mass consumer advertising is never accountable; it can't be measured in terms of a company's bottom line and so it patently cannot be managed.

This is not true of measurable marketing, i.e. of direct marketing. Direct measurable marketing allows you to see almost instantly what *is* working and what *isn't*. And if you know what isn't making sales for you, *you can stop doing what doesn't work.* You can even measure the degree by which an approach has failed and sometimes make effective corrections. But, mostly, you learn to cut your losses early and move on in a different direction. Measuring the success or otherwise of a direct marketing campaign is incisive.

On the other hand, measuring the effectiveness of mass consumer advertising is usually a very complex matter and is finally measured in an abstract way, which is called '*share of mind.*'

Share of mind is not exactly money in the bank, but it is as close as you're likely to get to measuring results with this kind of advertising. The theory of share of mind suggests that *the more people know about your product the more sales you are likely to make.* It works on frequency and the creative impact of your message.

In other words, should someone want a tin of soup, and your product name springs into their mind at the moment they require the soup, and if their perception of your soup is that it is at least as good as any other product on the market, then they are likely to buy your brand and not that of your lesser known competitor.

When this happens, it is claimed that you own, for your product type, a superior *share of mind.* This you have brought about by consistently spending a lot of money on advertising over a great deal of time. By so doing, you have earned *top of mind awareness* for your product in the soup category.

Buying *share of mind* is a very good theory and I have no doubt, in the final analysis, it works. The longer you do it, and the more you spend, the more likely it is to work. The one proviso always is that your product is at least as good as that of the competition.

But you can't measure this type of advertising. And if you can't measure it, you can't tell which part of your advertising is working and which is not. In fact 50% or even 80% of your advertising may be going to the wrong people with the wrong message.

The closest mass consumer advertising can come to measuring its own effectiveness is to work out how much it costs you to reach each one thousand people. This is called appropriately enough, *The cost per thousand.* While this is quite nice to know, because it tells you how many people you can afford to reach for the money you have to spend, in the long run it isn't very useful. Simply because it doesn't show you how many people in the thousand you have reached are *interested* in and are *likely to buy* your product type. It doesn't tell you how to get down to the *lowest possible cost* for each individual sale made.

Put very simply; if I can reach 1000 people with $1000 spent on advertising, the *cost per thousand* is obviously one dollar per person. But what I *don't* know is how many of the thousand people my advertising has reached, at a cost of a dollar each, will end up buying my product. I have no way of measuring this in terms of sales.

For instance, my product may cost $10 to buy, so, to break even, I will need to get 100 customers out of the 1000 people I reach with my advertising message. But, say only 10 people buy my product of the 1000 I have reached. Then, clearly, it will cost me $100 to make a $10 sale. The point, is that with mass consumer advertising there is no way of finding out whether your advertising is working, or whether it isn't effective.

And this is why measuring sales is a critical aspect of business management. It is why the statement: *If you can measure it you can manage it,* makes so much sense to financial controllers and chairpersons of the board or anyone else who is seriously in business to make money.

Mass advertising always talks about an *efficient reach and frequency,* but it never thinks in the measurable terms of how much it is going to cost to make each individual sale.

The salesmen at Freedom Pontiac loaded $250 onto the unit price of an auto, and this was exactly what they had to 'spend' in order to make the sale. If they lost the $250 by giving it away they were back on the unit price and they made no money. If they used it as an incentive to 'sell up,' that is to get more money out of the customer, they made money. So even here they had a measurement they could manage.

Direct marketing is *measurable* marketing. You know *exactly* how much you have to spend in order to get someone to buy something. The measurement is based on asking two very simple questions.

The first: What does it cost *for each customer* who responds by name? This is known as: *Cost per Response.*

The second: What is *the most effective proposition* you have to give your potential customer to make him or her want to buy your product or service? This is known as: *The Offer.*

Taking the first criteria, *the cost of response,* this is a measurement which divides the number of responses gained (interested potential customers) by the number of dollars you had to spend to gain them.

You are no longer interested in what it cost you to reach 1000 people. Who the hell cares what the cost per thousand is? What you are concerned with is whether they are the right thousand people? Are they the people most likely to respond to your offer?

This leads to the next totally important difference in direct marketing—the *quality of the response* you get. You don't have 1000 anonymous potential buyers; you have *suspects* about to become *prospects*. This *qualifying* of your response is largely dependant on the second of the two rules: the Offer you use.

Quality of response means how many of those people who have taken the trouble to respond to your offer will eventually buy your product or service and how *easy* is it going to be to make the sale? *Easy* means how cheaply and convenient for your organisation and *hard* means how expensive and inconvenient.

Getting responses isn't all that difficult; getting the right responses is difficult! For instance, Montgomery Ward, a large American Department Store which does a lot of direct response, should have known better when they decided to start an Auto-Club in order to sell automobile travel and touring. As an incentive to encourage responses, they offered Zsa Zsa Gabor's gold Rolls Royce as a sweepstake prize. More than 20% of the people who responded didn't even hold a driving licence and a further significant percentage either didn't drive regularly or didn't own a vehicle. This was obviously not a successful attempt to get a quality response for their Auto Club.

They may have gotten a much lower number of initial responses if, for instance, they'd offered *free* to every respondent a Personal Travel Folio—road map and driver information, motels, diners, petrol stations, doctors, hospitals, police, highway conditions for any holiday driving destination of the respondent's choice. They could have added to this a book of price-off coupons at various outlets along the way. These coupons would have a 'use-by date' of one year. The response would almost certainly have been lower than the offer of a sweepstake ticket for a gold Rolls Royce, but the *quality of the responses* would have been very high—and each *suspect* would have almost certainly qualified him or herself as a *prospect* for membership of the Montgomery Ward Auto Club.

The cost of the personal travel folio as a free premium may have cost no more than the outlay for the Rolls. Premiums of paper are excellent because they have a high perceived value, but are low cost to produce.

Which brings up the next point: be careful of an offer which brings a response which is bigger than the capacity of your organisation or staff to handle.

For instance you may want to get people to test drive the new Ford Capri and so you advertise that a new Capri can be won in a key lottery. People wishing to enter should send in their names and they will, in turn, receive a key in the mail. One lucky key will fit the winning car and all the respondent needs to do is to go to a nominated Ford Dealer and book a test drive, whereupon their key will be tested in the lock of the Ford Capri prize.

So far things look good, the entries arrive by the sack full, the plastic keys you mail out cost less than five cents each, for a relatively inexpensive mailing shot, you have all the booking you can handle for a test drive of your new Capri. 'Well done, young Kennedy, you've done it again!'

And then people start coming into your showroom and queueing around the block by the thousands for a test drive of the new Ford Capri—so they can stick their winning plastic key into the Capri lock. Your salespeople cannot begin to cope with the human traffic, let alone attempt to sell a Capri to a *suspect* who would rather like to win one free, but who, otherwise, has absolutely no intention of ever becoming a *prospect* and eventually owning a Ford. Your sales staff are soon worn out and your database has become completely clogged with useless names. Car salespeople learned a long time ago that you must go for a test drive with the prospect. This is the very best time and place there is to overcome the prospect's objections.

You have to find a way to *qualify your response*, that is, be pretty bloody certain that your respondent has some passing interest in buying a Capri in the first place.

For instance, with the trend towards soft-tops or convertibles you might look at people who already own a Ford and who belong to an upwardly mobile socio-economic group. You could then suggest that they test drive a Ford Capri as the second car in the family, the partner's car. The kids will love it, the male in the household can use it on weekends, and the female as her weekday car, or the other way around. Now you have a Ford for work and one for play. You could offer free membership to an Auto Club in return for signing up for a test drive of the new Ford Capri, provided both partners come in for the test drive.

Now you have found a way of qualifying your respondent, who you know is already predisposed to the Ford marque. As well, you know you can handle the number of test drivers without too much trouble.

So, now we see how the two rules work together: The cost of response must be affordable and the nature of the offer must be manageable and result in a qualified prospect. In this respect it is as well to remember that: *The offer always drives the quality of the response.*

As in the example of the Ford Capri test drive offer, a huge response is no measure of success on its own. A good direct marketing campaign could be a response of one tenth of one per cent of all the people you reached, but all of whom converted into a sale.

A poor response might be a 50 per cent reply from the people you reached, with very few of them having any intention of buying your product or service.

Response in itself is meaningless.

To improve the quality of the response, that is, turn your *suspects* into *prospects*, it is necessary to use *qualifiers.*

Qualifiers are tiny barriers to deter those people who are essentially, not interested in a new car but only in the free gift. For instance we may say that the offer of the free membership to the Auto Club in the case of the Ford Capri, applies only to 'Ford families' with no second car, or with a second car which has at least 60,000 kms on the mileage counter. These little *qualifiers* can be very important in achieving a high quality response.

Say you were selling a service and not a car. Perhaps you want to generate leads for retirement insurance, always a tough problem. To identify *prospects,* you ask *suspects* to send in their details in return for valuable information from your organisation. As an incentive to them to respond, you offer a 1943 SS Jaguar sports car fully restored to mint condition and certified by the Jaguar Owners Club. The age of car being 55 years to correspond with the ideal age of anyone buying retirement insurance. It sounds like a nice offer (the 55-year-old thing is a nice little qualifier) and there are all sorts of clever, creative things you can do with it. But there is still a very high risk that a great many *suspects* will respond for the chance to win the car, and not be potential *prospects.* Once again, you'd be 'up to your eyeballs' in administration with your database clogged with false sales leads.

However, if you offered a far less appealing premium, say a *free* Retirement Planning Kit, the chances are that you would get a somewhat lower response but a much *better qualified* one. Your *suspects* would almost immediately become *prospects.* It would be most unlikely that people would respond to a free retirement kit unless the subject of retirement was on their minds. Even if they don't buy our particular insurance offer at the time, you will have added a quality name to your database for a future offer or promotion.

In the end, using the two measurement criteria—*cost* and *offer*—it all adds up to what it cost you in money terms to make a single sale. And also, what it cost us in reputation to make a sale. A good direct response campaign is one which delivers the optimum cost per sale in both money and in goodwill terms; a bad one gives an ineffective cost per sale.

Costs, money and emotion are all important. But if you get the money one wrong, you do not live long enough to earn goodwill or to enhance your reputation.

As a general rule it can be said that an incentive or premium of some kind will always increase responses. This was true of Freedom Pontiac, with its offer of white walls, chrome side mirrors and pigskin seat trim, and it is true of direct marketing. People simply love to get something which they perceive to be free. In direct marketing terms, it is normally well worth using a premium (a reward for responding) providing always it is *cost effective.*

Cost effective doesn't simply mean that you can build the cost of the premium into the price of the goods. It also means that the premium offer attracts *more responses,* or suspects, who turn readily into *more prospects.* It must be a premium offer which has an *affinity* with the nature of the goods or services being offered, one which connects psychologically with the offer. In fact, the ideal premium could be referred to as an, *Affinity Premium.*

If you neglect this rule of the affinity incentive, or premium, and simply offer a free and totally unrelated gift for every response you receive from a suspect, you run the risk of a low, average-quality response.

It is one of the paradoxes of direct marketing, that the easier and more attractive you make it for people to respond to your offer, the lower the quality of the responses you will get.

You must always think the campaign through and not be carried away with a bag full of mail sending for a free gift in return for a name and address. **Example:** If the gift you offer is a cute fluffy toy, and the product you are selling is a set of spanners, the hundreds of schoolgirls who happily send you their names and addresses will not end up buying too many sets of spanners.

The offer you make drives the quality of the response. Think it out very carefully before you rush off to buy a gold Rolls Royce from a blonde Hungarian.

Freedom Pontiac got it wrong by rewarding a sale with the doubtful privilege of having lunch at Kitty O' Gorman's, and seeing Lottie the Body perform. Conversely, it was also wrong to punish the lack of a sale by making a public spectacle of the salesman by having him wear a dunce cap on the pavement during lunch break.

However, it is just as well to remember that you get it equally wrong when you get a bag full of replies in response to a misguided or silly premium offer. The result is likely to earn you the dunce cap and get you slung out onto the pavement for performing silly tricks that are not going to earn the respect of your customers or lead to a sale.

Your premium should drive the offer you're making and qualify each response. It is not the number of responses you get, but the quality and cost per response which counts. The final and only meaningful measurement is the cost per sale.

Chapter Six

*A philosophy for life born out of a paprika sandwich and a
hard boiled egg.*

★ ★ ★

In America I was learning a great deal about life. Though I'm not
sure they were all the right lessons. I was the youngest salesman
at Freedom Pontiac and, as an Australian, a bit of a curiosity. The
senior salesmen were happy to train me in the doubtful, if closely-
guarded, techniques of selling automobiles in the early '50s. I
suppose I was influenced by them. It was good playing with the
big boys who thought of me as a bit of a novelty. I quickly learned
how to make them laugh with my accent and Australian expres-
sions. For a while there, I thought I was pretty hot stuff.

But, in fact, I wasn't doing very well. There wasn't enough of
my Dad in me and I didn't flourish in the car salesman's environment. Then my father got ill and my mother wrote to tell me: 'He
wants to see you but doesn't know how to say so. Please come
home, darling!'

I was pretty disappointed with myself. I think I'd had just about
enough of North America. But it hadn't solved
anything and I was still pretty confused about my father. I still
thought I wanted revenge. You know, leave home a nobody and
come back a squillionaire so that you show your Dad that you're
bigger, smarter, tougher and better than him. You want to be able

to show him you didn't need any help from him to succeed. I suppose it's a sort of reverse psychology. You really want him to love you, but you've got to show him you don't give a hoot about him. Males play these silly emotional games with themselves from a very early age.

But now my mother wanted me home and I had precious little emotional weight to throw around and no success to take home with me. I'd been away two years and I barely had my boat trip home. I'd always imagined going home with an armful of hugely expensive, unobtainable-in-Australia presents for everyone, even for my Dad, and when they ooh'd and aah'd as they opened them, I would look modest and say: 'It's nothing, just a little thought from America.'

What I lacked in wealth I felt I might have gained in cunning. I decided to put my Freedom Pontiac experience to work to con my father into sending me the airfare home. The idea was to use the money to buy presents for everyone so that I didn't arrive home the prodigal son with a handful of air in my trouser pockets.

I devised this rather clever telegram: AM WALKING—BROKE, PLEASE SEND MONEY!

The Kennedy senior response came within twenty-four hours: KEEP WALKING—TAKE THE SHORT CUT VIA HONOLULU!

He may have been sick but nothing else had changed and no money arrived from Australia. I booked a passage home. By coincidence, it was the Orsova again. This time though, I had a six-berth cabin with a porthole. I guess it was the luck of the draw, for I bought the cheapest available ticket. My final night in America was spent on the roof of the Y.M.C.A. in the downtown L.A., the roof accommodation 'under the stars' being $8 a night while 'inside' was $12.

I awoke on my final morning in America to a thick choking smog, which burned the back of my throat. I have to admit that the thought of the crystal clean air, and a fresh breeze blowing across Sydney harbour, made going home broke a little easier to bear.

I wish I could say that the time in Canada and America had made me independently minded and uncaring of my father's regard for me. But it didn't. My father was determined I should amount to something, and that didn't mean my becoming a car salesman. To his chagrin, I'd abandoned economics at university in the first year. But he still harboured ambitions of a business career for me. He accepted that I enjoyed selling, but in his mind there was selling and there was *selling*.

I found myself working for a Jewish-Hungarian refugee named Albert Sheinberg, who has since become a legendary figure in the Australian manufacturing, financial and property development world. But at that time he was not long out of Hungary and was just developing his business momentum. In a land where the chairman of the board is usually known by his first name down to at least middle management, it was inconceivable that anyone would refer to Albert Sheinberg in any other terms but 'Mr Sheinberg'. In turn, even at my tender age of 23, he always referred to me as 'Mr Kennedy.'

Albert Sheinberg was to be the person who would teach me the real lessons in life I had been waiting for. He was kind, honest, dynamic, generous, very clever and he worked enormously hard. He made me his personal assistant. Why he would have done so is a mystery. I was the only manager in his organisation who was not a Hungarian-Jew and, in his terms of reference, I was abysmally ignorant. I knew about cars, pooey nappies and egg prickers and he was about to plunge me into the world of high finance, real estate and manufacturing, where he was already making a big name for himself.

Mr Sheinberg was a truly extraordinary person. I guess still is. He called me on the telephone only twice in three years. He rarely used the phone to do business. He was a one-to-one person and he trusted personal relationships and a handshake above all else. 'Mr Kennedy, always you should look a man in the eyes, then listen to what he is not saying … behind, in his head, is going on a very important conversation.'

His dress never varied, casual and business, it was always the same outfit, a white sports shirt open at the collar, with braces and a baggy suit. His hair was cropped to exactly one inch of steel grey brush-cut. Once, when I asked him why he had a German haircut when he was Jewish, he replied: 'Mr Kennedy, even a Jew

can learn from a German. In life, it is an absolute waste of time
to comb the hair!'

He would carry a large paprika sandwich on rye bread in his
right hand suit pocket, together with a hard-boiled egg. It never
changed, always a brown paper bag and in it a paprika and egg
sandwich. We'd go to auctions together and he'd look down-at-
heel, I mean worse than the male equivalent of a bag lady. He'd
be munching his sandwich and sticking up his finger bidding for
a building worth five or six million dollars, which in the '60s was
a huge amount of money.

He always had traces of white powder on his shoes and one
Sunday night, I asked George Farkas about it. George had also
escaped from Hungary and ran the jewellery factory they jointly
owned. He leaned over and whispered into my ear: 'He prefers
to 'dry clean' himself. That's Johnson's Baby Powder. He puts it
on all over his body and some of it falls through his underpants
onto his shoes.

If he looked like a derelict, it wasn't because he wasn't clean—
just the opposite. Albert Sheinberg was about as clean a man as
you'll ever meet. Everything about him was clean. The deals he
made. The way he treated people, his outlook on life. And, I
guess, talcum powder must be a pretty effective cleanser, because
he always smelt clean as well. It was just the suits he wore, they
were also clean, but they looked like they'd been thrown together
by a blind Afghan tent maker. His expensive car was just as
unkempt. He would stick it into low gear and forget to change
up to a higher gear en route, so that he lurched rather than drove
to any destination. Mr Sheinberg was much too busy living his life
to be in the least concerned about appearances or cars. I often
wished that he'd been my father.

Once a month he invited all his associates and managers to
meet in his house on a Sunday night. With the exception of
myself, they were all Jewish and mostly Hungarian. It was an
entirely different culture for someone like me and I learned to
really like Jewish people and thought them quite wonderful.
Everything was out in the open. They had a great sense of humour
and colour and eccentricity, and they allowed that they were not

perfect and helped each other in a hundred different ways that had nothing to do with business. I think it was Mr Sheinberg, more than anyone else, who taught me that relationships are built on trust and that they are very important and should never be taken for granted.

There I was, once a month on a Sunday night, among the shouting and laughter and protests, when they'd all come to talk to Mr Sheinberg about the month in business. I can't say they came to report to him, that would give quite the wrong impression. They came as friends, openly, they admitted mistakes, asked advice, gave advice, shouted at each other, lost their tempers, sulked, comforted each other, picked up ideas and shared each other's triumphs and disasters. I'm sure every man in that room knew he was never alone, never without love or help or comfort. That whatever happened his wife and family would be cared for.

There was Mr Buddae, who was just then starting Astor Glass, and the guy who ran American Bag Stores, and the one who ran Berryman & Company, the furniture manufacturer. Also, there was the partner who ran Swiss Leather Goods, and who was in competition with American Bag Stores, and the lovable Leslie Kritzler, from Goldstar Bakery, who, despite the racket, always fell asleep before 8 p.m. when the *loschin* soup arrived, because he got up at 4 a.m. to bake. Finally, there was the ebullient George Farkas, who, as a refugee, started driving a taxi at night and fashioned costume jewellery in his little Kings Cross flat during the day. His wife baked fancy continental cakes and made exceedingly good continental coffee before the days of espresso and cappuccino. George would invite his fellow taxi drivers home for a cup of coffee and a bit of cake. He would then get them working, fixing paste and glass into settings which he had cast from lead and dipped in gold and silver. Mr Sheinberg had discovered George one day while going home in George's cab and now they were in business together.

Mr Sheinberg taught me one of the most important lessons I ever learned about pricing merchandise. It's such a simple idea yet it took a genius like Albert Sheinberg to think of it. He had made me manager of Park Lane Handbags. At 24 I was probably the youngest person working there. I ran the show and he trusted me to make the day-to-day decisions for the 100 people who worked in the factory. But in one area, he made a rule which was never under any circumstances broken. It was the golden rule in the factory and I think it, more than anything else, turned this small handbag manufacturer into a huge enterprise.

When the new season's samples came in, we'd all sit around a large table and none of us was allowed to know the manufacturing price of the item we examined. We simply wrote down what we thought the handbag was worth as a wholesale and retail item. The point is, of course, that once you know how much something costs to manufacture you can't help but be influenced by this knowledge in pricing it.

In this simple way, by not knowing the manufacturing cost, items which cost quite a lot to make but were priced low by the people around the table were rejected. Conversely, items which may not have cost a great deal, but which were perceived by us to have a high value, were immediately ordered for the coming season. This allowed us to offer them at an attractive price to the retailer, while affording the factory a generous margin.

Such a simple idea, and one which I have used in selecting products for direct marketing ever since—sometimes with quite spectacular success. Perceived value has absolutely no relationship to cost price.

While Mr Sheinberg trusted his partners and managers to the hilt, he was not a fool and he expected his casual workers to attempt to steal from him. He was a realist. He taught me always to be conscious of pilferage.

While I was managing the handbag factory, a lot of handbags were being stolen. With over 100 employees, we simply couldn't find out how it was being done. Employees were searched every evening upon leaving the factory and regular spot checks made of the loading docks. The gates were manned with guards 24 hours a day. The garbage, which was collected twice a week, was inspected nightly. Garbage was often used to get goods out of a factory. But nothing we did was effective. More than 50 handbags a week were being illegally removed. It got so that I was beginning to feel personally responsible, almost guilty.

'Mr Kennedy, ' Sheinberg said to me, 'think simple, don't look for clever, look for simple!' This was before Dr Edward de Bono had sold the world the concept of *lateral thinking.* Albert Sheinberg displayed it in almost everything he did. The blind pricing of handbags samples being just one small example.

One morning, as I was coming into work very early, the garbage truck was parked in the factory driveway collecting the garbage from the factory bins. The yard man was using the hoist to bring the bins to the truck. As I entered the gates I saw him point to three bins and raise his thumb at the garbo. I knew immediately that I'd discovered the scam.

The stolen handbags were in three garbage bins which had been packed only minutes before they were to go out with the rest of the legitimate garbage. The simplicity lay in the process taking place in a matter of minutes early in the morning when nobody was about except the storeman and the yardman. It turned out, they were co-conspirators with the garbage collectors in what became known as, 'The Garbage Bag Connection.'

Just as Mr Sheinberg had anticipated, the scheme was almost ridiculously simple and virtually foolproof. Only by coming to work unexpectedly at 6 a.m. had I finally uncovered it—and then only because I'd been cautioned to look for a simple explanation.

Albert Sheinberg treated me, in fact all of us, like family. He was understanding to the point of benevolence. On the other hand, I was bright and liked to think I was efficiently running the handbag factory, but I was probably too big for my boots and rather arrogant. Eventually, I think to Mr Sheinberg's relief, I said that I felt I knew all about handbags and couldn't make much more of a contribution and would like to move on. Mr Sheinberg moved me into his major company, Stocks and Holdings, a huge financial organisation which had just started building exhibition homes.

I started as a salesman at Gold Star Homes and I used to sit in an exhibition home all weekend, way out in Ryde—a nearly tree-less, mindless, hopeless suburban development.

I'd try to sell these people houses—young people, not very sophisticated, ordinary working class kids with hope in their hearts and the dream of owning their own home showing in their eyes. They were prepared to make any financial commitment to get started in their first home.

It was by no means the worst of the developments taking place. It was within striking distance of the coast and the city with several middle-class suburbs abutting. This part of Ryde had what in real estate terms was called 'potential.' There were much worse suburban developments taking place in the West, where hundreds of acres of bushland were simply levelled. In the process, the topsoil was removed so that even today, more than 35 years later, they remain desolate, featureless, red brick suburban 'slums' with all the attendant problems.

The '60s was a sad time for the Australian suburban landscape: a time when bad taste ruled; State and local government corruption was alleged; ecological malpractice was everywhere and uncaring public instrumentalities let sewage flow straight into the clean, running rivers. Consequently, a swarm of financial opportunists, developers armed with fleets of bulldozers, and an army of bricklayers reaped havoc on the beautiful bushland surrounding Sydney.

This period, which I can only think of as the Ugly '60s, caused most of the present day sub-topia seen around suburban Australia. However, at the time, I was not sensitive to any of these issues. I thought only of learning how to make a buck.

The '60s also saw the advent of direct marketing in Australia. It was a business with an already dubious reputation in America, brought into Australia mostly by individuals who were ethically doubtful and unskilled—men in cheaply rented offices in dilapidated buildings in the sooty end of town, selling sex devices and horoscopes by mail order. They knew very little and were simply looking for the gullible section of any population to exploit for a fast dollar.

There were, of course, exceptions, but they were not plentiful. The best that can be said of these early years of direct response is that the small practitioners were ignorant and arrogant. They worked mostly in products that were over-promised in the advertising, and were of poor quality and value. The products often arrived in plain brown paper wrapping at an exorbitant price. Because of all of these things, the early direct marketers generally failed in business and probably ended up as second-hand car dealers.

Pornography, like every other kind of merchandise, has to be of high quality and well-priced—a point these early direct mail cowboys never understood. They regarded their customers either as stupid or as perverts when they were neither.

I have never worked in the soft-porn business, but I have met people who have. They say that pornography is not sold to doubtful-looking characters in dirty raincoats, but to people who wear three-piece suits and monogrammed shirts and send their kids to private schools. Pornography is a classless business and has replaced money as the favourite item under the mattresses of the nation.

From Gold Star Homes I was moved into Stocks and Holdings to learn the financial side of the real estate business and managing commercial properties. After a year and at the ripe old age of twenty-five I thought it was time to make a living on my own. I had lots of energy and ambition and I figured that Mr Sheinberg had given me the experience I needed to make it big on my own. We parted company, but not without a promise from him that if ever I should need help of any sort, I was to come to him first. Later, when I got into a spot of trouble, he came to me with an offer of money. I'm sure the offer still stands. He is that sort of man.

In those days banks were very reluctant to lend money to anyone wanting to buy a home. You practically had to own a home in order to get a loan for a mortgage. Times were a'changing and young people wanted their own homes. So I set up on my own as a finance broker. My job at Stocks and Holdings and Gold Star Homes had allowed me to meet solicitors who handled money for clients. So now I acted as the go-between—people who had money were connected by yours truly with people who wanted it. I earned 1% of the final loan, which sounds great, but wasn't. I barely made a living. And so I started to look around for other things to do.

As well as the brokering business, I opened a dry cleaning kiosk in the Imperial Arcade with a friend, David Ashcroft, who worked in insurance. Whenever Rosie, the girl we'd hired to run it, wanted to go to the toilet, or have lunch, she would have to call one of us and we'd leave whatever business we were doing and hurry down to man the kiosk.

We never thought to close it, or even give Rosie a sign which said 'Back in 5 mins.' We'd both learned that service was the name of the game and we intended to literally 'service the pants off' our customers.

On one occasion, I was negotiating a pretty big deal with a solicitor from one of the establishment law firms. I was in his office with his client to sign the documents. It was all very civilised with leather-bound books with gold stamping lining the mahogany walls, leather armchairs, portraits of founders—the usual intimidating city law firm environment. The very superior old fart of a lawyer and his client, a lady in her sixties with an imperious English accent, were formally polite. We drank tea and I remembered to stick my little finger out and it was fine—except that I had to man the dry cleaning kiosk at 12 o'clock because Rosie had to go shopping with her mum, who was coming in especially. Rosie had begged me not to be a minute late as her mum was apt to get tetchy.

When we'd finally finished being polite to each other, and had jointly signed the documents, I had only five minutes to dash uptown to the Imperial Arcade. I arrived just as Rosie was starting to wring her hands and jump up and down and look distressed, with a cranky-looking woman, presumably her mum, standing outside the kiosk.

At about 12.45 p.m., I looked up from tagging a bunch of things to go to the cleaning depot and there, coming towards me, was the lawyer and the old lady. He was obviously taking her to the Hotel Australia for lunch. The dry cleaning kiosk was a small island, slap-bang in the middle of the arcade, and it wasn't possible to hide. I could see the look of bemusement on the lawyer's face as he saw me. Both of them stopped at the kiosk and the lawyer said to the old lady: 'Doesn't he look remarkably like the young broker in my office this morning?' Then, turning to me, he said: 'I say, are you related to a fellow named Kennedy?'

I hadn't practised crossing the border at Buffalo for nothing. 'Kennedy?' I looked suitably quizzical, running the name through my mind, 'No sir! I'm from Toronto, Ontario.' My Canadian accent was flawless.

As they walked away, I heard the old biddy say in her loud upper-crust accent: 'Quite a good likeness, but the young man in your office was much more *refeened*, not so *coarse* looking.'

Talk about sticking your pinkie out when you hold a cup of tea!

If I had learned anything from working with Mr Sheinberg it was to diversify, to stay flexible, never to get yourself into a corner, never to put all your egg-pricked eggs in one basket.

'Mr Kennedy, learn always to look around. Don't be proud. Business is business; a little bit here a little bit somewhere else. When something goes wrong in one business, something is always going good somewhere else.'

Of course, Mr Sheinberg had a genius for picking his partners. I chose mine because they were just like me: broke with lots of energy, very little know-how and a great anxiety to make as fast a quid as possible. Together David Ashcroft and I were not a great meld of honed and polished talent. Besides, we lacked the refugee status of being essentially clever men, with a sound ethnic and religious network, willing to work like dogs to make a good life for themselves in a new land. I was just a kid, who was trying to prove to his father he wasn't a bum and not succeeding very well. David's personal agenda probably wasn't all that different.

In the money-broking business something seemed to always be going wrong. The people who had the loot were too greedy and wanted too high an interest rate, and the people who needed the loans were too poor to repay the interest rate. Nor was the dry cleaning business all that crash hot, with the profits having to be split two ways after paying Rosie's salary. I decided to take Mr Scheinberg's advice: David and I decided to diversify into food.

Apart from Cream of Wheat I knew very little about cooking and David knew even less. I'd seen Leslie Kritzler, of Goldstar, go from a hole-in-the-wall bakery to a huge enterprise. It never occurred to me that this probably had something to do with his knowing a bit about baking bread!

People, I reasoned, needed food to stay alive and we would supply food to what today would be termed a *niche market*—to late-night weirdos! We opened a restuarant in Kings Cross, situated at the quiet end, away from the sleazy, night club, strip-tease, neon-lit end of the strip.

We'd convinced ourselves, mostly from personal experience, that drunks and late-nighters don't really care what they eat. We would open a place that stayed open when everything else closed. We were, after all, pretty busy during the day. So a late-night eatery seemed ideal for the hours left over for making a fortune in quick, somewhat carelessly-prepared 'avant garde' food, which was closer to being inedible than it was to French cuisine.

We called the restaurant 'The Cafe Inferno' because it was next door to the fire station in Victoria Street. As it turned out, no establishment was ever better named. Just about everything we served was burned to a crisp and our salad wasn't just limp, it came with a tiny pair of crutches. I arranged a daily delivery from Goldstar Bakeries of six dozen left-over hamburger buns and a bag of breadcrumbs to mix with the mince topside. We used to pay the kid who delivered them two bob for delivery. The buns and crumbs were free!

The Cafe Inferno was, without question, the worst restaurant ever to open in Sydney—or, for that matter, anywhere on earth. It also sported a frenzied bongo drummer with very little talent but a great deal of stamina. Customers would sometimes beg us to make him stop.

The premises were in the front of an apartment block. In order to go to the toilet, customers had to cross a small internal court-yard in the centre of the block of flats to reach the toilets on the far side. The residents, whether because of the ceaseless bongo drummer or the fact that noisy drunks and weirdos were always crossing the courtyard, would sometimes tip a bucket of cold water over a customer as he returned from the toilet.

We got used to seeing patrons returning wringing wet, and with an astonished look on their faces, not quite sure what had happened but pretty bloody upset. We kept a large towel ready and also a plastic raincoat and umbrella, which we urged our clients to use when going to the toilet. This worked on the more sober ones, but the more inebriated would set off unprotected and come back doused and bewildered while the bongo drummer played on, never pausing for a minute, no matter what the crisis.

At that stage of my life I didn't yet understand the priorities, the three golden rules of direct marketing which also happen to be the same three rules for running a successful business.

In the case of direct marketing, the rules require:

1. The audience to be targeted.
2. A compelling offer
3. Irresistable creative execution.

Used for running an effective business the same three rules might be slightly modified to read:

1. The customers you need.
2. How you present your wares.
3. The advertising message.

In terms of The Cafe Inferno, let's begin with rule Number 3, the advertising creative message. Well, regarding The Cafe, the advertising creative message was to prove non-existent. We simply didn't have the means to advertise, except for a neon sign in the window which originally read: **Exotic Food—Open late**. Which is quite good really. It tells any weirdo, providing he isn't too stoned to read, that you're open and he can buy something to eat. Perhaps not terribly original, but clear enough—and clarity is the essence of good communication. Our advertising had one essential weakness: it required each prospective patron to pass our front door. In *reach and frequency terms*, it was pathetic. But, at least, it was some sort of promise which, under the right circumstances, could have been quite compelling.

Except it wasn't. Our main message became obscured very

early, soon after we got it, the neon sign, *Exotic Food—Open Late*
got bumped into by a huge transvestite and made a sort of frying
sound, which continued forever afterwards and which caused the
neon to somehow short-circuit on the capital letters so that the
sign read: **tic ood pen ate**

We told ourselves frequently that one of us was going to remember to call Rousel Signs and have it fixed. But, somehow, when
daylight came we always forgot. So our creative message must have
been particularly confusing for our main target audience—the
late-night misfits hanging around the Cross. They'd pass and hear
this peculiar frying sound coming from the neon sign. Then
they'd stand on the pavement outside, swaying, with one eye
closed, trying to work out what **tic ood pen ate** could possibly
mean. If they stood long enough, the smell of burnt hamburger
meat, and chips fried in rancid oil, would eventually reach into
their besotted brains and they'd be pulled into the place by the
nostrils. So, in effect, our major creative messages, while being
visually puzzling, could be said to have been more of an auditory
and olfactory nature, which worked with great subtlety at a deeply
subliminal level.

The next, or second rule is: *A compelling offer.* In this respect,
The Cafe Inferno could be said to have been up with the haute
cuisine establishments around town. We always tried to have some
sort of gourmet surprise on the menu, a 'Tonight's Special,' like
Grilled Hake Oriental or *Mixed Grill, Mexicana, two eggs, extra chips!*
The exotic content to justify the words 'Oriental' and 'Mexicana'
was a dash of soy sauce on the fish and a splash of Tabasco on
the mixed grill. I'm sure you get the idea. This was the equivalent
of Mr Sheinberg's blind-pricing policy, where the merchandise
always looked great value for the price.

I recall once becoming terribly excited about a special offer for
the cafe. My mother had taken me to a decent restaurant for
lunch. At the table next to ours, they were served a dessert called
Peach Tournado, which had brilliant purple flames leaping from it.
I thought this was absolutely terrific and conceived of an all-time
great special for the Cafe Inferno, which we'd call *The Grill Inferno.*

David agreed that it was a great idea, a bit of real class. So when a guy who wasn't all that smashed ordered it, we hurriedly threw together a mixed grill, into the centre of which I put a small container of methylated spirits. We were unusually full that night and I was in a hurry. Must have been a bit careless with the metho, as it spilt all over the sausages, steak, bacon, peas and whatever.

The waiter that night was David. It was my turn in the kitchen. I waited until the last moment and, just before he emerged from the swing doors leading from the kitchen into the restaurant , I threw a lighted match into the centre of the plate.

With a great *whoosh!* away he went, half-doors banging against the wall, flames leaping up towards the ceiling, the entire plate an inferno all right. David tried to look unconcerned, beating gently at the flames with the dishcloth he carried over his arm, which only seemed to fan them to a greater fury.

It was truly remarkable. David was pretty cool and didn't panic and kept walking, beating at the flames, trying to ignore what was happening, determined not to be put off and drop the plate and run for his life, as any sensible person would have done.

David put the plate from hell down in front of the astonished customer and said with as much aplomb as it is possible to muster with your sleeve on fire: 'You ordered *Grill Inferno,* sir!'

By this time, the flames in the plate had died down to a dull roar. The bacon looked like two pieces of charred elastic, the eggs had disappeared altogether, the tomato was black, the chop about the size of a ten cent coin and the steak not very much bigger. Only the beetroot and lettuce remained intact, though they were steaming beside the totally burnt-out chips.

What's more, the entire restaurant clientele, had fled into the night, never to be seen again. It had been one of our best nights ever—up to the point the *Grill Inferno* arrived!

I guess what this means is that we weren't too good at rule number two. For a start, the basic offer, that is the food, was pretty ordinary, and *specials we offered,* or in direct marketing terms, *the compelling offer,* caused our customers to stay away in large numbers. Either the bad food was the cause or the nearby Methadone Centre was doing a lot better job than we'd imagined.

Finally, there is the most important rule of them all: attracting *the right customers* in business or, translated into direct marketing terms, *The audience to be targeted.*

I guess making our major customer base late-night eccentrics, weirdos, freaks and those not too smashed to be allowed in, wasn't as smart as it had first seemed to us. There were several compelling reasons why this was the case:

- People on chemical substances don't have any money because they've spent it all getting stoned.
- They regularly fall asleep into a plate of spaghetti bolognaise and you can't wake them up when it's time to go home.
- They make a terrible mess of the toilet and they often stare at the wall for hours.
- They regularly start seeing things in the shadows and freak-out in public.
- A group of weirdos together can cause a lot of trouble and can be dangerous.
- They seldom if ever tip and often throw up, sometimes immediately after eating.
- They frequently say loud and terrible things about the place when they leave, such as: 'Now we know why there are no Chinese restaurants in the Cross, you guys have got the monopoly on serving up dead cats!'

In all, we'd picked a terrible customer base to work with: unreliable, often abusive, stupid, stoned, ungrateful and usually broke. In *target audience* terms, they were a complete disaster. What's more, other than giving them ptomaine poisoning, we didn't go to a great deal of trouble to encourage them to return or to remain loyal.

If you take the three golden rules, by far the most important is your customer base. Direct marketing is a methodology which is about customers, not about products' or services. In fact, in direct marketing terms, the customer is *10 times* more important than the creative component in your advertising and twice as important as the special offer you make. Here are the values of the direct marketing components in a campaign.

Audience = 10. Offer = 5. Creative =1.

Take your creative budget and multiply it by 10 in terms of hours. That is, take the time you spent carefully briefing designers and copywriters to make sure they have the concept right, then add the head hours they spent coming up with a creative approach, then the hours spent jointly reviewing drafts, roughs and visuals, plus the time required for final art or television, and *multiply all this by 10 times.* That is how much time you should be spending, proportionally, in getting your audience component right.

Again, for the time spent preparing and reviewing *your offer,* multiply the creative preparation time by five. Now, and only now, are you starting to get your emphasis right on the three major campaign components. The problem is that defining your audience is, generally speaking, dull work.

The Offer usually needs a bit of thinking, a bit of ingenuity. There are an unlimited number of options available, which makes it exciting. It's rather nice work inventing the offer you are going to make.

The Creative is just plain exciting, fun to do, working with long-haired people of both sexes, with the arse out of the back of their blue jeans and knee caps showing where they've carefully cut and frayed the denim. There is also lots of expertise to take a mediocre idea and dress it up to make you look good.

The Audience, on the other hand, is hard, hard work. Not any fun at all. You can't invite your associates over to see your brilliant breakthrough on *audience data* in quite the same way as you can with your great new advertising campaign. The guy who comes in to discuss your latest *regression analysis* doesn't wear Ray-Ban Alpine reflective glare lenses with leather hoods to protect the sides of his eyes, or drive a Porsche 911. And he never thinks to invite you to lunch at trendy watering holes, where the waitresses are moulded into black vinyl from neck to ankles.

And so, most of us find it too hard to work through the remorseless boredom it often takes to get your *audience component* perfect for the offer you intend to make. This is especially true of newcomers to the direct marketing industry—banks and insurance companies, car companies and other corporate hopefuls.

One, five, ten. They are the time multiplier figures which will often determine your success or failure in direct marketing. Have them tattooed on the back of your hand: one for creative; times five for the offer; and times 10 for defining the audience.

Let me expand for a moment on *the audience component* of your direct marketing campaign. A customer isn't simply a one-off user of your products, or service, in a single direct-marketing campaign: she, or he, is potentially a life-time user of your product or service. The *lifetime value of a customer* is the very foundation of any serious business.

It seems so very simple when you put it like that. Every time I go to the football I buy a hot dog after the match from the same lady. She is old now, her life with six kids and a husband who abuses her has been hard and it shows in her face. When I started going to the football 40 years ago, we were both kids. Once, it must have been 30 years ago, she prepared a hot dog for me. I didn't have any money on me and when I ruefully explained I was broke, she said: 'You're never too broke for one of my dogs,' and insisted I take it. We've been Ian and Rose ever since. I am a lifetime customer and I'd rather go without a hot dog after a football match than buy one from anyone else.

Here is a question: *Who is the most likely person to buy a new BMW?*

The answer, of course, providing they are satisfied, is the owner of a current BMW. Who, then, are your best customers? Quite obviously, your *existing customers*.

So here we are back at *relationship marketing*. I can absolutely assure you that the great majority of major corporations spend not nearly enough on relationship marketing to their existing customers. The airlines are perhaps the exception, having been forced into it by the travel agents who *owned* the relationship with the airline passengers.

The sad fact is, that most of us take our existing customer base for granted, we accept them as our right, like a wife or husband, and we spend pathetically little time considering their needs or showing them any corporate love and affection. We are all too busy chasing after new conquests.

Sure, we give lip-service to the customer loyalty concept: '*Honey, of course I love you! Have you seen my golf shoes?* Somewhere on the wall of the company is a grubby poster which says: *The Customer is always right!*, or some such euphemism for love. We can usually remember to find a line between the columns of figures in our annual reports to thank our customers for their loyalty. But that's about it.

Most major corporations using direct marketing have a *transaction mentality*, which means that, basically, they are more interested in a one-night stand than in an on-going relationship.

Your existing customers have a value to you which is worth a fortune. In marketing jargon, it is called the LVC, for *Lifetime Value of a Customer*. This is the value of a customer during their lifetime with you.

Once you start to assign a dollar value to this LVC, you will come to some interesting conclusions. On-going relationships, apart from doing your corporate image a lot of good, also become hard-headed, hard-nosed, sharp-eyed, bottom-line propositions. Your LVCs are the crown jewels in your direct marketing crown.

Some pretty impressive research has been done in the area of the *lifetime value of the customer*, most notably by Frederick Reichheld of Bain & Company, and W. Earl Sasser, a professor at the Harvard Business School. They jointly published a paper entitled 'Zero Defections' in the September–October 1990 Harvard Business Review, which changed the way companies look at their bottom line.

Their research findings showed that the move towards what they called 'Zero Defections' from a company customer database increased profitability by a hugely significant rate. They proposed that profits would increase by up to 75% by merely retaining 5% more of a company's existing customers. No, you didn't read that incorrectly—by keeping an extra 5 per cent of existing customers they contend that a company can increase its bottom line profitablility by 75 per cent.

They quote MBNA , an American credit card company in Del-aware, whose President decided in 1982 that he would do every-thing in his power to keep every customer he could profitably serve. He would do anything to keep them satisfied, providing it wasn't demonstrably unprofitable. He called in Bain & Company to conduct the programme.

To do this, Bain & Company began a process of '*Defection Anal-ysis*' for MBMA That's a fancy couple of words for simple customer detective work. If any one customer decided to defect from the company's customer base, they wanted to know why? They set in train a process to keep the customer by contacting him or her and adjusting the MBMA product or process to suit the customer's needs or expectations. Over five years the rate of customer defec-tions dropped from over 10 per cent to just five per cent, which is half what most corporations would regard as a very efficient rate of customer defection.

In the process of this *defection analysis* they learned what their customers wanted or expected of them. As a consequence, they sold a lot more MBNA credit card usage. In five years, their ranking as a credit card company went from number 38 in the industry to number 4. Profits increased 1600 per cent!

The same study was repeated in over 20 industries, all of which showed dramatically consistent findings. Over a five-year period in the industrial distribution industry, the existing individual cus-tomer profit of $45 per annum went to $163 per annum. In the car-servicing industry, the figure over this same period went from $25 to $88 per annum. In the credit card business, it increased from an average loss per customer of $21 per annum to a profit of $55 per annum over five years. The remaining 17 companies all had a similar profit growth.

Bain & Company's management consultancy division achieved such excellent results in advising clients on defection analysis, and in using other loyalty management techniques, that Bain & Company began a company acquisition business to capitalise on these techniques. Bain Capital was formed in 1985 to acquire com-panies, which were not practising relationship marketing techniques.

The results speak for themselves. Nearly 10 years later, Bain Capital has resold, or taken public, 17 of the companies it acquired. It realised six times the amount invested. Bain Capital currently holds 26 companies with $U.S. 2.2 million in revenues, giving an annualised return of 92 per cent. This company is phenomenal proof of the effectiveness of making loyalty management techniques in business.

The key to all of this is not complex analysis, but a simple understanding that people are people through people. That by knowing your customer, talking to her or him, asking them to tell you what they want, and even what they like about doing business with you, and then acting on this information throughout the company—from the chairperson to the delivery girl!

In one of the most successful Domino Pizza franchises in America, the manager makes sure that each employee understands that every regular customer is worth $5000 over the lifetime of a franchise contract. So, when the phone rings at the Pizza parlour, and a raucous voice somewhat rudely demands that you deliver a hot $10 pizza all the way across town in 15 minutes, the employee sees the voice as a $5000 silver-tongued demand. You will thus react quite differently than to a lousy $10, *hold-the-anchovy* order from a half-inebriated anonymous caller.

MBNA, the credit card company with the 16-fold profit after *defection analysis*, sends out its pay-cheques in an envelope stamped with the words: *Brought to you by the customer.* As well, they put bonus money into a kitty for all employees every day the defection rate stays below 5%.

It is as well to remember that existing customers are, on average, five times more profitable than prospective customers. How can you measure the profit in a customer you don't have against one you do? Well, quite easily really.

In most businesses, there is a cost for gaining a customer. Customers, or prospects, don't just politely knock at the door, ask to come in and gratefully buy your services. They are obviously the result of all sorts of influences—most of which you have set in train yourself, possibly an advertising campaign or a direct response or public relations campaign. The time making the sale would be a fourth influence. It all adds up so that the customer comes to you at a price, which can actually be worked out to a figure. In most companies, the ratio is 5:1 in favour of existing customers. That is, if a new customer costs you $100 to add to your database, and to make a purchase of a new product or service, your existing customers will cost you $20 to make the same purchase.

So, offering a new product to your existing customers first makes a great deal of sense in several ways. The more people buy from you and are satisfied, the more they will continue to buy. If your new product isn't up to scratch, your existing customers will let you know, allow you to make corrections, usually accept your apology, compensation and explanation, and remain with you. A new customer, however, will simply send the goods back, or disappear, never to do business with your company again.

Finally, the more *old* or *active* customers you have, the more stable your income stream will be. On the other hand, the more *new* customers you get, the more volatile your income flow will be.

It's all common sense or, as Mr Sheinberg would say: '*Look for the simple explanation*'. The simple answer is, that new customers are tentative with you and you with them; they are reluctant to take risks with you until they know you better, and you are reluctant to extent them credit until they have shown a regular capacity to pay. On the other hand, existing customers with whom you have an existing relationship, are confident in the corporate friendship they enjoy. They will, therefore, make higher-value, higher-profit purchases from you and you will be more relaxed extending them credit.

It's a bit like the partners Mr Sheinberg would pick in all sorts of industries, some of which he could not possibly have known much about. For instance, I am fairly sure he couldn't have baked a loaf of bread if his life depended on it. But he had a money resource, of if you like, a lending or investment capacity, so he stuck to his fellow Hungarian Jews, whose background, language and emotional needs he understood very well. They were in effect, his friends. He was doing business with his friends.

Now, if a friend wants to borrow a $100 from you, you can easily evaluate the risk involved. You can be fairly sure you'll get your money back, or be able to form a successful partnership to get your investment back.

But if a total stranger approaches you and asks to borrow $100, or wants a capital loan and in return offers you a business partnership, the risks increase enormously. You don't know him, his background, emotional stability, or his capacity to bring a joint enterprise to a successful conclusion. The risks become much greater and your natural caution, understandably, increases. The strong possibility is that you will refuse him the money.

If you take good care of them, long-time customers are money in the bank. They will refer business to you and get pleasure from doing so. A simple 'thankyou card', with a gift voucher *at your shop* for $50 for every new customer they recruit, will send them out actively canvassing on your behalf.

The operating cost of servicing an existing customer declines over time. For instance, you don't need to keep credit checking them, or adding them to your database, or buying new customer lists. You can quite often charge your existing customers a premium price. They will usually pay slightly more for a service or product they trust rather than shift to something they don't know, albeit at a slightly lower price.

Pleasing your existing customers, making them feel safe and secure and well liked and always welcome, is perhaps the most important task you have as a company. It is estimated that your average family life value customer (LVC) will spend $100,000 in a supermarket in her or his lifetime. That's what this type of regular customer is worth: $5000 for a pizza parlour; $100,000 for a supermarket.

My wife Suzi was a regular shopper at a well known Sydney supermarket. While shopping, some five years ago, she reached over for a bottle of liquid laundry bleach. The top came off in her hand and the container fell and spilled over her dress and shoes, ruining both.

Naturally, she complained to the store manager who told her

that she must have taken the top off the bleach and that he couldn't do anything about her ruined dress or shoes. She wrote to the company head office, enclosed the ruined garments and shoes and asked for $200 compensation, which was a great deal less than the articles cost her new. She received the garments and shoes back with a letter enclosed saying that the company didn't feel it was at fault and would not be paying her compensation. This went on for several months until one day the company solicitor wrote to say the matter was closed, and the company would not pay any compensation, nor would it enter into any further correspondence.

At this stage, thoroughly tired of the discordant dialogue about the supermarket, which had been going on at the breakfast table every day for months, I suggested that she sue the company. It was a perfect example of a company not understanding the principles of LVC and I was curious to see the final outcome of their stupidity. Well, we won the case, got costs awarded against the company, the judge gave my wife compensation of $500 and altogether the case cost the supermarket company around $10,000. They had lost $9,800 plus a potential $100,000 over my wife's supermarket shopping life-time. Alternatively, had they smiled, happily paid the $200, and replaced the bottle of bleach, they would have had a customer singing their praises—a captive for life (LVC).

This kind of corporate stupidity occurs all the time, usually because most corporations believe most people are cheats and not to be trusted. Whereas, very few people cheat and those that do are almost always 'strangers'. Regular customers seldom cheat. After all, what's the point in cheating a friend?

The concept of a 'no-argument' refund policy is a very sound one for a company to adopt—even if, occasionally, you are cheated. Jim Nordstrom, of the hugely successful Nordstrom Stores, on the West Coast of America, tells his staff: 'I don't care if a customer rolls a Goodyear tyre through the front door of the store and demands a refund. If they claim they bought it here, and paid $200 for it, take the tyre and give them the full refund!' Nordstrom, of course, doesn't even sell tyres!

In my company, everything is sold on a 12-month, unconditional, money-back guarantee, plus a three-month free trial. We
have proved conclusively, over 25 years of trading, that people are
honest and genuine in their complaints. Our total returns for any
reason, including lost in transit, damaged goods, returns etc. have
consistently run at less than three per cent of goods sold. You
simply can't have a public face which is different to your private
policy. It doesn't work, it's rotten business and, what's more, it's
unprofitable because you lose the *life-time value of your customer*
(LVC).

Your customer is for life:
An outward advertising smile and an inward corporate scowl, simply don't work together to make a long-term profit.

Chapter Seven

Trouble, wearing only a G-string and spangles, comes knocking at my door.

★ ★ ★

During our ownership of the Cafe Inferno, I opened a Jazz Club in the basement of the Boulevard Arcade in the centre of town. I called it The Hungry I, after the famous San Francisco jazz club. It wasn't the smartest move because, at that time, the city emptied around 6 p.m. My reasons for opening it were more because the rent was cheap, the kitchen more or less intact, chairs and tables came with the joint, and all it needed was a coat of paint and a few posters. It never occurred to me to monitor the traffic into town, or the distribution of the evening population. I shall talk about the Hungry I later in this book but, first, a little of my adventures and eventual downfall at the hands of Lulu Brown, alias *Miss Behavin*, the greatest little strip-tease act ever to come to town from the U.S. of A!

Quite how I met the famous stripper, I'm not sure. Though sometimes the night shift at the Cafe Inferno was so awful that going to bed was out of the question. And, as the jazz at the Hungry I was not enough to soothe my furrowed brow, and because I had the rather juvenile idea that I was a bit of a man about town, I'd drop into the Diamond Horseshoe, a night club owned by a rotund American of doubtful integrity, but with an outwardly respectable persona, by the name of Sammy Lee. Lulu was the star attraction, supported by five other strippers. I daresay I met her on my way home one early morning when I popped into Sammy Lee's establishment looking for a bit of spangle, light and laughter.

Sammy was what you'd call a real nice guy unless you owed him money, or reneged on a contract. But, at the time, the idea of having a real live American-type hood in Sydney was pretty exciting. He was seen as a colourful and a necessary part of the social scene. Also, he was a big contributor to the Police Boys' Club movement and to the various 'private' police superannuation schemes.

A second of these semi-legitimate imports was Lee Gordon, a promoter of events, American Jazz stars and, in fact, anything or anyone who could draw a crowd to the dilapidated, tin-roofed, wooden-benched boxing stadium at Rushcutters Bay. When it was built, in 1908, it was the world's biggest boxing stadium. At the time, it was the only large crowd venue available in Sydney. Lee Gordon brought to Sydney Frank Sinatra, Ella Fitzgerald, The Beatles and a host of famous American stars. He also promoted shows for some up-and-coming Australian Rock 'n Roll stars, most notably among them Johnny O'Keefe. One should not forget that he also championed the use of cocaine, and all sorts of little pills and substances that helped Sydney to become the big-time, sophisticated city it was trying so desperately to be.

Lee Gordon, Like Sammy Lee, was much admired. Their activities, so good for the pension plans of policemen, seemed never to be too closely scrutinised. There was genuine sorrow in the community when Lee Gordon over-dosed, or in the official police parlance of the day, 'committed suicide.' However, behind the glamour was a fair bit of sleaze. The bread and butter of Lee Gordon's operation were the strippers and small-time night club entertainers, the second-string show-biz acts that keep the night club business going 365 days a year in a big city.

Lulu Brown, alias *Miss Behavin* was one of the most famous of these strippers. She was pretty, firm breasted, tanned golden brown and smooth as cinnamon butter. All of this under lights.

In harsh daylight she didn't scrub up quite as well. I learned that a red spotlight on tired skin evens out the blotches and bruises, dents and imperfections and gives the skin a warm, tanned look. Stage craft and 'wet-look' lipstick does the rest. In those days, being a night club stripper was a pretty tough vocation—a hard life in which booze and cigarettes played a big part. I really liked Lulu Brown, but it wasn't in a sexual way. To use an American expression, she was a rough, wise-cracking broad, not terribly bright, but kind and sensitive, guilt-ridden and looking for a better life and hoping for one big and lasting relationship. I laughed a lot in her company and I was happy to call her my friend.

Most strippers, or at least the ones I knew, were the world's prime example of the female people who work from the shoulders down rather than from the neck up. As a consequence, they were generally horribly exploited by night club owners and, as well, had a pretty hard time with their managers, boyfriends, musicians, band leaders and the influential 'friends' of the owners of the night clubs. All of the afore-mentioned males have a tendency to think that a stripper is on duty for all 24 hours to deliver sexual favours in return for a half-a-dozen Manhattans and a gaudy box of chocolates, or a cheap trinket.

I was young, innocent, and had no thought of groping her. This may have been the basis of my appeal to Lulu. For my part, she represented glamour and sophistication. Having her walk up to me after her act, and sit down at the bar beside me, and say: 'Hiya, handsome!' made me feel like a man about town. All pretty child-ish, I suppose, but very important to me at the time.

Not long after I'd met Lulu, she had a row with her current manager and she asked me to manage her career, as she was having contractual problems with Lee Gordon. This was hardly surprising as it turned out her manager was in Lee Gordon's employ. He was not, therefore, over-inclined to serve Lulu's best interests.

At 25, nothing is impossible. So I agreed, too stupid to know that a strip-teaser's manager usually carried a gun in his shoulder holster, which was concealed by padded shoulders, which covered unpadded shoulders already so wide that their owners had to move sideways through doorways.

I went to see Lee Gordon about her contract. To my surprise, I found a small, bald, dark, little Jewish bloke who looked like the proverbial sand-in-the-face wimp. He smiled, asked me to sit down and tell him my problems. He must have been quite impressed with my negotiating skills, because he capitulated. I obtained his agreement to honour the existing contract and to give Lulu several small additional concessions, including a chance to protect her from management enforced after-hours 'obligations.'

What I didn't know was that he'd agree to anything, because he had absolutely no intention of honouring the agreement.

I was an instant hero at the Diamond Horseshoe for this supposed verbal victory over the 'Prince of darkness.' Then Lulu told me that the other five strippers had approached her and asked if I'd manage them as well. Some people seem to learn things only by compounding their stupidities and I agreed at once—flushed with my win over the big-time night club owner, who was known to be a tough sonofabitch. Talk about big time! I was 25-years-old, the manager of six strippers, joint owner of the world's worst eatery, intimate of all the Sydney night-life heavies, part-owner of a jazz club and, during the day, the slightly-tired operator of a finance brokerage and dry cleaning business.

One night, not long after I agreed to be manager of the 'Sexy Six,' I arrived at the Diamond Horseshoe after the Cafe Inferno had thrown out its last freak. I was there, ostensibly, to see my girls working, only to find that they'd had a terrible argument with the management. They had been ordered to mix with the customers—wearing their tassels and G-strings—when they weren't on the stage. The girls refused. They considered themselves professional strippers, not hookers nor bar girls. They were waiting for me to turn up and give Sammy Lee a working-over with my renowned verbal skills.

Sammy sat me down in his office, poured me a scotch without asking whether I drank and then leaned over his desk and jabbed a stubby finger into my chest while chewing at a big cigar. It was just like a bad fifties movie, with Jimmy Cagney or George Raft about to 'moider da burn.'

'Listen up, you young punk. This is my place and what I say goes. The girls do it my way or no way, you understand? You want trouble, I'll give you more trouble than you know how to personally handle!'

Given this ultimatum my famous verbal skills deserted me, but my stupidity remained intact. I left Sammy's office and told the girls we were walking out. They thought the trembling, terrified tone in my voice was due to my extreme rage. They loved the idea of strippers going on strike. Someone called the press and the next morning I was on the front page of The Sydney Telegraph, arms linked to three strippers on each side, posing in their G-strings and nipple tassels outside the Diamond Horseshoe. The headline, rather clever for the Telegraph:

G-STRING STRIKE!
NIGHT CLUB WANTS THE LOIN'S SHARE!

Well, my old man, no doubt with a severe hangover, would have shambled out to pick up the morning paper on the front lawn. He would have opened it before he was fully back in the house—and hit the flaming guttering! I'd only been home half an hour when he came bursting into my room and tore the sheets from my bed.

'That's it, that's finally *bloody* it! You've disgraced me and broken your mother's heart, you're taking drugs, associating with criminal elements, pimping for six bloody whores! You're out of this house and you're out of everything. You've got an hour to pack up and piss off!' He stormed out leaving me dazed and wondering what the hell I'd done.

The stupid part was that I'd thought all along, that in his peculiar eyes anyway, I was doing what a *real* man should do—a bit like, metaphorically speaking, getting syphilis at 16. But now he was appalled at me for the sort of thing I thought should have made me a hero in his eyes.

The truth, of course, was that Lulu and I, and the other six strippers, were just friends. I'd never laid a hand on any of them. I hardly drank and wouldn't have recognised an amphetamine pill, or line of cocaine, from an aspirin or a teaspoon of castor sugar. I didn't knowingly associate with underworld characters except, of course, Sammy Lee and Lee Gordon. Otherwise, I was totally and blissfully ignorant of anything going on in the Sydney underworld. I simply liked the bright lights, the late nights, the girls and the music. But, in my mind, I was trying to do the things Mr Sheinberg had taught me—to spread my portfolio and my risks. However, with no capital base, while I was doing the best I could, it wasn't all that crash hot.

Life seldom seems to understand the purity of one's motives and without free board and lodgings I was a dead-cert goner. I was stretched beyond any resources I'd ever had anyway. All the businesses I was involved with seemed to be going bad at the same time. Lawrence Dry Cleaners wanted their kiosk back, finance dried up for the small time brokers like me as the banks finally realized they were onto something by lending money to young people, the Cafe Inferno went so far downhill from a flat start that it was already a deep hole in the ground which threatened to bury me financially, and the jazz club had collapsed a week earlier due to a raid from the licensing squad. I was also having partner trouble in the jazz club.

At 26-years-old, I was broke and would have been bankrupt if there had been any bank to *rupt*. In fact, looking back at each of my businesses, not a single one ever ran properly. I always under-capitalised, but worse, I didn't really know how to run them. Each had been created without any forethought, nothing had been planned, everything just seemed like a good idea at the time. I had not invested sufficient time into any of them to understand the nature of what, in each case, I was required to do.

Suddenly, and for the first time in my life, I was afraid. I was a failure in my own eyes and most definitely, in my father's eyes (for the second time!) I'd always been a cocky kid and I really thought I was good at business. I thought I was a good salesman and then everything collapsed around me. I owed, what at that time seemed like a lot of money, to people who had been kind to me and who had given me credit when I must have been an obvious risk.

I must have had a bit of a breakdown and for three months I became a bum. Except that I hardly drank, so being a bum was difficult in the land of sunshine and plenty. I'm not sure how I lived. I know I didn't work and I had no money. I remember some of the time being cared for by a very nice air hostess, who fed me and looked after me and didn't ask for very much in return. I wish I knew her whereabouts today, because I'd like to say, thank you. At the time, I was much too sorry for myself to appreciate how very kind she was to me. (Nola, if you ever read this: Thank you for picking me up, dusting me off and sending me back into the ring to box myself out of my self-indulged bout of misery.)

Walking into the unknown on 'a wing and a prayer'—as I had done with every one of my business ventures—isn't very bright. But it is surprising how often it is still done, and this is particularly true of the direct marketing business. It looks easy and you can quickly get carried away with the idea that people are suckers, and that a large amount of money is to be made for the cost of a bit of stationary and a postage stamp. Huge organisations, with resources to research everything, quite often mount a direct response campaign with virtually no testing. They are convinced they know best and have a natural affinity for the direct-response medium. They don't test the merchandise, they don't test the offer, and they don't test the target audience. That's pretty well acting in much the same way as I did when, convinced I was a genius, I opened the Cafe Inferno, and all of the other businesses I hoped would make me a quick fortune with not too many questions asked!

In fact, the whole art of business, successful business, is asking questions. The more questions you ask, the more likely you are to get things right in terms of your customers and so, ultimately, in terms of your bottom line. In direct marketing, asking questions is the Holy Grail. **Test, test, test and then, just to be sure, test again.**

If you want to be in a position to measure results, than testing is the key to measurable marketing. I can almost hear some marketing manager reading this and saying: 'Yeah, but we're different.' Or 'I can't afford to do a test and a campaign as well' or simply, 'I can't be bothered with running a test campaign, going through all that tedious evaluation. We've got a damn good product and I know I've already got the media mix right.' My point, my *urgent* point, is that you *can't* afford not to test! Nobody gets it right on 'a wing and a prayer.'

If you go ahead without testing and you blow your whole campaign, not only are you up to your eyeballs in the proverbial, but you'll never know why. You may not have lost a great deal of money and gained very little useful experience in the process. If you must lose out sometimes, then, lose wisely. The information you gather in the process will eventually make you a winner.

Prior to the full blown campaign, if one, or even two tests indicate that something may be wrong with any of the three vital test components—the *audience selection,* the *offer* or the *creative* message which carries the offer—you can make an early and relatively inexpensive adjustment to any of these. Then you can test again until you are confident you have corrected the problem. You then *know* that the campaign has every chance of succeeding.

As a consultant, perhaps the most common problem I face with a client, who is anxious to mount a direct marketing campaign, is when I suggest we test. 'Thanks, Ian, but we have a time restraint. We really have to get underway with a big campaign, so let's forget about the testing, eh?'

That's a bit like knowing the petrol gauge in your car shows empty and, because you're running late for an appointment 20 kilometres out of town, you decide you'll chance it and not take the five minutes it will take you to pull into a service station and fill up the tank.

In direct marketing terms, you are making *the* classic error of judgement. It is both arrogant and presumptuous to believe *you* will be the one to get away with it, because nine times out of 10 you will not.

So, rather than argue the point, what should you test?

Well, remember the variables, the *1: 5: 10* rule. One for the *creative message, five for the offer you are making,* and 10 for the *audience selection.* You always begin by focusing on the audience selection. If you want to mess around with the three variables, always do most of your messing with the audience you have selected to receive your offer.

Secondly, it is essential to test the offer. You may have several different options, or opportunities for premiums, so don't simply take them home and ask the wife and kids which they prefer. Test.

Thirdly, test the creative approach. But, unless your copywriter is a moron (I've met some), and providing your audience is carefully and correctly selected, and your offer is attractive to them, than you are already more than 90 per cent down the road to a successful direct-marketing campaign *before* you test the creative component.

The environment into which you place a test is important. Some companies test in a captive group—that is, they simply get several small groups, five is the usual number, consisting of up to eight people whom they believe fit the audience profile, and test the offer, carefully noting the reactions to the offer and even the creative.

In my experience this doesn't work well. In the Cafe Inferno, we knew everything there was to know about eccentrics—except what they'd do after we seated them. Lee Gordon was perfectly willing to give me all the assurances I wanted that Lulu Brown's contract would be honoured, but he had no intention of keeping his promise.

Simulated audience profiles do not work as well as live testing. For the cost of simulating an environment through research, you can usually run a live test to real customers and get an accurate result. You may also sell some goods or services on the way, sufficient to pay for the testing!

Here comes another golden rule, the Grill Inferno rule. It goes like this: When you live test a product, test it on your existing customers first. Using your own familiar database is considerably cheaper than going blind into the media, or to a database with which you are not familiar. The logic is that providing you are selling a product which matches the aspirations of your existing customer database, you should be able to sell it to your loyal customers, the people who trust you. If you can't, you are unlikely to be able to sell your offer to a complete stranger.

It is important to know what are the logistics of a successful test. To be statistically valid, a mailing of 10,000 will be needed to generate 50 to 75 orders. Any number less than this is not statistically meaningful. In effect, you are converting about one per cent, which is a viable result.

However, if you are not doing a mailing you have to rely on advertising in a magazine that delivers sufficient of your target audience. Then, use a full page advertisement, or a loose insert, in the magazine, which should guarantee you a circulation of at least 25,000.

To put together a single communication mailing of 10,000, that is a mailing containing a single offer, including the creative work and the printing, will cost you in the region of $10,000 to $15,000. Now you may think that a test costing this much is rather expensive, but if you have a campaign budget of around $100,000 you are likely to be a great deal happier being disappointed on a $15,000 budget than on largely blowing the bigger sum.

Similarly, running a well-prepared, full-page colour, direct-marketing offer in a magazine will cost you between $15,000, to $20,000—a sortie which still beats blowing the lot in a blind assault on an unknown market.

There is sometimes a very good alternative. Look to testing your offer in a multiple mailing. That is, piggy-back your new offer on an old one, or several old ones. Your new offer then rides along in the same envelope and shares a bit of the glory. Your customers know about the old offers and know to trust them. So, some of the goodwill and credibility of these familiar offers rubs off on the new offer. Importantly, your costs are shared with the other offers—a $15,000 solo offer becomes a far more reasonable $5,000 multiple offer, or even less if there are more pieces in the envelope.

When you think about it, almost every business is a numbers game. The number of no-hopers the Cafe Inferno could attract to make a profit, the number of pairs of trousers the dry cleaning kiosk could take in to cover the rent and Rose's salary, and the number of bums I could get onto seats nightly in the jazz club, The Hungry I. Without the right numbers, we usually go broke.

Direct marketing is, quintessentially, a numbers business. Unless you can think numbers, or hire someone who does, you simply do not belong in the direct marketing business. Numbers, unless you're fascinated by them, are usually the tedious end of any business. These days you can usually get the computer to do the work of crunching the numbers. But you are still going to have to read them, understand what they mean, and make decisions based on them.

Thankfully, there is a formula, a secret but very simple method which will get you off the hook and guide you to a successful conclusion. In business management jargon they are called: *The Key Ratios.* These are the numbers which really impact on your particular business. Work within them and you are likely to remain happily in business; get them out of whack and disaster strikes like a sledge-hammer! While this is true for most business, it is especially true for direct marketing. If you can get your key ratios right, and maintain them like the royal rose garden, you will find yourself in control—that wonderfully enviable position all business strives to ultimately achieve. In direct marketing, measuring your success relies on the constant manipulation and management of your key ratios.

Here they are, all six precious little darlings. They will send you laughing or crying to the bank. It all depends on how you manage them. They can be broken down even more but these are the major ones.

1. Nett sales
2. Cost of goods
3. Fulfilment
4. Promotional Cost
5. Overhead allocation
6. Profit

Let's take one at a time because they're not quite as simple as they may seem. It is the percentage of the nett sales which they represent which is the key ratio that must be monitored constantly. Here is a model for a general merchandise mail order business:

1. Sales price (nett sales):   100%
2. Cost of goods: 40%
3. Fulfilment: 5%
4. Promotional cost: 30%
5. Overhead allocation: 15%
6. Profit: 10%

1. Sales price. This is the listed selling price, plus handling fees, less any discounts for, say, early purchase or multiple orders, less returns. (I must emphasise that discounting as a general rule should be handled with extreme care. In direct marketing discounting is the easiest way to damage the perceived value of your product or service. I try as hard as I can to avoid offering a discount, preferring instead to increase the over all perceived value of the offer in other ways. For example, an audio tape of bird calls free with each bird plate.)

To your listed selling price you now add the postage and handling charges. (Or, if you prefer, don't add the postage and handling—provided you are certain that the actual cost of the postage and handling cancels out the charge you are adding for this category.) If you add a $2.95 postage charge, your sales price may look like this:

Sales price: $100 + $2.95 = Sales price $102.95

But you're not quite through yet, we must now factor in (estimate) our returns rate to get our nett sales value. Let's say you add a 5% return of goods due to breakages, customers changing their minds, incorrect addresses, whatever. This time, the formula looks like this:

Nett sales value: $102.95 × 95% = $97.80

Putting it another way, just imagine how much Lee Gordon would charge Sammy Lee for *Miss Behavin's* strip tease act at $102.95 per session.

Now her employer has to expect Lulu will be indisposed for about 1½ days each month. So the cost to him is 5% of the total package. Thus, the nett sales value of Lulu to Lee Gordon is $102.95 × 95% = $97.80. How he shares this amount with Lee, is of course, a separate arrangement.

2. Cost of goods. This is the ready total cost of goods at the stage where they are in the warehouse to go out to the customer. Here is a typical list of items which make up this cost.

—the product itself
—freight
—sales tax
—duties
—extra packaging
—cost of financing
—insurance
—agent's fees
—royalties
—personalisation (adding initials or names—if any)

In fact, the only items which are not included in the cost of goods at this stage is the cost of storage, and addressing and sticking on labels for despatch. These are allocated to the fulfilment key ratio. The cost of goods component key ratio varies according to the commodity, eg. General Merchandise 40%, Collectables 35%, Books 20%, Wine 50%. You need to have your cost of goods, within these percentages in order to run a profitable direct marketing retail business.

3. Fulfilment. Fulfilment is a pretty standard set of costs though it is amazing how many direct marketers miss some of the key costs. They comprise:

—order processing;
—cost of storage;
—labelling;
—postage or delivery to customer;
—returns refurbishing.
—if you have added postage and handling to the selling price.

The last item, *returns refurbishing*, is one most often neglected. But it can be a meaningful cost to unpack goods and check for damage, mend or replace items, re-pack and despatch or send to the garbage tip, or back to the manufacturer. It is also just as well to include any disbursements incurred in processing any orders. You may have the customer-service staff on overtime, or have to pay for dinner on three nights for the warehouse packing staff who are working late. Costs have a nasty habit of sneaking up on you and you have to be constantly aware of what your fulfilment costs are.

4. Promotion. What is listed here is the 'raw' cost of the promotion and not the cost of the creative component, which is recorded separately. Cost of promotion encompasses the following:

—advertising space or inserting charge;
—outbound telephone calls;
—list rental (renting names and addresses);
—postage on promotional material;
—mailing house costs such as inserting and handling;
—air time on radio and, or, television;
—the cost of loose inserts in newspapers or magazines;
—printing leaflets, brochures and letters.

Of course, in this category you may have other costs. But they should only be special costs associated with a specific advertisement. For instance, you may want a scratch-and-sniff element on a panel in a special advertisement for a new perfume you are offering. You would include the production work necessary to create such a specialised advertisement.

Taking your key ratios, your objective should be to end up with a ratio of promotion cost to sales of between 25% and 35%. Or in the words of a successful advertisement should produce sales between 3 and 4 times the advertising cost.

Here now is a conundrum: in direct marketing you do not include your creative costs in your promotion key ratio. That is, you do not amortise the art direction, copywriting and production costs of your advertisements, brochures or letters. The reason for this is quite important to understand.

Every offer you make has a natural home, a perfect place where it should be characteristically found. As a direct marketer, you are always looking for this magic address—the magazine or newspaper that delivers the highest response for that particular style or type of offer. You will code your coupons with a key number so that you can see from which magazine the response came. This is a critical part of your strategy; wasting advertising money on magazines or newspapers, or on a TV programme which doesn't pull a profitable response, is simply throwing money away. You are, therefore, constantly involved in making a performance evaluation and if you *add a share of your promotion development to each advertisement* you run, while looking for the perfect home for your offer, you make a true performance comparison difficult to achieve as *it corrupts the cost per order comparison.*

What you must do with creative costs is to create a separate fund in your accounting which you can call 'Development Costs.' For instance, creating a new strip routine for Lulu Brown would go into such a category. You can't amortise it against each evening's performance, or each club she works in. You simply add it to the overall cost of being in business and amortise it every year. In a direct marketing sense, you do the same. You simply forecast then record these art direction, copywriting and production costs and then write them off over the life of the promotion. If the first promotion fails and you never try another one, then you write them off against this one unsuccessful promotion.

5. Overhead. Overheads really are a trap for young or careless players or for natural optimists. I am now convinced that *direct marketing business cannot operate with an overhead allocation of much less than 15% of sales.*

If this makes you whistle it's because we get back to that old contention—too little customer service ruins many a good programme. Your life-time customer value is your primary asset. Do not neglect it. This category is where you include the cost of your customer service, and I urge you to be generous. Customer service is all too frequently underestimated. So, begin with 15% as your key ratio and you'll have all the makings of a happy campaign.

6. Profit. Profit is what's left over after all the hard work. But it doesn't quite end there. Profit isn't a fluke; it is something which is carefully managed. If you keep all the key ratios in close to the percentages I've indicated, and there isn't enough left over, then the first thing you do is try to find a way to cut costs to reduce the other ratios. But you only have three major choices. You can:

- increase the price of the goods or service;
- increase sales;
- choose not to trade in any particular product or service.

You should be aware that if you are going to increase the price of the offer, the likelihood is that you will decrease your sales. Mail order is sensitive to price movements.

There is another way of looking at your ratios. This is by not initially costing in your promotional and overhead costs, and working out exactly what is the cost of sale of one item before you spend a penny on promotion. Put another way, you work out the cost of the goods and fulfilment and what's left over in your budget can then be allocated to promotion, overhead and profit.

This method is another way of looking at the key ratios. It is called 'The Allowable.' The allowable is the amount of money available to buy one order and either break even at a calculated sale figure or make a profit, depending on how you calculate.

So now your costing analysis, which originally you based on key ratios, will look like this:

1. Salesprice
2. Allowable.

Allowable. The *allowable* is the amount left over after you have calculated all the costs incurred before promotion, overheads and profit. These costs includes the following:

—Cost of goods
—Fulfilment
—Cheque charges
—Credit card commission
—Bad debt rate

Let us now look at the last four *allowable* items. Let's stay with our previous example of sales price of $102.95 and a return rate of 5%, giving us a nett sales value of $97.80. This figure now includes costs of goods and fulfilment and we now cost out the remaining four items which make up the *allowable*.

Cheque charges. Cheque charges are, of course, whatever your bank charges you to process a cheque. The cost can quite easily be worked out according to the percentage of your customers who pay by cheque. In my business, we find that around 60 per cent of our customers prefer to pay by cheque. The bank charges us 31 cents to process each one. Therefore we make the calculation:
$$31c \times 60\% = \$0.19$$
Thus, the added cost to each item sold is 19 cents.

Credit card commission. This is worked out in the same way. The cost of your customers doing business with a credit card is the rate the credit card company charges you multiplied by the number of customers who prefer to use a credit card to pay you.
$$\$97.80 \times 40\% \times 2\% = \$0.78.$$
Thus, the added cost of each item sold is another 60 cents.

The last item on your *allowable,* the *bad debt rate,* will not apply if your offer requires a single payment or is a money-with-order offer.

Bad debts. Bad debts vary from industry to industry and company to company, in my company we have been able to keep them at two per cent. If we are offering three instalments of interest-free terms, the bad debt will of course occur on either the second or last payment. The first payment had to be sent in to secure the goods. It is essential to get the first payment before you ship the goods, especially when marketing outside your database where you have no relationship with the purchaser. If we divide our $97.80 selling price into three equal payments of $32.60 then our bad debt calculation looks like this:

$$\$32.60 \times 2 \times 2\% = \$1.30$$

Thus, the cost of bad debt on each item sold is $1.26.

This is how a typical costs-before-*allowable* structure would look if we were making a single-payment, money-with-order, offer:

Single payment money-with-order calculation	
Nett Sales Value (NSV)	$97.80
Cost of goods (COG)	$40.00
Fulfilment (F)	& 5.00
Cheque Charges (ChC)	$ 0.19
Credit Cards (CC)	$ 0.78

When all this is added up and subtracted from the nett sales value, it gives us an *allowable* of $51.83. This is the amount we can spend on promotion, overheads and profit. So if it costs us $30 to buy an order (promotion cost divided by number of orders) we have $21.83 to put to overheads and profit.

You now know how much you have over to spend on promotion and overheads. But you still need to know how many units you have to sell to cover all your costs and reach a break-even figure. This is the most reliable forewarning you can get to indicate whether you are taking too great a risk, or simply a well-calculated one.

So, let's take a look at how you reach your break-even figure. To put it into financial jargon for a moment, it is the *sales price,* **less** the *unit cost* of the goods per item, **less** the *unit cost of filling an order,* again calculated per item, **less** your *overhead* calculation. Do this fairly simple sum and you will know how much you have to spend per unit to break even.

For example, using real figures in a campaign, it goes like this: We have a total sales price of, say, $100, a product cost of $40 and a unit cost of fulfilment of $5. We have allowed ourselves a 15%

overhead cost, which is $15. Add all that up and it comes to $60, which leaves $40 from our original $100. If we want a profit per unit of 10 per cent, than we take $10 of the $40 left over. This leaves us with $30, out of our original $100, to spend to make people buy our product. In other words, if we can buy an order for $30 and if the other costs are correct, we will have made $10. If we buy an order for $40, therefore, we will have broken even. Now, let's take an advertisement, or mailing, which costs $3000. In order to make 10 per cent profit, I have to sell 100 units (i.e. $3000 ÷ $30). In order to break even, I need to sell 75 units ($3000 ÷ $40). The judgement to be made, then, is whether or not this particular advertisement or promotion will generate between 75 and 100 orders.

The real beauty of *the measurable marketing approach* is that every promotion or campaign for every product can have a profit and loss account (P&L) of its own. This is enormously useful, because it means you can *measure by media, and by product*, every promotion, every day if you need to. You can see how every item in your direct marketing portfolio is performing in terms of either breaking even or making a profit.

What this means in practical terms is that you can look at each variable and see which are working and which are not. By emphasising one, and eliminating or downgrading another, you can get the most out of your campaign.

Remember, everything is based on your key ratios. If you get them wrong, you may think you're making a profit while, in point of fact, you are 'drowning by numbers.' Don't, for instance, pump in a lot more advertising because you think things are going well. The promotional ratio to your nett sales value (NSV) has to remain acceptable. Also, it is as well to understand that playing around with variables, and acquiring the information from them, costs money. Someone has to crunch the numbers, load the computer, create the spread sheets, and translate the result. Information, if it isn't needed, is pointless. So restrict what you want to know to what you can afford to know, or what you need to know to direct your campaign. In other words, only get information that will lead to action. The rest is, muscle-flexing by your marketing department, or wanking—call it what you like. It's a waste of money!

Nothing in life, or in direct mail, goes on forever. All the rivers finally run into the sea. Lulu Brown, alias *Miss Behavin,* was lonely and ours was a different friendship. But when my Dad gave me the boot, my connection with Lulu came to an end as well. Even the weirdos stopped coming to the Cafe Inferno, and the till closed forever. The 'trousers' that strut their way into dry cleaning kiosks, take a different path. As I mentioned previously, banks get smart and offer young people better loans than brokers working hand in hand with greedy lawyers. And, difficult partners in jazz cellars finally silence even the most persistent boy drummer. Knowing when the end has come is the true art of survival in almost anything.

In direct marketing campaign or promotion, knowing when the end has come can be critical to your bottom line. Many a good campaign has unexpectedly dived swiftly into the red. Watch your *allowable* like a hawk—every day, if necessary.

But before you end a campaign because it is no longer delivering a profitable return, you must know how to syphon off the useful information it contains. The information you can acquire during the on-going life of the promotion can be critical to its success at the time, and also enormously useful in the success of future campaigns. Do not think that a direct marketing campaign is over because you've put the media schedule to bed. A direct marketing campaign is over when the last advertisement you run fails to deliver a profitable cost-return per order. You can work a campaign to its death, but you also have to know when it is dying, and when it is finally dead.

Here, then, is what you should record during a promotion and for use after it is over. This is the information you are going to need in playing with your present campaign, and for use in yet unthought-of ideas, and unborn direct marketing campaigns. This is why newcomers can't buy this information; you simply have to have access to historical records.

I have always regarded the Big Person in the sky as a bit of a 'number cruncher.' A record keeper. I see Him high up, bent over the earth, which is his book of records, with a great celestial quill in His hand—the sharp end forged from lightning and the feather the great cumulus clouds. The Great Creator knows that recording facts, observations and behaviour is an essential part of the creative approach. We have to know where we are in the present, and where we've been in the past, to know where we are before we attempt to go into the future.

The facts of the Almighty's database are all there: seven days for making; the division of time into days and nights; the seasons precisely planned; phases of the moon controlling the tides; comets passing to the chime of a giant celestial clock; just enough of this and that mixed into a brilliant air formulae we can breathe, the weight of the air above us sufficient to keep our feet firmly planted on the ground, yet keep our step light; keep ratios for everything and an obsession for dates; growth rings on trees; calendars in rocks; the layers in the earth's crust as the corridors of time itself. God loves to keep records. So should you.

For instance, when we destroy the eco system, the trees, animals and birds, the rivers and the lakes and our chimney stack economies pollute the sky, we are in fact using the present to destroy the records. And so ecologically, we are destined to walk blindly into the future.

In direct marketing, I call the set of records required the Campaign Evaluation System. These contain the 22 things we need to record about the product and the campaign if we hope to benefit from the lessons we learn each time we go into the selling environment. You may simply call them your Campaign Management. This is the heart of your numbers game and you can't be effective without it. It may be a bit tedious, but remember, making money is never tedious—and this recording system is what will make it for you in the end. When you collect these records over the years, you will have an invaluable history of direct marketing that works in your market.

The Campaign Evaluation System (CES)

The following CES points are used singly and together in various formulae to evaluate the exact performance of the campaign, promotion by promotion, product by product.

1. **The date of promotion or advertisement**. By recording the date you can gauge how long the promotion is delivering responses. You discover whether the results are consistent, or better, or worse, or about average, compared to the previous occasion(s) you may have used that medium (magazine, newspaper, direct mail, TV program). You also could track the order flow for comparison with future ads and other publications. When assessing a magazine advertisement's effectiveness, make sure you record the on-sale date, as well as the publication date, because they can differ significantly. Sometimes you are testing a new medium with a known product and, at other times, a new product with a known medium. In other words, you may use a popular women's daytime TV show for a product which you know sells very well in a popular women's magazine. Alternatively, you'll use a new product on a TV show you know had responded well for another product you think will be similarly interesting to the target audience profile offered by the show.

The experience available from our past records can tell us whether we should quickly abort or continue a campaign.

2. **The medium we used**. Don't assume you will remember. Record whether you selected your target audience from your own lists or an external list. Was it a magazine? Which magazine? A newspaper? Which newspaper? TV? Which channel and which programme? This way you build a data bank which on *which* media seems to work well for *what* product type. You will, of course, have this information on your Profit & Loss (P&L) account. But campaigns and their records tend to get buried in filing cabinets. So store past information on your central data bank, where it can be retrieved as a planning resource when you are preparing a direct marketing campaign.

3. **Code each promotion.** Coding is the key to all promotional analysis. Every order coupon for every product in every medium, carries it's unique key number. We can call anything up on the computer database simply by feeding in the code. We will thus obtain a complete picture of what we did on any particular promotion. Or, call up all the codes for a category like luggage or bird plates, and compare them with other categories.

4. **Advertisement Type**. This tells us precisely the components of the media selection. For instance: a full-page colour magazine advertisement; solo mailing; multiple mailing; loose insert into a magazine or newspaper; and so on. If it was an advertisement then it should be noted as a left or right hand page, with any other information which might *qualify* the response. The word 'qualify' in direct response means those elements in an advertisement which are different from the norm. For instance, a right-hand page in an early part of the paper, or magazine, is considered a superior position to a left-hand page in the same place. Readers, when flicking through a magazine, spend more time on the right-hand page and, besides, it is easier to clip a coupon from a right-hand page than from a left-hand one.

5. **Nett-sales value**. This is a repeat of the example given earlier under *key ratios*. But just to remind you, the NSV is the price of the offer, including postage and handling, after deducting returns.

6. **Circulation quantity**. How many people we have reached with our advertisement or mailing.

7. **Advertisement cost.** This is purely the cost of buying the space or the cost of mailing through the mail and does *not* include artwork, development, design time, overheads etc.—unless it applies only to that advertisement: e.g. the cost of artwork to accommodate an unusual ad size.

8. **Unit orders received to date.** This is the reading from the latest

order intake print-out, or simply a manual count. Looking at units ordered is critical in a campaign and is done as often as you like but, at the very least, once a week, so you can get an accurate picture of the movement of product. Sometimes, this needs to be done daily if large amounts of money are involved, or you have to order products more frequently. As the CES is a promotional report it has no regard for whether the item is in stock and assumes every response became a sale. A response or an order should only become a sale when it is shipped to the buyer.

9. **Per cent response to date.** (In percentage terms this is **Circulation** (CES Point 6) divided by **Units sold** (Point 8). At 1 per cent, it means one in every 100 people who have been reached with our offer is responding. This may look like a very small haul, but in direct mail could be very profitable. A single mailing based on an in-house list (your own known database) will score best of all. Multiple insert mailings, loose inserts or even full-page colour advertisements, can generate response figures of just a tenth of one per cent—i.e. one person in a thousand responding to your offer. But if your circulation is large enough, and your cost per response low enough this can be a profitable outcome.

10. **Cost per order to date.** How much is it costing you to buy an order? To find out what your cost per order to date is divide Point 7 by point 8 i.e. the cost of your advertisement divided by units sold. This figure should be looked at frequently and compared with your *allowable* as a check to see how effective your offer is, and how to play with your campaign and fine tune your media selection, especially if this is a test.

11. **Final response (F).** At the start of your campaign the final response will be a figure you estimate based on your budget—the 11 per cent return you budgeted broken down to a number of units. But as your campaign gets under way, your estimated final response must be adjusted based on how well your campaign is going. This is, therefore, a dynamic or *rolling forecast*. When the responses stop coming in, the final response section to your

computer is marked with an 'F' to indicate to you that the pro-motion is completed.

12. **Final cost per order.** This is done in exactly the same way as point 11, immediately above, and is a *rolling forecast*, and of course a $ figure.

13. **Conversion rate**. This applies only to an offer that has two steps for the customer to take. For example, you make an offer which says: '*Free 30-day trial offer! Send no money with your order.*' On receipt of the order you send the invoice. This is a good way to get a customer to respond but it is not without its problems. So you calculate your conversion rate only *after* you have their lovely little cheque in the bank. Promoting outside your database can lose you up to a third of the orders.

14. **Break-even allowable.** This is the amount of dollars we have left to spend on promotional costs, overheads and profits, which we covered in more detail earlier. It is in essence, our *gross profit* on the item.

15. **Break-even units.** We discussed this earlier but, to remind you, this is the number of units we need to sell to clear all our costs, but make no profit.

16. **Budgeted units.** This is your original budget for the number of units you hoped to sell at the beginning of your campaign. Take this figure and compare it to the actual or updated final response figure and you will get a good picture of the three variables: How many units we thought we would sell; how we are doing at the present moment; and what we expect the final outcome to be. By looking at these figures you can determine if you have a disaster or a success on your hands. But, more importantly, you can often see how to avert the former and enhance the latter, as you move from media to media.

17. **Updated units sold**. This is our real, up-to-the-minute, latest

number of units sold. In the early stages of the campaign you will be watching carefully to see how this figure compares with the one in point 8—units sold to date. It will eventually become the estimated or final number of units sold.

18. **Projected nett sales.** This is the income of your current results projected to the end of the campaign. The formula for this is: Point 5 × Point 17; i.e. nett sales value of the item offered multiplied by updated units sold.

19. **Projected contribution.** Contribution is the amount left to pay profit and overheads after all other costs have been deducted. Just like our *rolling figures*, in points 11 and 12, this will be a continuing adjusted figure based on units sold (point 17) until the end of the campaign is reached. The formula for this is Point 17 multiplied by the Allowable, less the Advertising Cost. By the time new orders have stopped coming in, and returns have stopped, it will be the same as the contribution-to-date figure. i.e. it shows you the projected gross profit, before overheads.

20. **Contribution to date.** This is simply how much contribution we have made to date. The formula for this is: Actual Unit orders received (point 8) × Allowable less the Advertising Cost.

21. **Advertising to sales ratio.** This is your *advertising cost* (point 7) as a percentage of your *projected nett income* (point 18) and is one of the key ratios. You simply divide your income by your promotional cost and calculate it as a percentage. This will vary according to your industry, and the kind of campaign you run, but as a rule of thumb, 30 per cent or lower is a good yardstick. That means you spend 30 cents to generate an income of $1.

22. **Contribution margin.** This is your *projected contribution* (point 19) calculated as a percentage of your *projected nett income* (point 18). This figure will vary according to the type of business but, using a rough margin, you should aim for around 40 per cent.

CAMPAIGN EVALUATION SYSTEM – A WORKING EXAMPLE

PRODUCT: AIR MATTRESS (DOUBLE)   **PRODUCT CODE: AMD1**   PROMOTION RESULTS TO 22/08/95

1. Date	2. List Medium	3. Promotion Code	4. Adv Type	5. Nett-Sales Value $	6. Circulation Qty (000s)	7. Adv Cost $	8. Units Sold	9. Response %	10. Cost per Order to date $	11. Final Response %	12. Final Cost per Order $	13. Conversion Rate %	14. Break-even Allowable $	15. Break-even Units	16. Budgeted Units	17. Updated Units Sold	18. Projected Nett Sales $	19. Projected Contribution $	20. Contribution to date $	21. Adv to Sales Ratio %	22. Contribution Margin %
25/01	BOND	W51B	MULTI	80.75	10	320	8	0.08%	40.00	0.08%	40.00	100%	41.28	8	22	8	646	10	10	49.54%	1.59%
25/01	BOND	W47B	MULTI	80.83	10	310	18	0.18%	17.22	0.18%	17.22	100%	41.32	8	21	18	1454	433	433	21.3%	29.81%
25/01	BOND	W44B	MULTI	80.80	10	243	15	0.15%	16.20	0.15%	16.20	100%	41.35	6	19	15	1212	377	377	20.05%	31.13%
25/01	BOND	W59B	MULTI	80.86	100	3200	130	0.13%	24.62	0.13%	24.62	100%	41.34	78	216	130	10511	2174	2174	30.44%	20.68%
25/01	BOND	W60B	MULTI	71.75	10	233	8	0.08%	29.13	0.08%	29.13	100%	30.24	8	13	8	574	8	8	40.59%	1.55%
11/03	BOND	W81B	MULTI	71.85	24	770	33	0.14%	23.33	0.14%	23.33	100%	31.89	25	43	33	2371	282	282	32.48%	11.91%
12/04	BOND	W79B	MULTI	80.86	160	4053	125	0.08%	32.42	0.08%	32.42	100%	40.88	100	230	125	10107	1057	1057	40.10%	10.46%
					324	9129	337		27.09		27.09		39.73	233	564	337	26875	4341	4341	33.97%	16.15%

1. **Date** Mail date or date advertisement appeared
2. **List Medium** List mailed or media used
3. **Promotion Code** Code on response device
4. **Adv Type** Solo, Multi, Full page colour
5. **Nett-Sales Value** Price of the offer, including postage and handling, after deducting returns
6. **Circulation Qty** Quantity mailed or circulation of media
7. **Adv Cost** Cost of buying space or mailing not including design, artwork, overheads, etc
8. **Units Sold** Actual units sold to date
9. **Response %** Percentage response to date
10. **Cost per Order to date** Cost per order to date calculated as Adv Cost divided by Units Sold (7./8.)
11. **Final Response** Estimated final response percentage
12. **Final Cost per Order** Estimated final cost per order

13. **Conversion Rate** Percentage of customers with paid orders
14. **Break-even Allowable** Amount of dollars left to spend on promotional costs, overheads
15. **Break-even Units** Number to be sold to recover all costs
16. **Budgeted Units** Number targeted to sell at the beginning of the campaign
17. **Updated Units Sold** Latest estimate of number of units which will actually be sold
18. **Projected Nett Sales** Projection of total sales based on current number of units actually sold
19. **Projected Contribution** Calculated as Updated Units Sold X Break-even Allowable less the Adv Cost, ie 17.X14.–7.
20. **Contribution to date** Actual income to date calculated as Units sold to date X Break-even Allowable less the advertising cost, ie 8.X14.–7.
21. **Adv to Sales Ratio** Advertising cost as a percentage of the projected nett sales
22. **Contribution Margin** Projected contribution as a percentage of projected nett sales

This table assumes that every order taken is a sale. That is, stock or out-of-stock is not taken into account. Strictly speaking, an order does not become a sale until it is shipped, but this is an evaluation system and not an accounting record.

I daresay there are other elements you may wish to include or some you want to exclude. But the ones I've given you are those we've developed over years of practice. They seem to be the elements most essential in evaluating a direct marketing campaign. The point to remember is that the most important information you will ever need, is the rate-of-response and the cost-per-order. i.e. How many people for how much money. All business is the same—you need to know how much you have spent, and how much you have earned, and how much you think you are going to earn in the future.

To have this vital information at your finger-tips in direct marketing means always tracking the order flow, i.e. counting the orders as they come in from day one. Days in which you receive no orders are still counted as order days, though you must exclude weekends and public holidays. With a little experience, and a few campaigns under your belt for similar products or services, you will learn how to keep track of this order flow so that you can compare what is happening in your current campaign with similar campaigns, similar products and similar media selections, This, in turn, will help you greatly to estimate what percentage of orders have come in, what are yet to come, and when your campaign is likely to end. Don't put your faith in this year's highly creative campaign. The creativity, with very few exceptions, is not a hugely critical factor. Providing always it is well done, your results will remain consistent.

In terms of managing your campaign, you need to be constantly aware of how well you are doing so that you can intervene if necessary. You have to be able to change some aspect of the campaign if it seems to need correcting—perhaps use a different kind of promotion.

The report explained above totals all of the columns, so that you have an on-going record of how well all of your promotions are performing. This means the bottom line addition of all the columns accruing all your promotions are on the sheet, is giving you a moving profit and loss statement, from day to day, or week to week from a promotional viewpoint. It won't tell you how much your overhead is, or if your product costing is correct, but these costs are an accounting exercise. It will tell you how your promotional judgement is working, which is anything but an accounting exercise.

I don't suppose that at 25 I had the intelligence to do the analysis required to find out why my business empire fell flat on its face. But each component—the Cafe Inferno, the dry cleaning kiosk, my brokering business, the Hungry I and my management of Lulu Brown and her spangled G-stringed sisters—all contained lessons, from which someone smarter or older might have profited.

Post-evaluation is not only a necessary part of business, it is every bit as essential as pre-campaign planning and budgeting. In truth, it is the best possible opportunity to learn, to note down your mistakes, put them on record on your promotional database, so that you, or others following you, will not repeat them in future campaigns. In direct response marketing, I find I learn more from my failures than I do from my successes. Perhaps this is because I analyse the failures very carefully, while briefly acknowledging the successes as I search for the next success. No matter how skilled and experienced you are, post-campaign analysis remains essential to success because, as humans, we simply never stop learning and, verily, in direct marketing, new surprises lurk around every corner of each new campaign.

When you fall on your face; pick yourself up, dust yourself off, and before you start all over again, analyse what went wrong. Then record your findings. The past is always the key to the future.

Chapter Eight

★ ★ ★

The night I discovered life is not about the song but all about the singer.

★ ★ ★

When I look back on my earlier disastrous excursions into business, it's clear that the Hungry I, the jazz club I opened on a wing and a prayer, came closest to being a success. The reason was that I knew quite a lot about jazz. In other words, this time I had a reasonably informed point of view: I sensed that the people of Sydney might like a jazz club and would go almost anywhere to hear good music in reasonable surroundings with food you could reasonably expect to eat. So I decided to open one and call it after the famous San Francisco jazz club.

Fortunately for me, Australia, and Sydney in particular, had produced a few excellent jazz musicians. But apart from the hotels, night clubs and jazz dives, where the music was the interruption between the strip teaser and the funny man, there was no like-minded place for them to play. Only the Silver Spade Room, at the Chevron Hotel in the Cross, could get a proper response to good musicians and music. But the Silver Spade's prices were well beyond the average jazz lover's pocket.

For once, I seemed to have understood all the messages coming in. The Hungry I's opening night promised to be one which would be scribbled indelibly on the calendar of the culture-starved Sydney of the mid-sixties.

I had taken a great leap into the dark and somehow managed to get the great Gene McDaniels to perform on the opening night—without having to put down a deposit with his agent, or make any guarantees. I simply promised him a share of the gate. He was out here for Lee Gordon's jazz festival and I guess he too was hungry for his own kind of people. When I asked him if he'd play an extra two nights at my jazz cellar, I must have made it sound rather more big time than it was, because he most generously agreed.

Jazz musicians are among the nicer people in this world and there is a sort of brotherhood that works among them. If you know and love jazz it shows and I think Gene was just one very decent guy who was travelling without his manager. So he didn't have some hard-headed money man pressing his buttons and trying to make a deal. He just graciously agreed to be my big, opening-night star.

The kitchen I'd inherited in the Hungry I was positively Dickensian. It would have worked well on a set for Oliver Twist. Most of the gear was missing and the gas range, installed in the early '20s, was well named. It was called an Early Kooka, with a picture of a Kookaburra in enamel on the oven door. The pots, such as they were, were chipped. The frying pans and griddle were caked with ancient fat, baked to a tar-like substance a quarter of an inch thick. The whole place smelled of rancid oil and insecticide, from when the Flick man had fumigated the joint. Dead cockroaches lay in untidy heaps in the corners, where you could still see the original pattern of the linoleum. It had once had large yellow and red triangles, but now it had a pattern of large black paths from years of kitchen traffic. The huge walk-in freezer, designed to carry several carcasses of frozen beef, made weird bubbling, gastric-type sounds like a giant with the tummy rumbles. They shook the wooden floor upstairs so that the place vibrated in a small earth tremor every few minutes.

But, still, it was a definite improvement on the Cafe Inferno and it was all my own, except for a silent partner who later proved

to be rather more furtive than silent. But I saw it as my own
success or failure. I felt sure that I'd finally latched onto something I could do. I told myself that if the kitchen wasn't that crash
hot, it was better than the Cafe Inferno's. Anyhow, jazz was food
and drink to the kind of people I hoped to attract and they probably wouldn't even notice what they were eating—providing it was
edible. I spent a small fortune cleaning the kitchen up and getting
it working properly.

Opening night was a sell-out, though the audience was seeded
with 'freebies' for anyone who was anyone in Sydney. We could
have sold the tickets four times over. With a premium on the grog,
I figured I might even break even on my first night! Wowee! What
a businessman I'd turned out to be. All day long the city radio
stations were pumping out Gene McDaniels' numbers and there
wasn't a Disc Jockey in town who hadn't pre-recorded his evening
programme so that he could be present at the opening of the
Hungry I.

With Gene McDaniels available for two nights, I had also con-
tracted the Australian Jazz Quartet, Bryce Rhodey, who had
recently returned from a successful concert tour of the U.S., and,
the Three Out Trio, who had backed Frank Sinatra when he'd
come out to Australia for Lee Gordon. I'd open with a bang, but
I'd continue on with far from a whimper. You couldn't have put
a better programme together anywhere outside New York, San
Francisco, Chicago, New Orleans or Paris, or so I told myself. Jazz
circles in Sydney were buzzing with high expectancy and for once
Kennedy looked like he was going to be a hero, the young entre-
preneur with the heart of a jazz purist. It was heady stuff, I can
tell you.

I hired a Cockney chef with one eye and a nasty scar down
his cheek, who told me he'd cooked on the Queen Mary and
could handle 200 meals on his ear. He wasn't pretty, but I wasn't
looking for beauty in the kitchen. He sniffed and huffed a bit
when I showed him the facilities, but finally decided that he
could work some combinations around what he called demi-
French cuisine: Soups with croutons; sophisticated omelettes;
little specially stuffed herb sausages; duck with paté de foie gras;

and; of course, the ubiquitous steak. He promised the steak would be eye of fillet with a special pepper sauce, that was *piquant.* Other menu items were oysters natural, grilled or kilpatrick, and 'angels on horseback,' and prawns, which he announced as barbecued shrimp on the shell with a *soupcon* of extra virgin olive oil. There were other bits and pieces, as well. If it all sounds pretty dreary in these days of heightened food awareness, at the time this menu was really rather avant garde.

I readily agreed to his suggested menu and asked him to order the stuff he needed through a food wholesaler, with whom I'd made a deal. 'Mind,' he said, 'this ain't exactly the kitchen on the Queen Mary. I can't absolutely guarantee everything will turn out perfect, now can I?'

'Well, it's got to, mate! This is an upmarket jazz club I don't want my patrons eating shit! guv'nor!'

That's an insult!' he cried, 'I was sous chef and then second chef on the Queen M, I don't cook no shit, guv'nor!'

'I'm sorry. The menu looks great,' I apologised and then, to reassert my authority, I added: 'But remember, I won't tolerate drinking on the job. No grog in the kitchen except what's used in the cooking!' I said this looking him in the eye as I shook his hand to conclude the deal. We'd had more than one drunken cook at the Cafe Inferno and while it didn't matter too much up there, I intended running a classy joint here in the Boulevard Arcade and I wasn't taking any chances.

'Quite right, matey, not a flamin' drop, I promise, Gawd's honour.' He did a sort of boy scout salute and then turned and winked at the two kitchen hands I'd hired. 'Hear that, lads, no piss on'a job or you're kaput at the Cafe de bleedin' Paris … or is it Le Club Jazz on la Rive Gauche?' he sneered.

'Are you taking the piss?' I asked in my best stripper's manager voice, indicating to him that I was not willing to take any lip from a one-eyed, scar-faced, Pommie bastard! (You do learn a thing or two hanging around a night club in the early hours.)

He backed off immediately; bluff is usually better than cuff. 'No, no, just askin', guv! Now, what about me knives and uniform, you ain't said nuffing about them?' I gave him a sour look, which cost me an extra $10 a night for the supply of his own private set of chef's knives and starched uniform.

With the kitchen arrangements finally settled I was satisfied that Sydney jazz fans would not go hungry and, with a bit of luck, we might even get a reputation for our food.

We'd sold or given away 250 tickets, which was the total capacity of the cellar, according to the fire brigade. By 7 p.m., close to 1000 people were queuing around the block on the street level. It was at this point that I began to feel a little uneasy.

At 7.15 the chef appeared at my side on the pavement where I was trying to persuade people without a ticket to go home. He was in full chef's uniform, starched and rigid as a rolled-up poster. He took one look at the queue stretching into infinity and said something unprintable. He then announced that he was slipping out for a packet of cigarettes. He never came back.

By 8 p.m., I was in a state of panic. The place was packed to the rafters: people were banging on the tables demanding food. Downstairs, I had two kitchen hands who probably couldn't boil water. Fortunately, the music was good and the mood of the crowd held and they drank enough grog to temporarily forget that they were hungry.

I couldn't get a cab so I ran all the way up to the Cross and took the temporary chef (they were always temporary) out of the kitchen at the Cafe Inferno. I gave the only patron in the joint $20 to leave and put the cardboard 'Closed' sign on the door. I frog-marched the protesting cook down to the Boulevard Arcade and demanded that he cook for 250 hungry, Hungry I, jazz fans. All I can remember was that he started to get the shakes. He then broke down and wept and said he was on Methadone.

Then a detective-sergeant stationed at the Darlinghurst police station, a member of the Drug Squad, arrived and demanded to see me. Fortunately, I knew him—a decent sort of bloke, a big Irish-Australian named O'Leary. He was a friend when I worked for George Farkas, of Goldcrest Jewellery, in the Mr Sheinberg days. He sometimes dropped in at the Cafe Inferno and claimed to enjoy the food. Like all the restaurants at the Cross, our food was free to any cop who cared to drop in, so he had no need to make such an absurdly ridiculous claim unless he *actually* meant it. I can only think that he must have had a very sad childhood.

'You got a bloke called Gene McDaniels singing here tonight, son?' he asked.

I explained to him that Gene McDaniels was the star turn, the big time, the top of the bill, Mr-Jazz-in-lights himself. He was my number one man, and the entire future of my infant jazz club.

He scratched his chin. 'Dunno about that, son, cause we just put him on a plane back to the States.'

'What!' I screamed, 'You did what? Now, c'mon, Sarge, tell me you're joking?'

'Sorry son, we caught him with some of that marijuana in his possession and the commissioner thought, rather than make, like a fuss, him being a Yank an all, we'd just quietly put him on a plane back to America. Make the best of a bad business, eh?'

The band playing would soon want a meal break, the place smelled to high heaven of old grease come back to life, new paint, sweat, cigarette smoke and the acrid smell of 'pot' mixed with bacon and eggs, some of which had started to appear from the kitchen. I was in deep shit.

Detective sergeant O'Leary's nose twitched: 'I think we'll give this place a miss tonight, don't you think, son? I can see you're in enough bother as it is. We'll drop 'round Tuesdee night. What's the grub like? Smells okay. Stay clean, ya hear?' he grinned, 'Particularly on a Tuesdee!' He wrote, '*Hungry Tuesnite,*' in pencil in his note book and took his leave. He then turned back and said: 'You fixed up with a liquor licence?' I nodded. In fact we had no liquor licence. In those days, it was nearly impossible to get a liquor licence for a nightclub or restaurant and you simply had to pay the police to stay in business. Every restaurant and nightclub in town took this for granted. Detective Sergeant O'Leary was simply making sure I wasn't going to bump my nose unnecessarily.

The Gene McDaniels news was devastating. People had come to hear him and, without any food in their stomachs, they were getting more and more pissed. They were likely, at any moment, to turn nasty. I half wished O'Leary would stick around, but then a cop in a jazz club is never good for business, even when he is being helpful.

Then David Ashcroft, my partner at the Cafe Inferno, arrived. He'd decided to look in at the Cafe to see how things were going and found the 'Closed' sign on the door. He arrived at the Hungry I only minutes after Detective Sergeant O'Leary had departed. I could see from the look on his face that he was a trifle miffed. He accused me of having no regard for him, or our joint business and, without waiting for an explanation, he promptly hauled back and punched me severely on the nose, splattering the front of my starched evening shirt with blood. Then he turned and ran down the stairs to the kitchen below. Minutes later, he stormed out of the club: 'Inconsiderate, bastard!' he shouted back at me as he frog-marched the whimpering Cafe Inferno cook down the road and headed back towards the Cross.

It was 10.30 p.m., almost time for Gene McDaniels to appear. The crowd was getting restless. I knew I would have to go onto the stage, hush the band and make the dreaded 'no-show' announcement. I thought that, maybe, with the blood on my shirt, they might feel sorry for me. But then, on the other hand, the sight of blood might send them crazy and they'd tear me apart.

I waited at the door, sniffing and smoking like an iron foundry trying to summon up enough courage to stop the band and make the announcement when a striking-looking black lady walked up to me.

'Hi,' she shouted above the din, 'I'm Nancy Wilson, haven't we met?' She looked towards the stage, 'Where's Gene?'

Nancy Wilson wasn't all that famous at the time, but I'd met her briefly, heard her sing, and thought she was marvellous. Even then it wasn't hard to tell she was going places.

'It's my night off and I thought I'd like to hear the great man.' She smiled winningly up at me, 'You will find a place for me, won't you?'

I explained what had happened, fingering my tender, swollen nose and hoping she would notice the blood on my shirt.

'Would you like me to sing?' she asked.

Nancy Wilson sat under a spotlight and the crowd hushed as

the Three Out Trio fingered the opening bars to 'Bye, Bye, Blackbird' and then the crowd simply went beserk. Nancy sang her heart out without a break for nearly two hours and the Hungry I Jazz Club was not only saved but became famous overnight.

The two kids in the kitchen had come good and got stuck into making onion soup, omelettes, bacon and eggs and baked beans. When we finally closed in the early hours, there had not been a single complaint about the food.

The opening of the Hungry I was a huge success and, by sun-up, tired almost beyond endurance but feeling about 9½ feet tall, I crept into bed.

Nancy Wilson, you are a great, great lady and I never miss your show if I happen to be any city in which you are performing. As they say in your vernacular: 'Thank you, ma'am, for saving my ass!'

I guess in all my business adventures up to that date, I had only once got the audience mix right and that was at The Hungry I. And the only reason I got that one right was that I'd guessed right for once and established a Jazz Club in a city which needed one badly. In other words, the audience found me and not the other way around. In business, I was to learn, this is an extremely rare occurrence.

At the Cafe Inferno, the weirdos were usually too drunk or stoned to find me and often too broke to buy a meal when they did. As a potential target audience for a business, they were a dead loss.

Because of the high rate of interest private capital demanded, the brokerage I ran attracted only desperates who were mostly turned down the by sharp-eyed lawyers who administered the private funds. Another poor choice of target audience.

The strippers were, of course, not an audience, but the audiences they appealed to for their living were very big on lechery and not so big on cash. Most strippers live from hand-to-mouth so my payment as their manager was, to say the least, inconsistent. Poor audience choice number three.

Even the dry cleaning kiosk was, in audience terms, a poorly-conceived operation. The kiosk was tiny and sat like an island in the middle of a busy arcade with the service window facing the street outlet. In people terms, these two factors proved a disaster. For a start, people bring their dry cleaning into the city from home. They're usually in a tearing hurry in the morning and they had to queue for service facing the line of morning commuters bearing down on them. In this way they were bumped and shoved and generally ruffled up by commuters running late for work. Next, we had no room in the tiny kiosk to hang dresses and jackets, so our specials for dry cleaning were always men's trousers and for laundry, men's shirts.

Now if you've ever stood in a mid-city street in the rush hour and counted the ratio of men to women, you will discover about one man for every 10 women.

If the man was single he might avail himself of our special on trousers or shirts, but most seemed to be married. But the married guys expected their wives to take their dry cleaning into the local suburban dry cleaners. There are not too many men who will stick a dirty pair of pants into a briefcase and take it into the city to face a horde of young women determined to mow any man underfoot in an attempt to get to work on time.

So, once again, I got the audience and their needs all wrong. Thus, we eventually went broke and Lawrence dry cleaners closed us down.

Almost everything in business begins with people. In direct response, the business of finding the people who are most likely to be attracted to your goods or services, is always the top priority.

The graveyard of direct marketing is littered with the corpses of companies who sent excellent propositions to the wrong people. e.g. Lawn mower offers to people who live in high-rise apartments. The right information to the wrong people is simply the most common mistake made in direct marketing, or any other marketing for that matter. Identifying and planning *who is the right target audience for your product or service, and then how to reach them, is the essential starting point to any marketing process.*

Let me refresh you memory:

Audience: 10

Offer: 5
Creative: 1

The audience factor is *10 times* as important as the creative element in the ultimate success of the direct marketing campaign. This means that, compared to creative, you should be devoting 10 times the resources of time, effort and money to getting the audience right.

However, let me give you a typical boardroom response to this critical equation.

Imagine you are addressing your directors with the details of your new direct marketing campaign. You show the artwork for the glossy brochure. You get the usual nod of approval and a couple of critical comments, which you carefully note. The ads look great, but the chairman wants the logo bigger.

'How much is this costing?' someone asks. 'Around $10,000 with photography but not the finished art, that will be about $4000 and the printing another six grand. We're home and hosed for $20,000.' A few people nod. The ad budget is through and the board seems happy. The preliminaries are over and you get ready to announce the really exciting news.

'To make sure this campaign works like no campaign ever has before, we propose to spend $200,000 on making sure we've got the audience exactly right. Not a stone will be left unturned until we know the geography, demographics, psychographics and every other living detail that makes up our target audience segment. Gentlemen, we are about to create the most specific piece of data about our audience this company has ever seen.'

The boardroom suddenly grows very silent and you can chop the atmosphere into large blocks of ice with the edge of your hand. The chairman clears his throat.

'Good God, Kennedy, that's bloody 10 times more? Ten times, ferchrissakes!'

'But, sir, we must know to whom we are selling our product,' you protest.

'Everyone!' he shouts, 'We sell our bloody product to everyone and we don't need to spend $200,000 to know that!'

Nothing sells to *everyone*—not even Coca-Cola or even electric light bulbs. The golden rule in marketing is that you always have to sell to *someone!*

Who is *everyone* anyway? Are you everyone? Patently, there is no such collective noun as everyone in marketing. How could you possibly appeal to everyone in an average household, let alone an entire city or country? There is always, in every circumstance, a *someone.*

Now, if you agree with me that we need to know precisely to whom we are talking, then please don't get a message out of this example of a typical board meeting that the creative expression of a direct marketing campaign isn't important. Because it is, very, very important. But for too long we have believed that people (everyone) are swayed by our commercial eloquence, seduced by our words and pictures to buy what they neither want or need. This is simply not true.

I once saw a very pretty ring on the finger of a woman whom I sat next to at a dinner party. She was classy-looking, well groomed and obviously well off. The ring looked old, an heirloom I supposed, and I commented on it. She told me how it was made from gold dug in Cornwall; it was ancient gold, not the same colour as most gold. She said it was the same type of gold used in the wedding ring given by Charles to Di and she cherished it. Several months later I was shown the same ring by a direct marketing colleague as an example of a very successful offer he had made the previous year.

The point is, of course, that in the woman I'd met he'd found his prime prospect. The creative, which was obviously well done, had worked and she was very proud of her ring. The facility with which she told the story of the rare and differently-coloured Cornish gold indicated that she'd told it often to a great many casual admirers of the ring. The ring, too, was a genuine article, beautifully crafted and though not inexpensive, great value for the money. My colleague lamented the fact that his client couldn't get any more of this special gold or they would have happily continued the offer, which he declared to be an absolute winner.

In the case of the ring, there had been no deception in what was said in the creative. The copy had obviously been excellent and the customer satisfaction enormous. If you are going to be successful in your marketing, your creative and your offer have to be good. But, most of all, you must choose and locate your target audience with precision: 1: 5: 10 is still the golden rule.

This brings me to the next very important aspect of direct response—the way people make decisions. I have stressed that a direct marketing offer appeals to one person at a time. You are not talking to a mass consumer audience, but to your Uncle Roy, your mum, cousin, the dry cleaning lady, or the cashier in the petrol station, all as individuals. You are are not talking to everyone, you are talking to someone. The appeal is never collective, it is always tailored to speak to one person. But this doesn't mean that only one person makes the decision to buy your merchandise or service, or even that the person who uses it is always the prime decision-maker.

As a general rule, the lower the price tag and the more simple the purchase, the more likely it is that only one decision-maker will be involved. Conversely, the higher the asking price, and the more complex or life-involving the purchase, the more likely it is that at least one other person will be involved.

The term we use for this multiple decision-making is appropriately enough: **The Decision-Making Unit (DMU)**. We shall refer to it from this point on as the DMU.

The DMU is predicated on the notion that in many decisions there is more than one player involved. Perhaps an example may be helpful.

You are selling hotel rooms to business people. But as any reasonably experienced hotelier knows, hotel rooms may be, but very seldom are, booked by the business person who will use it. The three most likely situations which occur in the booking of a hotel room are a call from a secretary, a travel agent, or it may be that a corporate deal exists where the user, the business person, has several choices of hotel within a price limit. Here, once again, the secretary, or 'gate-keeper,' as we sometimes call them, may be involved.

Within this very simple and oft-occurring example, lies a very fundamental point. This is that unless you have a good idea of the dynamics of the decision-making process, you would easily find yourself talking to only one part of the DMU and perhaps the least important part at that.

If, for instance, you realised that the user is relatively unconcerned about the choice of hotel, provided it is close to where he wants to do business, and the room is clean and comfortable, and the water in the shower hot—then his or her personal assistant could well be the key to your hotel being selected. You would then promote an offer to a PA of a weekend for two at Surfers Paradise with every eight nights booked in your chain of hotels. You could also make an offer of a free air ticket for the boss's spouse and weekend accommodation for two for every eight nights spent in the hotel. This way, you have gratified the secretary and absolved any possible guilt she may feel about booking your hotel and, at the same time, made her boss happy as well. You have also used the whole of your DMU effectively.

Recently one of the world's most successful niche publishers, who catered almost exclusively for the academic library market, came to us for a direct response programme. One of the first questions we asked was: 'Who makes the decision to buy a book or journal, the academic librarian or the heads of department?'

They scratched their heads and admitted they were not sure. We conducted a relatively simple piece of questionnaire research and increased their orders for books and journals by almost 25%. We looked like heroes by simply doing something that is so fundamental to a direct marketing programme, that it shouldn't even be questioned. Success, as it so often does with organisations, had made them lazy and perhaps even somewhat arrogant. Assumption is the enemy of effective marketing.

If assumption is the enemy, than careful target audience segmentation may be the greatest friend a direct marketer can have. We have already agreed that 'everybody' doesn't exist, that people have different needs and backgrounds and fall into different groups. Groups? Well, yes, people may be individuals but they are often individuals who have common habits, loves, tastes, enjoyments, needs. As marketers, it is our challenge to decide how these segmentations come about. Who they are (our audience) what is likely to interest them so that they act (our offer), how best we can reach them (our media selection) and, finally, what is the best way to stimulate them to act immediately on our solicitation (our creative approach), and then to look for the differences between them. Mass marketing looks to averages, but direct marketing looks to differences.

It's quite easy to become confused about your potential customers because some look alike, speak alike, act alike but really think very differently. Here in Australia, my company is the largest seller of porcelain collectors' dolls. But before porcelain dolls became big collectables, as they did recently, porcelain collectors' plates were Australia's number one collectable. Plate collectors seemed such a perfect target for porcelain dolls. After all, the plates were hung on walls, displayed in cabinets, rested on side tables and performed many of the same decorative functions as the dolls. It was a reasonable assumption that they would be the same people. But it was a completely wrong assumption. Plate collectors do not automatically become doll collectors. We didn't know why this was so, so we set out to find out.

Well, we knew why people collected plates. Plate collectors are concerned about the decorative appeal of the art, not unlike people who collect paintings. Though unable usually to collect original works of art on canvas, they want original plates. They are after the authentic thing. They want a limited edition and they love the idea of scarcity and the appreciating value that this will eventually produce.

Doll collectors, we were to find out, had an entirely different set of physical and emotional needs. They collected dolls as if they were people. They talked about them as personal friends. They also hated to think that their dolls might be lonely, so they bought more dolls to create a happy family of dolls. This may well be a leftover from a lonely childhood, or simply the need in all of us to be a child again. Porcelain dolls could satisfy this need without them appearing to collect soft, cuddly Raggedy-Ann dolls, or dolls that wet and cried 'mama,' which would make them seem immature, or child-like, to their friends.

The point is that doll collectors are light years away from plate collectors. They are an entirely different market segmentation. Sending an expensive and attractively prepared offer of a collector doll, using your plate collector database, would be a direct marketing disaster.

And so it becomes very necessary to segment your customers into pre-defined groups, to put them into boxes. Oops! That's not a politically correct term and you should be careful how you go about this, not all people can be fitted comfortably into a designated box. And it's never a good idea to become too smug about your ability to segment the market.

However, marketing theory has provided us with a series of convenient categories into which we can place our customers. To do this it uses several criteria with rather ominous names. The more common terms are: *Demographics, Geography, Sociographics and Psychographics*. Not exactly a cuddly bunch of terms. We will explore each in turn.

1. **Demographics:** This is the breakdown of the population at large, their age, sex, income etc. Now this doesn't tell us a great deal, although it's not entirely useless. For instance knowing someone is 25-years-old doesn't say a great deal about them. We obviously need to know more. But knowing someone is 55 can often be a little more useful.

For instance, in Australia, as elsewhere in the Western world, we are seeing a great increase in the so-called 'grey market' of people 55 and over. These customers want all sorts of things, primarily based on their age: retirement accommodation, financial advice, holidays with their own kind. In fact, new opportunities are occurring every day to the live-wire direct marketer. For instance, no motor car manufacturer caters for the old person. Cars are advertised as fast or roomy, no automobile manufacturer has come up with a car that's easy to get into, is an ideal touring car, has a hoist on the boot to pick up heavy shopping loads, or even something as simple as a small trolley to carry shopping to and away from the car. There are a dozen other features which could easily make a motor car more comfortable and ideal for the older driver. Today, you can get a car practically custom built, yet no manufacturer has thought to custom build a car for the older driver. Direct marketing could very easily fill this gap.

New products and services are being created every day with marketers becoming more and more aware of the needs of individual customers. There was a time when direct marketing was the lowest rung on the selling ladder and it is still, in some respects, a business which could do with a bit of a cleaning up. But more and more smart direct marketers are asking themselves not only what they can take out, but what they can put back—how they can win the customer's approval with their corporate good manners.

Just 10 years ago in the U.S., Gun Denhart started Hanna Andersson, a direct marketing company selling children's clothes by means of a catalogue. Today, she has one of the leading children's catalogues in the U.S. Baby and infants' clothes are one of the most competitive businesses in any marketing environment. Yet Gun has prospered hugely, growing Hanna Andersson an average of 25 per cent each year. Gun is a master at the art of understanding her customers' values and appealing to these values. She understands 'The Value of Values.'

For a start, she calculates how many trees are felled to make her catalogue, and plants twice as many each year. She puts her toll free phone number on the label of her garments so that if the customer loses the washing instructions or needs help they can call for advice. She also promises to buy back, for 20 per cent of the original price, any garments in good condition which the children have out-grown. These are then given to charity by her company. Gun believes emphatically that she is marketing to an individual, and she is careful to find out what the needs, beliefs, value systems and aspirations are of the individual family members who shop through her catalogue. She also realises that the purchase isn't made simply by the young mother, but by a collective family of other influences—grandmothers, aunts, cousins, friends. Every new baby and every toddler has a large extended family and they are all direct marketing opportunities. She also asks her customers to let her know when they are getting duplicate catalogues and she pays them $5 for giving her this information. As an unsought bonus, their cancellation often comes with a new address of a mother-to-be, a recommendation that makes for her another customer friend and replaces the one she has just lost. Treating your customer as an individual, and appealing to his or her values, can be a very profitable business.

When a marketing organisation tells you that their audience profile is typical woman aged between 25 and 50, they may as well tell you that all their customers once broke a thumb. The information is practically useless unless you're trying to select candidates for a Ms Pretty Hands contest. The differences between a woman of 25 and 50 can be, and often are, mind boggling.

2. **Geography:** Neighbourhoods can be very different. They may differ in income, ethnic composition, single or family residences, old or young, typical occupations, type of dwelling and a host of other clues as to how the people who live in the area go about spending their lives.

A gay community living in an inner city suburb will differ enormously from a migrant, or ethnic community, which may live in a similar-looking inner-city suburb.

Geography is an important start-up clue to the composition of your audience, yet it is often neglected. A number of often ignorant, and even racist, assumptions can be dispelled by a stroll through the area on a Sunday afternoon. Your eyes can often be a very intelligent researcher and you don't have to have 10,000 questionnaires fully completed to come to some very relevant conclusions after the stroll or a Sunday afternoon drive through your target area. Finally, a great deal of information is available from published census statistics and newspaper circulation profiles. A little looking goes a long, long way.

3. **Sociographics:** The art of knowing how people lead their lives; their habits, hobbies and loves. Gardeners need lawn mowers, plants, seeds, hoses, gloves, shears, trowels, forks, spades and books. Golfers need clubs and clothes and shoes and lessons.

Young mothers need baby clothes, books, nappies, a whole range of new household products, and so it goes.

It makes perfect sense to monitor the births in the newspaper notices for your database and then cross reference them with your census list to see where the heavy baby belt is situated in every city. Similarly, if you want to sell a very expensive set of golf clubs, you might buy the list of the country's 2000 richest people and match it with the membership list of the most expensive golf clubs (not an easy task). The more you know about the way people lead their lives, the more accurate you can be in meeting their needs.

4. **Psychographics.** How do your customers feel and think? A community of Irish immigrants will feel and think very differently from one of Greek or Asian. Blue collar workers tend to hold different political views than do white collar workers. More importantly, what benefits from your product or service do they anticipate? If you have a customer who lives in a steel town, or industrial suburb, and does physical work with little permanent job security and no superannuation plan, then the chances are that security and reassurance will begin to be important to them from their late forties as the end of a working career is in sight. They will be excellent candidates for life insurance, but they may also be customers for disability insurance, fire insurance and holiday insurance.

In a polyglot society like Australia's, the assumption that all Australians will think and act alike is a very dangerous one. Never make sweeping assumptions about an Australian city or a suburb, as you are more likely to be wrong than right. Should you think there is an opportunity in a Vietnamese community, then learn something about the value systems these migrants have brought with them from Vietnam. A Buddhist does not think in the same way as a Baptist. If you know what people value emotionally, you can match their needs far more easily with your product or service. How your customers feel and think is both the key to their heads and their purse. Remember, their aspirations are more important than their lifestyles.

Can you see your customer clearly in the flesh?

All the above is valuable information but until you get to know your customer 'in the flesh,' it is difficult to do business. People are people through other people, and it is important to feel you know your prospect in much the same way as you know your neighbour. Visualise your inner city customer sitting at the kitchen table having a chat over a cup of tea or a drink. Visualise how she looks. You have her age, nationality, background, community, religion, income. You now should be able to see her clearly.

Most direct marketing copy-writing is written to some abstracted customer in a vacuum. The language can be dry, tasteless, odourless and deodorized. The copy writer simply cannot see his or her prospect further than to know what sex they might be.

Training your copy writer to visualise the prospect is a skill which is often lacking in today's direct marketing environment. Yet it remains important. Many sales barriers fall if the prospect feels that you are speaking to him or to her in his or her language. Direct marketing is predictive—you have information and you make predictions from it. You have to learn to think through the information to the actual person, and know how he or she will react to a situation. This is easier said than done so here are a few hints on how to go about it.

Start from the position that nobody wants to hear from you, that they have a scant interest in what you have to say, and even less in the offer you are making. In other words, they don't want to hear about *yourself,* they want to hear about *themselves.* Ten words about you and the offer you are making is infinitely boring; but 200 words about them is absolutely fascinating. People are ego-centred. You are; I am. We want to know what's in it for us and we assume that you are already looking after yourself very nicely, thank you. You simply cannot begin making commercial love to your prospect if you cannot visualise her, if you cannot see her clearly; it is like trying to woo someone you've never seen through the keyhole of the front door.

In Australia and New Zealand they should be treated with great caution. They have been collected for a different purpose to yours. This is simply because *they* are often too abstracted. That is, they contain the bare essentials and make it almost impossible for you to visualise your prospect. If you can't see her or him properly, you've got very little chance of talking in a sympathetic and persuasive manner. The system of finding people in the first place, and then getting to know them, should be managed with great intelligence and sophistication. Names culled out of a telephone book is not a sophisticated technique. The art and science of database marketing is compiling relevant detail. Look for quality, not quantity. A list should be up-to-the-minute and a lot of rented lists are hopelessly out of date. The reason for this is obvious: people who rent a list and find out information about the people on the list, do not add that information to the list when they return it. So it never accumulates relevant prospect data and detail. That's why they're called lists and not profiles.

Your best option is always to develop your own database of real and active customers, with whom you speak by mail or phone on a regular basis. You do this by asking them frequently to do something and in this way they respond to you. This is the simple business of keeping in touch. It isn't all that different to sending a postcard to a friend when you're on holiday.

Real database marketing, as opposed to renting a list or collecting names in a file or on computer, is the essence of relationship marketing. Without the data how can you commence the relationship?

Name acquisition and management is the first process you have to master. Names have to come from somewhere and you only have two choices—rent a list or collect the names yourself, one by one.

You rent a list through a third party, usually a mailing house or a list broker. In other words, you never get to see the list as the renter doesn't want you to transfer his set of names onto your list. He wants to know he can rent it again to you and to others.

Thus the smart list owner will also want to vet your mailing. The reason is to see whether your are making an offer which will not offend the names on his list. A ridiculous example for want of another is a Christmas ham offer to a list of prominent Jewish people. Silly as this sounds, people do some very strange things with rented lists. They can alienate the people on the list and so spoil it for the list's owner. The original owner of the list always wants to be in a position to say that he genuinely thought that *your offer would be of interest to his names.* He also wants to be able to assure the people on his list that photostats were not made of their names, and the list circulated willy nilly to everyone in the direct response business. No-one wants junk mail piling up into bonfire proportions at the front gate. Complete confidentiality must be maintained. The mailing house or broker will protect that confidentiality and never allow you direct access to the list. The usual list rental is 15 cents to 20 cents for every name on the list, every time it is used. This is something you can do yourself when you have your own database.

Never forget to approve *everything* that is to be mailed to your list. Do not, under any circumstances, abdicate your approval rights to your broker or mailing house. Someone might just construct an offer that is so appealing (e.g. a free entry into a sweepstake simply for sending back a name and address), so that a high proportion of the names on your confidential list end up on his new list. It has happened.

Generally, when people respond to your offer via a rented list, you can usually put them on your own database. Anyway, you have to have their name and address to fulfil the order and to provide customer service. But not always. If they responded by credit card or cheque, then the credit card company, or the bank, will usually demand that the name is wiped from your records once the order is filled and the customer satisfied. Furthermore, the names cannot be used a second time for promotion without approval.

The name that comes from a response to any offer is obviously a lot more valuable than one you picked out of the phone book, or from a rented list. The name is, still 'hot' and you immediately know something about the person behind the name. Such names are referred to as a *response list.* Conversely, the names you get elsewhere, which are 'cold,' are known as *compiled lists.*

Ideally, when you are in the business of creating your own database, you want to do this with *response names* to make a *response list.* A list of *compiled names* in a database is usually compiled from telephone books, electoral rolls, association members, or club memberships. These lists show a surprising rate of attrition. They are usually out of date almost before you've used them. The natural attrition rate in Australia through moving, death, marriage etc is 20 per cent per annum.

So don't be tempted to use a rented list unless you know precisely why you are doing so. *In over 20 years of selling mail order merchandise in Australia,* I've never made a rented list work for mail order. I'm sure I could do so if my competitors would rent me their lists but, of course, they'll do no such thing.

However, I have found that it does work to swap lists with other well-managed, non-competitive mail-order traders. This is because, like your own carefully-compiled database, theirs also is detailed and well maintained. It contains only the names of people who have bought product from that retailer recently. Of course, you can only do this with companies you trust, otherwise you never know, until it is too late, whether they are swapping names of equal quality with you.

It's important to know whether a list is '*alive*' or 'dead'. It's usually dead if you don't know where it came from originally, how up-to-date it is, and if it contains little or no specific detail. It is 'live' when it is obtained from any of the following sources, which you know to be active and recent:

- phone response
- coupon response
- purchases in retail outlets
- guarantee cards
- credit card lists
- salespeople's prospects and customers.

If I keep stressing the problems with rented lists, it is because they have very often let me down. Business lists, in particular, suffer most from dating quickly. Look to your own company and see how many people in your organisation have changed jobs, titles, departments or left in the last 12 months.

In fact, our experience shows that a rented business list can be redundant by as much as 50 per cent in a year. That is, if the renter assures you his list is only one-year-old, you might get this kind of failure rate from it. These lists are termed *static information*, because a very large percentage of the *names on them are 'dead'* on their feet. It is well worth phone-verifying a percentage of the names to check the degree of accuracy.

A *response list* is quite a different matter. This is *'live' information*—living, breathing, responding names. They have been active quite recently—a credit used, a guarantee card completed, a phone call made requesting further information. It is sometimes possible to rent a *response list.* If you rent one, make sure that you find out from the owner of the list: when, why and how the names on the list responded; and what offer was made to cause them to respond. If you are confident you can trust this information, then a rented reponse list can work well.

There are several ways you *evaluate a response list* when you are selling merchandise by means of direct marketing. Listed below, in order of preference, are the six ideal criteria for the names on the list:

1. Bought a similar product or service at the same price by direct response.
2. Bought a similar product at a different price by direct response.
3. Bought a different product at the same price by direct response.
4. Bought any product at any price by direct response.
5. Took any direct response action requiring money.
6. Took any direct response action.

This criteria will help you *qualify* (evaluate) any list you are given to consider. It's pretty logical, really. The best customer you could possibly get on a list is the one already doing what you want them to do, though perhaps not yet with you. But remember: *A response list will always out-perform a compiled list. Furthermore, the best lists of all are the ones you build yourself from your own responses.*

How then do you go about collecting your own database? Well, of course, it depends on what kind of business you are in, and what you are selling and to whom. If you have an existing business, then you should collect the marketing data of the customers you already own. This is rather easier said than done. For instance, many banks and insurance companies have mountains of data, but it was collected for accounting and not marketing purposes. Often, to get the marketing information you need, it is easier to start again from the beginning and build what is known as a *Relational Database* because it relates different information. It's not quite as onerous as it sounds, because you already have the names and, presumably, a fair amount of co-operation from your existing database. By interrogating them, you get the marketing information you need. If you are a general marketer expect about a 20 per cent to 30 per cent response to a well-planned questionnaire. You will get a much higher response if you are a financial organisation and can tell your respondents that the completion of the questionnaire is beneficial to a continuing relationship.

If you are a retailer, you should have the names of all your customers. But, lamentably, many Australian and New Zealand retailers do not have this basic data. This is simply unforgiveable! If relationship marketing is a data-driven form of advertising, and you are missing the data, then in short, you're stuffed!

In addition to any data on existing clients you might have, or can acquire you don't have much option in Australia if you are a direct marketer but to 'buy' the names out of the media by running coupon-response advertisements.

I have been nursemaid to half a dozen overseas companies, who are accustomed to working from lists in their own country, and who decided to build their start-up business in Australia out of lists (despite my advice). They have failed miserably and eventually had to resort to coupon response.

However, even when a major new direct marketing organisation tries to build a list by 'buying' it from the media it can be risky. It is made difficult because the media itself is of such a high-risk nature, with no really tried-and-true direct-response magazines, newspapers and TV programs in many segments of the market.

Here are some guidelines to help you.

You have to create advertisements which make an attractive offer but which are really designed to collect names. Advertisements in selected publications which invite a direct response can be very cost effective in bringing you good quality names for a highly responsive list. In a way, it's using a sprat to catch a mackerel. Let me give you an example.

With the Australian Bicentennial coming up in 1988, we wanted to collect a response list of people most likely to purchase commemorative merchandise. We set up an exercise in 1987 to break even which would allow us to get an early start in the following Bicentennial year. Keeping the cost per order low is important. If desire for profit overwhelms your name-gathering exercise, you can often diminish the response and end up with a much less effective response list. If you break even, you have acquired a good name without it costing you a cent. If the name is good, and you can make a profit in the process, then you have the best of both worlds.

We created a collectable plate with great emotional appeal developed from original artwork commissioned from Australia's leading marine artist, Ian Hansen. It showed The Bounty anchored in Sydney Cove on a glorious summer's day on January 17th, 1788. It was important that the article we used be seen to be original and valuable as well as good value for the asking price. We achieved this situation with a perfectly splendid-looking plate. It was a plate that people would hang on their walls, or display in their cabinets, rather than store away as a future asset.

Each plate was numbered and carried an official backstamp with a commemorative inscription. It came with a signed certificate of authenticity. In other words, while we wanted a broadly-based list of people who would be interested in buying Bicentennial merchandise, we made sure that the plate would fit the expectations of the most serious-minded plate collector. This is an important point to make: people often think that by collecting names by means of an offer of cheap and relatively shoddy or valueless merchandise, they will achieve a high response. But this approach seldom, if ever, attracts a quality response list. Name collecting is a very serious business and it is all about quality responses. Don't try to get good names with poor products because responses to cheap, shoddy products will always be the very best responders to cheap, shoddy products.

Once we had created merchandise of a very high quality at a very attractive price, we tested the offer using our own house list. We mailed out a brochure which would be very similar to the print advertisement we would eventually run in selected media. This worked well and gave us the confidence to place our Bicentennial plate offer using two basic methods—space ads placed strategically in magazines and loose leaf inserts in newspapers and some selected magazines using the brochure. These generated 1,500 orders at a slightly lower than break-even cost. It was a nice result. We had the basis of a response list of names who might be interested in buying Bicentennial merchandise. This was then increased to other mediums to give us a very effective response list, which allowed us to capitalise handsomely the following year on a number of Bicentennial offers. Other direct marketing organisations, using rented and mostly compiled lists, reported that they had fared very badly during the Bicentennial year.

As an aside, it did occur to us that by offering a superb plate we might be gathering names of just plate collectors and not people generally interested in Bicentennial merchandise. So we used the new list to make a straight plate offer of a good quality collector's plate without a Bicentennial motive. To our delight, the response was very ordinary, which meant that we had the right target audience for Bicentennial merchandise.

In a different exercise, we took as a test offer one of the most successful, medium-quality, low-priced plate offers ever made in the US market. It comprised four Currier and Ives Four Seasons plates. With it we ran a name-collecting exercise to try to get future serious plate collectors. As sometimes happens, we broke the bank. The exercise was designed to break even, but it brought in 10,000 orders at $29.95 for a set of four plates. It gave us a superb future response list and a handsome and unexpected profit. Sometimes, if you're lucky, you can do a lot better than break-even on a low-cost name-acquisition exercise. But don't set out to do this; the object of the game is to collect names for a response list, which you may use next for a 'SERIES' selling offer. It's all about selling 'upwards.'

A series selling offer is pretty well what it says—the sale of more than one thing in a series. For example, one of our most ambitious, though successful, offers was the Wedgwood Kings and Queens of England 120-part thimble series. You can get some idea of the life-time value of such an offer, when you realise that it took a collector 10 years of receiving one thimble a month to complete this collection. Some collectors died before the series was complete.

Sometimes, a series might seem rather a formidable task to the collector. When they realise that, over a period of time, the outlay is considerable, they baulk at the offer. When you think this might happen, you can structure your offer as a 'silent' series: that is, you don't promote it as a series, and there is no obligation to buy more. At a future date, you simply offer an additional piece that fits nicely into a set.

The maths of a successful 'silent' series works with four products as follows: If you have 100 customers who buy the first offer in the series, you will find that the next offer will generate 40 orders, the third 25 and the fourth, because you tell them it is the last in the series, will generate another 40 orders. In terms of your bottom line, you have done very well. The cost of gaining the first 100 orders will have been considerable, but the following 105 will have been gained at a very low cost. A nice little promotion, to say the least! The most attractive item in the series should, of course, be offered first in order to attract the most initial response and, therefore, the most names.

It is curious that people don't often respond to an offer of similar sort of merchandise, which is perhaps in a different configuration. For instance, porcelain plate collectors may buy a vase or figurine with the same motif, but won't buy the same motif on a cup and saucer or a porcelain doll. Knife collectors are dedicated solely to the blade. They will only collect knives and cannot be tempted, for instance, by a replica of a 17th century hand-gun, or a replica of the Colt .45 Billy the Kid used in his train hold-ups. Just as sadly, doll collectors *only* collect dolls.

What a customer will and won't buy is, of course, priceless information for your database. When your base is loaded with sufficient relevant information about your customer, it will greatly help in the cost effective management of future promotions.

There are several other ways of collecting quality names other than through a media offer. One is *using a telephone bureau.* You give a detailed brief of your desired target audience to a telephone bureau and they will respond with names which will cost you under $10 each. But you must be quite specific. If you have an offer which you think will interest computer programmers, then give the relevant profile details you want: e.g. programmers who drive a luxury car, play golf, have one or more children, and have been in the same job for more than three years.

Yet another good name collecting device is to offer an incentive to your known customer base to introduce a friend. This means you are asking your customers to be advocates for your firm. *Advocacy*, is, of course, the top rung of the Loyalty Ladder. The good news is that people are reasonably self-selective. They will choose to give you the name of a friend who has much the same taste and aspirations as they do. This gives you a good chance of a valuable new customer.

Remember, you must keep '*topping up*' the names on *your database.* It will not remain plump and ready for action unless you nourish it constantly. Natural attrition is constantly eroding about 20 per cent of your database. The best way to top up your response list is through media advertising. That is, making an attractive offer where you budget to break-even in return for new names to place on your response list or *data*base.

And don't forget, it is all about relationship building. If you don't use your database it will grow stale. If you don't call a friend on a regular basis, she or he will eventually drift away. It is no different with a response list. Pay your customers the courtesy of a regular friendly visit with an offer, or a communication, which

Ian on Bondi beach, circa 1942

Sally Kennedy with her son, Ian.

'Witt' Kennedy, father

... and son.

Ian Kennedy (front centre) captain of Sydney High School debating team.

Racing 'B class' catamarans at Rose Bay, New South Wales

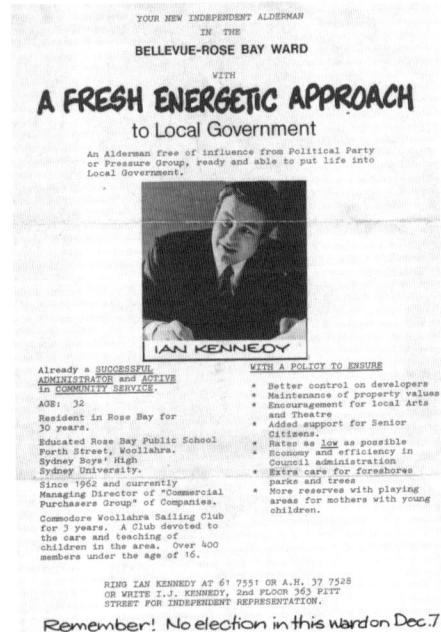

Before being elected to Woollahra Council courtesy of his first direct marketing exercise.

One of Ian's less successful night-life ventures in Sydney, the short-lived Jazz club, The Hungry I.

Peter Cook and Dudley Moore, the legendary comic duo, on tour with Ian in New Zealand in the 70s.

Ian and his son, Sam in Spain, 1995.

The Eagle Knife - A solid gold replica of the American Eagle Knife presented to Ian by the Japanese manufacturer in 1984 to commemorate the 2 millionth knife manufactured. Sales grossed 40 million dollars at retail.

The two most successful items from the Australian bicentenary in 1988. The watch at retail A$59.90 sold A$4.4 million worth and was reformatted in five other countries.

VALET-PAK

holds all your travel needs...

Keeps two suits on **locked-in hangers** so they'll stay wrinkle-free.

Takes shirts, sweaters, underwear, sleepwear and toilet articles. You name it. Withstands more scuffs, more stains and more hard wear.

Fashionably styled in rich, leather-like vinyl and superbly finished with double-stitching and double-riveted straps.

You take less effort to lift and move it about because new Valet-Pak luggage puts **lightness and flexibility** in your hand. It folds down into a compact 49.5 cm x 59.5 cm (19½" x 23¾") size and weighs only 2 kg (4 lbs).

Time to pack and unpack is less. Valet-Pak's heavy-duty, full-length diagonal zipper gives you easy access. **Three special zippered storage compartments** mean your clothes can be organised quickly and neatly carried wrinkle-free.

Space is at a premium when you're on the move. Valet-Pak folds up into a **compact brief case shape.**

The **built-in hanging hook** saves valuable time and allows you to hang your clothes when travelling, or, when you arrive at your hotel, so that your clothes are always neat and clean.

THE IDEAL GIFT FOR ANY MAN.

Carry it with you like a briefcase.

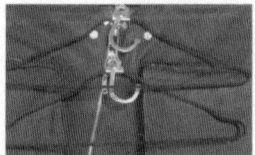

Special lock-in hangers hold suits in place.

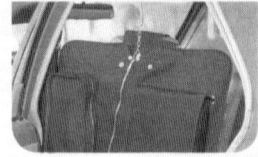

Hangs up like a garment bag and keeps clothes wrinkle-free.

The very first mail order merchandise offer inserted with Diners Club statements, 1975. The response rate of 11.6% was staggering.

On of the first Bond International direct marketing ads in the early 70s.

The hugely successful Onkaparinga blanket promotion, shich made Bond International the biggest buyer of single bed blankets in Australia.

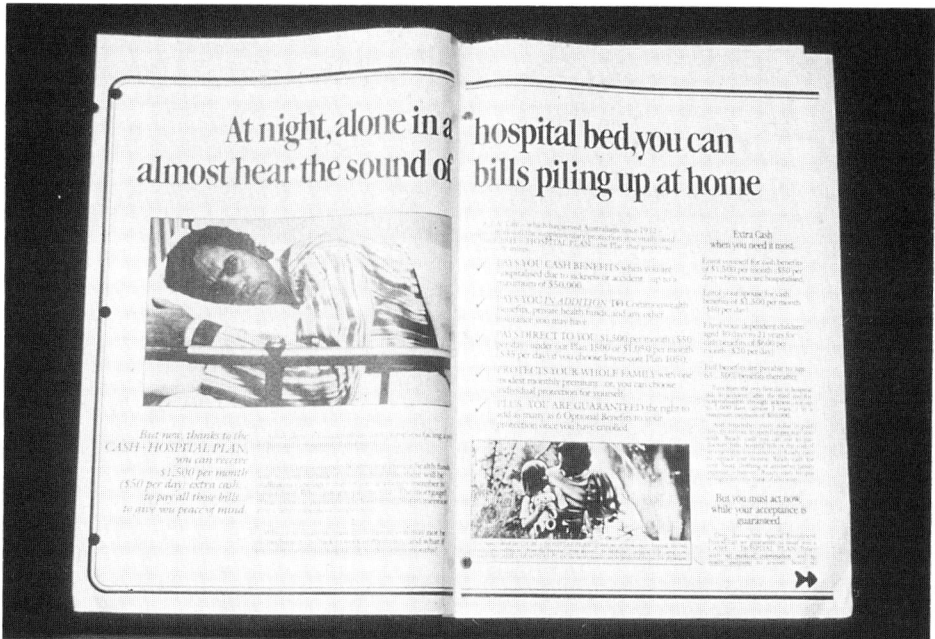

One of the most successful insurance ads of its kind in Australia written for APA by Mel Gottleib and one of the only four page response ads ever.

The In Home file, a metal box that never sold well in retail stationers, was turned into a successful mail order product first in Australia and then in nineteen other countries.

Montreaux, Switzerland, Ian becomes
the first Australian to speak at the city's
famous Direct Marketing Symposium.

In Zurich with Jerry Reitman, Executive
Vice President International, of advertising agency, Leo Burnett, Chicago.

Galloping Gourmet days. From left, Ian, Graham Kerr, Marilyn Lapidus, Paul Talbot
(founder-owner of the Fremantle Corporation) and Walter Cran, President of Cresca
Foods, in Conneticut, USA.

'The three amigos'. Ian with Murray Raphael and the bearded Jim Rosenfield, two leading US direct marketing speakers.

Ian receives the prestigious US Echo for direct marketing in Boston.

Working in the Tokyo office with US partner Michael Harrison, the original co-owner in Bold International.

Ian with Japanese, American and Australian colleagues at the collectable plate supplier's office in Nagoya.

Celebrating with Walter Schmidt, founder of the great Montreux direct marketing symposium.

George Patterson links with Bond International

By SUSAN HELY

Australia's biggest advertising agency, George Patterson (annual billings $260 million), will link with the biggest direct marketing company, Bond International Pty Ltd, which has direct sales worth $10 million and billings of the same amount.

It was the first link of its kind and Bond International would provide consulting services for George Patterson clients and, in turn, Patterson would recommend Bond's services for the direct marketing needs of its clients, the chief executive of Patterson, Mr Geoffrey Cousins, said.

The direct marketing facility was an adjunct for existing com-panies and would not replace other forms of advertising. His clients had pressed for a direct mailing service. Patterson felt it was better to link with the best rather than try to establish its own.

He said there was no exchange of equity between the two compa-nies at present and he declined to comment on future plans.

Bond International, which is itself an importer and exporter, has a data base of 300,000 customers and numbers among its clients Diners Club and Qantas.

It owns the Heritage Collection and is in a joint venture with Wedgwood Australia, the Wedg-wood Collectors Society, and is the Australian agent for the Bradford Exchange Ltd, which is the largest collectors plate com-pany in the world.

Mr Cousins said the most attractive feature of Bond Interna-tional was that it was a trader in its own right and its data base was one of the most sophisticated in Australia.

Bond International is headed by Mr Ian Kennedy who founded the company in 1972.

Mr Kennedy has been the winner of the Direct Marketer of the Year award and has been a member of the international advi-sory board of the Direct Market-ing Association of America for more than nine years.

The announcement of the link between Bond International and Australia's biggest advertising agency, George Patterson, in 1986.

With two other direct marketing Hall of Fame inductees, Eddy Boas (left) and
Vin Jenkins (centre).

Interviewing Phillip Adams on stage at the Pan-Pacific Direct Marketing Symposium
in Sydney in the mid-80s.

makes them feel wanted. This means you should be in touch with them at least four times a year. Treat your database as a list of cherished friends and they will continue to respond. **Seventy per cent of customers who disappear from a database do so for non-hostile reasons**. Keep in touch and keep 'topping up' your list.

I think it is important to differentiate between a list and a database. A list can become sophisticated and so is called a response list. A good database provides us with *qualifying* information—that is, enough information to evaluate the potential of an offer to the names on the list. This evaluation, or qualification is obviously, a desirable sophistication of the 'live' response list. There is a rather convenient way of measuring the common ground between you and your customers which we call the FORM guide. All database segmentation is based on some kind of scoring system so that you can 'rate' the names. Your form guide is the simple beginning of what will eventually be a far more sophisticated system. Here's how to 'do the form':

F is for **Frequency**: *How many times have the customers on your list responded to an offer you have made to them? What proportion or percentage is that of the number of times you have invited them to accept an offer from you?*

O is for **Order**: What have they been buying? Is it always the same thing, or related products? It is unlikely that they will simply buy anything; people have product preferences which are usually pretty consistent.

R is for **Recency**: When was the last time they ordered or responded to an offer you made? Make a time comparison between this order and the previous time they ordered and then compare this with the period they have been on your response list.

M is for **Money**: The monetary value of their total spend with you. Take this figure and divide it by the total number of responses they have made to an offer. This gives each customer an average response value, and play an important part in the scoring system.

You should keep your FORM guide up to date and revise it before every mailing. The information, with a little extrapolation, can tell you a great deal about your regular customers and keep your response list 'hot' and database fresh. It is also the single most important function of any database segmentation, as it determines to which segments you should be mailing. Most importantly, this affects your profitability.

There is a phenomenon in direct marketing which seems to defy scientific analysis. It is called *Stamina.* This refers to a customers' propensity to spend again and again with you. This is yet another reason why it is so important to record the original source of the name on your database.

Here is an example of how stamina and source are linked. I track one set of names obtained over, say, five years, from the Australian Financial Review, and another set from Business Review Weekly. If, after analysis, I find that the customer names from the Financial Review spend, on average, 30 per cent more than the names from BRW, then I have to take notice. I then assess this 30 per cent increase using the two critical criteria of 'cost per response', and the 'quality of the response.' If the assessment reveals that the Financial Review delivers a higher-quality bigger spending responder for my goods or services, then this *greater stamina* response means that I can afford to pay more for the Financial Review customers and I should attempt to attract more of them.

No direct marketer can tell you satisfactorily why one of two publications, which seem to have an almost identical target audience and editorial content, will deliver a quite different result. Why one will deliver a more fickle on-going response than the other? Theories abound, but hard facts are pretty thin on the ground. Accept this as a phenomenon and exploit it by measuring it and using what you find.

Here is an interesting though perhaps logical piece of information. We have found that the *more emotional* a response, the *less stamina* the responder will have. For instance, television, as a direct-response medium, tends to be more emotional than, say, a brochure mailing, letter or print advertising. It is a great deal easier to grab the phone and place the order than it is to find a pen, a pair of scissors, fill in the coupon, cut it out, put it into the envelope and remember to post it. Television, though often brilliant for the quick, or emotional response, is low on stamina. With the telephone being used more and more for direct marketing, it is likely that it, too, will not be as good a medium to create customers with stamina.

You must be very careful, and on your best behaviour when sending your goods, or delivering your services, to your customer. This is, literally, where the promises end and you have to 'deliver the goods.' The name for this, as previously mentioned, is *fulfilment*. Fulfilment is a wonderful source of information for your database because, if you get something wrong, you should encourage complaint. You learn very little from a compliment, but a great deal from a complaint. Research shows that the complainer, who's complaint is satisfied, is twice as loyal as a future customer than one who never complains. It almost makes you want to build in a complaint factor, though perhaps that's getting a bit too smart for your own good.

For instance, if 5 per cent of your customers complain about the packaging of your merchandise, change it immediately. The point is that a 5 per cent complaint factor could mean that as much as 50 per cent of your customers were dissatisfied but haven't bothered to tell you.

Treat your customers as prized people. They are, after all, money in the bank. You don't have to go looking for them, you know who they are, where they live, what they like, how much they'll spend, how frequently they'll make a purchase and how loyal they are to you. They're already paid for, and they've proved themselves to be friends. To neglect them in the pursuit of new, expensive and unknown names is a pretty silly business decision. Yet, every day, people are out there in the media looking for, and paying for, new names. At the same time, they are neglecting their own customer 'family.'

Remember to use your database to research the value of an offer you intend to make in the media in order to recruit new names.

However, most name-getting exercises are low-profit offers. These offers should not be made to your own database simply because it cheapens your relationship with your customer friends. You should offer your database customers, those people on your response list, your higher-margin, best quality items. They already trust you, and they will respond to a valuable offer.

But if you do have a superb offer, and want to take it to the media because you believe it will deliver both names and a profit, then make sure you offer it to your own list customers first. Make them a private offer, even one with an added value premium, because they are valued customers. *If your response list responds to a media offer* it makes them feel unwanted because they were not offered the product before you made it widely available. Also, you want the responses from the media to be new names and not old ones. Moreover, you can reach your regular customers at a lower cost per sale than you can buy new sales from the media.

As to the telephone, it's not a good idea to badger your response list on the phone. But an occasional call to see how they're going, or follow up on a mail offer, is a good idea. If you have the right approach, you can ask customers what they think, what they want and what they do. Most customers will give you heaps of information if you're not too personal, and seem to be taking a genuine interest in them.

Never ask them research questions on the order coupon. It confuses their decision to buy and substantially reduces response.

Ask and you will receive. When we started to work with porcelain dolls, we had an almost empty database. Dolls of this kind were a new idea in Australia and we needed to know more about our customers. We knew a great deal about plates so we made a number of intelligent assumptions. Plate collectors want certificates of authenticity and certainly doll collectors would too. Limited editions were important to plate collectors and owning a rare doll must also be important to people who collected dolls.

We were wrong. Assumption had once again proved to be the prime enemy in the direct marketing business. Our research showed seventy-two per cent were not interested in certificates or limited editions. They simply liked dolls for the company they provided. We also found out what they were prepared to pay for a porcelain doll and how many, on average, they were likely to collect. Nor were they interested in the dolls as an investment, or for gifts. Forty six per cent said they just wanted them around. Unlike plates, where the investment motive is fairly high, less than 7 per cent of doll collectors considered investment, or future value, important. However, they liked the idea of passing the dolls onto their grand-daughters one day.

By the way, we never promote any collectors' item as an investment. It's a cheap trick and we think unethical. No person can decide in advance what will be a valuable item a few months, or years, along the track. The investment decision has to come *unprompted* from the customer.

Database marketing is all about keeping a relationship alive and, in many respects, it is a marriage of sorts. 'They are not interested in me any more and take me for granted,' is the most common complaint you hear from direct-marketing customers. 'So bugger them, I'm leaving!' is the most common result.

Research among your good customers is not expensive. It's essential and, in the end, very cheap. It is a silent, private and on-going dialogue between you and your customer friend. It makes them feel comfortable dealing with you and it helps you to serve them better. Many organisations, who employ direct marketing in their communications mix, use an in-house magazine or newsletter to keep in touch with their database. They include a questionnaire in most editions and offer prizes for sending it in. Philip Morris, in the U.S.A., used to register a 40 per cent response to this method of research. Phenomenally useful stuff for a database! It's all about giving in order to receive.

Austin Rover in the UK used to maintain direct communication with it's one million strong database through their in-house magazine, Catalyst. In every issue was a survey form requesting information on the customer's purchase intentions. Pretty blatant stuff, but in return they also asked the customer which sections in the magazine they most enjoyed or did not enjoy at all. Was it gardening, entertainment, fashion, female pursuits, sport, hobbies, travel? The future editions of the magazine were then specially tailored to their most expressed needs. Not a bad way to win friends and influence people while practising one-to-one marketing! What can possibly be more effective than asking customers what they want, and then providing it for them?

We send out best customers Christmas cards. We are always surprised at their response. Letters come back to us detailing holidays, how the family spent Christmas day, what they ate for Christmas dinner and even what gifts were exchanged. These really nice letters are addressed to me because my hand-written signature appears on every card. These are not lonely people responding to any sort of outside stimulus. They are just ordinary family people pleased that they enjoy a relationship with me. It is a genuinely nice exchange and we enjoy doing it. And, at the risk of being commercial, some of the information in these pleasant replies goes into the database. *When your customers start writing back to you, then you know your relationship marketing is working '13 to the dozen.'*

Remember, God is in the details;
your database is your Bible.

Chapter Nine

★ ★ ★

How I learned to bring dead money back to life
with a label attached to my big toe.
&
It's very difficult to shoot a deer
when it's licking the salt off your brow.

★ ★ ★

One of the many jobs I was given by Albert Sheinberg was to be the salesman and marketing manager for the Goldcrest Jewellery factory. This was the ultimate expansion of former taxi driver George Farkas, who used to make costume jewellery in his kitchen. With an injection of capital from the great man, George's home-made jewellery business had become a pretty big enterprise—although the original kitchen sink method of manufacture hadn't changed an awful lot and the base metal of almost all of the jewellery was still lead.

As the salesman, I would drive around visiting shops, showing my samples. If the shopowner placed an order I'd go to the nearest phone box and instruct the factory to fill the order, promising the paperwork when I got back to the office. Albert Sheinberg liked to make the credit loop as short as possible. There would also be a big incentive for cash payment. But even if we sold on consignment, which was often enough, George and I believed that the sooner goods were on display in the jeweller's window, the sooner they sold. So George wanted the orders filled fast. As he would say: 'Credit saved a day means interest we don't pay.'

I'd often have to pick up the order from the factory and deliver it to the various shops. However, the problem with this method of near-immediate delivery was that lead is very heavy. As we got more and more successful, I would carry increasingly large amounts of stock and the car springs were always collapsing. This meant I'd lose a couple of days out on the road while they were being replaced.

George Farkas was not a man who liked this kind of inefficiency. So he went to a car auction and bought a second-hand hearse. It seems hearses have heavy-duty truck springs, though how he knew this I can't imagine. (Maybe he drove hearses before he drove taxis!)

So there I was, driving up to suburban jewellery outlets in a hearse. This proved to be a wonderful bonus, because the proprietor would almost always buy something from me in order to get the hearse away from outside his shop. I suppose he correctly assumed that people don't get excited about buying an eternity ring with death knocking at the shop door.

We also discovered another invaluable use of the hearse. As is inevitable in the jewellery business we would sometimes acquire a bad debt. When this happened, as was not infrequent, George would tut-tut a bit and then he'd go and change out of his factory clothes into a black suit, white shirt and black tie. We'd get into the hearse and drive to the the shop that owed us money. We'd stop just before we got there and he'd wrap a white sheet around me—a bit like an Egyptian mummy with only my head sticking out of the top. Then he'd remove my shoes and socks and tie a standard label to my big toe in the way you see it done to a stiff on a slab in a mortuary in the movies.

We'd draw up outside the shop with me lying prone in the back, seemingly as dead as a kangaroo hit by a bull bar, the label prominent on my big toe. George has a gift for languages and, whatever the nationality of the offending shop-owner, George would loudly complain in the offender's mother tongue, listing various unsavoury character traits which led to their current defaulting behaviour. Not one of them enjoyed the hearse being parked outside, with its dead cargo, and most paid up quickly. Then I'd spring back to life, causing the shop-owner even further embarrassment and amusing the local crowd.

George's apartment, which despite his sudden upward mobility in the world he never changed, was one of my favourite places. His wife cooked superbly and her pastries were divine. We'd sit around at night having a drink with several of his friends. Two of the more regular of these was a seven-feet tall guy called Lance and who was later to be Sergeant O'Leary, of Hungry I fame. (This was before my jazz club days.) George used to refer to Lance as 'The Human Split-pin' I never did get to know his surname.

George was also mad about guns and had a large collection. Not all of them were lethal, a part of his collection consisted of air-pistols in all the configurations of the real thing: Lugers, Brownings, Colts, Police snub-nosed pistols and more. All just as deadly looking as the real thing, although they fired pellets rather than bullets.

There was nary a pigeon to be seen around George's apartment block, as the itinerant Kings Cross flock had all seemed to realise that cousins and aunties and old-man pigeons and brothers and sisters had fallen to the soft but deadly plop of one of George's air pistols. George called them flying rats and took great delight in bagging an errant municipal pigeon, which may have foolishly strayed into Elizabeth Bay from the safety of Kings Cross.

One night, when we'd been at his place drinking Schnapps with beer chasers and getting steadily more and more pissed, George, as usual brought out a paper target and pinned it to the bedroom door. The more we consumed the less interesting the target became and soon we were betting on hitting the plastic daffodils, then a small Hungarian vase and then we began to nominate an individual glass bead on the chandelier and when one of us suggested George's cat Sergeant O'Leary, who was not yet on the Drug Squad, or even a detective, intervened and said: 'Let's do it proper, lads. Let's go shoot ourselves a deer for breakfast!'

'Where, ferchrissakes? It's two o'clock in the morning and we're in a flat at Kings Cross!' I exclaimed.

'Royal National Park, son,' O'Leary said with great authority. 'The place is crawlin' with the bastards!'

While George loved guns, I don't think he ever associated them with killing anything but Germans or Russians. For my part, I hated guns and, as for the Human Split-pin, he confessed in a loud whisper that he'd never really handled a proper gun.

We were pissed and a bit uncertain, but Sergeant O'Leary was determined that it was deer steaks for all over a campfire in dawn's bright light. At 2.30 a.m., we found ourselves, armed to the teeth, each with a gun from George and a dozen rounds of ammo, heading for the Royal National Park in the hearse.

It was bitterly cold when we got into the park and Lance, the giant Human Split-pin, was elected to wear O'Leary's leather jacket and stand on the roof of the hearse. He was equipped with O'Leary's eight-battery police torch. He was to be our early-warning system, with two taps on the roof indicating a deer sighting.

It never occurred to us that Lance wore thick pebble glasses, and that creeping down a narrow dirt road in the dark wasn't going to help his myopia much either. I was at the wheel of the hearse, crawling along in low gear, when we heard two taps and our eyes immediately followed the beam of the torch.

It was a bit misty, but there, almost within shooting range, was a deer grazing. Instantly George and O'Leary cocked their rifles and took aim, in a whisper, O'Leary instructed me to drive very slowly along the light beam. We were soon within shooting distance with George and O'Leary sighting down the barrel at the hapless deer when I screamed, 'Stop!' braking violently, just as the first shot rang from O'Leary's rifle.

What we'd thought was a deer turned out to be a Volkswagen with a couple inside making love, the car was rocking violently, which accounted for the movement the short-sighted Lance had seen. I could see a white bum firmly pressed against the windscreen just as Lance, unbalanced by my sudden braking, came crashing down onto the bonnet of the hearse to send the torch in a high beam of arched light flying into the nearby bush.

Nobody was hurt and the couple made a hasty getaway.

'Jesus!' O'Leary exclaimed, 'Dead set, mate. If you hadn't

braked suddenly, I'd have layed a round right on his Sharon-eye!'

We fell about laughing, too pissed to realize how close we'd come to a major disaster. Lance had sprained his wrist but, anaesthetised by alcohol and the cold, felt nothing until much later.

Then suddenly O'Leary stopped laughing. 'Where's me torch?' he asked, looking worried.

This seemed very funny at the time and we all broke up again.

'It's fuckin' police issue; we gotta find the bastard,' he announced, no longer too pleased with the mirth around him.

So we all went scrambling around in the bushes to find Sergeant O'Leary's police issue torch, which must have gone out as it hit the deck. I was hunched over, beating feebly at the bushes, looking for something long and silver in the night, when I felt this large wet thing across my face. I very nearly died of fright, some monstrous huge wet rough organism was wrapping itself around my face in the dark. I jumped up and ran screaming from the bush. I ran up the road, past the hearse, as fast as my legs could carry me—to be followed by a rather sad-looking old deer, who'd come to investigate the sound of rifle fire and the sudden acceleration of the Volkswagen.

The deer propped and snorted, reluctant to chase me. Turning, he walked back to the hearse and started to lick at George, who'd given up looking for the torch and had come back to sit in the front seat of the hearse where he'd fallen asleep.

Finally, O'Leary, being a cop and I suppose used to looking for corpses and things in the bush, found his own torch and returned to the hearse and flashed it onto George, who had his arms around the neck of the deer and was sobbing: 'Oi Vey, to think maybe we could kill such a be-ootiful deer person already!'

Then we all patted the deer and cried a bit as well at the very idea of killing such a friendly old bastard. Then we poured a large bottle of Resch's Dinner Ale down the dear old deer's throat and went home to bed with terrible hangovers.

In direct response marketing, the closer you get to your prospect's heart, the more likely you are to win his or her attention. Personally-created stimuli are always going to win over the impersonal approach. It may seem a strange analogy, but a visit in the hearse with a live corpse had a much more direct emotional effect on the average shopkeeper owing money, than a traditional threat to take action by means of a letter from a lawyer. The point is that we knew what was the most personally-effective medium to hit him where it hurt, and we used it well.

Knowing the relative strengths of the various direct response media is an important part of the technology of direct marketing. Also, how often we mistake one thing for another—a Volkswagen for a deer, so to speak—simply because we do not know the territory in which we are operating.

Getting to know what works in the external media and why it works is a vitally important aspect of direct marketing. Why, in the case of insurance, is a Shirley Temple movie the best vehicle for a direct-response TV campaign aimed at selling financial services to women?

Actually, I haven't a clue, but every time we ran a high-powered financial package for the new, financially independent female in an old Shirley Temple movie, it out-performed any other movie or programme by two to one.

Why are handwritten envelopes more likely to be opened than typed ones? Why are right-hand pages in magazines and newspapers more effective in direct response than left-hand ones? It is all a matter of knowing the territory, so that when you go beating around the bush looking for the light, you come up with a real live deer.

Once you have clearly identified your target audience, and have the right offer to make to them, then you need to decide how best to reach them. Generally speaking, the medium you choose is most likely to be one of the four main media methods used in direct marketing: (1) mail; (2) print (newspapers & magazines); (3) broadcast media (radio & television); and (4) the telephone. There are many others, but these four major mediums are the usual choice.

You have another medium which, if used correctly, will make any outside medium you use more effective. It is, of course, your own database. Think of it as a magazine filled with the loves and lives and intimate going-ons of thousands of people you know as friends or, (at least) customer-friends.

With your own database, you control the content of the so-called magazine, it's frequency of distribution, the circulation and, best of all, the costs. This database 'magazine' is your most powerful marketing asset. Increasingly, all over the world companies, especially retailers, are comparing the costs and benefits of buying a piece of an external medium, such as a newspaper advertising page, against the costs of contacting their own database as potential customers. We have, of course, dealt with the extreme importance of your database in the previous chapter.

A good direct-response campaign should, as a general rule, use at least two different mediums: sometimes, there is justification for using all four. It is much better than depending on only one.

A direct mailing followed up by a telephone call is particularly effective in Australia. The follow-up phone call can often double or triple the mail response.

Some very effective peripheral media exists, such as signboards, bill boards, 'take ones' (the little folders and pamphlets left on counters of banks etc), or even sponsorship.

However, most campaigns will depend on the four major external media categories we've mentioned which, when used together, are commonly referred to as *integrated marketing.* Ultimately, they should all feed into, and be nurtured by, your own personally controlled, powerful medium: **your database**. All the behavioural responses, new names and purchase records should be carefully fed into your database so that you have a 'living,' day-by-day record of the promotion.

I am constantly bemused by the casual attitude a great many companies embarking on a direct marketing campaign take to the four major external media. They think of the mail as sending out a simple letter, television as a commercial, print as a press advertisement, and telemarketing as the switchboard lady asking someone to buy the company's product or service. Media buying is totally different for direct marketing than it is for mass market advertising. It does not rely upon the ratings, or the number of people out there in consumer land, but rather on their response to the salutation, or if you like, their propensity to respond.

It is always interesting for direct marketers to think about the mood of the media. By this I mean that each medium possesses a set of qualities, a definite personality, which can be used to enhance or present the salutation: TV, for instance, is a very broad and emotive medium; whereas radio is chatty, specific and local; print, magazines and newspapers are great for imparting information; and telemarketing is totally interactive and a truly great follow-up medium to a salutation or direct response letter. Finally, the mail is the most personal medium and allows you to tell lots in a friendly, personal style.

Each medium has a number of components that you need to understand if you are going to use them successfully. So let's start with the traditional medium, the most personal of all, the good old letter in the mail box.

1. Mail media. The mail is, of course, the most used medium in direct marketing. (This may not continue as, in America, the telephone has replaced it as the major direct marketing vehicle.)

There are three main ways to use the mail in Australia, New Zealand and most other South-East Asian cities:

● Solo mailing
● Insert mailing
● Letterbox drops

Solo mailings are, of course, the delightful business of directing your letter to a specific person by name and address. Hopefully, you know enough about them to make this letter effectively personal. This kind of letter nearly always delivers the best response, though not necessarily the best cost per response.

Insert mailings, also known in the vernacular as' *free rides*' or '*ride alongs*' is mail that hitches a ride along with something else, such as your electricity bill or monthly credit card statement. In this way, someone else pays the postage. Also, you can put your offer on the outside of the reply envelope continued in the *host* mailing.

In this way, you may not even have to do an insert. You may even get the reply postage paid by someone else. For reasons everyone seems to have long forgotten, this clever little mailing device is known as a 'bang-tail', or in South Africa it is known as a 'hot potato'. But, in Australia, don't use it just to save money because often it won't; the special tooling required to make the envelope and print it with your offer can increase your cost over a plain insert by as much as 50 per cent. An envelope, compared with an insert, is an expensive production. Nonetheless, a very common method of 'piggy-backing' on someone else's mailing is to offer to *supply the envelope free in return for the right to reprint on the outside back and inside flap*. Bang-tailing can be a very effective way to do a relatively inexpensive mailing, because you don't have to pay the postage.

Letterbox drops are impersonal mail shots, which may even be un-addressed except perhaps for the words: 'The Householder,' or, 'In business to Business.' 'The Office Manager.' They are simply left in your letter box.

The mail is still the best way to create continuing loyalty and to stay in touch with your database, there is simply no more cost-effective way to build and maintain relationships. You can still, at this time of writing, *put a personally addressed envelope in the mail for less than a dollar*. Even if you don't have your own database and have to rent a list, pay for paper and envelopes and have a fulfilment house do the stuffing and handling, you can still come in under one lousy dollar! In relationship marketing, you need to stay in touch with your customer at least four times a year. So, for just $4 you can maintain a presence with each client. Now, if you have all the other things right—target audience, your offer and the creative elements—that just has got to be tremendous value. Reaching the same person by telephone, using a telephone bureau, will come to approximately $5 per contact. Reaching the same person by making a personal sales call is estimated to cost around $300.

Perhaps I'm talking a bit too much about saving money. You will recall how earlier I stressed that quality of response was more important than cost per response. A cheap response that doesn't work very well isn't cheap; but an expensive one that works magnificently can be the cheapest way to go.

However, if you can afford to *combine a really good mail campaign with some quality telephone contact,* that is about as close as you can get to making a personal call on your customer without actually knocking on the front door and introducing yourself.

As a general rule, personal solo mailings work better than inserts or letter-box drops. It isn't too hard to figure out why this would be so. For a start, personal looking letters get opened with some anticipation whereas letterbox drops and inserts can often be ignored. Secondly, from a good database, the more personal you make the letter, the better the response, and the closer the future relationship.

That's not to say the others don't work. Letter-box drops, because they are so cheap, can cover a very wide audience and, depending on the offer, will produce a very satisfactory cost per response. Though it should be remembered that letter-box drops are prospecting devices and not relationship-building excercises.

The same is true of inserts, which can be even more effective than letter-box drops because they allow you to select your target audience more accurately. Also, they get into the target's house and are often read when the reader is relaxed. The technology, sometimes called 'intelligent inserts', now exists to target audiences in a precise environment within a magazine or particular section of a newspaper. For instance, an insert for a travel offer can be placed in the travel section, often with a knowledge of the lead stories in that section. This gives your insert a relationship to the editorial content. Another example is where a credit card company inserts a travel offer into the statements of those members who have a consistent overseas spending record.

Having satisfied yourself that your know-how extends to working all three mailing techniques, you may want to test all three on a cost-per-order basis. You can then make a decision on how best to go. For example, a solo mailing may cost 90 cents per single mailing while an insert costs no more than 30 cents a piece. The question then is: 'Is my my solo mailing going to pull three times the response of an insert?' The answer may well be: 'Probably not.'

One more important point on inserts. In a magazine *free-ride*, a loose insert will always out-pull a stitched one by 100%! And while I'm at it, never listen to a load of codswallop from a media sales rep that loose inserts don't work because they fall out all over the railway station platform or newsagent's floor. Loose inserts work twice as well as stitched ones, which are sometimes as much as double the cost!

Another tip. I've already mentioned the personally addressed envelope, but the hand addressed one is even better—and for most of the same reasons. Handwriting usually denotes a more personal contact, someone you know, a friend perhaps. No-one throws away a hand written envelope. But it's an expensive option unless you're a charity with lots of free hands to help. Charities use this method to great effect. But, for most of us, it's not a viable option so what is the next best option?

If you are doing a mailing to a business, this is the 'package' you would use to create the very best chance of it being opened and read:

- A plain white envelope of reasonably good quality;
- Typed name and address, (not a stick-on address label, though it can be laser printed.);
- A real stamp and not a postmark;
- Stamp the word '*confidential*' on it.

But when you put the word 'confidential', or 'private', on the envelope, make sure that you mention something which can be construed as confidential in the first paragraph of your letter. Nothing maddens the recipient of a direct response letter more than the phoney 'confidential' trick on the envelope. You can often blow the whole mailing in a single word, and end up looking like a huckster to boot.

The personalised letter—self-addressed, postage stamped and 'confidential'—is the most expensive way to go with a mailing shot. Of course, every element of it you discard will lower your costs, but, almost inevitably, it will also lower the response.

Putting a mailing shot together is hard and expensive work. It is easy to underestimate the cost of typing, folding, stamping and sealing the letters. Marketing departments these days are pretty lean places and direct response organisations have long learned that staff salaries are their biggest overhead. If you employ a high-calibre staff, it is much better to use them doing a high-calibre task. In putting a mailing together, you should always ask: 'How much of this should I do myself, and how much should I sub-contract?'

One of the major sub-contractors you should use is the Mailing House, which is very much like a factory. This is an organisation which will undertake, at a quoted price, to collate the various pieces in your mailing—fold, stuff, address (often laser print), stamp and despatch—in the most economical way. They will qualify you for the bulk mailing or item-size discounts available and, at the same time, observe the postal regulations.

However, there are a few traps for young players in the mailing house connection. These usually come about through ignorance or misunderstanding between the parties.

As with any sub-contractor, a proper briefing is essential. Even if they appear to be experts, and assure you they've done your kind of mailing a thousand times before, tell them *exactly* what you expect for your mailing. Tell them your offer, the key dates and deadlines involved, and ask them to give you a complete breakdown of deadlines and expenses—i.e. precisely what you can expect for your money, and put it on paper.

The art, some call it a science, of dealing with a mailing house and specifying exactly the levels of service you require, is hugely neglected in most organisations.

It is logical to assume that *they* know more than you do about the task and should be left to do it without interference. True, don't interfere unnecessarily with your mailing house, but leave them alone only after you have given them the perfect brief and observed that they are following it to the letter. Many a mailing has been ruined because the letters didn't arrive on time, or the follow-up was bungled in the mail, or a key element was left out of the mailing, or most commonly the brief was misleading.

Qualify and quantify, the what and the when, take advice by all means, even demand it, but then spell out in single-syllable words just precisely what you expect from the mailing house.

Conversely, the biggest whinge you will hear from a mailing house is that you came to them too late. Wherever possible, talk to them early in the campaign-planning stage . They can often give you good advice on design and production and save you a heap of money. For example, by making a piece slightly smaller than your designer indicated, you may qualify for a postage concession. It is common for an advertising agency to design an envelope that is bigger than standard size and so the increment in postage costs shoots up. Or the same mail ignorant designer may create a fold that can't be made by machine and has to be hand folded, or one which can't be picked up by an inserter and so greatly increase the cost of the mailing. Create a number of dummy mailing packs first and test them. Select the paper carefully—will it run through the laser printer, will it fit easily into the reply envelope etc. A good mailing house, called in early, can become a very useful partner in business.

For any mailing of less than about 2,500 letters, a mailing house is probably not economical; however, above this amount, it may well be the intelligent thing to do.

Another useful partner in the mix is the post office itself. These days the pressure is on the postal services to run a business and there are a number of discounts you may qualify for in a posting. Pre-sorting large consignments into the various postal codes is just one such discount. Currently, posting 500 advertising mail items at the one time, earns you the minimum discount of 20 per cent and 2500 items earns you 26.5 per cent discount-providing you apply for a permit for advertising mail. Here too, if you have a reply-paid envelope insert, you can get up to 50 per cent discount. In Australia, this is called ADPOST Direct Mail Discounts. Yet another way, is to pre-sort mail. With facsimile and electronic mail taking away a great deal of traditional post office business, the postal service wants your business badly, and will be happy to send around one of their business managers or representatives to talk with you. It's time well spent and I urge you to avail yourself of their advice which often leads to considerable savings.

2. Telecommunications media. It may be because of the tyranny of distance, but Australians have taken to the telephone more than any other people except, perhaps, the Americans. Australia has the highest per capita penetration of mobile phones in the world and we are in the top three users of the facsimile machine. But the phone is rapidly assuming a major importance in direct marketing.

Telecommunications really grew up as a marketing medium with the introduction of the toll free 008 (now 1–800) number in Australia; 800 in the US and 0800 in the UK. What it meant was that you could strike while the iron was hot: 'Why not call us at this very moment and completely free of charge?' At last the direct marketer could grab the moment, and use the emotion, while the customer's undivided attention was on the offer. It was powerful, even heady stuff and from 1975 on the toll free 800 number has dominated direct marketing in America. As the battle for the ears of the nation grows between the two competitive Australian phone companies and as New Zealand sees the same sort of competition evolve, we will see increasingly attractive offers made by phone companies to direct marketers.

With the almost universal adoption of the fax machine, not only on business premises but, increasingly, in the home as well, we are going to see a great increase in inward and outward bound marketing. We are simply getting closer and closer to the individual customer, which augers well for the future of our business.

This brings up a point I've been meaning to make: change is something most people fear, and this is also true of business. A great many businesses simply fail to grasp the the changes in the world around them and, as a result, slowly fade away. Direct marketing is business where change is almost constant. This is because it is driven by communication technology, which is changing almost too fast for most of us to fully utilise. The only thing that is certain about our business is that it will change more rapidly than any other, because it is at the cutting edge of communications technology. And our business will greatly benefit from these changes. I believe that the changes which will occur in the next five years will be more significant than those of the last 50 years.

However, one old-fashioned business technique will never change—the need to properly service your database or customer. People are people through other people, and it will be ever thus. Therefore, one of the *nicer improvements* in direct marketing via the telephone is the *help line.*

If you can offer a help line for your customers then do so with a passion, even if it is rarely used. A help line adds great credibility to your offer and the more comprehensive the scope of the help offered, the more credibility it suggests. Research shows quite clearly that the offer of a 24-hours help line can be a major reason for a customer's decision to purchase—particularly for a service or product which might seem complex. What you are saying to your customer is: 'Don't worry. We're with you day and night. You'll never be left in the lurch.' It's a powerful persuasion to buy because it indicates continuity and confidence in the product.

In America, it has become so very much a part of doing business that, some years ago, a friend of mine in New York heard his eight-year-old son complain that his Lego didn't have a help-line number on the box. Now, of course, it does. In just 20 years, the Lego Builders Club has come to dominate the U.S. toy market. Seven out of every 10 American families, with children under 12-years-old, own Lego construction bricks and receive a newsletter and catalogue.

Now, just think about it a moment: your objective as a direct marketer is to get as close to your customer friend as it is possible to do. A voice asking for help at the other end of the line is a gift from a benign God, even if the voice is somewhat anxious or even angry. It gives you the opportunity to cement a customer friendship and to turn a customer into an advocate if you get it right.

The General Electric Answer Centre is just such a model help line. It receives an average of 4000 calls an hour. 'For God's sake, help. My refrigerator is defrosting all by itself and I've got the thanksgiving turkey and all the holiday food inside the freezer!' If two minutes later you've solved that problem, you've made a friend for life. In fact, just such a problem occurred on a GE help-line and the operator established that the client's refrigerator was 18-years-old and beyond help. Thanksgiving was a day away and they arranged for a new GE refrigerator to be delivered that night fully stocked, the food compliments of the staff at the help-line. Not bad public relations, what? It does not seem surprising that the GE Answer Centre has often been called the best of its kind in the world.

GE Operators are well trained and have computer terminals which, at the touch of a button, will give them the answer on screen to almost any query a customer may have. If a help-line operator can't answer on the spot, they guarantee they'll be back within 48 hours. Their records show that they can answer and remedy 90 per cent of all questions on the spot and that they're improving. The GE help-line is open 24 hours a day, seven days a week: 'Like your GE appliance, we never sleep!'

GE research shows that 91 per cent of their customers are fully satisfied with the service. Of those, 96 per cent say they pass on the good news of GE back-up and service to friends seeking to buy an appliance. In other words, they have reached the pinnacle of the loyalty ladder and have become advocates for the brand. GE use their Answer Centre and their operators as one of the mainstays in their corporate advertising. They readily acknowledge that it has played a major part in their market share. Today they are the biggest and one of the best-managed companies in the world. It all begins with a willingness to give as well as receive.

Which brings us to complaints, which occur when the customer bought something with high hopes and now feels let down.

There is an old cliche in business, which says that the only real job a complaints department has is to make itself redundant. Nice thinking, but not terribly realistic. People complain for all sorts of reasons, and these are not always caused by the product or the service.

The key to dealing intelligently with complaints is to delegate the responsibility of dealing with complaints to the people who actually serve customers. A service-person, who is well trained in damage control, will do a much better on-the-spot job than some officious clerk behind a telephone who is having a bad day. The people who are in closest direct touch with your customers are the first in the line of fire. These are the ones who should be taught to deal with the customers' anxieties and problems.

It is important, perhaps vital, not only to deal with complaints, but to listen to them carefully. You should capture them and study them and, if a pattern is emerging, you can pick it up and remedy it. So complaints should be logged for study. Remember, a complaint is a magnificent opportunity to do something exceptional so that you revitalise the customer–supplier relationship. Time and time again, research into complaint handling shows that a complaint well handled will generate a disproportional brand of customer loyalty—well in excess of what can be expected from a customer who has never complained.

Some U.S. mail order companies, knowing this, have created deliberate problems so that they can convert complaining customers into advocates and loyal brand users. Let me show you what actually takes place in the customer's mind when a complaint is lodged and well handled. It puts the customer in an irresistible psychological position if you have apologised and asked how you may redeem the situation to the customer's benefit. Everyone likes the thought that they can be generous in victory and magnanimous with their forgiveness. It is a rare feeling of power for the 'small' over the 'large,' the individual over the giant corporation. That is why you should be grateful that customers feel strongly enough to complain—a complaining customer has gone to considerable trouble on your behalf. They have alerted you to a possible problem in your product or service and they have cared enough to let you know what's on their mind. How very much easier it would have been for them to have simply walked away from your service or brand forever. **In fact, 70 per cent of people who leave your database do so without an argument**. They just drift away. You have to remind yourself that you simply cannot afford such a rate of attrition and so you will field every possible complaint and deal with it in a personal and considerate manner.

Also *Root Cause Analysis,* or *Defection Analysis,* as it is often known, is becoming popular business practice among companies who seriously practise relationship marketing.

Root Cause Analysis requires that you interview every customer who leaves you and find the root cause behind their defection. In the process of conducting this analysis, you can often convince the respondent to reconsider their decision to leave you. But the main reason remains: you must find the root cause which has lead to their decision to leave you so that it can be corrected. If you act swiftly when you first note a trickle of defections, you can often correct the problem and so prevent a flood.

It is interesting that companies which conduct root cause analysis frequently find that their employees have a different perception as to why a customer is leaving than the reality. This alone is a sufficiently compelling reason for conducting the research, as the company employees may inadvertently be contributing to the demise of the customer. By identifying the real reason, damage control can be instigated and the problem corrected.

However, sometimes there isn't a great deal you can do to make a correction as many of your customers may see as an advantage what others see as a disadvantage. For example, one credit card offers you frequent flyer points with every purchase you make. Obviously, frequent flyers will like this idea. But, people who don't fly may feel they should receive an equal advantage, and decide to use another credit card to 'punish' you. If you note that a customer's credit card has been inactive for say, three months, you might have reason to think that this may be an early warning sign you should think about investigating. Once you can identify the causes of a problem your customer has with your product or service you can make amendments, or make them a special offer to get their business again. This is called *taking anti-attrition measures.* It's a sophisticated term for giving the customer a phone call and asking them if they are completely satisfied with your service or product.

I am reminded of my time at Goldcrest Jewellery when, on occasion, someone would come in and complain that a pair of earrings, or a bangle, gave them a touch of lead allergy. This was fair enough, the stuff was made of lead after all and some people, it seemed, were more allergic to it than others. I always found the way George Farkas dealt with these complaints totally mystifying. He would make a big fuss over them and then say that, as compensation, they could pick any two objects from the factory display case for free. As these, too, were made of lead, I could never understand why this psychology worked. But it did. Customers would leave with two pieces of lead jewellery happy that their complaint had been generously dealt with. No one ever rejected the offer on the basis that they were simply getting more of the same and would now become three times as poisoned as they were before.

Studies not only show that *people become more loyal* to you *after you have satisfied a complaint,* but that this loyalty is both qualitative and quantitative. *They will become twice as loyal as they were before.* Conversely, the customer who walked away from your database thoroughly disenchanted (though without ever complaining), will tell an average of 10 people how thoroughly disreputable your organisation is.

Teaching customer-service staff to handle complaints has to be a top priority in your company. Because complaints, properly dealt with, are among the most powerful marketing opportunities you will get. Moreover, don't have a token fight just to show the customer you're no push-over. That sort of psychological master-minding doesn't work. You simply lose all the goodwill, even if you do give in and satisfy your customer in the end. People are generally nervous about complaining. If you make them feel that you are privileged to be able to deal with their complaint, they will respond with generosity. Always ask yourself: 'How do I send this customer away with a smile on his or her face?' And one of the best ways is to tell the truth. Don't invent some cock 'n bull story about how remarkably rare the defect is—a chance in a million in a product that has to pass 132,000 tests from 2000 unsmiling, white-coated Swiss inspectors. Admit that you've had a few similar complaints and are very concerned and intend doing everything you can to remedy the situation.

I have always taught my customer-service people that they

must, under no circumstances, lie to the customer. If they feel the need to lie then we have obviously let the customer down in some way. Sadly, many a new employee expresses astonishment when reprimanded for telling an untruth, pointing out that they have been trained to 'avoid the exact truth' in handling customers with complaints, when there is a known problem with the goods or services.

Invite your customer to help you by asking them if they have observed any other faults. Your customer-service people should also be allowed to admit fallibility, and be taught how to turn a complaint into a customer opportunity. They should also know that they will be backed to the hilt by their senior management.

It is one of the most common sins in direct marketing that the customer-service people are not fully briefed on the products they are installing or maintaining. They should be constantly updated. Your customer services manager should be present when you brief your creative people so that he or she knows precisely what you are offering, and what the expectations for the product or service may be from the customer.

The telephone is an increasingly popular response medium. In a sense, what used to be the coupon in a print advertisement is now a telephone number. The day is fast coming when the telephone is going to be 'boss of the wash' in direct marketing. What has been made to work on broadcast media has now been transferred back to print.

Over the last few years, people have gained confidence in the direct marketers' use of the telephone by responding to commercials immediately they've been broadcast. It was only a single step from here to take this confidence back into print by eliminating the process of a coupon and substituting a phone number. In Australia, when they are given an option, (that is, both coupon and telephone number,) about half still respond by mail. My advice is to allow for both ways to respond to your offer.

While a telephone number in a print advertisement is somewhat easier to handle than one in a TV commercial, it is, in both instances, a more expensive way to do business than the old method of mailing back a coupon.

Instead of the leisurely method of opening envelopes and processing coupons, telephone use by the customer means you have to man a phone, or a battery of phones, for long periods. In Australia, these phone answering and processing bureaus are not as readily available as they are in the U.S. As most people respond in the evening, setting up a phone-answering service yourself means staff have to be brought in on overtime rates. This can make your offer a very expensive one to service. Initially, the 008 numbers came with complicated instructions and weren't toll free in Australia. It was also rather stupid of the postal authorities to have in the 008 number a prefix so close to the 08 number, which is the prefix for South Australia. Mrs Penny Curuthers received 2500 calls when we were running a campaign advertising women's financial services for the A.M.P. People inadvertently dropped one of the zeros in the 008 prefix. For several weeks we sent our apologies, accompanied by numerous large bunches of flowers, to her Glenelg home—though I'm not sure she ever forgave us.

However, with the coming of a competitive phone system, things have simplified. We can now largely offer a free service, similar to the one which has revolutionised the direct response business in the United States.

Before you think that the smart answer for the marketer is to install an answering machine with a pre-recorded set of instructions to the customer, let me tell you that it won't work. People simply do not like to leave personal details on an answering machine. When placing an order they prefer the security of speaking to a live person on the other end of the line, and they want to be able to ask questions. We know this because up-to-date equipment used measures the number of disconnects.

However, an answering machine can be useful in some other aspects of your business. For instance, you can use a 0055 number if the offer is to give information. The point here is that the customer has decided to call for more information, it has cost something to do so, and so they feel in charge. They are therefore, happy to listen to the information coming back to them and then to leave their names and phone numbers if they want to accept the offer or avail themselves of a free sample or get more information.

We have the technology now, as they have had in America for several years, to show the number of any person calling in. In private homes in America, this service has been positively sold as a protection against nuisance calls and has proved very popular. In Australia, it has been tested, to see whether people feel it is an invasion of privacy or whether they believe there are sufficient nuisance calls to justify the service.

In the U.S., there have been several developments which indicate that all is not well with the system. In Australia, there is a great deal of controversy over the privacy issue.

Telecom has been testing Caller ID (as it is known) in more than 3000 homes and businesses in Wauchope, a country town in NSW. Most residents felt that first identifying the caller, gave them a measure of freedom from intrusion. It also reduced the incidence of hoax calls and obscene calls. However, at the end of the trial, 25 per cent of those participating, were still opposed to Caller ID.

In a strange twist, several Consumer Associations in the U.S. are claiming invasion of *their* privacy. Consumers, it seems, want the right to check on companies with whom they are already doing business while remaining anonymous in the process.

Several U.S. companies, with large inbound telemarketing centres, don't let the caller know that they know who they are and simply mail them a catalogue or further information after they receive the call. Curiously, the caller doesn't seem to object and this I-won't-tell-you-I-know-who-you-are-system is proving to be a very lucrative source of new business.

When the phones 'run hot' in response to a good offer made on TV, or through a print advertisement, you'll need a system that enables you to qualify the calls and make the sale. Otherwise, for every customer you convert, perhaps 10 others will have given up trying to get through and you will have lost them forever. The trick is to capture essential information as quickly as possible. This should be carefully planned before the calls come in, and not suddenly invented in a crisis situation. All the good phone bureaus simply get the name and phone number of the caller and promise to call back when they are not over-loaded. Very few callers object to this happening and most prefer it to hanging on, waiting to be processed. With this 'quick' information, you can process them either by calling back after the rush is over, or writing with a full explanation of your offer. With their name and phone number you require one further piece of information— you ask them when they will be at home to take your call. If you don't do this, you can expect 50 per cent of your return calls to be wasted.

With more time, your questions can become more exotic and expand into tastes and preferences, options, add-ons, or whatever. This is known as 'selling up.' In the U.S., the average sell-up rate is 20 per cent of customers. That is, if you try to sell a more expensive version or an additional product to every customer who calls in, you can increase your overall sales by 20 per cent.

Cellarmasters, Australia's largest bottled wine outlet, sells wine directly into homes. And they greatly prefer to work with a telephone because they can gather information from the customer as to their tastes, the sort of wine they thought they liked, what they'd tried in the past, or hoped to experience in the future. In other words, they can add to their database in a qualitative way, something they could never hope to do using a mail-in coupon. As a consequence they have developed a very efficient phone bureau called Telemasters.

However, it should be realised that while the phone is a terrific way to get to know your customer, and his or her needs, it can cost three times the cost of a mail-in coupon to process the response. Sophisticated phone bureaus have a mask, which appears on the V.D.U. (Video Display Unit), in front of the operator, as soon as it is triggered by the phone number connected to a specific offer (the *unique* phone number). On the mask is a series of questions, which the operator asks the caller and, depending on the answers given, moves the operator to the next question. The answers the caller gives are automatically married to the softwear that processes the order and, as well, maintains the database. Whatever method you use, make sure you have a good system for processing and storing the information you have coming in.

On out-bound Telemarketing, a technology which is called *predictive dialing* has halved the cost of making the calls. Cellarmasters claim they can now make a phone call for nearly the same price as they can mail. This innovative direct marketing wine company was started by David Thomas about 15 years ago. It is a truly great success story in relationship marketing and is today the most sophisticated and successful direct marketer of wine in the world.

Remember, if you're going to use the phone, your operators must be skilled at developing relationships and in obtaining quality information. But before you ever try to set up your own phone response centre use an outside bureau until you understand the problems, and what resources you require. Indeed, it should not be uncommon for a caller to ask for an operator by name, as often happens with Cellarmasters.

When you have a direct response business, which involves customers frequently calling in to place orders, your database is critical to your success. As soon as a customer calls Cellarmasters, they display his name and tasting notes on the VAU. This enables them to immediately suggest new wines which fall into the customer's preference categories, and which are likely to please.

If you set up a sophisticated response mechanism, for God's sake test it before you go into battle. We usually find an average 15-year-old test customer to 'dry-run' our system. If she manages to confuse your operator, start again and simplify the system. By the way, it's not a bad idea to get the same person to 'dry-run' a print coupon you may have designed. If she becomes confused with the information on it, then start again. Rehearsal calls are an essential part of any effective telephone response system. You **must** be confident that your operators can handle the offers you are making, despite the many difficulties presented by the customer's call. And if you are using a bureau call in orders yourself, frequently.

The telephone can be made to work both ways—for in-bound

calls such as we've just discussed, and for *out-bound calls*, or spec-
ulative calls. Out-bound in America are a menace and you need
to be careful how you go about them as they often offend people.
There has been a strong reaction against them in Australia and
New Zealand, even though 'cold-call' canvassers are sometimes
the most reputable banks and insurance companies.

In many US cities, the habit of answering the phone directly
has been abandoned in favour of an answering machine just so
that the householder can avoid this kind of call. In San Diego,
where cold canvassers seemed to have been very numerous in the
past, 60 per cent of households now have a silent number.

That's the down side of out-bound calls. In the beginning, persistent salespeople with slick telephone techniques, and an immediate transaction mentality, attempted to badger and bully and
generally provoke people into buying. This kind of 'hot' selling
can damage your corporate name, or the brand you sell, and leave
your customer very browned off indeed. It simply isn't good direct
marketing.

But, more and more, these phone hucksters are disappearing
and responsible direct marketers are using the out-bound phone
quite differently. They have come to realise that the initial cold
call is an unwise technique, that the name of a potential customer
(the suspect) must be obtained through other means, and with
the customer's prior consent. When this is done an out-bound
call is much more effective. In other words, the idea is to establish
a long-term relationship and this takes time. But once the relationship is in place, the out-bound telephone call to a customer
who trusts you is an excellent way to do business. That's the good
side of out-bound calling. Used with sincerity and patience, it can
be a very powerful marketing tool and is extremely profitable to
the companies who do it well. After all, a phone call from a business friend can be a useful and welcome addition to the day even
though, I suspect, the average person would prefer not to receive
these calls.

I am constantly surprised at the lack of interest most business
people in this country have in calling their customers. Australians
and New Zealanders are the most travelled people on the globe.

This means that we spend a great deal of money on tickets, accommodation and the general business of travel. Yet, how many times have you heard spontaneously from your travel agent in the past five years? Have they called to ask you how you enjoyed your holiday—the one that cost you several thousand dollars spent through their agency? Did they ask your advice about the places you visited, how you found the airlines, hotels, cities? Did they send you a postcard saying they hoped everything went well?

Of course not! They simply closed the books with a sigh after you'd paid up and forgot all about you. Yet the very best way to sell the next holiday is immediately after you've returned from the last one. Then follow up a few months later with an out-bound call which politely asks if you'd like some information on a new destination, or on a place at which you wished you'd stayed longer. All of this information, is snugly kept for further use in your database. Out-bound calls with a customer you know can be a very good way of doing business.

The opportunity to pick up the phone and make an out-bound call to someone you know is available to most businesses. Tom Peters, one of the great management gurus, tells the story of a man who attended one of his lectures on the topic of his famous book, 'In Search of Excellence.' After the lecture the man came up and simply asked: 'What exactly do I do?'

Peters, a little tired, sighed and started to go through the principles of excellence again. 'No, no, I heard all that, ' the man replied, 'but what exactly do I do. How do I go about doing this stuff?' Peters, replied, 'Tomorrow, when you get to work, call your 10 best customers and invite them to lunch and then ask them to tell you what the hell they think of your business.' 'Great, I'll do just that and thank you,' said the man, delighted with this *real* advice.

Sometimes we forget to do the simple things a phone can do— a call every Monday morning to a client to ask if he has anything special coming up during the week where you may be able to help? The opportunities to build long-term relationships with intelligent out-bound calls are always there. Then, when you have something interesting to sell or a proposition to make, you can do it easily, knowing you will be welcome.

3. Broadcast media. The two major broadcast media are quite obviously television and radio. Let's begin with radio.

My advice to any direct marketer who wants to use radio as the major medium for his offer would be to think very, very carefully before doing so. As a primary response medium it simply isn't all that effective. Radio reaches people while they are busy doing other things. They seldom sit down to listen to the radio, as they might to read a magazine or newspaper or watch television. So radio is background and not foreground media. People simply don't rush for the telephone to make a response to a radio sell.

Perhaps, with the advent of the mobile telephone in the customer's handbag, suit pocket or motorcar, things might change. It would certainly be worth testing once in a while. But I know of no direct marketer who can claim that radio worked better for them than any other direct marketing medium. Certainly, while we have tested it rigorously, it has never worked for us. I have even been given the most ideal circumstances to prepare a radio offer, where a radio network has offered me every possible facility—the best programmes, an advertising fee based on results, a hand-picked and carefully-nominated target audience, and an announcer who had the complete trust of his audience. In addition, we ran a tested offer, which we knew would appeal to his listeners. We got a fairly good response. But when it was measured in quality and cost against alternative media, it simply did not hold up.

However, as a secondary medium, radio can be made to work very well. For instance, if a network has a listener's club, or a special interest group, you can mix a radio campaign with a mailing to the club members and get a very good response. Alternatively, you can use radio to get people to pick up information from a given outlet, such as a bank, or even to direct their attention to an advertisement in a newspaper, or to check their letterbox for a free sample. All very useful stuff, but not the real backbone of a direct marketing campaign.

Radio is such a pleasant and personal and local medium that it surprises me that it doesn't work very well for direct response. But, it wouldn't hurt to keep testing it from time to time. The telephone which was formerly too difficult to get to, is now often in your potential customer's shirt pocket or in the car and this could make a big difference to the medium in the future.

Television, if used properly, is quite another matter and it has to be taken very seriously indeed as a direct marketing medium. It is still one of the great direct response opportunities in Australia.

Television has long been the province of mass media advertising of the kind known as image advertising. Goods and services were advertised not for immediate response, but for brand recognition and image. If people are familiar with a brand name and reputation, they will select it next time they go to the supermarket. Because this was the way advertising agencies sold their product they have always been wary of direct response marketers. The claim that goods and services could be sold directly to the public immediately after the transmission of a TV commercial, did not sit as well with the agencies. Getting the two sides to agree on almost anything to do with the selling process was difficult. Formal media image advertising groups remained antagonistic towards direct response. The two were natural enemies and, in commercial terms, never spoke to each other.

It was, therefore, with some trepidation that I sold my company to one of the world's largest advertising companies—one whose network in Australia makes it the country's largest advertising agency by a country mile. George Patterson Bates saw the inevitability of having a direct marketing arm and so they made me an offer I couldn't refuse. Nevertheless, I was worried that the two cultures would clash.

What I wasn't to know was that the result was to be one of the most intellectually stimulating adventures I have ever undergone in business. Together, Australia's most successful advertising agency and direct marketing organisation forged a partnership and a new concept for marketing goods and services which was to earn us world-wide acclaim.

In hindsight the concept was simple enough. Instead of agree-
ing that image advertising and direct selling were opposed to each
other, we suggested that they might work very well together. We
contended that it might be possible to create a new type of TV
commercial, whose message was split 50/50 between direct
response and branding, or brand image. But, until we could
measure it, it lacked credibility, and conventional wisdom denied
that it was possible to do.

Now, obviously, the direct marketing side was easy to measure—
tracking responses is the whole meaning of this discipline. But
how do you measure brand image recall, and on-going brand
awareness, when it is mixed in with a direct selling message?

When we first came up with the solution it seemed rather silly.
But the more we thought about it the more obvious it became.
While the people who responded to the direct marketing offer
could easily be counted, those influenced by the image advertising
could also be measured; they would be those people who didn't
respond! In other words, we would measure positive brand recall
and brand awareness among the non-responders to the direct
selling proposition.

In doing it this way, we had created a discipline whereby the
impact of the brand awareness advertising among non-responders
could be measured in accepted qualitative and quantitative methodology. The direct selling proposition would also be processed
in the normally accepted manner, as outlined elsewhere in this
book.

In each instance we ensured that the budget allocated for each
component, that is, the brand image and the direct selling, was
predetermined by the client. The success of the campaign was
to be measured in image terms by research, and in selling terms
by the cost per lead generated, and the final cost of every sale
made.

It was the first time in the history of both kinds of advertising
that both disciplines had been combined in this way; brand awareness connected with direct response brought a new and powerful
combination to marketing.

The name we gave to this combination is Power Response

Advertising. Alex Hamill, then the Managing Director of advertising agency, George Patterson, called it the most exciting selling innovation in Australian advertising, since the advent of television.

In terms of new television selling concepts, we have seen the rise of the home shopping channels via cable television in the USA. This method of selling should not be confused with Power Response Advertising. It is a separate way of doing things, which has not yet come to Australia or New Zealand, and is likely to bump it's nose a few times before it does.

Basically, a home shopping channel is one which does nothing but sell goods of every description directly to customers who have tuned in to respond. It's like a giant auction sale, except that the prices are fixed and the customer simply phones through and orders. There's rather a lot of hype involved and impulse and emotional responses are very much the name of this particular game. Be careful before you rush into this medium. While HSN and QVC, two national cable home-selling networks, have sales of more than $U.S. one billion per annum, a great many other attempts have failed. In France, the Mintel network is in four million homes and has been very successful, though this was only achieved when the French government decided to give the terminal free. It also came up with the idea of putting telephone numbers on the medium, a phone book. The result was that people became used to using the network and eventually began to respond to it in other ways as well.

We should be careful not to dismiss cable and in-home selling, but for quite a while yet we can expect the more conventional use of mass media commercial television to dominate direct marketing sales.

The introduction of the 008 number in the 1980's has made television a serious choice for direct marketing. If there are a series of golden rules, that is, the do's and don'ts of direct marketing on television, then the most golden of all is the prominent inclusion of the 008 number on the screen.

The next essential advice is to initially use a telephone bureau to handle the responses. The telephone bureau will be able to advise you on how to manage the incoming response, whereas your own learning curve, if you decide to go it alone, could cost you your campaign, or at the very least, a great many disenchanted callers who are lost to you forever.

As your volume and knowledge grows you may decide to bring this answering facility in-house. You may even do this in conjunction with your help-lines, if you have established this facility. But always begin with an outside telephone bureau. When the time comes to own your own, there are many organisations who will help you to build an effective in-house operation.

The 008 number has brought a huge excitement to the direct marketing business. Perhaps my greatest 'high' in direct response was to see the mail bags coming in stuffed to bursting with coupon responses. But I was to discover that wonderful as this was, it was nothing compared with the effect of a television 008 response.

My first experience with response television was with a product called Netski-Knife, a set of four kitchen knives. Netski was a name I invented myself based on the Japanese Netsuke, the traditional tiny but exquisite ivory carving of a human, or a beast, which is much treasured by Japanese collectors. Why I thought this was a clever name I'm not now sure. But about 99.9 per cent of the human race had never ever heard of a Netsuke, so the name derivation was a complete piece of nonsense. However, I was sure it would work and thought myself very creative.

With the help of Telprom at Channel Ten we created a 120-second commercial in the classical American direct response mould. We used a Sous chef from the Suntory restaurant as a demonstrator. The commercial ran off-peak on a Sunday morning in January 1981 in a non-rating period, together with a 30-second follow-up commercial as a reprise of it's longer counterpart.

Then, sitting at a bank of phones in a phone bureau, set up as an experiment in Camperdown, Sydney. I watched all hell break loose. The tension waiting for the phones to ring was extraordinary and then, suddenly, the first RING! It sounded like the 'clappers of hell'. Then lights everywhere as the switchboard went beserk.

Netski-Knife literally blew up three telephone exchanges in Sydney that Sunday morning. So many calls came into the exchanges, that they triggered the overload cut-outs, which killed the whole board before the equipment was permanently damaged. A day later, by special delivery, we received a stern rebuke from Telecom, warning us that we were damaging public property, and should not put the commercial to air without consulting them.

However, there are spills as well as thrills in power response television. One of the most common of these is not understanding that 'less is more' in direct response television. The set up for Netski-Knives was lazy Sunday morning on a dozy programme going nowhere, except filling time during a non-rating holiday period. Any traditional advertising practitioner would tell you that this was the zero condition for effective advertising—and they would be entirely wrong when it came to direct response. **Prime time television rarely works for direct response advertising on television.** And the reasons are obvious.

You're watching a heavyweight boxing match, perhaps a world title fight. The fighters come out for the 10th round. This is the critical round and both boxers are tired, with one just leading the other on points. Each round is three minutes and the world champion begins to unleash a few punches. You see the contender take a left and begin to stagger. On comes a two-minute power response commercial for a set of four lousy Japanese knives. By the time it's finished, the champion and not the contender is flat on his back, out for the count. You don't know whether to hurl the TV through the window or simply burst into tears. But you do know that there is no way on God's earth you are going to rush to the phone and buy a set of four knives.

The least effective way to run a direct response TV campaign is in prime time or on an exciting programme. You will get a minimal response and often generate a great deal of aggravation, especially in a sports program. All the experience on U.S. television suggests strongly that this is true, and our experience over some 30 campaigns confirms this in Australia and New Zealand.

I can't tell you how many times I have had to persuade a large client not to put his offer on prime time television. Because he or she is conditioned to basic image advertising, they simply cannot reject the notion that more people watching will deliver better direct response results. But it won't. The first great lesson in direct response advertising is to run mainly off-peak. Ideally, you should run in an old movie, or a mid-morning show or an afternoon serial—providing this last option isn't the kind that makes the blood pound. Always select the programme for your direct response offer where the condition of the viewer is relaxed and not totally absorbed with the content.

The time you run your offer can also be important. In America, the best time for direct response is late at night. Americans are tuned to the concept of service and expect that it will continue around the clock. If they see a response offer at midnight, or beyond, they have absolute faith that the bureau at the other end will be manned.

Not so in Australia or New Zealand. We don't seem to be able to comprehend this kind of service. Why would someone sit up all night to answer a dumb telephone, unless it was the police or ambulance? Though this may change in time, and with competition from the phone companies, you should be wary of going to the expense of a night bureau. **The very best time for Australians and New Zealanders to respond at home is in the morning, or mid-afternoon.**

Yet another important rule to observe in your direct response television commercial is the length of time you keep the telephone number on the screen. **The number *must* be available to the viewer for a minimum of 30 seconds, though preferably 45 seconds**. Don't under any circumstances *FLASH* the number or jump it around the screen; simply let it sit fat and bold and contented for the required time, so that your viewer can see it, inwardly digest it and, finally, write it down. As I said earlier, God is in the details.

A fewer number of long commercials will out-perform a series of more frequently-run short ones. That's not only because they can demonstrate the product more effectively, and allow your viewer more time to think about the proposition you're making with more concentration, but also because they are more unusual in character. People are less used to them on the screen, and so appear to pay more attention to them. In fact, research shows clearly that, among non-responders, the message retention is 50 per cent higher in a 90-second commercial than it is in a 60-second one.

We have also found a very effective pattern for direct response commercials. It is one long commercial, 90-second or 120-second commercials, followed by a 30-second commercial in the next commercial break. The 30-second commercial in the number two spot is, of course, a reprise or paraphrase, of the longer commercial. It also contains the 008 telephone number for the entire duration, just in case the viewer missed it in the preceding longer commercial.

You will recall that I mentioned Shirley Temple earlier as an effective television vehicle for an offer directed at women. We now know that movies with a strong female lead, which also have a poignant and easy-to-absorb story, are the most effective when making an offer to women. We also know that old movies work better than modern ones. But we don't know why Shirley Temple beats the pants off all of them, often by a factor of two or three.

I once attended a seminar where a prominent psychiatrist pointed out that women and men had quite different abilities to absorb information. The male brain seems to be singular. It can only adequately concentrate on one element at a time. The female mind can effectively respond to up to four or five different stimuli and pay attention to each simultaneously. This, he pointed out, was why men get so terribly upset with women when they talk over the television. The male can't attend to both topics at the same time while the female has no problem doing so. He went onto say that this difference between the two minds and, in particular, the problem with the television, was one of the major sources of domestic fights. Women simply cannot get it into their heads that the male attention span is singular and esoteric.

If what the psychiatrist says is true, then this explains the old movies, the old black and white movies, and even perhaps the old, black and white Shirley Temple movies. They do not call for a great depth of concentration as they are already old, familiar friends. They can simply run as part of the domestic background, while the female viewer gets on with other more important tasks, quite capable of responding to the content of the movie, and presumably our commercial, while she does so. If the movie were new, in colour and attention-grabbing, she might be forced to pay closer attention to it, therefore become emotionally bound up within it, and so give scant attention to the direct response messages during the commercial breaks.

Well, in the absence of a better theory, it's an explanation anyway. Someone is certain to think that what I've just said is anti-feminist, though I can't think why they should do so.

The real issue is that the environment into which you deliver your message is critical to the successful response you get. It is as well to remember that a peak hour block-buster movie isn't going to do a damn thing for you. Television is, by its nature, an emotional medium and the state of mind of the viewer will largely determine the response you get. The state of mind you are ideally looking for is one of calm interest. This can, of course, lead you to some bargain TV buys. When we booked every Shirley Temple movie, with the prospect of running our ads the whole year, the TV stations thought they've just died and gone to heaven.

So, not only do you match your products target audience with the most likely audience of the television programme, but you also *take into consideration their state of mind while watching*. That's why you would stay out of high-tension, high-interest sports events, current affairs and news.

A great many marketers work hard at getting the selling mix right, but then neglect that actual process of fulfilment. The process of handling the phone-calls in response to your ad should be every bit as sophisticated as any other aspect of your campaign. If you lose a large percentage of the calls coming in, you have defeated the whole purpose of your campaign. You need a call-handling bureau which is sophisticated and knows how to handle the peaks. It must have a queuing system built in to the answering system, and it must be able to identify the disconnecting rate—that is, how many callers are hanging up and how many calls are being answered per minute. A healthy balance will ensure that the system doesn't blow up. The main thing to ensure is that the phone bureau is adequately handling the load of calls coming in.

Generally speaking, buying the media is a difficult task. The TV stations are only interested in rating points. Media buying shops, with very few exceptions, have little or no understanding of buying for direct response television. Every TV network salesperson will concoct some highly plausible explanation as to why your advertisement will work better on a particular programme on their station. They know that there simply isn't any way to prove what they are maintaining except by rating points. And direct response television isn't too interested in rating points.

When you suggest the absolutely finite measurement of sales to them, like their cousins in the print media, they become totally disinterested. When the 40 to 100 channel household becomes a reality in the very near future, the present rating system will disappear and stations will have to come up with a much more accountable method to justify the purchase of time.

At present, by watching a TV campaign like a hawk and analysing the cost per response per individual spot you can, by adjusting your TV schedule often halve your cost per response. It is still vitally important to have a flexible schedule until the early results are known and the response pattern is formed. The TV stations don't cater for this flexibility and it can be a constant battle, but you should persevere because it is well worth it in savings.

When you know you've got the potential to handle all your incoming calls you're just about set to go, except for one more critical thing. *Consider testing the campaign.* That is, do a test run of every element in your campaign.

Almost no direct marketer tests TV campaigns and it is true to say, to do so is far from an exact science, but we have found it worthwhile and here is how we go about it. Run your TV direct marketing test for two weeks in one capital city as a live test. This is called your *phase one* and you mainly test all sorts of program combinations before you roll-out nationally in *phase two.*

You might think that this is an ideal time to test some different versions of your direct response commercial as well. In fact, it isn't usually practical. These days, a sophisticated direct-response commercial costs a great deal and it's far too expensive to go changing it extensively or doing a new one. Remember, if you have the target audience right and the offer right (both previously tested), then you will get the creative right by simply using commonsense. So what you're really testing is the program mix. By exploring program times and types, and measuring cost per response, you will, in two weeks, get a very good idea of what schedule will deliver your optimum cost per response.

However, sometimes there is a major issue to test. For instance, in a campaign we ran for a large insurer on women's financial services, we thought that the sex of the presenter might be a very important aspect of the offer. The commercial had been made using a well known male news reader, on camera and we chose a very competent, authoritative female presenter, so that we had two identical versions of the same commercial. We ran each one every alternate day for the two weeks of the test market so, over the fortnight, we had a direct comparison, day-by-day of each presenter. In fact, there was absolutely no difference in the response rate.

Consider carefully the advantages of a test run. It is not uncommon to improve the cost of response from phase one to phase two by 50 per cent. It is also a good test of the phone-answering methodology and of the fulfillment material you are sending out. Altogether, it is a very sensible thing to be doing. At least consider the first two weeks of these two as a test.

Television doesn't only work for product, it also works very well to generate sales leads. For instance, you might be a bank or an insurance company with a special retirement package or investment opportunity. You run your advertisement suggesting that people simply phone in for more information and no obligation. The names and addresses that come in are, therefore, already qualified: you know the people who left their names and addresses have already indicated their interest.

Now you go into action as fast as possible: speed is of the essence. The names and addresses which come to your telephone bureau should be on disk to your fulfilment house that same day. *There is a definite correlation between speed and conversion.* Ideally, within 48 hours, your first responders should have a personalised letter and information booklet in their mailbox, or they should have received a phone call from your firm. Quick contact is absolutely vital in lead generation.

If you have a sales force, then the leads should be shared between them. The letters that went out should also be personalised so that the salespersons' name and signature is on them. This gives your sales force a sense of being involved and also the added incentive to convert more prospects into customers. The argument is, of course, that all sales leads have an equal weighting when they come from a television commercial. The conversion rate therefore should depend on the added ingredient—the salesperson. The letter will, of course, promise personal contact with the recipient within a few days. The joy of this approach is that you provide your customer with genuine service and you make your salespeople very happy at the same time. Salespeople like nothing better than a qualified lead, and customers like nothing better than a prompt reply.

In working with large corporations who are convinced they need both a direct marketing approach, and an image building one, we have had great success in suggesting that both commercials be shot at the same time—with a strong element of the image commercial incorporated into the direct-response commercial.

This is how it works. The company prepares a normal 30-second-image building commercial, which is run on prime time television, perhaps even during a sporting event. The 90-second direct-marketing offer is run in movies in off-peak. The two have a strong family resemblance and, therefore, the image commercial works to give reassurance to the direct-marketing commercial. It integrates what for many organisations is necessary brand image advertising with a call-for-action offer. Furthermore, with '*ebb and flow*' studies, you can set up a study to establish a schedule which will give you a high degree of overlap between prime-time and fringe-time audiences.

The result is great economies in production and the buying and use of time on the box. One reason is that in buying a big schedule of fringe-time television, you can get a bonus-priced number of peak time spots. Alternatively, if you're a big buyer of prime time, you can get your fringe-time schedule for peanuts if you negotiate carefully.

Direct response television continues to be one of the great untapped new business opportunities in Australia. Many major corporations, conscious of the mail order image, are nervous about using direct marketing on television. In their minds they see the ubiquitous 'steak knives' commercials and grow shy of the medium. Yet a financial services programme for women is about as far as you can get away from such a prosposition. And the campaign we ran for Australia's biggest insurance organisation was one of the most successful new business opportunities ever achieved by that company in direct response.

This campaign—for the AMP—might never have happened had it been left to the usual reactionary elements always present in a large organisation. But, fortunately, it was driven by Ms Laurel Jackson, a remarkable woman, at that time one of the very few AMP senior female executives, who with courage and determination championed the direct response campaign through a maelstrom of politics and objections. It was an outstanding commercial success.

4. Print Media. The last of the big four media categories is, of course, *Print*, which covers the following major opportunities:

- Mass circulation newspapers
- Magazines, male and female mass circulation
- Specialist magazines (fishing, trade, health etc.)
- Business newspapers and magazines
- Free & suburban newspapers and magazines.

There are, other opportunities for printed material with direct response marketing, but I'm sure you get the idea. If there is a target audience you want which is large enough to bring in a viable cost per response ratio, almost any printed medium will qualify for use.

However, you should be warned—buying print space for direct marketing can be very different to space purchased for general brand image, or even retail, advertising. Here are several rules you'd be foolish to ignore.

The first rule is to correctly evaluate an unknown print medium. You do this by removing all the other possible variables. This means that you test a known product with a known offer using a successful creative approach. You take this proven package into the unproven medium without changing a single element, not even a word, with perhaps the only exception being page size. However, even in this, if you're testing a magazine with a full page newspaper advertisement, then make sure you use a full page in the magazine to do so. The relationship of space to effectiveness is well known.

A full-page, direct-response advertisement is initially expensive. But it will almost always out-perform anything less than a full page. That is, on a cost-per-order basis, a full page is usually much more cost effective than any smaller size. If you have to down-size, the general rule is to go no less than half-page. It's difficult to get your customers to take you seriously in a small size direct response ad. I have not had much luck in Australia with broken space, as it's called. Basically, it's difficult to get the impact you require, combined with the credibility you need, in less than a full page. *Remember the two essential criteria for direct-response promotion: cost per response & quality of response.*

The essential difference between buying for a brand image campaign, as opposed to a direct marketing one, is that in general advertising media is purchased on the amount it costs to reach a thousand readers. This is appropriately termed *the cost-per-thousand,* When you buy on a cost-per-thousand basis, you take into account two important factors: the multiple page exposure of the newspaper or magazine, (that is, the number of times an individual is likely to see your advertisement during the time he or she owns it) and, secondly, the number of readers who will read it after the original reader. This second figure is known as the *pass-on* value. It is for this reason that the readership of a magazine or newspaper is quoted as much larger than the number of copies sold. It is an important factor in selling the magazine or newspaper to an advertiser.

However, in direct marketing the criteria is somewhat different. You are primarily interested in response. The response measurement far outweighs the cost-per-thousand, number of impacts, or pass-on value of brand image requirements. One can be measured as a general characteristic and sold, while the direct-response measurement is one of an individual case history. One product will work splendidly in a certain magazine and another, not terribly dissimilar, will bomb. You simply can't measure an over-all direct response potential for a newspaper or magazine.

Response characteristics for the print medium can only be gained and measured by experience—that is, from recording and measuring each medium. It is for this reason that advertising agencies not familiar with direct marketing are unable to evaluate the responsiveness of the various print media. They simply do not have the historical data.

Direct marketing in print is like buying a personally tailored suit, while brand-image advertising is an off-the-rack purchase. When you place an advertisement in a print medium a whole range of measurements come into play: the name of the publication; the size of the advertisement; the position by page number; the day of the week in which the offer ran; the time of the year; even the weather on the day. If you record all the contributing variables, a properly-coded order coupon will give you a lot of this information. Over a period of time, you will know which are the best publications for what offers, and even which are the best specific issues to use.

Here is a whole list of well proven generalisations for direct marketing offers which involve cash-upon-order:

- Weekend newspapers work better than weekday ones
- Saturday morning newspapers work best of all
- Tuesday works best for the Australian Financial Review
- Afternoon newspapers generally don't work
- Free newspapers do not work well in the metropolitan area
- Specialist sections in newspapers don't work as well as the general news section. Special supplements barely work at all. Don't be tempted to buy space in a travel, fishing or similar

supplement. Choose the general news section of the same paper instead. People seem to know that special supplements are a newspaper initiative to bring in revenue. They generally contain long and tediously-written advertorials for the people who have taken formal advertising space.

- Specialist magazines can work very well as they attract a specialist audience. Put your fishing offer in a specialist fishing magazine and it will work.
- In Australia, the three most responsive mail order magazines for women are New Idea, TV Week and Woman's Day. They have remained at the top for 20 years and show no sign of being unseated.
- Sports-dominated newspapers and publications do not work well.
- The period between mid-November and mid-January is usually the best time to take a vacation as direct response is just about dead in the water.

Nothing is absolute in direct response and while these are my findings over a long period, they should be no more than warning lights for you. Your business may respond differently and you are urged to test your advertisement in any publication where, your commonsense tells you, you may get a worthwhile response.

In testing your offer it is important to be able to track your responses by each source, as you may be running offers simultaneously in a number of publications. You should always code the response coupons, usually done with a small (10 pt) number at the bottom of the coupon. If you're taking telephone responses make certain that the operator asks for the origin of the enquiry. Or allocate a unique phone number to each media.

Lester Wunderman, usually regarded as the founder of contemporary direct marketing, developed a simple and highly-effective technique to measure the cross-over between different media. This is how it works. If you are using television to highlight a print advertisement which carries the bulk of the information, you place a small box somewhere within the print advertisement without explaining why it is there. In the television commercial, you mention the little box in the print advertisement and offer the viewer a free gift if he or she ticks the box and sends it in to you. The only possible way the person responding to this instruction could know about it is through the television commercial, thus giving you a precise cross-over measurement. Of course, you can set up the same kind of measurement between any two media, for example a print advertisement and a mailing piece.

You've heard it before, the three maxims of effective real estate, are *position, position, position.* What holds good for that business is equally true of direct marketing in the print medium. After the choice of magazine or newspaper, position is the most important variable in determining response.

Again, here are a set of rules to take pretty seriously:

- A right-hand page is up to four times more responsive than a left-hand one. Given the choice, never buy a left-hand page even if you have to pay a loading for one on the right.
- An early right-hand page is the big daddy of them all and will be much more responsive than one which occurs later in the publication.
- Advertisements which are not a full page should always appear on the right side of a right-hand page. This is because of what is known as *the perceived difficulty factor.* The reader simply sees the job of clipping a coupon from the centre of a page or from the left-hand margin as too difficult, even though it might take only moments longer to do so. Furthermore, a coupon clipped from the extreme bottom on the right-hand side of a right-hand page does not mutilate the newspaper or magazine for the next reader.

Public relations has a role in direct marketing, and there is a plethora of books on the subject which are readily available to you.

It is said that a column of favourable editorial comment is worth about six of formal advertising. While I don't think the ratio for direct marking is quite as valid, public relations can, nonetheless be a very useful addition to a direct marketing offer. The reason

LOCATION, LOCATION, LOCATION

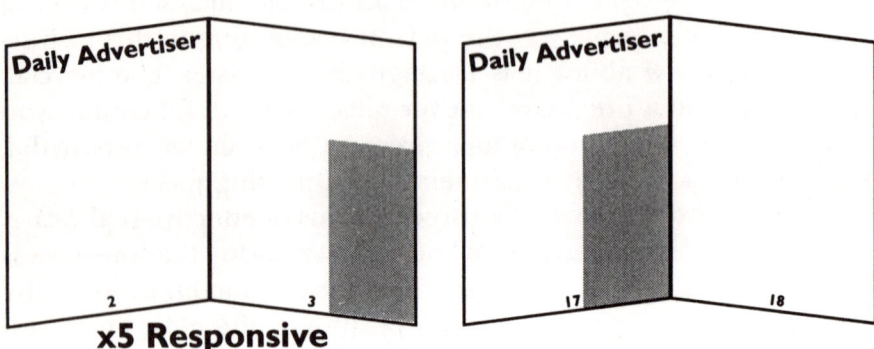

x5 Responsive

Location, Location, Location—Right hand pages can be five times more responsive. Never buy a left hand page if you have a choice.

is, as you will have surmised, because editorial is considered impartial whereas the self-interest in an advertisement is obvious. An editorial comment is like a personal reference, it is supposed to have no axe to grind or involve personal gain for the referee.

So how do you go about getting it?

Well, for a start, don't buy it in the kind of advertorial you'll be offered in a newspaper supplement. But do buy your advertising space in a special interest magazine, which will somewhat less blatantly editorialise around the subject of your offer. For instance, a motoring magazine depends very largely on automobile manufacturers supplying them with merchandise to test as well as favourable product information. This is a sort of quid-pro-quo the reader understands and is likely to forgive, so that the slightly advertorial nature of the magazine is accepted, and does not greatly diminish the worth of the editorial content.

Free magazines are, of course, another source, where paid advertising, just as in television, pays for the free circulation and of course for the editorial salaries. They too can be a reasonable source for publicity. Though there is a margin of credibility in this kind of publication, it is somewhat offset by the obvious nature of the magazine. These magazines, as well as car or special interest magazines, are usually run on an editorial shoestring. They are simply waiting to welcome well written and not obviously partisan stories of genuine interest to their readers. They often have a new product section created almost specifically for this purpose and in return for a full page they will run an editorial comment in it.

However, if you want to work the national or mass media, you are generally advised to hire a specialist public relations outfit or bring a professional one onto your staff. This is not an area for amateurs. But if you're small and can't afford either, here are a couple of tips on writing a press release:

- Follow the same rules as you would communicating with your customers.
- Visualise your prospect, which in this case is an editor with an audience of his own. Visualise him and his target audience.

- Frame an interesting headline and write copy saying something interesting about the reward the readers will receive from the product. The press release should never be about you. 'I'm proud of our all-Australian pencil factory,' says Perfect Pencils Pty Ltd Managing Director, Woody le Pointe, is not the way to go. 'So what?' is the likely retort from the editor. 'Apprentice engineer invents a million dollar 'intelligent' pencil' is more like it.
- Always start with news. Fresh information that the reader does not know about your 'intelligent' self-leading pencil. Then tell them what's in it for them—the benefits they will get from owning one. News that is highly exciting to your board of directors may not thrill the world outside.
- Don't over-sell or over-promise. 'Bottoms Up revolutionises the office chair may look good in a release. But if it is simply announcing a new range of office chair colours, the editor is not going to give you free space in his paper or magazine. This kind of nonsense is the hallmark of the amateur public relations release and is far too common not to be spotted a mile away.
- Write the press release in the style of the magazine or paper. This means that you should get a copy, see how it presents in copy and layout and what sort of picture it takes, and fashion your release accordingly.
- Follow up the release with a phone call. It helps to get your release to the top of the slush pile and you can often add a little information which will push it into the publication.

Now a word about the future of the print medium. Magazines and newspapers have, as a general rule, been slow to innovate and to make the most of technology. This is especially true of Australia, which has only recently introduced full colour capacity into newspapers. The publishers are only now beginning to look at the real needs of their own readers. This new technology has a real application for direct marketing.

I have a friend in Brazil who publishes a magazine not unlike Time Magazine. He constantly surveys his readers and asks them to identify areas of special interest to them inside and outside the magazine. He might get a big response for say, photography, whereupon he will run an in-depth supplement on photography, which will go *only* to those readers who answered the survey. Bingo! He can sell space in that particular supplement to photographic suppliers at a premium price and everyone wins.

The point is, of course, that from a direct marketer's viewpoint, he is offering a qualified prospect, practically a customer, and if I were in his country and had an offer in the field of photography, I would be happy to pay a premium for space in his supplement. This sort of smart, applied, logical marketing doesn't even require sophisticated technology. It simply needs a well maintained database of his subscribers. Moreover, my friend in Brazil can use it once or twice a year forever.

In the U.S., some publications use Selectronic Binding. This goes one step further than my friend in Brazil in that it electronically reads database and couples it to the binding machine. For instance, The Farm Journal goes out to 800,000 subscribers and has over 7000 different versions of the same journal every month. A pig farmer gets a section on pigs and not the one on cows. New farmers will get different versions than established ones receive. The subtleties are quite remarkable if worked correctly from a sensitive database. Parent magazine tracks the age of your child and binds special supplements specifically for parents like you, who have children of the same age as yours. If you have three children of markedly different ages, you get three supplements bound into the magazine.

For direct marketers, the advantages of this sort of technology are obvious. A car manufacturer can print the name of his regional agent and salesmen in the same town or region as the customer. With the use of *inkjet printing* it is now possible to put the name of the subscriber into your direct response advertisement. Open up to page five and there's your name in the headline:

Mr Backhoe,
it's time to call us about
our special tractor deal!

Now that's what you call targeted marketing. Here is another example. The U.S. edition of Time Magazine devotes an entire page to tell each subsciber how their congressman/woman voted on current issues. This innovation has real sociological implications and is making elected representatives a lot more visible and accountable to their electorate.

To conclude this chapter, it is obvious that the opportunities available to direct marketing are increasing rapidly. Technology is paving the way and all it takes on your part is a little imagination and a lot of testing. Your success will be built on the care you take to:

- Set clear objectives based on your goals and the aspirations of your target audeince.
- Review the media which seems to best meet these objectives.
- Remember, in media, just like in a letter, the more relevant it is to the reader the better the response.
- Test, monitor, test again.
- Evaluate results and feed all the information into your database. The campaign isn't completed until you've extracted the last ounce of information from it for future use.

*If God hadn't been in such a hurry
to rest on the seventh day and
had tested a few more concepts,
His results would, almost
certainly, have been a lot better.*

Test, test and test before you rest!

Chapter Ten

Jesus doesn't make a souffle rise any higher but He sure can curdle the sauce on the top.
and
How to sell a Pontiac with a strip of brown paper and a leaky pen.

★ ★ ★

One of the best breaks in my life came from England, via the Air Force, to New Zealand and then to Australia. His name was Graham Kerr, a tall, good-looking, young, bon vivant chef. He had great charm, was irresistible to women and was, and perhaps still is, the best cooking personality television has ever seen. He caused a sensation on Australian television and got the sort of ratings for a cooking program you'd expect for a grand final.

Graham's style was infectious. He'd slosh a bit of this, add a dab of that, swig from the bottle of wine he used for cooking, and generally make cooking seem not only like fun, but dead easy. I've never seen anyone do it better. Even men liked to watch him. He was also making a fortune. He was managed by Harry M. Miller, another New Zealander who had made a huge reputation for himself as an entrepeneur. Harry was responsible for revolutionising Australian pop culture by mounting and promoting a locally-produced version of the pop musical, Hair. Then, he produced an even more brilliant production of Jesus Christ SuperStar.

In fact, Harry M. Miller embodied the spirit of the '60s. He was in tune with the Flower generation and Woodstock and as a

showman he spelled an end to the wise-guy generation represented by Lee Gordon and Sammy Lee. Clean, good looking
enough to be a movie star himself, with a well modulated voice
and a stunning blonde Hollywood film star for a wife, he was Mr
Clean on top and tough underneath.

Harry was a man with a golden touch and he managed Graham
Kerr so well that The Galloping Gourmet, the name invented by
Len Evans when he and Graham undertook a promotional tour
of Australia, lasted well beyond what might have been the expectations for such a property. Finally, however, the time came when
The G.G. had exhausted his potential on Australian television and
it was time for him to move on.

A friend of mine, Paul Talbot, who ran Fremantle International,
a very successful television distribution company headquartered
in New York, had lusted after Graham Kerr from the moment he
first laid eyes on him. I mean, of course, in a purely commercial
sense. Paul was an American who grew up in network television
in the US and he knew potential when he saw it. His past credentials included the Davis Cup and the Melbourne Olympic Games
in 1954. Graham Kerr would be, he knew, a positive sensation in
America. He formed a syndicate, of which I was a member, and
bought out Graham Kerr's contract from Harry M. Miller.

Paul took The Galloping Gourmet to North America as an Australian cooking expert. My job was to market all the cookware and
food and assorted products that emanated from the program.

Paul was proved right. Graham Kerr's The Galloping Gourmet
became the most widely-watched program ever in the history of
food and wine. The Americans went ape over the slightly risque,
naughty-but-nice Australian with the beautiful blue eyes, who
could sell the pants off a recipe and, with it, train-loads of cook
books and cooking merchandise.

For three years The Galloping Gourmet was running five days
a week on 170 television stations in the U.S. and another 48 stations in Canada. There had simply never been anything like it on
American television and we all thought we were in clover. Here
was one man, on a simple set, no gimmicks, no supporting cast,
in front of a camera doing his own thing in front of 40 million

Americans five times a week. It was an extraordinary performance, most of it ad lib, by an astonishingly talented performer.

At the very height of his success in 1972 Graham Kerr went into a Church in Baltimore, Maryland where he saw a vision of Christ. In fact, it was Graham's maid who had first seen a vision of Jesus in the church and rushed home immediately to fetch Graham to have a look for himself. Christ had waited and Graham was converted on the spot. He came directly up to New York and announced to us all that there would be some changes to his program. Firstly, it would begin and end with a prayer. Also, there would be no more wine or strong drink.

One of the joys of Graham's program was its lack of inhibitions. By the end of many a program his generous slurping and sloshing of the wine he used in cooking gave him an irreverent air. It was his trademark and the thing that research showed endeared him most to his viewers. Being pragmatists, we figured we could probably get away with the no-drink clause and pick up a whole group of new viewers in middle America. We thought that Young & Rubican who syndicated the program, would agree to the idea—when Graham announced that the new series would be called, 'Cooking for Christ.'

We were done for! The good Lord might be good at baking loaves and cooking the odd fish, but he made a lousy souffle. Not even the Bible Belt wanted to know about Christ's culinary expertise. We kept going for a while by re-hashing programs and making the odd special, you know, 'the best of..' that sort of thing. But the cream had curdled; it was time to go home.

Today Graham is still a star, though not nearly as popular as before. But, who knows, the second coming of Graham Kerr may well be nigh.

I think the direct marketing lesson I gained out of The Galloping Gourmet is obvious—when you're on a good thing, stick to it. A format that works, providing always you keep it up-dated, and you research your target audience, can be made to last a long, long time. Changing something because you feel a change is due, or you're simply bored with the old format, or even if you have a vision, can be disastrous.

The offer is what drives the quality and quantity of the response. Viewers didn't want a prim and proper lady cook, or even a fat French one to show them how to cook. They wanted a slightly irreverent Australian, who you'd like your daughter to marry or to marry yourself. That was the offer, not the food he cooked. When the offer was changed, well the good Lord didn't make the souffle rise any higher, and He wasn't why people would have enjoyed the program. The offer has to be matched as closely as possible to the aspirations or even the fantasies of your audience.

Direct marketing is all about getting a response that converts to a sale. If you don't have an interesting offer then what are you giving people to prompt them to respond? If you don't excite people enough for them to want to respond immediately, then they probably never will. It's that easy and that tough. Once they've put the advertisement down, or passed the phone and think about making a cup of tea, watering the garden or taking the dog for a walk, you can mostly kiss the sale goodbye. Direct marketing is a now-or-never proposition and how you present the offer is very important.

That's why the offer is ranked second in the relative weightings. The joy is, of course, that offers don't have to be hit or miss. They can be controlled simply by testing an offer against all the other known variables. You soon learn what works, what doesn't and what is likely to work best.

The psychology of the offer is important. 'Buy one, get one free!' is about as spot-on as you can get in couching an offer. But '50 per cent off this month only' is about as misguided as you can get in stimulating that part which presses the human want-to-have button, and makes the phone ring.

The '50 per cent off offer' talks your audience down, not up. It creates a negative image of the merchandise, which consumers think must have been bought as a remainder lot, or which has some imperfection, or was over-ordered and everyone has one. 'Buy one, get one free' does just the opposite. It suggests a genuine bargain and a bonus. It is an 'up' offer which research shows consistently works twice as well as the 'down' offer of half-price merchandise.

The 'buy one get one free' concept has been used for everything from soap to sunglasses. But I was astonished when recently a man stood up in a seminar I was conducting and said that he'd learned of the concept at a previous seminar I'd conducted and then claimed it worked just as well on automobiles.

'Sure,' I said tentatively, 'but how the hell do you stay in business?'

'Simple,' he replied, 'we sell expensive cars with a big margin. So I go out and buy basic second-hand cars, do them up and make this offer: 'Buy a new car and get a second-hand one in good condition for your son or daughter,' he grinned. 'We can't keep up with the orders coming in. We can't find sufficient cheap second-hand cars to give away.'

How many times have you been offered a $2000 reduction on a new car, or an extra $2000 for your trade-in. It's almost a standard offer in the prestige car business. But a good car for the kid thrown in, a two-for-the-price-of-one offer? Well, you don't see that kind of opportunity coming along every day, especially as the kid's car carried a 12-month fully guaranteed warranty! The sums are the same in the end. But the one offer captures the imagination, while the other one is expected and, therefore, boring. It is also a much more personal offer.

At Freedom Pontiac we were each allocated a certain time on the floor. That is, we were allowed to sell from the showroom. With one or two tricks such as I outlined in an earlier chapter, this was more or less money for 'old rope'. People came in looking for a car, or at least looking, and the rest, well you know the story.

But it was much harder when we were required to go out among the population and search for leads. This was the hardest kind of work. Imagine approaching a slightly older or beat-up car in a supermarket lot and asking the owner if he or she would like to buy a new Pontiac?

But it wasn't done quite like that. We would all go out with a roll of brown wrapping paper and a pen with a tendency to leak. We'd hit a busy supermarket parking lot and whenever we saw a car that looked a little worse for wear, or was an older model, we'd roughly tear off a strip of brown paper and in scrawled hand-writing, preferably with the odd ink blot, we'd write: Call me urgently about your car. Terry, LA 674 2800.

We'd do this all over the parking lot, trying not to let the owner of one car see a similar slip of paper under the windshield of another car.

The result was, of course, predictable. The owner would come out of the supermarket with a load of groceries, a bit hot and bothered and read the paper on the windshield. Then they'd go all over the car to see where the ding was, find nothing and grow increasingly curious as to the reason for the hastily-scribbled number on a piece of wrapping paper. In many instances, by the time they got home, they were itching to know who and why and they'd dial the number and ask for Terry.

Meanwhile back at Freedom the switch knew that this call belonged to the Terry team—that is, one of five salesmen who sold under the Terry name.

'A Terry call!' she'd announce on the broadcast system and any salesman in the Terry team, one whom was always on the sales floor while the other five were out canvassing, picked up the phone.

'Hello, Terry speaking.'

'Ah, Terry, you er left a note on my windshield, you know, to call you?'

'Oh that's right, Mrs ...?'

'Reynolds, Martha Reynolds.'

'How very nice of you to call, Mrs Reynolds, may I call you Martha?'

'Yes, of course, but what is it?'

'Well, Martha I may just have a nice surprise coming your way!'

'Surprise? I'm not sure I like surprises left on my windshield?'

The salesman laughs: 'Nothing to worry about. You see, we've been looking for a Chevy just like yours, same year, colour and model, a customer of ours wants one badly and is prepared to ...'

'It's not a Chevy, it's a Chrysler Imperial! What is this?'

'That's funny,' he laughs, 'Hey, was this today? Did you get the note today? You did? Well then that explains *everything*! Two days ago we had a request for a Chevy and today for a Chrysler. Same collector, he does them up and sends them to the Samoan Islands. He gets firm orders, very specific, a Chevy here, Packard there, a Chrysler somewhere else. You see there's a big rust problem in the tropics, sea air, salt spray, the islanders don't like to buy new cars but they won't buy a heap either.'

'Well, I can't see what this has got to do with me?'

'I'm glad you asked Mrs Reynolds, er Martha, we are in a position through this buyer to offer you a trade-in deal on your Chrysler you simply couldn't get if you took it anywhere else!'

'A trade-in, why I never thought to … it's only five years old …'

'On a brand new Pontiac, state of the art, not only a trade-in but a boot full of groceries to the value of $500!'

I won't go on any longer, I'm sure you get the idea. Always make an offer your customer feels he or she can't afford to turn down. This doesn't have to be bigger and better, but simply, a more imaginative use of the trade-in margin, or discount, you were prepared to give in the first place. And if you can make it seem personal, that is, a one-off offer to an individual customer, then it is going to be very hard for them to refuse. For example:

'Only for collectors who wisely purchased the first edition of the Windsor Castle plate, we now make you this offer: buy one, get one free—two royal plates for the price of one—the magnificent changing of the guard at Buckingham Palace plate, and the Hampton Court plate, both for the price you paid for your Windsor Castle plate—$49.99! Each plate comes complete in a royal blue, velvet-lined, walnut veneer collector's display box fitted with sterling silver hinges and antique design lock. More, you will receive an additional English crafted display box for your Windsor plate to make up a three boxed heirloom collection. We regret, only one order per collector is available in this offer.'

Qantas has used the 'buy one trip, get one free' on the London route with the free trip being to selected European capitals. Cellarmasters do it all the time for wine, order six bottles and get six free, it works a treat and has been the most successful offer they've ever made.

Of course, 'buy one, get one free,' is not going to be suitable for all products—like wedding receptions or appendix operations or heart transplants. But for a great many products it is a much stronger inducement than simply discounting, which may add up to exactly the same end price, but which devalues the product in the mind of your potential customer.

Which brings us to the next well worked and successful offer turned into a powerful inducement; *The free trial offer.*

Free trial is an essential component in mail-order. This is because the customer has no opportunity to meet the seller and make an assessment on a face-to-face inspection of the premises and of the salesperson. I guess humans are naturally suspicious and the free trial ensures that the offer is on the level. If it isn't and you've over-glamourised your product, then keep your warehouse doors wide open as the goods are going to come back to you in truckloads.

Porcelain dolls are a big collector's item and as Australia's biggest direct response marketer of porcelain dolls, we take enormous care to ensure that the picture of the doll in the brochure is a true representation of the actual dolls. No clever retouching, size enhancement or clever photography. We try to represent as accurately as possible the merchandise we sell. Less than five per cent of people send the dolls back, which is one of the lowest return ratios for porcelain objects in the world.

Did you know that it costs almost seven times more to put an item back into inventory than to send it out in the first place? It's simply dumb to try to deceive your end customer. If you won't do it for ethical reasons then, remember, you're in business a long time.

Some prestige motor vehicle dealers have offered doctors and lawyers and other upwardly mobile professionals, a free trial of an expensive model, usually over a weekend. It seldom if ever works, because two days is simply not enough time to get to know and feel a new car. Dealers, on the other hand, are afraid that the car will be abused. New cars have a very high ratio of accidents as people learn to handle them. Also, car companies have learned

that it is unwise to allow a prospect to trial a car without a salesperson present as there is no one to field questions and answer
the objections.

The ideal length for a free trial is 30 days. We see people offering 10-day or 14-day periods, but this is not sufficient. Short
periods of free trial often reduce the response rate. People are
busy and worry they won't have sufficient time to make an assessment of the product and return it within the free time period and
so they don't order it in the first place. The difference in cost
between 14 and 30 days is nothing. But the response rate difference can be significant.

Don't be nervous about offering a free trial. It doesn't increase
the number of people who will abuse your offer. And if your
product won't stand the wear of a 30-day trial, you ought not to
be selling it in the first place.

We used to run a mail order business in Hong Kong with a
Chinese partner who had little trust in her fellow citizens. She was
adamant that we never allow a free trial until one day, at our cost,
we tried it on a substantial offer. Of course, the percentage of bad
debts and returns was no higher than elsewhere, but the response
rate slightly more than doubled.

Offering interest free credit will always increase your response
dramatically, often doubling or tripling it. Of course you carry the
bank loan interest and there's always a bad debt risk. But it
doesn't seem to be very much higher than giving 30 days to pay.
In fact, bad debts in our experience are not a significant factor
in doing business and are around 2 per cent of our receivables.
That's better than most banks! The longer you are in business,
the better your database becomes. This enables you to cull the
bad payers. The good ones, who buy from you regularly, regard
your invoice no differently than they would a retail account from
a department store.

However, be careful about offering credit through the media,
either on television or in a print advertisement. Both attract the
unscrupulous like flies to honey. You don't lend money to a complete stranger, and you would do well not to offer interest-free

instalments to strangers in a direct-response offer.

The method that seems safest is to ask for a first instalment up front, say 25 per cent of the selling price before the goods have been delivered. This sorts out the outright crooks and also, as a general rule, if people are going to default it's with the first or second payment and not the final one. Like everything in direct marketing, you should test market your interest-free offer thoroughly by running it right through the entire payment cycle, before throwing it open on a national scale.

Remember always, the world is full of people trying to 'stretch a buck'. Payment terms are vital to a customer at the lower end of the market and critical to response. The price point you set for the monthly payment is every bit as critical as the end price. If we are making an offer of an item that is around $40 in TV Week or New Idea, the two middle-income women's magazines, we would offer the option of splitting the whole price down the centre. Then we'd make it two equal payments of $19.95 and this could increase response by up to 50 per cent.

On higher-priced merchandise, you would always feature the monthly payment and bury the full price somewhere in the copy. Featuring the full price invariably reduces the response.

Then there is the 'send no money now' payment offer which you can use in the media. The great advantage with this offer is that you can make a feature of it in your advertisement. There is always something rather grand about an offer that seems to implicitly trust the potential customer. In fact, once you receive the coupon you send in an invoice before you ship the goods. The default or drop-out rate at this point is around 25 per cent. You send one follow-up letter and then quit as any more contact is a waste of postage. Historically, we find that the initial loss of around 25 per cent is more than made up by the increase in initial responses.

If you want to go for the jackpot then combine **free trial, send no money now, interest free credit and a free gift** in your offer. This is a very powerful motivation and will work very well if you are prepared to take the risks.

I recall a very successful offer we made for a series of plates featuring Australian songbirds. The initial research showed that the plates were ideal for our database and that we could expect excellent results. But we added an element to the offer which cost very little, but it added romantically to the whole concept.

We prepared a tape cassette of the artist recalling her childhood in the Dandenong ranges together with the actual songs of the birds we were to feature on the plate. I'm afraid it was a job on the cheap and we sent Bjorn Valsinger, our joint Managing Director, to record the narrative and the birdsong. Unfortunately, he also recorded by mistake the snoring of the ancient labrador asleep at the feet of his mistress. The artist had a pretty dreary sort of voice and the dog's snoring kept cutting over it, and the birdsong, well that was quite nice if you like that sort of thing. I ran the finished tape in the car one day and damn nearly had a collision as I drowsed off.

We marked the tape at a retail value of $9.95 (cost to us $2.00) and shipped it as a free gift with the first invoice on a send-no-money-now offer. We called it 'Birdsong & Labrador snoring' and the customers loved it and the offer worked brilliantly. All it takes is a little imagination and an ability to teach an old dog new tricks!

Not such a new trick these days is the use of the credit card in direct response. Achieving this facility in Australia took years of negotiation with suspicious credit card managers. In 1975, when we first approached Bankcard, the then major credit card in Australia, they simply refused to allow mail-order selling. They finally agreed on the basis that we would be responsible for paying back the amount if the card member defaulted. This provision still exists, despite over a million direct marketing transactions with no higher default factor than normal Bankcard retail trading. But some banks are like that, once they've got what they believe is an advantage; trying to change the rules is like trying to refute the act of creation in the book of Genesis.

Today it is essential to offer credit card facilities to your own database and to media promoted customers. You'll find that roughly half your responses will want to pay using a credit card. A good way to offer credit card 'terms' is to ask your customer to sign an automatic authority on the order coupon using the following statement:

'I authorize you to debit my credit card with $ ... amount each month over the next six months.'

It may be important for you to know which of the credit cards are the best for your business. All work but some are a lot more expensive to operate than others. The two I put on my 'no' list are two travel and entertainment cards, Diners and American Express. These two, while being excellent logos to put on your offer, charge you almost twice as much as Visa and Mastercard to operate. Now that Visa and Mastercard are universally established, it doesn't make a lot of commercial sense to promote Amex and Diners at a trading disadvantage to yourself. But it is something you ought to test before you make a final decison. Diners and Amex will argue that their card gives you greater credibility than the others and will buy you more response. I invite you to test this for yourself, though don't hold your breath.

The direct marketing business is one of taking chances. Risk is, after all, a pretty relative business and you can be absolutely safe with only three customers, if that's what makes you happy. But risks should be undertaken only *after* you've done everything you can to ensure you have all your elements right and this includes your offer. Test several offers to see which one works best for you. While testing in the media is expensive, it's essential if you want to stay in business. We have 22 variations in the terms of our offers (that is 22 payment options) and each requires a different piece of software. It drives the computer people crazy, but then you can't let a computer programmer run your business for you—although they'll try. Oh, how they'll try!

Creating a sense of urgency! A sense of excitement is essential. You want your customer to respond immediately and so you have to act accordingly. If you make a *limited time offer* then you're obliged to stick with it. If an order comes in a day late then you must send it back with a note regretting that it arrived too late.

It doesn't matter if you have a warehouse filled with merchandise, you must maintain your credibility. Moreover, you will also miss the opportunity the effect of being rejected has on a potential customer. The effect of saying 'no' will work for you. The very next time you send out an offer, the person you rejected in your last offer will be the first to mail in a response coupon. We all desire what we have been told we may not have.

The closing date of your offer should be sufficiently in advance for people to make a decision and take an action. But it should not be so far removed that they can postpone the action through inertia or procrastination. Always close your offer at the end of a month. If you open an offer at the beginning of October, then you should close it at the end of October. But if you open it on the 15th of October, then you will close it at the end of November. People will simply not remember middle of the month dates. But they will clearly register an end of the month closure. Be specific. Don't say: 'Offer closes in two weeks'; put the end of the month date down clearly: 'Offer closes 31st of October.

Out of fairness to your customer always use the date of the postmark. If you are in Sydney and the offer comes from a small mining town in Western Australia, it can take some time to reach you. So don't penalise for distance. If the response envelope is marked 30th of October, then the coupon is valid even if it reaches you on the 7th of November.

If you want to keep your options open, yet still get some sense of urgency then you can prompt your customers to: *'please send your order by the end of October'*. It's a reasonable compromise between urgency and procrastination, and it works quite well as the request itself implies a sense of 'do it now!'

We've discussed the concept of the 'free gift' offer. You saw how it worked in the songbirds of Australia example, with the free tape relevant to the main offer, which is a critical ingredient in all direct marketing. Positioning the free gift is very important in the juggling act of maintaining equal emphasis on both quantity and quality. The point is that the gift should not be the main reason for responding to the offer, but a nice little bonus, a thank you for responding quickly—the little extra the customers need to push them over the edge.

Your customer's thought process should go somewhat like this:

'Hmm, looks interesting. Could be a good magazine to get, keep me informed. Hey, what's this? A free ticket in a sweepstake for a Lexus. Let's see, what are the conditions? Oh, that's easy enough. Get my subscription in by the end of October. Hell, why not? It's a good mag anyway and I'm getting 12 months for the price of ten.'

Quite the wrong positioning would be:

'I'll have a crack at the Lexus, you never know your luck. If I miss out I'll cancel my subscription. Boring magazine anyway.'

When this happens what you get is a low-renewal rate and an uncommitted reader. In other words, your database is corrupted by sweepstake contestants instead of readers.

I have used the example of a magazine subscription because there is a strong school of thought within the publishing and advertising industry that the profusion of irrelevant gifts (a free hair-dryer for a business magazine) has actually changed the nature of the readership profile of some magazines and, therefore, the ability of the advertising within it to influence the readers. The wrong free offer can be dangerous to the outcome in more than just responses.

The *free gift* offer is a fulcrum, a balance between quantity and quality. The quantity of responses you get against the quality of those responses. Therefore you must always determine whether two criteria are in place:

- **Value**
- **Affinity**

The value of a free gift must be judged very carefully. For instance, in business-to-business marketing, a high-value gift may be seen as a bribe. Management becomes suspicious, particularly if the gift is offered to the manager of the purchasing department.

However, in marketing to the public at large, the value of a gift which is a critical part of the offer, is the key factor in driving the quality of the response. That is, a creative and compelling gift will be the major factor in the *quality* of the response.

Now this doesn't have to be an item of great value as long as it is seen as a gift that is relevant to the potential customer's desires. Another way of looking at it is to offer a free gift that is relatively or completely boring to the public at large, but would be fascinating to your prospects—the bird call tape to bird plate collectors, a train whistle tape to model train enthusiasts.

We were once approached by a manufacturer who custom-built vans for industry. He was interested in getting into the courier van market and gave us the brief to find out what, ideally, a courier company wanted in a van. We developed a questionnaire, which we sent to courier companies and asked them to distribute it to their drivers. It asked the drivers to design the ideal van. In return for their ideas, we promised to send each van driver a small pocket torch which glowed in the dark, so they could always find it if they put it down while handling a delivery. A torch was a nice idea, one that glowed in the dark was an even better one. Both cost very little as a premium offer but, for a courier who works at night, the glow worm torch made a lot of sense.

Couriers from all over Australia sent in complete designs for vans. It was information of high quality, and in terms of the courier business, pure gold. Where to put a tray to carry forms, where the ice box should go to carry their drinks. Things you simply wouldn't think of unless you were a busy courier. They also gave us a whole heap of information about themselves: how many vans they or their employer owned, when they bought new vehicles and, of course, their full address. Today, based on this one questionnaire and a small glow-in-the-dark torch, the van manufacturer has made large inroads into supplying courier vehicles in Australia and New Zealand. When later he needed some specific information, we already had our next free gift, a small cool box for drinks, which fitted neatly behind the driver's seat.

It is important to select a gift which appears to have a direct affinity with your potential customer-tapes of birdsong, torches for couriers, calculators and data diaries for financial services. With a little imagination, you can get it right almost every time. And when you do, you can be confident that the right gift, positioned nicely between quality and quantity, will give you the best possible quality response and, therefore, the lowest cost per sale.

The early bird offer is yet another way to go. Offering some sort of relevant reward for the first 100 orders or enquiries received, or all orders received by a certain date, has the effect of not only increasing your total responses, but in getting people to respond more quickly. This again is a demonstration of the principle that the sooner people can be made to act the better the end result. It also increases the over-all response as it compels some of your customers, who may not otherwise get around to buying, to order immediately.

There are, of course, endless ways of phrasing this *early bird* offer. One particularly nice way was shown by The Reader's Digest, which combined an *early bird* offer with a *sweepstake* and a *closing date*. 'One thousand dollars a day for every day you beat our March 1st deadline' (If you win the sweepstake, of course).

The same principle of no back-sliding applies here as it did for the free gift and limited time offers: the gift must have an affinity to your product or service *and* there must be strict adherence to the rules of the offer. If you state it as the first 100 orders received, that's what it is, no matter how hard your 101st customer pleads with you.

I learned this the hard way. We ran a campaign for a home beer brewing kit and offered a free pewter tankard to the first ten respondents. It was a truly magnificent piece, beautifully engraved with the image of the ship, 'Parmelia', which brought the first settlers to Western Australia. It would have been worth $150 retail. A truly-desirable offer, custom-created by Selangor Pewter to our own design.

It was hardly surprising that the beer kit offer pulled it's head off (Oops!). One elderly lady wanted the tankard so badly that she had travelled to our office, at enormous inconvenience, from a great distance away. She took the bus and then the train, walking the last two miles from the station. She arrived hot and exhausted, with her entry in hand, only to discover that she was entry number 15.

She stood in the customer service centre and complained bitterly at the unfairness. She'd read our advertisement within minutes of buying the magazine on the day of it's delivery to her newsagent. She'd filled in the coupon immediately, grabbed her hat and coat and left for town so that she could be in the first 10 entries. She had the money for the beer kit in her bag and didn't want any interest-free terms, she wanted the TANKARD!

I broke down and gave it to her, robbing number ten entry of his. After she'd left with a triumphant smile on her face, the place went wild. The customer services staff started ranting and raving; some even threatened to resign. How could I, of all people, break the rules. Didn't I know what it was like, day after bloody day having to say 'no' to a customer? Didn't I appreciate how badly they felt when they faced such bitterly disappointed customers and yet, in fairness to all the other customers, stuck to the rules?

They were right, of course. I had given in for all the wrong reasons—to get out of trouble. I'd acted this way to stop feeling bad, to stop the old lady from crying. That's no way to run a business which you maintain has perfect integrity. And it's simply not fair to your staff or to your other customers who have done the right thing. I was wrong. Quite wrong.

Strategic discounting, by any other name, is still discounting. I know it's done quite a lot, but I am most reluctant to suggest that you use discounting an offer as one of your marketing platforms unless it is your entire platform e.g. a discount warehouse catalogue. I keep asking myself why I am offering a discount? Is it because my product is over-priced? In which case I should price it more reasonably. Or because I think it will make my service or product more attractive? In which case I haven't presented it correctly. In either case, I tell myself, I'd better rethink the proposition.

Australian and New Zealand marketers seem to make a habit

of building themselves into a corner on price. Why this should be is difficult to understand. Used continuously, discounting is the last ditch stand of a salesperson lacking confidence in his or her product. It does nothing for the customer and often, the few dollars saved results in the product quality being devalued in her mind. Price isn't everything provided the goods or services are competitively priced. But the belief that she is buying a good product, is a great comfort to your customer. Think very carefully about what you are saying about your product or service when you repeatedly offer a discount. Having the odd sale as an event is a quite different matter and can be very effective.

Adding value is much the better approach. It takes more trouble, it requires some creativity and extra thinking, but it means a great deal more to your customers than the knee-jerk reflex to cut your price. Mail order should not be seen as a cheap option but as a very convenient way to shop for an enormous array of goods and services. The convenient difference is they can be brought to *your* door, rather than you having to *schlepp* over to a huge, noisy and confusing suburban shopping mall. Direct marketing is a value-for-money option, but not a source of cheap goods or services.

It is always tempting to continuously offer a discount because it does seem to get results in the short term. In the long term, it will build you into a corner where you are perceived as a cheap option and your discount becomes the norm and you have to keep increasing it. It is an unfortunate position to find yourself in and an even more difficult one to change. It only seems to work for traditional retailers at the bottom end of the market and especially with food sellers. Your image in the eyes of your customers is everything you own that's valuable. David Jones, Australia's premier retail department store, has got it right; they have built a solid and abiding reputation for value and if they are going to discount they do it only twice a year. The sale contains genuine bargains and maintains the concept of value-for-money. The evidence that such a sale is considered important and genuine is the fact that people queue outside the doors from the previous night—as they also do in London for the twice-yearly Harrods sale.

If you decide to offer a discount always couch it in dollar terms and not percentages. 'Save $10!' is infinitely better than 'Save 10 per cent' is. Money, not fractions, equates with what people understand. Ten bucks buys the kids dinner at McDonalds, or is almost the price of a movie ticket. So $10 means something—'10 per cent off' has much less impact.

The limited quantity offer. Placing a restriction on quantity appeals to the snob in all of us. We all want to possess something that is thought to be rare or difficult to obtain. It gives us a sense of being somewhat special, discerning and informed. A nice feeling. Some companies promote the spend on a limited edition offer as an investment opportunity. In my opinion, this is quite wrong, even immoral. Most limited or special edition mass-market offers are *unlikely* to become hugely valuable within the life time of the purchaser—a fact which is well known by every direct marketer.

Again, if you are making a limited quantity offer, you must stick to it. If you make the claim that only 500 pots signed by the now dead master potter are available, then you'd better make sure she is dead and that, despite the 360,000 coupons you received, you send out only 500 signed pots. This is no time to do a *Lazarus* on your customers.

It's quite common for marketers using the limited edition ploy to hover on the fringes of the truth. Some of the very famous European plate-makers create limited editions on the basis that they are made, say, in the Bicentenary year, or whatever the celebration is for that year. What they don't tell you is that they intend to sell the plates made in that year for years to come; nor do they say how many have been made.

One of the more common ways to limit an edition is to say that the production of these highly significant plates or porcelain objects is limited to 50 firing days. This tends to suggest that only a few plates are made on each of the 50 days and then the mould is broken. However, some European factories can turn out 10,000 plates in a firing day. Some limit!

One of the better ways to limit an edition is to have a closing date beyond which you do not accept orders. Like any closing date, this serves to heighten the response and is fair to the customer who orders within the time frame. It is also great from the marketer's point of view because you are limiting the edition to the number of orders you receive by a certain date.

The popularity of 'collectables' in the direct marketing business has totally confused the public about limited editions and the words have lost much of their currency. The Franklin Mint, with their mass market collectables, turned the limited edition into an art form. Our own research on porcelain dolls suggests strongly that our customers don't buy dolls because they are a part of a limited edition but simply because they like the look of the individual doll, the doll has a personality of it's own and they don't care if it's a limited edition, with its own certificate of authenticity.

However, if you want to work a full-blown limited edition offer correctly, then you must *do it* correctly. You must individually number your merchandise in the following way 27/500 together with the artist's signature. This simply means that this is the 27th item in a total collection of 500 items. The numbering by hand adds another touch of mystique to the product.

The difficulty, of course, is to judge just how many your limit is going to be. Genuine limited editions in the mass market usually have a secondary value. You must put sufficient items into the market so that this secondary value can operate in trading terms. If you only put out 10 items on a limited edition offer then this is probably too few, unless the item is of enormous collector value. If you put out 40,000 it's probably too many to give the item any resale value. Finding the optimum is difficult, but we have found in plates in the Australian market that 10,000 is an ideal number. You may miss out on a few orders, but you won't be left holding the bundle.

Our Australian Bicentennial plate was the biggest selling of all the plates available. We had it specially designed and produced after a great deal of research into what people wanted on such a plate. To add an urgency element, orders could only be taken until midnight of the anniversary. But, in fact, we'd sold out long before this time. Sure, we missed a few sales, but it's always nice to know that the warehouse is empty, the bank loan paid back, and your profit margin safely in the bank.

Giving away information for free. If you are trying to generate sound leads for your sales force, or for an upcoming mailing, than giving away good information is a great way to go about gathering them. Banks have used this method successfully to attract home loan borrowers: '*A free guide to buying a house—the what, why, when and where of buying and setting up a home.*' A booklet such as this will attract only people buying or renovating a house and so will be in the bank's mainstream target audience. It works just as well for an insurance company; '*Free guide to superannuation and planning for retirement.*' This material is self-selective, it's dead boring for someone not interested in retiring and fascinating to those who are. Research shows clearly that when information is original and well conceived, customers prize it highly. Also because it is produced on paper it is inexpensive and looks like a great free gift.

Competitions and prize draws. Greed is an excellent way to generate information provided you are after as much raw response as possible. That is, you want names, as many names as you can get. Boys Town Sweepstakes, a huge charity for orphan children operating out of Queensland, is after as many names as they can get. They select the quality of their response by the high price of the sweepstake ticket. But, in return, they offer huge prizes, usually spearheaded with a magnificent home and surrounding property. This particular sweepstake is a testament of how effective such an offer can be on the international market. Boys Town has been very successful in mailing their sweepstake to the Japanese from Australia. Fortuitously, a Japanese entry did win on one occasion. This received great publicity in Japan and vastly increased the interest in the sweepstake. Reader's Digest does the same thing with big prizes of a general nature anyone would want to win. Names are very much the name of this game.

For most marketers, this kind of headlong splash offering riches in return for the raw material leads isn't sufficiently qualified. If you want to go the sweepstake route to generate good leads, then you should offer a gift or prize that has an affinity with the merchandise or service you ultimately intend to offer.

We were given the job of selling advance tickets to EXPO 88, a giant exposition to be held in Queensland, which was intended to attract Australians from other States to the Sunshine State. The organisers wanted to have a sweepstakes prize of two first class air tickets to London, a five-star hotel holiday, with chauffeur-driven Rolls Royce and a generous spending allowance. If you bought advance tickets to EXPO, you were to be automatically entered in the sweepstake. When we said we were opposed to the prize, they were very huffy. Someone had gone to a lot of trouble to organise the trips.

'But why would you have a lottery prize which sends people away overseas when the whole idea of EXPO 88 is to bring people to Queensland?' we asked.

They didn't seem to see the connection, the obsession Australians have about getting out of their own country and seeing the world dominated their thinking. We persisted and finally got our way. We made the prizes several luxury holidays within Queensland. We organized one of the biggest household drops ever in Australia, which was backed up by television. Just over three million homes received the mailing and 24,000 responded giving us a response rate of 0.8%. Our target had been 0.5% and we were laughing. These advance sales we know made a huge difference in creating awareness for Expo, particularly outside of Queensland. The sweepstake offer proved to have been a very effective hook. Though, I should add, we offered a second incentive. We combined it with a 'buy two get one free' offer, a three-day pass to EXPO for the price of two days if you bought in advance.

Just a reminder that stringent laws apply to the competition and prize draw business, and you should do your homework before you plunge into the deep end. Find out precisely what the rules are and then abide by them. Many an elaborate campaign has been brought undone after all the money has been spent, simply because someone thought they could bend a rule just a little or sidle unnoticed past a regulation. It might be a pain, but it's a lot better than the major operation you'll be involved in if you break the law.

The money back guarantee. Don't think of a money-back guarantee as a clever idea: think about it as essential to your business. Your product or service *should deliver* what it promises and if it doesn't—even if the customer merely *thinks* it doesn't—then you *must* refund the money involved. Besides, if you're a fair trader the risks are very small. If you're a crook, you wouldn't be reading this book anyway. 'Money-back' not only reassures your potential customer, it's a sound reason to do business. It says clearly that you are a reliable trader and that you stand behind your merchandise.

A money-back guarantee should operate for all legitimate business, but in direct response it's absolutely essential. After all, the customer buys everything from you on trust. You have no shop front to impress, no merchandise on display, no touch, feel or see facilities, no retailer or query or question. All you have is a money-back guarantee and not to use it is a foolish oversight.

The free sample. Soap and shampoo manufacturers have been using free samples for yonks. It is almost built into the ethos of the business. People love to try new things and, therefore, free sampling is a sure-fire way to get their interest. But, with a little imagination, it can have other interesting applications outside the foot or cosmetic business.

Once I decided to try selling blankets by direct marketing, an ambitious undertaking to say the least. But the blankets were Onkaparinga, a brand with an excellent reputation in Australia, which made it a little easier. With a quality blanket, price is obviously very important. But perhaps of even more importance was the notion that, if you didn't like what you got, the idea of lugging a couple of blankets back to the post office could be a major psychological obstacle to purchasing in the first instance. So we sent a swatch of the blanket attached to the mailing. Simple enough, but now respondents could actually put the blanket between finger and thumb just the way they would in a retail outlet. The swatches, of course, came from the off-cuts on the factory floor. In the tests we ran, the mailings with swatch, increased response by 25 per cent. Within 12 months, we became the largest single buyer and seller of one-size blankets in the country. Where traditionally blankets are sold in pairs or different sizes, we sold them in triplicate and in one size. 'A pair and a spare,' said the promotion. All it takes is a little imagination!

We ran a free sample offer for a dog food and, in the television commercial, the dog picks up the phone and dials us for the free sample. It worked wonderfully and although the telephone staff at the phone bureau were coached in the correct **dogma**, they had a lot of trouble understanding the Scottish terriers who rang in (only kidding!). The free samples were sent out packed in Styro-foam bones, with a questionnaire about the customer and the family dog.

Lovely stuff! We got back a huge amount of information for the dog food manufacturer about the eating patterns and other domestic habits of just about every type of canine.

The deluxe option offer. Why not trade up? That is, get your customers to buy the deluxe edition or take an extra service instead of the standard one. A great many people can be tempted to trade up. For example, a hotel suite for $50 more than a standard bedroom? Why not, it's a second honeymoon after all. We have found that around 60 per cent of customers when the option is properly presented to them, will trade up to a deluxe option. People love to spoil themselves. The theory is simple: you've already convinced your client or customer that she should have the standard product, now why shouldn't she, as someone with discrimination, receive the best?

Michael Cansdale, the founder of The Heritage Collection in England, is a master at the art of the deluxe option. He was the king of the collectables market in the U.K. in his day and he understands the need some people have to show off. He will often simply add a line of copy, almost as an afterthought, at the bottom of an offer for, say a solid silver objet d'art, which reads: Also available in solid gold for five thousand pound sterling. This is perhaps *50 times* the price of the silver piece he may be selling. It is truly astonishing how often he will receive an order for the gold version.

Introduce a friend, or **The membership offer**. You don't need to be told that we all need to feel we belong. Belong to something special, different, exclusive, interesting, advantageous. Hence all the clubs, wine clubs, book clubs, sewing clubs, automobile clubs and art clubs. Membership makes us a little different from the rest of the crowd, a little special and, of course, it has other more direct advantages—newsletters, free samples, special offers, free gifts and early-user privileges.

What is happening is that you are building a relationship. It's called, *Relationship Marketing.* It works best in direct marketing where you have a one-to-one communication. You are putting together like-minded people and nothing makes a better database. You are not simply taking their money with a polite 'thank you', you are putting something back into their lives. It's a very solid business way to go if you have a service or merchandise that works for relationship marketing. Inviting your members to introduce new members is ideal recruiting and can often be done with quite a small incentive. As I have mentioned before, this is the most cost-effective form of recruitment possible.

The negative option offer. Not all shopping is fun. Lot's of it can be deadly boring, even to someone who appears born to shop. Pantyhose, while not being one of life's major shopping decisions is a pain in the bottom (or is it the crutch?) A hosiery manufacturer in France worked out a way around the problem by offering to automatically send six pairs of pantyhose a month in the configurations their customers desired. They called it 'Le Club.' Most women go through five or six pairs a month anyway and know precisely what their colour and size needs are. The negative option offer has a lot of potential if you'll think it out carefully and you deal in a fairly mundane necessity. The Americans call this: 'Ship 'til forbid.'

The Positive Option offer. This is the opposite to the offer above. It offers the things people like to have brought to them in a trouble-free manner on a regular basis. Your potential customer receives a rather nice initial gift, or free membership, in return for an agreement to accept one offer a month from a wide variety of merchandise they know they are likely to use. Wine clubs, book and record clubs are typical of this kind of offer. Some people have trouble choosing, or simply lack the time, and as your data-base tells you the sort of thing they prefer, you can simply select it for them. For instance, if their information shows that they like jazz, a new compact disk offer (the selection of the month) is automatically sent to them. You make the choice for them and they are billed. It is up to them to advise you by a certain date, if they *don't* want the selection of the month. In effect, what you have done is to combine a positive offer with a negative offer.

The Yes/No offer works best when some sort of relationship already exists between you and your customer. For instance, a bank might use it to issue a new plastic ATM card to existing customers:

'Your new plastic ATM card has been reserved for you. So all you have to do is to tick the 'Yes' box on this form. If you do not require an ATM card then tick the 'no' box so that we can amend our records.'

Yet another way of using the Yes/No box is by stating that you have been fortunate enough to obtain a limited number of valu-able *somethings* and are allocating them on a priority basis to past customers. If the customer does not want one of these *somethings*, would she kindly tick the 'No' box so that her specially reserved *something* can be allocated to someone else.

Incidentally, you keep the records of these 'No' customers and mail them with your next offer. You remind them in a follow-up phone call that they refused your last offer, but that they may be interested in this one. You will find that your rate of response with the 'no' customers is higher than from people who have never responded at all.

What, in effect, you've done is to keep your lines of communication open. Following up the 'no' response with your new offer by phone, gives you an opportunity to talk to the customer, remove any doubts they may have about your new offer, and help them to consider the potential purchase with more care.

In a campaign we conducted for a major Australian bank we asked older people if they wanted an automated teller machine card (ATM). If they didn't want one they were asked to tick the 'no' box. The 'lift letter', so called because it lifts response, said on the outside: 'Open this letter only if you've decided not to avail yourself of this offer.' The letter virtually said: 'Look, we don't want to insult your intelligence by trying to convince you again to take an A.T.M. card, but we would be grateful if you could take a moment and tell us where we went wrong. Of course, this approach not only causes the customer to reconsider (and therefore, increase acceptances) but it provides a huge amount of useful information. Follow-up phone calls from bank staff showed that all sorts of doubts existed in the minds of their older customers. People were afraid that they'd be confused by the technology, or that they'd be attacked while trying to operate the teller machine in the open standing on the pavement. These calls allowed the bank to change the communication and explain more fully how the card worked and why it was unlikely to lead to an attack or a robbery.

Responses to the 'lift letter' give you an excuse to follow up, by mail or phone and provides you with priceless research which can help to correct any misconceptions or poor direction in your communication, or even in your product.

It is important that you understand that causing people to think carefully about why they are saying no to your offer is infinitely preferable to having them simply consigning your brochure to the rubbish bin. If they consider their reasons for rejecting your offer for only a few seconds, you have an opportunity to help them to change their minds. You may even cause them to reconsider their decision to reject your offer and so increase the acceptances. Lift letters and 'no' boxes always increases response.

A final word about the phone follow-up to a mailing. A skilled salesperson on the phone can double your sales. The call should always open with a pleasant enquiry as to how the customer has found your products or service. It will eventually get around to trying to convince your customer to reconsider the mailing they already have, or to presenting your latest offer. The phone is an abstracted medium and always requires a fairly gentle approach, or you could end up with a clunk in your ear as your customer decides to terminate the conversation. Remember, you don't have to get out of the bath to open a letter!

It is as well to remember that all of these offers work, but that some work better for some products than others do. You will decide which combinations work best for your product or service. Every successful direct marketing company has its own special blend which they have tested, analysed and measured against their objectives. It has proved to be the approach their customers most prefer.

The statement:

'I'm going to make you an offer
you can't refuse!' works well
for the Mafia
But in direct marketing
it's you who gets blown away
when you get the offer wrong.

Chapter Eleven

★ ★ ★

The Manager's Row
&
Pulling live lobsters out of Jane Mansfield's bum.

★ ★ ★

The show-biz bug bites deep and once you are bitten its divine poison stays in the blood for life. The romance of the Hungry I Jazz Club had never quite left me. In 1970, I was persuaded by Col McClennan, a well known Sydney showman and promoter, to go into a joint venture with him to bring famous international television artists to Australia to perform on the stage. Our premise, not always a correct one, was that people would flock to the theatre to see artists they'd known on television and film.

In what at the time was a remarkable coup, a miracle really, Colin convinced Dudley Moore and the late Peter Cook who had not worked together for several years, to work together again for a special Australasian tour. They were to create a show which was called 'Behind the Fridge,' a spoof of their famous BBC show, 'Beyond the Fringe'.

Just in case the show didn't work, we decided to take it first to Canberra for a try-out. After all, if you want to bury something effectively in Australia without it having any impact whatsoever on the population at large, the nation's capital is always the ideal venue.

In fact, the show proved to be an enormous success and we

toured around the country and then onto New Zealand, where I took on the role of Road Manager. That is, as everybody's pal, keeper of the peace and general factotum.

On the New Zealand leg of the tour we appointed Phil Warren, a truly famous New Zealand impresario and ex-mayor of Auckland, as our agent. I owe a great deal to this canny and delightful man who taught me a lot about the business of show business.

It was Phil who taught me to physically count the rows of seats in the theatre and check them off against the theatre box office seat plan to ensure there was no 'manager's row.'

He explained: 'There's often a 'Manager's Row,' even in the best theatres! It's the row that's in the theatre but isn't marked on the plan; the row that exists for the benefit of the theatre manager's personal pocket.'

Albert Sheinberg always cautioned me against the scam, the lurk, the dishonest employee, the syndicate with a conspiracy to defraud management. Here it was again in a different version. It works in theatre because the takings are always reconciled against the theatre plan, which is marked with the number of seats sold. Who knows, the manager's row may have started in William Shakespeare's day.

When I lecture to marketing groups, or hire or promote someone into a position of authority, I always caution them to *look for the manager's row*. It's really not a question of going around suspecting people; life is too short for that sort of nonsense. Besides, playing detective and sniffing around people's desks and into their files and waste paper baskets, leads to morale problems among your staff. Most people are pretty honest, but there is always a manager's row in every business. You'll spot it sooner or later without having to conduct a monthly witch hunt or develop paranoia about being cheated.

The 'Behind the Fridge' New Zealand tour was nearly a month long. It was a small, tightly-knit show, just Pete and Dud, (with Peter Cook accompanied by his model girlfriend, Judy Huxtable) David Tobin, our producer and two lighting experts and electricians, and me.

A single woman accompanying a two-man show, unless the

female member is a saint, is never a good idea. There was soon a fair amount of friction between the two actors. One of my many roles was to try to keep them happy. We travelled together, ate together every night and were in each other's pockets most of the time. So, if they weren't talking to each other, the atmosphere got pretty fraught. It became my unenviable job to chivvy-up whomever was having the sulks at the time.

One evening, when we were staying in a rather ordinary Wellington Motel, Judy came into our pre-show chat pretty huffy. She wasn't too happy about the hair-dryer or shower or something. Whatever it was, it had resulted in a fight with Pete, who now sat at the table, with his arms crossed, looking decidedly disenchanted. Show time was an hour away and, in a desperate attempt to humour the two of them, I recall turning to Dud, who was wearing his angelic 'don't-get-me-involved-in-this,' expression, and recounting the story of the worst job I ever had.

I told the story of The Toronto Towel & Linen Supply Company and, in particular, the ringworm episode. Dud thought it was hilarious and, despite themselves, Pete and Judy started to laugh as well. Then Dud told the story of the worst job *he* ever had, which was collecting all the phlegm Winston Churchill spat into a bucket while he was writing The History of the English Speaking People. Peter then countered with his worst job: retrieving live lobsters out of Jayne Mansfield's bum.

There, in front of my eyes, the material was born for what was soon to become the famous '*Worst job I ever had*' recording. It became one of their best known skits and is treasured among Pete & Dud followers as quintessential Peter Cook and Dudley Moore. A wonderful piece of comedy born on a dull evening in a second-rate motel after a quarrel over a faulty hair-dryer!

The rate at which the ideas for the skit came was truly astonishing. These two highly creative minds had the scenario completed in a matter of minutes and the more excited the three of us became, the faster and wilder the stories came.

Dudley Moore was a truly wonderful guy and we became good friends and stayed in touch for a number of years after the Behind the Fridge tour. He would often talk to me about the psychoanalysis he was undergoing, and he would recount some of the difficulties of his childhood, and his very humble beginnings.

He never talked as though he was over-involved with himself, but rather as if he was slightly bemused at how life had selected a little bloke like him and dished out so much of the good and the bad at the same time.

Dud was very close to his mother, whom he described as a very ordinary, very wonderful woman. He would often get letters from her while on tour and he'd sometimes read parts of these to me and chuckle. The influence of this very ordinary, extraordinary woman was quite pronounced. I'd be watching the show that night and I'd recognise something Dud had read to me from his mother's letter earlier in the day. When this happened, Peter Cook wouldn't miss a beat, and would pick up and run with these impromptu lines as though they'd been carefully scripted and exhaustively rehearsed until the timing was perfect. They were the perfect example of Shakespeare's lines from As You Like It (Act II, Scene VII): '*All the world's a stage, and all the men and women merely players.*' Pete and Dud would bring their real lives onto the stage with a humour and spontaneity and a special genius for knowing what worked in the normal human heart.

Dud once told me the story of going for an interview for some small musical part. He was very young and rather nervous and sat in the waiting room of the casting agent's office with his hands clasped together between his legs.

'Tea or coffee?' the rather glamourous lady at the desk asked.

Dud had never tasted coffee and grew quite excited at the idea. 'Coffee, please,' he said timorously.

'White or black?' the voice came back. It had never occurred to Dud that coffee came in two distinct formats. 'Er, black, please, miss,' he replied.

When the coffee arrived a few minutes later he looked into the cup of dark liquid he'd been handed.

'You wouldn't have any milk would you, miss?' he asked.

Dud would laugh at his own innocence, but it was this very

quality of bewonderment at life that made him such a sensitive and remarkable man. He never lost his sense of humility at the fact that life had been exceptionally wonderful to this very normal and unassuming man.

Which, of course, he wasn't. Everything about Dudley Moore was talented but never phoney. Later, when Cuddly Dudley was to become a genuine sex symbol and could have the choice of many of the world's most desirable and beautiful woman, I would imagine him sitting with me and having a quiet chat, looking slightly confused as he talked about himself in the somewhat astonished way he had of seeing himself—the kid from nowhere going, well, just about everywhere, the beloved friend of kings and queens and the beautiful people. I could see him talking about it while, at the same time, never forgetting who he was, happy to be thought of as ordinary, like everyone else from a small industrial town in England.

I remember well a lovely incident when we had a Saturday afternoon to kill on tour and found ourselves playing in a small hamlet named Invercargill. It was a place even more isolated than it's namesake in Scotland. It contained a handful of people tucked into a corner of a cold, and windy coastline on the absolute bottom of New Zealand's South Island, where the next stop, except for a few pinpricks of blustery islands, is the frozen wastes of Antarctica.

To our astonishment we discovered that, 'Bedazzled', the first movie in which Pete and Dud had starred, was playing at the local cinema. The three of us promptly decided to get out of our hotel and attend the matinee session. The effect on the local population of fishermen and sheep farmers who'd come into town for the show was truly amazing. They couldn't quite believe what they were seeing as we stood in the foyer at interval munching chips. Several shook their heads and thumped their temples. But, of course, it was New Zealand, and a long way South where the population is about 100 per cent descended from the Scots (and so are all the world's most mind-your-own-business-people). Though we received a great many incredulous stares, not one person actually confronted us.

On the way home, a short walk from the picture house, we were laughing about the movie and the way the audience hadn't wanted to stare at Pete and Dud but couldn't help themselves. And how both of them acted as though absolutely nothing strange was happening, and that they were oblivious to the looks, and thought of themselves as blending with the Harris Tweed jackets and gumboots.

Peter Cook once told me that the first two minutes on stage would decide the entire evening. 'If you don't win the audience in the first two minutes, it's going to be a long, long night,' I recall him saying.

It's really the same with direct marketing. In fact, you have got precisely five seconds to attract attention to your product or service. The time it takes to sneeze and then blow your nose. Five seconds!

That's how long it takes your prospect to look at your communication and decide whether to continue, to read more, or leave the television to make a cup of tea, or return to a book, or to hang up the phone in your ear, or to turn the page of a magazine or newspaper. If you lose your potential customer in the time it takes to count moderately slowly up to five, you've lost him or her forever.

It seems so unfair. The offer may be a very good one and if the reader, viewer or listener would only take a few moments to make a cup of tea and study your message, surely they would be handsomely rewarded with the pleasure and benefits bestowed on them by your remarkable product?

I recall recently arguing that a headline one of my clients wanted on his direct response copy was too 'clever'.

'You mean our customer's are too stupid to understand it?' he remarked.

I had just demonstrated how a simple and direct headline would communicate the benefits of his product clearly. He seemed unimpressed.

'No, not stupid. The customer is your wife, or someone very much like her. She just has better things to do with her life than to read volumes of mail, or to stare wide-eyed in amazement at a headline proposition that makes a neat and very clever pun!'

I once interviewed a young English copywriter for a vacancy we had in our copy department. 'Show me the advertisement you are most proud of,' I asked.

He turned the pages of his portfolio until he came to an advertisement for a restaurant at Heathrow Airport called, The Frier, a fast food outlet that promised quick meals as you came off the plane before catching a taxi into the city. The ad, run in airline magazines, showed a businessman with a tray filled with a plate of bacon, sausage and eggs, toast and steaming cup of coffee. The tray was balanced like a circus act on the palm of one hand, while the customer glanced at a well pulled up sleeve cuff, below which a large wristwatch said 7 o'clock. The expression on his face denoted clearly that he was well pleasured with the lightning service he'd only moments before obtained from the friendly staff and, despite coming all the way from Lapland, he would still be first to arrive in the office that morning.

The headline read:

'Out of the flying plane into The Frier'

It was a rather brilliant pun, from a nation of copywriters who are famous for their puns. But it was precisely what I wasn't looking for, despite the fact that it had won several awards from his fellow advertising practitioners and had, no doubt helped to increase his salary demand beyond that paid to the British Prime Minister. He didn't get the job.

A couple of years later on a routine trip to London I happened to enter The Frier for a quick bite before going straight into a board meeting in the city. There on the wall was a framed version of the same advertisement. I asked the manager whether it had worked for them. Had they attracted more airline customers with the ad? 'Naw, he said, 'not a sausage. Won a 'ole lotta awards though, 'ead office likes it. Bloody stupid, if you ask me!'

A 'Clever Dick' approach to copywriting is bad enough, but worse still is the direct response operator who wants to do all the writing himself and simply does it badly. Initially, poor quality mail gave direct marketing a bad name. This is the sort of mail which bears no relationship to the real needs of the reader. It is usually of the over-clever kind written by an under-sensitive 22-year-old copywriter.

Then there is the kind of copywriting that extols the virtues of the product to the point where it is unrecognisable. I have a friend who's wife will only drive a Honda 500. She is convinced that it is the only car she knows how to drive and no amount of persuasion can get her into another model, or even a newer car. The Honda 500 is a model which last came onto the market about 10 years ago and, as his wife is pretty rough on her car and parks essentially by touch, she needs a new car every so often. This task of providing one in a fit condition to drive is proving more and more difficult as, increasingly, the Honda 500's 'die' and go to the great car wrecker's yard in the sky.

Recently, he had the task of finding another one. At the same time, he wrote an advertisement for his wife's Honda in the hope of making a few bucks from some callow youth looking for a first car to do up. A day or so later, his daughter excitedly pushed the morning paper over to him at breakfast: 'Dad, here's one. It sounds perfect for Mum!' The advertisement in the paper was, of course, the one he'd written for his wife's old and completely clapped-out Honda 500.

The old biblical adage, '*The truth will set you free,*' should be physically carved into the surface of every direct response copywriter's desk. Poor writing with exaggerated or self-boasting claims is inexcusable, simply because it is so easily avoided. The reader has needs and presumably you have a product which can fill some of those needs. How then is it possible to describe these benefits in such an unwieldy and gauche manner as to be offensive. It is not the customer who is stupid. We insult her intelligence far more often than we appeal to either her emotions or her intellect.

This book is about the power of one-to-one communication—the ability to talk in such a personal or meaningful way with your potential customer as to cause her to not only want your goods or services, but to anticipate the trusted relationship she will enjoy with you.

An advertisement or brochure talks to one person at a time and always in terms of that person's needs or aspirations. It never talks about you. It sets out to stimulate, interest, educate, persuade and inform for the ultimate perceived benefit of your individual customer. The perpendicular pronoun 'I' should never be used in copy, the word, 'we' very seldom and the word 'you' lots and lots.

It is essential that we talk in the customer's language and in doing so clearly denote that we understand her, or his problems, and think alike, and can help with a solution. People respond to a piece of communication with which they feel comfortable.

For instance, Australia and New Zealand are a long way away from anywhere and the letter has always been a very important means of communicating. Not so very long ago, it took a month to six weeks to get a letter to Europe by sea. The tyranny of distance has always been a factor in the way we see things. The printed word has also always been important. Australians and New Zealanders read more magazines and books per capita than any nation on earth. The reason for this is simple enough, the personalised word has always brought them comfort in a land where a simple letter a couple of decades ago would take a week to go from Sydney to Perth, and 10 days to reach New Zealand from Australia. Americans, who have had the phone on in many homes since the early thirties, became a nation of catalogue users. They could talk to the people they loved by phone so the impersonal nature of the catalogue suited them just fine.

Not so Australians or New Zealanders. When I was a kid, the phone was still something you only found in the big city and then only in affluent homes. Letters were how people communicated and you only received a telegram if someone in the family was getting married or your uncle Percy had died in Oodnadatta.

Perhaps this explains why Australians didn't take quickly to the impersonal ways of the catalogue, and much preferred the individual brochure and covering letter to do mail-order business. We often send 20 different brochures in one envelope when it would seem obvious to combine all the information into one neat little catalogue. We'd do it in a flash if we thought it would work! The

Australian and New Zealand customer took a long time to feel comfortable with a catalogue probably because they had never been trained to use one.

I have witnessed more disasters in catalogues here in Australia than in any other branch of direct marketing. Catalogues, in general, have not worked until recently, but have always been strong in North America and Europe. Myer Direct, a huge retail organisation, has spent many millions of dollars developing a catalogue which is the first to survive three years. Perhaps it will continue to grow to their target of $200 million, but it takes a lot of pioneering dollars to change the buying habits of a nation which likes the personal solicitation in the selling process. Only since 1992 has there been any real indication that the catalogue might be here to stay.

Even when it is successful on a cost-per-order basis, never forget that nothing in the printed word works better than a personally-addressed letter or brochure in a single envelope. It's the age-old format of a letter, a letter from a friend. It is *always* a question of the cost of a response and what you have set out to achieve in your relationship with the customer.

It all comes back to what you are trying to say and to whom you are trying to say it and, then, how to most effectively win that person to your offer. We are, of course, talking about co-operation and not coercion, about relationships and not confrontation, about romance and not ambush. Making your customers feel comfortable in your commercial presence is absolutely essential in effective relationship marketing. And the most important element in this personal communications mix is reassurance. Direct marketing demands trust of a very high calibre. Trust is something you have to write into your copy and show outwardly.

If you have been in business for 20 years, then say so in a line printed on your stationary, or in a prominent position on your brochure. If you are a member of the national direct marketing association, use their logo or seal and spell it out where your customer can see it.

Using an anonymous post office box is most inadvisable. People want to know how to get to you and where you are. Some potential customers see it as a device to hide your identity. If you are in a small building and are the major tenant, try to get the naming rights. 'The Bond International House, Established 1972,' has a nice secure feeling to it. Your full business address, telephone and facsimile, stated clearly, are all meaningful credentials. If the office building is impressive, put a small picture of it somewhere in your brochure. It all adds up to trust.

After all, your customer may never have heard of you, and would almost certainly never have seen your premises or talked with a staff member over the counter. Apprehension and misgiving must be quickly replaced by familiarity and trust if you are to succeed in the business of direct marketing. But, remember, showing a picture of the factory is done only to reassure your customer and not to talk about yourself in a boastful manner.

Establishing a climate of trust is the first task of your copy. How would you feel if you looked up from your lounge to see a masked man waving a fully automatic toothpaste dispenser in front of your face and shouting that your teeth are practically green and need the immediate and just-in-the-nick-of-time attention of Clean 'n Gleam, the toothpaste that turns a fetid, evil-smelling swamp (your mouth) into a fresh snowscape (your mouth one brushing later)? If I appear to exaggerate, it is only to make my point, because confronting the customer is what a great many direct marketers do in their headlines and copy.

Communicating with the public by using direct marketing methods, means that *you are going to have to interrupt their lives.* This interruption is seldom invited and may well be unwelcome. How then do you get away with it? It must, of necessity, be intrusive, and so it really is up to you to make the experience a pleasant one. You must make it the intrusion of a young woman's smiling approach and not that of a six foot, 18-stone, scar-faced thug cracking his knuckles in your face. Your approach must be seen as a rewarding experience designed to spark a chord of interest in your potential customer or, if not, elicit a polite refusal.

The very basis of direct marketing communication is to interrupt in a responsive way. Image advertising, as opposed to retail or direct response advertising, is usually designed to be pretty passive. It may delight, amuse, explain and impress with images as soft as a mouse, while the technique for direct marketing must be as hard as diamonds. That is, hard but very valuable and desirable. The very definition of direct marketing is that it is marketing that is direct and unequivocal; you are interrupting someone's life in order to elicit a response. While it must be forceful, it doesn't have to be loud and it certainly doesn't have to be ugly.

In fact, the raucous and ugly days of direct marketing have done a great deal to chase customers away. Headlines which screamed at you and were backed up with star bursts and flashes and three dimensional prices zooming towards you in a superman comet-flash, are tired and forced. While they may still have some application in certain kinds of offers they should largely be put to one side. The words, '**you**', '**free**', '**now**,' etc. are still very powerful. But the way they have been used is old-fashioned and hardly belongs to the messages good direct marketing is fashioning today.

Much more important is the need to construct the right tone of voice for your target audience. Business people (consumers behind desks) respond the same way as Reader's Digest readers, but the tone of voice used is usually exactly the opposite.

The brashness, and with it the crassness, that typified so much of yesterday's direct marketing creative communications, has been shown to alienate a large proportion of potential customers. As well, it has discouraged the big brand owners, who found both the image and the construction of the direct marketing message totally incompatible with the impression they wanted their customers to have of their own products or services.

Direct marketing itself had an image of being down-market, crude, undesirable and tainted. It's emphasis on the hard-sell plunder of the customer's mind had no style, grace, rhyme or reason. This lack of subtlety, head-banging, steel toe-capped approach, also kept the good writers, the talented copywriters and art directors the industry so desperately needs, out of the business.

The really successful direct marketer today is perhaps one tenth part salesperson, and the rest is behavioural psychologist. What such people are doing is carefully analysing the potential behaviour of prospects and what the outcome is most likely to be to the stimulus they have put out. While humans are complex, and prediction is still a science quite often confounded, this approach is far more likely to succeed than trying to break the door down with your shoulder. Nobody ever shouted a door open and found a willing respondent inside unless they carried a warning that the roof was on fire. If you want to influence anyone, and you are not in a position to exert force, then you can only obtain a response by offering them a stimulus.

When you are creating a communication you are, in effect, wooing the intended partner in that dialogue. You infer that getting to know you will greatly benefit the reader, listener or viewer. The creation of this phantom lover or customer is essential. You have to imagine them seated next to you, asking questions, raising objections ('But we hardly know each other?'), looking bemused, smiling or pouting, thoughtful or pensive, or all of these things. Always answer questions in the order in which your prospect would logically ask them, and then predict how they will behave with the answer you give them.

Receiving a letter is highly indicative of how people behave. The work of Dr. Siegfried Vogele, Managing Director of the Institute of Direct Marketing in Munich, using eye cameras which track the movement of the human eye, show that when someone reads a letter they first look at the letterhead or address and then turn to the salutation. (They simply cannot resist their own name). Then they scan quickly down the right hand side of the page and note the signature and the postscript, if there is one. Then they return to the beginning and commence to read if they are interested enough to do so. That is, if they are *stimulated* sufficiently to respond.

Knowing this, we can design a direct marketing letter to take advantage of the natural flow of the eye. Here is a fairly simple example. Note the difference between a sentence beginning with:

Dear Ian,

   Buying our product today will make you eligible for a prize draw to win a cruise for two on the QE2.

or a sentence which begins:

Dear Ian,

   You and your friend will cruise the Pacific on the QE2 if you win the first prize in our exclusive customer draw.

Again, note the difference between a postscript at the very end of the letter which reads:

PS. Send the coupon in now while this offer lasts!!

or this approach:

PS. You could be spending Christmas day on the QE2, so send in your coupon today!

The essential difference between the two approaches is, in each instance, that the second is centred on the prospect and the benefit to her or him. It is fashioned in the form of a *stimulus* and so it is made a lot easier for your prospect to respond with excitement. '*You and your friend*' means laughter and fun and dancing the night away under a tropical sky, as well as a whole heap of other things the imagination might instantly conjure up. Also the epicentre of the offer in the first sentence is based firmly on the product ... '*Buying this product will ...*'

   Knowing how the human eye scans a letter we can now position the *stimulus,* or to use jargon, the *primary prospect-focused statement,* where it can do the most good.

Working with brochures and keeping in mind that we hope to predict and influence the behaviour of the prospect, the cover becomes vitally important and *must* be designed with the singular intention of getting your prospect inside; it's the welcome mat outside the front door and if it isn't, then it should be at the very least the main purpose of the cover. Any other message on it is secondary. The brochure cover is the door made of candy in Hansel & Gretel—so irresistible that your prospect simply has to take a peek inside to see what's coming next. How you go about this is in every way conditioned by what you know about your prospect. If she is a lady over 50 and a possible collector, it could be the picture of a smiling and very beautiful doll with the words: '*Can you remember when you were only five-years-old?*' If it's a lawyer, it is more likely to be a statement on an expensive looking cream paper which reads in an elegant legal typeface: '*Inside is a computer disk offer that will enable you to summarise, in no more than 50 words, every Workers Compensation case since Federation!*' In either instance, the need to open the cover is irresistible.

Having involved your prospect sufficiently for them to open the brochure, you now have to determine how next you wish them to behave. Your next step is to line up all the elements—the photographs, copy pointers, sub-heads and illustrations—to take the reader easily and naturally to the order coupon or to the phone number. What you are resisting with all your might is that, having concluded reading your copy, or having gone some way into it, your prospect consigns the brochure to the bin. The wastepaper basket is your natural sworn enemy and to remind yourself of this while you are preparing copy you should give it a good kick on several occasions.

What all this means is that the *first impression you make is always the most important one.* Research quite clearly shows that people buy things from people they like and trust. That's why sales people are selected for their personalities, for their charm and friendliness. This is no less true of the printed medium. If you like and enjoy an author, you will buy his or her books without inquiring as to what the story is all about. Printed information is no different although, in a brochure or letter, you probably have to start from scratch almost every time. You simply want your reader to like you, to like what you're saying, to end up feeling stimulated by you and be responsive to your offer.

In the list of rules The Reader's Digest uses to keep their copy stimulating for their readers they have this adage:

*Ten words about **me** is infinitely boring to **you**, a thousand words about **you** is infinitely fascinating to **you**!*

The language should also change as you think through the way the customer herself would talk, rather than the way you would formally present your offer. You will discover different words that work on a more personal basis. What you are really doing is moving the language from being feature-orientated (which is about us) to benefit-orientated, which is about the customer. Here are some typical conversions:

Features:	Benefits:
Me, we, us	You
Seller	customer
Sale	relationship
Buy	own
Apply	accept
Cost	value
Price	worth

What the product is, is always boring; what the product does for you is always interesting. Humans always think in terms of themselves. It isn't selfish, it's how we survive and always have done. In aircraft, when they tell you how the oxygen mask will fall into your lap from the ceiling should it become necessary, they always say: '*In the event of a child, always place your own oxygen mask on before attending to your child.*' The point is, if we don't look after ourselves first we may not be in a position to help others. Your job is *always* to talk about your prospect and how your product or service will greatly enhance their status in life. There are no exceptions to this rule in direct marketing.

All this is, of course, pretty much a matter of commonsense. Try using this personal-benefit technique in your everyday dialogue when you are trying to influence someone whether to do or buy something. It's the basis of most sales training programs but we tend to forget this. It is a good idea to be meticulous about the things you say to customers and you should think very carefully about their 'silent questions,' which must be anticipated and answered in your copy. Whether you write copy or leave it to someone else, it is a good idea to attempt to write it yourself. It's a great discipline for getting the marketing right, as long as you don't decide that you can do it better than a professional, which is very seldom the case.

Here are a few important things you ought to be aware of:

The headline is the power and the glory. Almost everything begins with a headline. '*In the beginning, God created the heavens and the earth,*' is a great headline. You immediately want to know more. The headline drives the offer and it is the stimulus that gets your reader to want to know more.

A good headline works on the AIDA principle—an acronym about which you could write an entire book. Effective direct marketing copy must have this discipline and if the AIDA principle can't be contained entirely in your headline, without making it seem clumsy or contrived, it must operate throughout your body copy. We call it AIDA because, like the opera of the same name, it is the only way to write direct marketing copy that positively sings.

A is for **attention** which must be gained
I is for **interest** which must be raised
D is for **desire** which must be created
A is for **action** which must be incited

A headline should be read and understood in five seconds. Your reader owes you nothing, no loyalty, duty or sympathy. When you introduce yourself to him or her you meet as strangers. The first eye contact and handshake will determine whether you get any further in the relationship. It has to be incisive, positive, interesting and fast. The same is true of any headline, except that the prospect is not captive. The introduction is not forced upon your prospect and she can relinquish your outstretched hand without feeling in the least embarrassed about doing so.

An almost foolproof way to get anyone's attention is to make an impact on them by dramatising something that relates to their lives. Again, it's not very different to an introduction:

'I can't tell you how very much I have been looking forward to meeting you!'

There would be very few people who could resist such an opening statement providing you are respectable in appearance and it is made with politeness and warmth.

In your headline you want your reader to say just as they would with the introduction to a very pleasant looking stranger: *'That's me! He wants to like me? He knows something about me. I want to know what he knows. Something good may come of this! I very much like the look of this person.'* People are people because of other people.

One of the best known direct-response advertisements ever written was by the famous American copywriter named John Caples. More than half a century ago he wrote a full page newspaper ad for piano lessons by correspondence. The headline read:

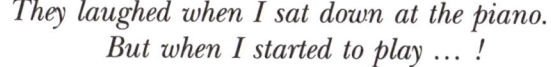

They laughed when I sat down at the piano.
But when I started to play … !

John Capel's famous ad, selling piano courses by correspondence, claimed to be the most successful direct response space advertising ever.

It's all there in one deceptively simple headline. **Attention**, because
we immediately identify with the situation. We have all wanted to
surprise someone with our talent when they thought us to be ordinary. **Interest**, because we immediately want to know more. How did
this situation come about? how is it resolved? **Desire**, perhaps we too
could achieve mastery of the piano and become popular and in
demand. **Action**, because all I have to do to change my life is to fill
in the coupon at the bottom left of the page.

Now look at the copy as it takes you through the process with
a number of sub-heads:

- Then I started to play
- A complete triumph
- How I learned to play without a teacher
- Play any instrument
- Send for our free booklet and demonstration lesson

All this worked in an advertisement written over half a century
ago, and it's as new as tomorrow simply because situations may
change but people don't. This same approach is often copied and
it still works. I saw a version of it recently in a business magazine
and called the marketer. He assured me that the advertisement
worked very well with senior business people who felt themselves
alienated by the technology of the desk-top computer and intimidated by the younger executives who could use one. Computer-
phobia in executives over 40 is very common and the headline
below worked extremely well for a marketer advertising a computer training seminar for senior executives.

'They laughed when I sat down to use a microcomputer.'

A similar idea worked brilliantly and consistently for Phillips language courses:

'No one believed I could speak French until we got to Paris.'

This type of headline evolves from knowing your prospect very well and finely judging their needs. If it's badly written or too clever, it can result in making your prospect seem stupid, or be forced to recognise a disadvantage they have been hiding from a hostile world, in which event they will not accept your offer to eliminate it. Puns and trick meanings and double entendre should be avoided; even when they are understood, which is seldom enough, they mostly irritate in headlines.

Headlines that work often have the ability to capture the reader's imagination. A very successful advertisement for Greenpeace showed a pleasant picture of a dolphin family frolicking in the waves:

'You can help save lots of other families with a $50 family subscription to Greenpeace.'

Here is a headline in the classic 'How to' idiom. This one is famous in certain kinds of men's magazines all over the world and has been running unchanged for 20 years.

How to pick up girls
A scientifically proven method

This headline, of course, offers a promise every pimply-faced adolescent going through the mumble-and-grunt stage of his adulthood will find almost impossible to resist. His hormones are screaming for action, while at the same time his brain turns to jelly every time he comes within 10 metres of a member of the opposite sex. The scientifically-proven method tells him this paralysis will be conquered by the miracle of science—*Pheremones*. This is the excretion of certain animals which, when rubbed on by the male sends women crazy. Some promise: so simple; so stupid; so successful.

Nearly 200 years ago Samuel Johnson said: *Promise, sheer promise, is the soul of the advertisement.* Nothing much has happened since to contradict him.

I recall conducting the very first mail-order offer inserted with the monthly statement for Diners Club in 1975. The item involved was a carry-on valet pack, which held a suit and a couple of shirts, with a place for socks etc and a wet bag for toiletries. The whole get-together was ideal for the busy executive away for a single night. It would have been tempting to write a headline which told the prospect all this. Instead, we wrote:

'You'll never have to wait at airports again.'

The single benefit of never having to hang around the baggage carousel after a flight was far greater than a description of the bag itself, which we later outlined in the copy and illustration. This particular offer was the first 'syndication' product ever in Australia and it pulled a staggering 11.6 per cent response! Syndication is where you make an arrangement, usually with a credit card company, to offer their members a product endorsed by them and using their credit card facility. You've probably seen one: 'A special offer only to Diners Club members.' The combination can be highly effective. I have on occasions been credited with inventing syndication. This is not true, it has been around the U.S.A. for at least 10 years, though I was the first to bring it into Australia.

Head-lining the price factor is always a tempting way to go, but it is often badly done, resulting in a screamer which looks and feels cheap. A price benefit in the headline should be done with care and is best contained within a promise. A price headline should always be more than just about price. Here is an excellent example used by a very successful UK mail-order company:

**Real hand-worked leather. Italian combination locks.
Open or shut, this case is worth over £60. Our price, £34.95.**

This advertisement sold 12,000 suitcases, which was, at the time a mail-order record for this kind of merchandise. When you look at it, it is not very clever. But it does add promise to price—the assurance that the article is first rate despite being offered at almost half price.

The value of putting a price into the headline raises another good headline-writing technique—the use of numbers. Numbers can add to the power of words if you know how to use them correctly. Most humans like to quantify things and feel secure once they know the numbers involved in almost any proposition they need to evaluate. We all like to measure things in a way we can relate to them as I've mentioned previously. Hence, 'Save $10 works better than, 10 per cent off.'

Here are two headlines, one with and one without numbers. Both are well constructed and talk about recycling cans. Both appeared below a picture of a mountain of aluminium cans.

At $200 a tonne, some solid waste should not be wasted
Some solid waste is too valuable to be wasted

The first advertisement proved far more effective than the second because the reader, using imagination, could start to put a value on the tin-can mountain instead of seeing it as an unspecified pile.

It's always good to be specific. It usually tells your prospect that you know what you're talking about, that you've measured the results and your comparisons are valid. An example:

51 per cent of Australians prefer Diet Pepsi.
Most people prefer Diet Pepsi.

The first headline works a great deal harder than the second. It also is more believable and certainly more actionable.

Panadol pain-killing tablets are safety-sealed three ways against child tampering.

Disprin pain-killing tablets are sealed against child tampering.

Both the headlines above work but the 'three ways' qualification just works a fraction harder. And in the few seconds it takes to make a decision to buy, a busy mother with children is likely to grab for the Panadol.

Remember, a headline is not an isolated incident on the page. What it says has to be explained out in the copy. The *three ways* the Panadol is safety sealed must be shown in an illustration or further elaborated in the body copy. Sustaining the interest and elaborating the message contained within the headline is critical in well-written copy. The headline is the five-second hook, the copy that follows is the coat you're going to hang on it.

Let me elaborate the principles within the AIDA formula for you when writing a headline. These are the things to keep in mind:

- A headline should contain news: *good news for the reader.*
- Appeal to people's self-interest: '*What's in it for me?*'
- Write in the language of the reader: *Don't use jargon.*
- Use a benefit in the headline: *Promise is the soul ...*
- Use words that have the power to move, such as: *you, new, free, now, save, great, amazing, quick, simple, secret, warning, breakthrough, latest, news.*
- Ideally, a headline should be no more than 14 words, but long headlines that say something are always better than short ones that say nothing. *Don't be vague, specify.*
- Headlines should be read and understood in 5 seconds: *Don't be a smart-arse.*

Gaining attention and understanding in the first five seconds is just as valid in a direct marketing television commercial or in the first paragraph of a letter, or even in the first five seconds of a phone solicitation.

Good copy, even great copy, will not rescue a bad headline. Work until you have a headline that's right, even if it takes you days. Time spent on a good headline is money in the bank. A good headline is three quarters of the work in motivating your prospect. Quite obviously, if they are not attracted to the headline the copy will not be read.

But this doesn't mean the copy that follows should not be taken very seriously. If the body of the message lets down the head, then nothing happens. The body copy has to drive the offer home.

Here is a basic rule for writing good copy.

One of the most common mistakes in writing copy is to tell people what they already know. Writers seem to think that they need to warm up the reader by telling him or her stuff with which they are already familiar. Good copy starts always with news, stuff that the reader does not generally know, and then takes the prospect on a journey of discovery. As a rule, always eliminate the first two paragraphs of your copy after you've written it and see whether it still stands up, or, with the addition of a single new sentence, can be made to work. If you do this as a matter of discipline you will be amazed at how often you have improved your copy out of sight.

Next, reduce your copy by 50 per cent and see whether you have taken away anything of critical importance to the reader's ability to evaluate and act upon your offer. The chances are that you haven't. Keeping copy sweet doesn't mean it has to be short, but the path to sweetness is usually in the elimination, refinement and culling of worthless words.

In the process of writing your copy, think through what your prospect is feeling. Very few things are wrought by logic alone, People have feelings and emotions as well as logic and common-sense. Use all these very human attributes. Copy that works always reflects the writer's understanding of the reader's behaviour, desires, habits and even fantasies. Lead your reader through a proposition which, whether logical or emotional, is clearly presented and helpful to read and which will not be critical of the reader's behaviour, or confuse or irritate.

People new to writing copy often get worried that they can't effectively judge the emotional or intellectual dispositions of their typical target audience reader. How can a 22-year-old female writer, who doesn't know a rose from a daisy, understand a 65-year-old male who likes to potter in the garden? You can grasp the essence of behaviour in humans by understanding two simple concepts.

People are: **Selective** and **Subjective**.

What this means is that people increasingly select for themselves what they want to see, hear or read. And they will remember and interpret the information they gather in their own particular way. This is known in behavioural science as **Selective Perception**.

1. **The selective process**. A pick-pocket working among a crowd of saints will see only their pockets and not their halos. People habitually choose to see only what they wish to see. A typical example is three witnesses of the same accident standing in the same spot. While they will all agree that the accident happened, they will differ widely in the details. The assassination of John F. Kennedy is a classic example of this. Interestingly, it is precisely the detail differences in the witnesses stories which helps to convince a jury that a witness is being truthful. A number of witnesses brought into court who tell, in absolute detail, the same story, is a sure indication that they have been collectively rehearsed.

A very good commercial example of selectivity occurred in a Benetton poster which ran in a multi-racial society. It showed two little girls smiling, the one black and the other white. Some black consumer groups became outraged by the poster and claimed that the pigtails the black child wore looked like horns, and that she was being depicted as the devil, whereas the soft blonde curls of the white child made her out to be an angel. When the picture was researched this viewpoint persisted among some black groups, but not once when shown to groups of whites. When the poster was changed to show the same children, but this time both wore pigtails, not a single black group saw horns on either child.

People bring their innermost emotions to bear on everything they see and so they become selective in their perceptions. If you know the culture you will already be half-way to understanding the selectivity of your prospect. If you belong to the same culture, it's not a bad idea to examine your own selective perceptions to see if they match those of your prospect in a broad sense, if not in the details. The chances are that they do.

You may not know anything about gardening. But you will know that, in your grandfather's day, gardening was a very important idea and meant a lot of things to do with survival, love of land, remaining close to the soil, lack of pretension, a sense of nature's bounty, satisfaction, religious understanding or faith, sharing and stress release. Not a bad bunch of assumptions for a start. Understanding even this much about your target audience, will cause you to write better copy for a gardening offer.

2. **The subjective processes**. We each have our own ways of looking at the world. In combination, we call this our culture. Cultural differences are the only real differences between people and they often dictate how we subjectively view the world around us. The attitude to the female form is always a good way to examine a culture. What happens to women in a society will tell you a great deal about it. Americans, in magazines such as Penthouse and Playboy, have taken the vicarious view of the female form to it's ultimate limit and this is also reflected in their movies. We call this a permissive society and equate it with the freedom to choose. While this has an up-side it also has a down-side. America, with its permission for any citizen to carry arms, is one of the most violent societies on earth. But you shouldn't simply look at this set of subjective criteria. There is a lot in U.S. society which contradicts this notion. There are more people who profess to be Christians in America than in any other society. For instance, of about 400 major television networks in America, some 147 are owned by right-wing Christian organisations. Looking at America from this perspective makes it one of the most conservative cultures in the world, where nudity, homosexuality and abortion is mainly against the law. In one or two States, an advertisement cannot show a man and a woman in bed together unless their wedding rings are clearly visible.

The point I'm making is that while there may be quite clear cultural indications that stamp a society, the behaviour within it can vary widely and is always subjective. You have to be aware of this subjectivity, or put into plainer terms, you have to know where your customer is coming from and to use this information to communicate with him or her.

It is not your job to change the subjective viewpoint of your readers, listeners or viewers. You have to start where they are at the moment of contact, and try to move them to where you want them to be. This is never done by telling them they are wrong, stupid or misguided, and that you can help them to change their ways. You have to communicate in terms of their subjectivity, their world. You have to get inside their heads.

Let me tell you the story of how I came to launch the Ralph Lauren Polo brand in Australia.

I had always admired the Polo brand, which was started in New York by a good Jewish boy named Ralph Lipshitz. He started out designing ties that were a little different. While Ralph Lauren was not his name, fashion under his adopted name came to represent old money and true conservatism of the sort young upwardly-mobile achievers thought highly desirable. The look conjured up images of old leather chairs, the kind you found in English clubs, country breeding, the horsey set, fox and hounds, picnic races. It was casual to the point of being snobbish but not unattainable, though still decidedly upmarket. It was a look you could have which said 'money' and a taste which was better than your own. It also came in both men's and women's fashions, so that it became a dual look: the Ralph Lauren duo statement.

This was extremely clever and I admired the marketing behind it immensely. I felt that the Polo brand would be enormously popular in Australia. Country Road had tried to emulate Polo for years. My friend and mentor Murray Raphel owned a menswear shop in Atlantic City and his way into the direct marketing hall of fame was through this retail shop. Murray had stocked the Polo brand for nearly 20 years. In fact, he was the only retailer in Atlantic City with the privilege. For, indeed, it was a privilege. The Polo brand is not given lightly to any retailer.

I started checking around the major upmarket stores in Australia to discover that they'd all tried unsuccessfully to obtain the Polo licence, including this country's leading upmarket retailer, David Jones, which had made several attempts to get the licence and which would have seemed ideally qualified to carry the Polo name in their range. Their executives had even, on one occasion, flown to Hong Kong in the hope of meeting the elusive Ralph Lauren but without success.

I asked Murray if he could try and get me an appointment with the Polo people in New York and he worked for nearly a year without any success. Murray was one of their oldest and most respected retailers, but he could do nothing for me. They simply claimed that they were too busy to consider opening in Australia, and, anyhow, a small turn-over country like Australia was well down their list of priorities.

Murray is a good friend and nothing if not tenacious. He finally persuaded them that they owed him a minute for each year he had traded with them to see his friend. Finally, after five years, I was given a 20-minute appointment in New York. Murray agreed to fly up and meet me to hold my hand.

I was going to get only one crack at the prospect and so I did all the things we talk about in this book. I visualised the prospect until I was pretty sure I could get into the head of the person to whom I was trying to sell. It's never easy to put aside your own ego and get the needs of your prospect firmly implanted into your own head. By the time the appointment came up, I thought that, finally, I was ready to meet with Edwin Lewis, executive vice president and the number three honcho in the Polo empire. 'Find out what's important to him,' I kept telling myself, 'forget your own needs, what does he need?'

From the moment I entered his office, it was obvious that Mr Edwin Lewis's needs were different to mine. What he definitely didn't need was some person from Australia, (or was it Austria?), pinching 20 minutes from his day. It was pretty obvious that the only thing on his agenda was to terminate my 20 minutes in 10 minutes. He immediately started to lecture me on how busy his organisation was and how time-wasting the various proposals from my country had been. Working himself up to a sort of executive dismissal, he opened a drawer in a filing cabinet and produced a crammed file at least six inches thick.

'Putz, that's what this is, words, thousands of words', (he pronounced it 'whoids.') I ain't got that kind of time, we're too busy. You understand?'

I knew quite suddenly what I had to say to him.

'Look Mr Edwin, you don't know who I am, but I've got all my credentials on a single sheet of paper, not too many words, which you can check out later. I'm also Murray's friend and you know him. I really don't even know whether I'm the right man for you in Australia … '

He stopped in his tracks and gave me a surprised look, 'What do you mean, *you* don't know, you don't know then who's gonna know?' He looked at Murray and jerked his shoulders.

'Well, what I know I can do, possibly better than anyone you'll ever find, is solve all this hassle you're having with enquiries from Australia. You give me that file and I'll look after it for you. On my way out, I'll give your secretary my business card and anyone who calls you from Australia, you can have her refer them to me. You never have to talk to anyone about Australia again. I'll write a full report and give you a summary of every person who calls, and after a year or two, when you feel you might be ready to do Australia, I'll find you the right people or the right group of people to do it, which may or may not include me.'

It was a promise, a benefit and a wonderful convenience all wrapped into one. I had solved his problem which, I guess, he found irresistible.

'He okay, Murray?' he asked Murray Raphel, who nodded. 'You got it,' he said, handing me the file.

'You've saved five minutes,' I said taking it.

I did exactly as I promised I would do. I let it be known in Australia that I was looking for a partner or partners and with the help, advice and many introductions from Eve Harman, the publisher of Vogue Magazine and Vogue Living, had many discussions with potential partners. This went on for two years, during which time I had no written agreement with the Polo people, though they honoured their agreement with me to the letter. All the people who approached them were referred to me.

On just two days notice, two and a bit years after we'd last met, Edwin Lewis arrived in Australia and urged me to put a group together. Polo are people, people and they prefer the right people to the right experience, they prefer good entrepreneurs, rather than good garment trade people or retailers who have fixed ideas about how to sell clothes.

I put together a syndicate consisting of Oroton, Ganton who are Australia's best shirtmakers, and myself. We formed a partnership named, Polo Ralph Lauren Australia, which has been a highly successful enterprise and continues to be so.

When you are making a sale, or marketing a product it is *always* the customer's agenda that is important and never your own. Take care of their needs and you automatically achieve your own ends. If I hadn't known enough to volunteer to solve Edwin Lewis's problem, he would not have given me the file and I would never have obtained the licence for Polo in Australia.

Don't use jargon. The really powerful words in this world are simple. This is because your reader understands them, relates to them and usually chooses to use them.

Here are some *simple* examples: use (not utilise); write (not correspond); help (not facilitate); so (not consequently); due (not attributable).

There are dozens of others, but the general rule is to use the word with the least number of syllables. This is not because people are stupid, but because they are busy and good-selling copy always has the common touch—unless it is making an offer to people who would expect you to use a more sophisticated nomenclature.

Sentences should, as a general rule, be no more than 16 words. Paragraphs should contain only one idea. The moment you change the subject, or write of some other aspect of your product, you must start a new paragraph. The ideal paragraph in normal 12pt type should be no thicker on the page than the tip of your index finger.

Keep it simple. The KIS principle is very important, yet writers often like to show off with words and constructions which people find difficult to understand. You can render even the most elegant and simple sentences to absolute rubbish by using the wrong words.

George Orwell, the great English writer, once demonstrated this with a quote out of the book of Ecclesiastes, which is one of the most beautiful passages in the English language. First the original version from the St James version of the Bible:

'I returned and saw under the sun, that the race is not to the swift, nor the battle to the strong, neither yet bread to the wise, nor yet riches to men of understanding, nor yet favour to men of skill; but time and chance happeneth to them all.'

Now to Orwell's version put into the contemporary jargon of so called sophisticated English:

'Objective consideration of contemporary phenomena compel the conclusion that success or failure in competitive activities exhibits no tendency to be commensurate with innate capacity, but that a considerable element of the unpredictable must invariably be taken into account.'

It is not entirely unfair to say that a great many copywriters aim towards the Orwellian version in an attempt to be clever and erudite. What in effect they are writing is unreadable nonsense. Not that the original Biblical version sings with the voice of an angel. Keep it simple and you will harvest much; complicate your copy and the seed you sow will prove to be barren.

Create a picture in the mind. We all love to hear stories and every product has a story which, if told in terms of the selectivity and subjectivity of your customer, will be seen as his or her own. *'They're singing my song! They're telling my story!'* We identify more strongly through stories than in any other way. Creating pictures in the mind is what copy-writing is all about. Your customer must, in her imagination, see, touch, smell and feel the stimulus you are feeding her with your words. *'Can you remember when ...'* is not a bad way to begin a piece of copy.

Keep it crisp. Incite your reader to action with your words, keep them crisp and sharp and not long and laborious. Even short descriptions can often be 'brightened' . *'Wax bright floors'* is a lot better than, *'floors are brightened by wax.'* *'Want to know more? Call me now.'* is a lot crisper than, *'I may be contacted by telephone should you require further information.'*
    Of course there are differences in tone. If you are writing to a

teenager you would adopt a different approach to the one you would use if you were writing to a lawyer. In neither case should you be stuffy or laborious, but you will want to use the appropriate tone of address. You will have to make this decision yourself but, if having completed your copy, you don't clearly understand what you are saying, then start again from the beginning. Though some people might argue with you, lawyers and teenagers are human too. Remember, you are never going to have the chance to tell your reader what in fact you *really* meant to say.

The picture. If the picture you construct to use with your copy doesn't clearly tell a story then don't bother to put one in. Pictures are the mirrors into your customer's heart. They show them that you understand them, care about them, have high hopes for them and enjoy them. You should always put your customer into the picture, that way the reader knows the copy he or she is about to read is about him or her.

'More people pictures!' is an almost constant instruction to our creative people. People are people through other people. People like to look at people, particularly when the people in the picture could damn nearly be themselves, or a slightly more glamourous version of themselves, anyway. They like to see people doing something with which they can identify, or being somewhere they would like to go. But don't use a beautiful 17-year-old model to show off a set of earrings, necklace and bracelet you know is likely to appeal to a 55-year-old doctor's wife. Pictures that sell are all about relating by understanding your reader's aspirations, identifying with their needs and predicting their most likely behaviour.

Don't exaggerate in your pictures. Don't make the situations larger than they are in real life. The brand of toilet paper your wife chooses is not one of life's major decisions, yet the pictures depicting it often treat it as though it is. One of my favourite advertisements for income protection in case of illness has a headline which reads:

'At night alone in your hospital bed you can almost hear the sound of the bills piling up at home.'

Ouch! But the headline was made even more powerful by showing a man in bed with just the right degree of pained expression. This particular advertisement, created by Mel Gottleib, the Canadian consultant for the A.P.A., was enormously successful. A competitive insurance company did a similiar ad and while the headline remained similar, the picture showed a man in intensive care with tubes protruding everywhere and a look of near terminal pain on his face. The ad was a hopeless flop for two very sound reasons. Firstly, a man in that much pain is concentrating hard on staying alive and is unlikely to be thinking about bills mounting up back at his home. Secondly, the picture just put people off. Horrific situations induce inertia in the reader. Do not exaggerate, always put your customer into a picture with which he or she can easily identify. People are not stupid and they don't go about life grinning like idiots, and running through fields of daffodils in slow motion, because they wipe their bums with a certain brand of toilet paper.

Clearly show the product. In direct marketing, it is essential to clearly show the product and to do so in some detail. If you're going to show it being used by your target audience then show it at closer range somewhere else. The reader has no reference point other than the picture you show them. And, remember, they know all about trick camera shots and retouching and other product-glamourising techniques.

If you're selling a suitcase, or a valet pack, then show the stitching in close-up to impress the reader with its strength. Similarly, if you were selling a set of copper pans, you would show a close-up of the copper rivets that hold the handle to the pot so that your prospect sees that the pot is well made in the traditional way. God is always in the details.

When we photograph a doll, we might take up to 50 different shots, moving the doll's head or the camera position, sometimes only fractionally, after each shot. The idea is to show the doll's personality to its very best effect . There is always one shot that does this and that's the one you are after.

Feel is important. In many products the way it feels is important. You will recall the swatch of blanket we sent with our mailing for Onkaparinga Blankets. Because you can't always do this, it is important to show the fluffy nature of the product, or the depth of pile of the carpet, or the softness of the teddy bear, with an extreme close-up shot. It even helps to show the tips of the fingers buried in the pile, or fluff, or whatever, so that people can sense the softness by imagining their own hands doing the same thing.

The importance of colour. There are two aspects to colour. Full-colour photography works best in brochures and you should use it at every opportunity. The other colour consideration is for the product itself. Don't offer your product in a dozen glorious colours unless this is part of the overall selling proposition and essential to the purchase, such as in a set of lipsticks. Choose instead only the basic colours, deciding which one you think will be the most popular or readily obtainable, and feature this in your advertisement. If you offer more than three or four colours, you will not get any more orders from the wider variety. You will simply spread the six or eight colours across your orders and compound your inventory problems.

   Providing the colour you choose isn't so unusual as to be gross or outrageous, or ethnically incorrect (white to the Chinese means death) your customers will most regularly order the colour used in your main product shot (always assuming your photo looks great in that colour.) This will *always* be the case and should dictate how you order your merchandise.

Photographs versus artwork. A well-taken photograph gives the customer a sense of truthfulness about the product being sold. Colour artwork, sketches or line drawings of the product are, generally speaking, ineffective. People have a need to relate, to put themselves into the picture, and a photograph does this infinitely more effectively than a drawing. An artist's impression is simply no more than that. It is one more barrier between the reader and the product. 'Let me see it with my own eyes,' is the silent request your customer always carries for your product or service. Artwork is always fantasy and photography, despite the knowledge that photos can be faked, is always reality. You may, on occasion, need to use artwork to illustrate lifestyle simply because photography is too expensive. When this happens, use an artist who can give you as close to a photographic likeness as possible.

Glamourize the shot but never the product. More product returns come from a disappointment in the actual look of the product than for any other reason. It is just plain stupid to make a product look better or bigger or more expensive than it actually is in real life. The temptation to do so is always a strong one. Instead, make the situation into which you place the product look glamourous. But don't, under any circumstances, 'doctor' the product to look more than it is. In the direct marketing business, what the customer thinks she sees is what she expects to get. You'll be loading half your stock back into your inventory in 30 days time if you don't take this advice.

Of course, this doesn't mean you forget that you're selling a dream. If you're selling luggage you're really selling an exotic or romantic destination, or both. You want your customer to feel that she or they will be walking through an airport feeling special, the way they imagine the very rich do. If you're selling cookware, you're selling the glamour and sophistication of an exclusive dinner party where your prospect is the heroine of a fabulous, delicious evening.

> **Remember always,**
> **that the proposition that ends in the**
> **head**
> **always begins in the heart.**

The How of the What. The coupon and the order form. The coupon or the order form is the moment of truth. Your prospect has decided she wants to buy and you had better know how to make this process very damn easy or you could still lose her. Remember always, you're interrupting a life, you want to make the interruption as painless and short as possible. The coupon is an opportunity to build a new relationship. It is a surrogate research document and the shortest possible route to making a sale! The intrusion into her life will simply not be tolerated if it becomes difficult or boring to complete—or you treat it as a real research questionnaire and ask too many questions.

Where is the damn thing, anyway? Your order form or coupon should always be placed where your customer can see it and would naturally expect to find it. Conventionally, this is on the inside of the brochure and not on the outside back of the final page, or fold. If it is in an advertisement, then it should be in the lower right hand corner for reasons I've previously explained. Never, under any circumstances, place the coupon in the centre of the page.

But be sure that the magazine you choose is 'coupon friendly'. If the magazine is regarded by your customer as 'precious', or as a collectable, then she won't 'cut' the page. Typical of such magazines are The Reader's Digest, National Geographic, Vogue or Vogue Living. There are others and they're not hard to figure out. With such magazines, you would insert a stitched-in perforated coupon card as a separate order form, or use an insert to advertise, rather than buy a page.

Your coupon should always be easy to cut or tear. Don't make them into circles or triangles, even though a pyramid shape is somewhat better than a circular shape. Rectangles and squares are perfect, with a stipled line around it and perhaps a tiny drawing of a pair of scissors which appears to be clipping on the dotted line to encourage your customer to take the big plunge.

Take note of the colour of the coupon. I recall seeing an offer in a magazine some years ago. It had a wonderful picture of two Japanese Samurai swords on a stand against an inky black velvet background. It looked expensive and very, very desirable with the all-black background elegantly set off with reverse white type in a

TV WEEK SAMURAI SWORD OFFER.

Please complete this coupon and send, together with your payment, to TV Week Sword Offer, GPO Box 70B, Melbourne, 3001. Make your cheque/ money order payable to TV Week and endorse with your name and address.

Please send me .... Set(s) of 2 Samurai Swords and Stand. @ $89.95 per set. Please add $5 to your order for packing and postage. Overseas orders please add $10 to your order for packing and postage.

Name _____

Address _____

_____ Postcode _____

I enclose my cheque/money order for $_____ which covers the full cost and delivery of my order.

OR Please charge to my ☐ Bankcard ☐ Mastercard Account No.

Signature of Cardholder _____

The famous black order coupon to which you can only respond using white correction fluid.

beautiful copper-plate type. The offer was reasonable and the coupon was in the correct position and looked good enough to tear out with your teeth. But what kind of pen writes on black paper?

I traced the advertisement to the direct marketing company who had prepared it and discovered that they received seven orders—five of them written in white correction fluid. The break-even for the offer was 150 sets. They had blown a hugely expensive advertising campaign because a precocious and screwed-up art director wanted his advertisement to look beautiful—and the direct-marketing client didn't have the good sense to fire him on the spot.

Always print your coupon in white or a very pale, warm, businesslike colour, making it a distinctly different colour to the background—unless the background is plain white. Your coupon or order form should be instantly recognisable. Never let the artwork in the advertisement protrude across the dotted line into the coupon.

Don't give your customer too many choices on the coupon. This may be very tempting, but remain circumspect. Your coupon or order form should be directly linked to the offer you are making and as free as possible from the mental tyranny of choice. Making a decision can be very traumatic for a great many people, who would much prefer that you take care of the details for them.

Tell her in the copy what she is going to get, then make the coupon simple. Don't confuse: '*Well, let's see ... I want the handbag and ... ah ha, the matching organiser. What colour now? When will I use it,? What dress or suit? Bum! It's got a detachable shoulder strap or a brass or silver or mock tortoiseshell handle! Which will I choose? Do I want the matching address book or the wallet, or for an extra six dollars, both? I'm confused, Help! Ah, forget it! I've got to go pick up the kids from school! What is this—20 questions? I'll think about it and come back later with a roulette wheel!*'

Bye bye birdie! She's gone, escaped. Just when you had her in the palm of your hand, she's flown the coop, out of your life forever.

Keep choices limited, selective and clearly identified **and don't forget to tell her to fill in the coupon**! Don't laugh, I'd hate to tell you how many times a neatly-clipped, perfectly-blank coupon has arrived in the mail.

Quite recently, I witnessed a rather sad coupon neglect incident. The young son of a friend decided that rather than trudge the streets, he would do a direct-response campaign on himself to try to get a job with an advertising agency. He listed the 50 or so agencies he thought might be interested. Then, using virtually his lifetime savings, he got a designer to make up a direct-marketing kit which included a stamped, return-addressed envelope. The reply card was a real winner. He'd selected a series of options, not too many, not too few, of the simply-tick-the-appropriate-box kind.

You can imagine how delighted he was to receive five replies with the ' I am interested. Please call for an appointment' box neatly ticked.

There was only one small problem. He'd neglected to leave a space for the reader to fill in the name of the company he was to see. No doubt the personnel manager thought this the cleverest trick of them all. The kid had taken the trouble to save him the trouble by pre-coding the cards so he would know from which agency the response had came.

Well he hadn't. Sad, sad story.

Another sad story is when you forget to put your own name and address on the order coupon. This happens too often. A really keen buyer will, nevertheless, send the coupon back to the publication. Clearly, this becomes impossible with a mailing. Another hint is always put your name and address in the body of the ad as well as on the order coupon. All publications have a pass-on factor and, if the coupon is missing, the next reader-prospect is lost unless your address is elsewhere in the ad.

All these coupon catastrophes can be easily avoided by *always* getting someone unconnected with your campaign or your business to fill out the coupon or order form first. As I mentioned earlier, my preference is a 15-year-old. If he or she can complete it to your satisfaction, it will pass almost any test known to humankind. Always, always, always, test a mock-up of the whole offer before it goes to the printer and, of course, especially before it goes out to your customer. It is far better to find out at this stage that you've goofed than when the orders fail to come in.

The envelope. Not all envelopes are created equal and you should be careful about which one you use. Once again, when thinking about the correct envelope to use think about to whom it is going. Who is your customer? Window faced envelopes that look like accounts, or an important document or letter, are unlikely to be thrown out unopened. A customer of a bank won't throw away a letter if it has the bank's address on the envelope. Despite conventional wisdom, there are a great many people who enjoy getting promotional mail and here the envelope message is very important. The envelope does not have to be plain; some of the best have a message. My personal favourite is by one of the all-time great direct mail writers, Bill Jayme, who, writing the direct mail launch campaign for Psychology Today Magazine in the U.S., had this message on the front of the envelope:

**'Do you close the bathroom door
even when you're the only one at home?'**

It was irresistible! And the mailing was a huge success. The envelope is an opportunity to be creative, but the message has to be connected with the offer inside. A message that's clever but leads nowhere will get you nowhere. People like things to be related. In direct marketing, continuity is essential to the offer you make. The message on the outside must lead to the goodies inside.

A final word about the letter. There is an assumption by people in management, who are not direct marketing specialists, that the shorter the letter to your prospect, the better the response is likely to be. It seems logical, if you follow their thought process, which goes something like this: 'Direct mail is boring. People don't like to be bored or waste time. Give them a short letter and they are more likely to be grateful to you and to respond.'

Of course, no such thing happens. If the offer is boring or wrong, short or long, the letter won't work. But if the offer is a good one, and the copy which announces it is well written then a direct mail letter can be two pages and sometimes four. If the letter is to a busy executive, and is sent to his office, then shorter is better. Ideally, it would be only one page.

If the letter is all about the reader then the copy can go on for yonks—providing, always, that it remains interesting and relevant. Try to keep the reader with you, tease him, encourage him (or her) to go along with you, to turn the page to solve an interesting problem, to learn more about the benefits and the rewards you are promising. Give your readers a reason to turn to the brochure, and explore it thoroughly, and finally make them anxious to fill out the order form or call TODAY to place the order. My business associate and friend, Eddy Boas, once showed me a highly-successful letter, which comprised eight pages selling a trip from

North to South around the globe. It was mailed to executives on the Fortune 500 list. In direct marketing, long can be beautiful if you have the talent to write a great letter.

Briefing an agency. In the beginning God made heaven and earth and he did it without a briefing, perhaps that's why things haven't always gone as well as they might have on the blue planet.

Too many good direct marketing writers and art directors are badly briefed by their clients. This is understandable to a point. The creative is not the priority in getting the selling mix right, although it is an element which can make a tremendous difference.

By the time you get to brief your creative team, the campaign should be almost completely formulated. At this stage, it is often difficult to step back to think through a proposition objectively.

You've probably been living with the offer for some months and the media for several weeks, and you think you know precisely what ought to be said and pretty well how to say it.

It's at this point that you need the discipline to brief your creative team very carefully, and to be prepared to listen to their solutions without deciding first that your answers are the best ones anyway.

Information is critical in a briefing. Information about the market, the product and, of course, the target audience. You need to become an information addict. You should collect all the information you can possibly find on your product, similar products and any competitors' products which may be out in the marketplace and directed at your target audience.

Living in Australia makes this information-gathering very important. We are still a long way away from the big markets in America and Europe and it is easy to slip behind the important trends, latest products, services and ideas.

Collecting information doesn't mean you have to subscribe to every magazine in the English-speaking world. A clipping service can be hired to send you advertisements from the areas of greatest interest to you. The service can be expensive. We use retired people, who for a reasonable sum do the job for us both here in

Australia and elsewhere. It isn't all that hard to arrange. There are a great many older people around willing to take on the task.

Collect all the information you can find and put it into the biggest envelope you have. This is the goldmine for your creative people. To this should be added a list of every single product feature with its corresponding benefit.

The next task is to get your creative team to meet your major target audience. The best way to do this is not only to give them a demographic, or even a psychographic description, but *also* to allow them to read your correspondence. Let them hear the language of your customers and read their letter of complaint or congratulation. Let them see what pleases the customer and what to avoid because it doesn't work. Then make sure your customer service manager is at the agency briefing. He or she is probably the person closest to your customer and is generally a wealth of information.

Of course, a fair bit of commonsense is needed—people are people because of other people. But never judge your customers by your own taste. Keep it simple and direct and interesting. Creativity in direct marketing is always characterised by these three axioms:

That's the briefing. Now you sit back and chew your nails. Usually the first draft from the agency, or the first rough visuals you get, fall far short of your expectations. Don't get impatient, hang in. If there is something you like, start to develop it; if not, encourage your writer and artist to try again. But remember, the yardstick by which you make a judgement has little or nothing to do with your personal taste. Nor should you show the creative solution around the office—everyone feels compelled to have an opinion and it is much easier to be critical than it is to be constructive. The classic mistake is to show your creation to your friends, colleagues, family or your butcher. Test if you can and don't go into the market until you are sure you have the best offer presented in the best possible language, with the most personalised, consumer-identifying photographs.

When finally you get an advertisement, letter or brochure that pulls its head off, don't get bored with it or fire the agency because they can't come up with another which tests better than yours. A letter the famous Bill Jayme wrote for Life Magazine lasted for over 10 years until another one came along and out-performed it.

Before repeating an offer you know works with a letter, brochure or advertisement, always test it against a new entrant. A new creative approach that your agency has worked very hard to perfect. Never mail out without testing something new on the smallest scale. Then you are always ready for the next one. We always tell our advertising agency that there is a crate of French champagne for the team that comes up with a new creative solution that out-performs the old one. It's a nice incentive to keep 'them *hombres*' honest.

If
you
can keep it simple
and you can keep it straight
with copy that lets your prospect relate
and photos that show the reader
herself,
your product will leap off the
warehouse shelf

Chapter Twelve

★ ★ ★

The day The Ziff Dog pissed on the Robot
&
the first time I met Speedy Gonzales.

★ ★ ★

Michael Harrison lived in a beautiful Brownstone on 62nd Street, between Park and Lexington Ave, New York. He has been my American partner and one of my dearest friends for 25 years. The Brownstone became my home on my three or four visits to New York each year. Michael is rather wealthy and a wonderfully sophisticated businessman. But in his head he is still a school-boy—somewhere between eleven and puberty—and so has all the toys known to man and Macy's toy department. This makes it very difficult to buy him a birthday present. I arrived on one occasion to celebrate his birthday with him when his wife, a senior flight attendant, was away. As I was inserting my key to the front door, his wife's birthday present arrived from Hammacher Schlemmer, the wonderful shop in New York that sells every kind of oddity you can imagine anything, from a gold-plated Rolls Royce to a clutch of live crocodile eggs. The huge parcel turned out to be an almost life-size robot which had to be personally assembled. This was just the kind of toy Michael loved best, complicated, interesting and programmable.

Michael, who is somewhat eccentric and the world's greatest loner, wasn't the sort of guy to have a birthday party, though he seemed delighted that I'd thought to drop in. He opened a bottle of Chateau Margaux, which would have cost a middle executive's monthly salary, and together we began to assemble the robot.

Two bottles later, and after an hysterical two hour session, we got the thing moving, though we couldn't get it to go upstairs as it was meant to do. It could answer the door and take people's coats if there ever was any people and, it could deliver a limited number of messages, such as: 'MICHAEL WANTS COFFEE' to the maid who came in to clean.

We also programmed it to chase Michael's dog, a strange little creature of Tibetan origin, called a Lhasa Apso. It is Pekingese like in appearance, with a fringe over its eyes and a tongue which permanently lolls. Even in New York, a city of strange and exotic collector dogs, Michael's dog would cause people to stop and ask about the breed.

Michael and his wife, Lyndsey, always referred to this tiny hairy creature as, The Ziff Dog. She was never simply, Ziff, because the dog, a highly intelligent bundle of pink tongue and untidy hair, refused to respond to anything but its full title. The Ziff Dog didn't care to be chased by the robot, which had a heat-seeking device together with a system for recognising shapes. It seemed to find the Ziff Dog wherever she happened to be hiding. Cowering, is perhaps a better description.

However, The Ziff Dog got smarter and smarter at avoiding the robot, carrying its blanket in its mouth or some other object to confuse the robot. How it worked this out I can't say. But the robot was no idiot either and soon a very large hatred grew up between the dog and the robot.

Finally, The Ziff Dog, realising that the robot couldn't climb the stairs, dashed upstairs for a bit of privacy. All this took place over a period of some hours while Michael and I got more and more smashed on the third bottle of good French red.

Michael, perhaps a little cruelly (but the drink was to blame), carried the robot upstairs where it immediately set about electronically finding The Ziff Dog. But this time the dog was too smart and after leading it a merry chase it quickly ducked over the top of the stairs and lay, head on paws, along one of the carpeted steps. The robot came lumbering after it and crashed downwards to break into a thousand pieces at the foot of the staircase. Whereupon, The Ziff Dog, yelping in triumph, dashed down after it and, gently, because The Ziff dog was a lady, squatted over the electronic wreckage and weed upon it.

I have often seen the same principle applied to Direct Marketing, when people chase their customer prospects ruthlessly not caring in the least for their sensibilities. The public becomes The Ziff Dog, fair game to be chased and cowered and bullied with all the electronic know-how we have at our disposal. We hound them relentlessly wherever they go. This kind of remorseless tracking, without concern for the feeling and privacy of our prospects, always ends up the same way—the public finally has had enough and finds a way of putting you out of business: pissing on you à la The Ziff Dog.

Direct marketing is about building relationships and not about creating a public nuisance or developing the idea of *junk mail.* Whole forests of trees are turned into unwanted mail every day because, like the Robot, we never developed a liking or understanding for The Ziff Dog and we go about chasing her in a remorseless, robot-like manner.

It is essential for direct marketers to get to the point where the people on their database actually like and respect them. Yet how often have you received three letters on the same day containing the same data with your name spelled slightly differently—a computer spitting out the letters in a robot-like fashion? How often have you phoned the company and asked them to correct the error, only to receive no reply and then be the recipient of three more identical letters the next time they do a mailing. Or worse … received a solicitation to join something that you already belong to … like a credit card. This is one of the single biggest problems in Australia. People are not numbers and statistics and demographics and psychographics. They are doll collectors and joiners of book clubs and crazy about rock 'n roll or classical music. They are mums and dads, worried about the future, the weather, retirement, or life in general. They are you and me and, just like us, they feel they have a right to command a little respect from the people who wish to benefit from selling them goods and services. If you don't know, like and enjoy the relationship you have with your database, you will never really be any good at the direct response business, simply because people are people through other people, who like and respect them!

Let me tell you about the day I met Speedy Gonzales. My former wife Suzi and I attended a sort of working holiday in the form of a very low-key conference of people we knew and liked in the direct marketing business. The conference was held at a place in Mexico named Cabo San Lucas, which is on the very point of the Baja Peninsula. It took hours and hours in a hired bus to get to the little town, which was supposed to be famous for watching migrating whales as they swan past the peninsula. But, in fact, it was famous for the very pleasant little luxury hotel, about 60 kilometres along a rutted road beyond the town, where you were supposed to watch the whales while you enjoyed a week of solitude and good Mexican food at, by any standards, exorbitant prices.

We were dead tired and dusty from the long journey and Suzi was practically dying of thirst, having refused to drink straight from the canvas water bag that hung from the radiator of the bus.

'Ian, will you call room service and ask them to send up a large bottle of mineral water and plenty of ice,' she called from the bathroom as she undressed to take a shower.

I searched high and low for the phone, in drawers and cupboards, even under the bed. Finally I stormed the several hundred metres past giant cacti and ornamental pools, filled with huge coloured carp, to reception and demanded to know where they'd located the phone in our suite.

'Senor, we 'ave not got telephono in 'otel!' the woman behind the desk smiled. She pointed under the counter and I leaned over to where her finger pointed, 'Short-wave rah-dio!' she exclaimed, pleased that she could help me if I had a communication problem.

It was a charming and quite beautiful hotel in a simple Mexican way and we learned that there was a bell cord in every room which, when you tugged it, produced someone at your door within 15 minutes. We soon got used to the slow and measured pace of the place, as we ostensibly waited for the whales to appear, and I was enjoying the rest enormously.

The following evening as we were watching the sun setting over the end of the peninsula and drinking a well salted and perfectly-limed Margarita, the gallop of horses hooves could be heard in the distance. Soon, out of a cloud of dust, a lone horseman came thundering at top speed up to the hotel and pulled his foam-mouthed horse to a dramatic standstill beside the front steps.

He looked like a cowboy, with a large Sombrero hat and a big bushy moustache that seemed to occupy the larger part of what was visible of his face, which was in shadow under his huge hat. Nevertheless, he had the hint of country official about him, a certain confidence which was emphasised by the bandolier of bullets and the revolver strapped to his waist. On the side opposite to the gun hung a large leather pouch. From where we were seated, I could see he was very hot and dusty and had obviously been riding hard for several kilometres.

You can imagine our surprise when the woman from the hotel reception who'd come out to meet him brought him over to us. He bowed deeply and then very solemnly announced that his name was Gonzales and that he had ridden all the way from Cabo San Lucas with an urgent message for, 'El Presidente, Senor Kennedy.'

Maybe the news of President Kennedy's assassination more than two decades earlier hadn't yet reached Cabo San Lucas, but he looked at me very suspiciously when I told him my name was Kennedy and that the message was undoubtedly intended for me. You could see that he was trying to re-visualise the pictures he'd seen of JFK and sort of super-impose them onto my face, the task becoming more difficult for him in the rapidly encroaching dark. Finally, he handed the slip of paper over to me. It was half a lined page from a school exercise book and wasn't even in an envelope. I opened it and it read: **Cal pliz Karen offeez pronto**! Which I took to mean: *Please call Karen at your office urgently!*

We offered Speedy Gonzales a drink and after five cans of Bud-weiser, which he guzzled by throwing his head back and holding the can up to his moustache and emptying the contents non-stop,

Popeye fashion, into his open tobacco-stained mouth. Finally, he wiped his foam flecked moustache with the back of his hand and gave a great weary sigh. 'Gracias, senor El Presidente,' he sighed in the voice of a man who has just been saved from drowning.

Whereupon he helped himself to three more cold cans, which he placed in his big leather messenger bag, then he bowed somewhat woozily, 'Buenos nachez, senors, senorinas,' he said to the others present and gave me a foot-clicking salute, which nearly knocked him off his feet. Then he staggered off to mount his still-panting horse. He shouted what seemed to be some sort of obscenity at it before he galloped off into the starry Mexican night.

Knowing nothing about short-wave radio reception, I got to the receptionist before breakfast to inquire how I might fix up some sort of radio link with the nearest post office in order to call Karen, my PA in Australia.

This proved impossible, the technology being quite wrong for this kind of thing.

'What will I do?' I asked.

'You will catch the bus, senor,' she offered, 'then you go into town. In the town is a phone!' She turned away, busy with other things.

'What? You're serious, I go into Cabo San Lucas, 60 kilometres away, in the bus and find the only phone in town?'

'There is two phone, senor … in the phone shop!'

So I said a hasty goodbye to Suzi and only just caught the bus, which was straight out of Viva Zapata, complete with fat sweaty matrons, evil-looking men with droopy black moustaches, snotty-nosed big-eyed infants and crates of chickens, baskets of vegetables and bundles of sugar cane and dried fish, the latter smelling bloody terrible, though nobody seemed to notice.

I arrived in Cabo San Lucas exhausted from the journey with the mid-morning temperature already well into the thirties. The phone shop wasn't hard to find. It was the one with the long queue outside it.

It was a shop which actually sold phone calls and had just two phones and two large women sat, one behind each phone, and worked out a price for your call. There was always much protesting and slapping of foreheads from the caller as the price seemed to be completely arbitrary, but the woman behind the phone remained impassive, completely immune to persuasion. I decided, that after queuing for nearly two hours with people who were making arrangements by phone for shipping drugs, and guys who looked like pirates, when I finally got to the front, I wasn't going to argue.

Finally my turn arrived and I announced I wanted to make a call to Sydney, Australia. The large, sweaty woman with the moustache looked towards the ceiling, rolled her eyes, and then simply imagined a large sum of money of the kind American *gringos* in the movies habitually carry, and then demanded this sum in return for my making the call. I think it remains the most difficult and expensive phone call I've ever made, and after speaking to Austria finally I was connected with Karen in Sydney Australia.

Karen has been with me for years and doesn't mind giving me an earful of her vexation on occasion, 'Where the hell are you? I've been trying to reach you for days! Have a little consideration will ya? You've no idea what I've been through to find you!' She was properly steamed up and her voice sounded like a mixture of radio static and ground glass as she yelled at me down the phone.

'Yes, well, it's been a bit of a problem on this side as well,' I said.

But she wasn't listening, she was mad at me and almost hysterical from chasing me around the world, 'It's urgent, they must know by tonight!

'*They* know what? Who is *they*?' I shouted back. I watched as a fresh drop of perspiration rolled slowly down the cleft of the monstrous bosom of the phone woman seated in front of me.

'Dave Barratt, of the South Australian Direct Marketing Association, wants to know if you will speak at their lunch on the 15th of May in Adelaide and I *have* to let him know by tonight at the latest!'

I sighed, too weary to fight back: 'Tell them, yes, okay.'

'How can I contact you again?' she asked, somewhat mollified by my ready acceptance of the luncheon engagement to take place in eight weeks time.

'Please, Karen, I beg you, *don't* even try!' I pleaded.

How very much we have become used to the technology that drives our lives. It seems almost impossible to think of a world without phones. In fact, just that one experience shows how far we've come and how much we take for granted.

When you think about it, ordinary people today, such as most of the people who read this book, will have travelled further in their lives and seen more wondrous things than Marco Polo did, eaten more sumptuous meals than the Queen of Sheba, and consumed more exquisite wines than King Solomon. We wear clothes softer and more closely woven, use perfumes more highly refined and sensuous than Cleopatra experienced, and sleep on better beds and on cleaner sheets than Marie Antionette.

Yet we want more—more experiences, more indulgences and more things. But most of all, as the world gets more and more complicated, we seem to get more isolated, lonelier and more in need of relationships.

Direct marketing is about building relationships. They may not be the loving family kind of relationship, but they are relationships nevertheless and they contain and require all the ingredients of a good relationship.

The need for frequent contact. Keeping in touch, letting your database know you are there and are thinking about them is paramount. They need to know they are special and that when something good comes along, which you think will interest them, you will make it available to them first and on some sort of privileged basis. Don't let your database get away from you so that you lose contact. Every time you lose a customer, it will cost roughly 10 times as much to replace him or her with a new name as good. And it will cost many times more to build a new relationship as good as the one you've just lost. Good customers become your advocates and they are what makes your business grow and expand. Keep the relationship going by being constantly in touch. Losing a long-standing member of your database is like a death in the family.

Show them you care. Lovers bring home flowers and families celebrate events and anniversaries as a way of showing they care for
each other. Your business relationship is no different. You must
show your customer that you care about him or her. If they have
purchased a doll from you, remember the doll's birthday—that is
the day the doll was shipped out—and send a card with a picture
of the doll with a Happy Birthday greeting on it. It may seem
corny to someone who doesn't care about dolls, but to someone
who collects dolls because they are lonely, or think of them as a
part of their family, such a card is a treasured item and it shows
that you care. It will also make your customer a great advocate
for your dolls. With a little imagination and a not very big budget
allocation, there are a great many things you can do to show your
database that you are thinking about them and care about them.
At Christmas time, send a card wishing your customer friend a
happy Christmas and thank them for their custom over the past
year. Explain that you've made a donation to the Starlight Foundation in their name. Simple, caring stuff.

At Bond International we have sent a Christmas card to our
best customers for nearly 20 years, always a piece of original art
specially created for them. We don't ask them to do anything
except to have a great Christmas holiday. In reply, I get dozens
and dozens of letters, some with personal photographs and, literally hundreds of Christmas cards. When this happens, you know
your relationship marketing is working properly.

Make them seem important. People love to feel important. They
love to feel a part of something that stands for something—some
expertise or special interest that sets them apart from their neigh-
bours. To carry the doll idea further, why not start your own
version of the loyalty club for doll owners—The Porcelain Doll
Society of Australasia. Invite your own customers to be members
at half the annual membership fee as loyalty or foundation
members. Invite them to have friends join, who will pay the full
price for membership but you allow a concession on the fees of

the introducing member. The new member becomes a loyalty member in two years and is then allowed to introduce other new members and obtain the same concessions. Once you start this kind of club or society the merchandising ideas will simply go on—and on and so will sales.

Be friendly. To be friendly doesn't mean you have to be syco-phantic, just friendly in the casual, easy Australian sense of the word. The words you choose to use in your letters should not be too formal, unless the kind of offer you are making dictates this approach. Very few do. Use easy, familiar words, the kind people hear around them every day. Make sure your switchboard and your staff do the same. Anyone who deals with people on the phone should be trained to do so. The phone can damage a rela-tionship before it's even started and all because a clumsy kid without phone training. It astonishes me how often this is done in huge organisations such as banks. Your phone manner and your media manner should reflect the same organisation.

Be generous. Don't argue over a refund, even if you know the mistake or the breakage occurred at the customer's end, accept the responsibility anyway. We've talked about this earlier, so I won't go on, but 'pay up and shut up' is by far the cheapest and best way to behave. Good salesmanship is not about making a single sale, but in beginning a relationship which will lead to many more sales in the future. Generosity is the hallmark of a good company and, besides, it takes a lot of pressure off your staff.

Be available. When your customer wants action, she would like it right away. But, in her heart, she knows it's going to take some time for you to call back. The trick to call back the same day, even the same hour if you can. Don't let your company or staff sleep on a query. A quick answer will almost always diffuse an irritated customer and most often will delight them. How often have you heard somebody say: 'They called me back immediately. I was impressed.' The longer you leave a customer query or enquiry the more likely it is to turn nasty. Moreover, make your management available to make a decision on the spot. Don't have a customer *complaint* department, have a customer *opportunity* department and then give them the authority to make the big decisions. Why would you put someone into a customer query area if you didn't implicitly trust their judgement? We always try to keep our reply to customer correspondence down to 48 hours.

Be convenient. This is an area very often neglected by direct marketing departments or organisations. They get going with a campaign, build it to a fever pitch, watch it go out into the market. Enjoy reaping the reward, and then close down and get on with something else. While this is inevitable to some degree, the doors must be left open for your customer to come back to you and the way they do this should be very easy. A toll-free 008 (now 1-800) number, supplied as a stick-on label they can paste into their phone book when they get their merchandise, is usually all it takes. Hanna Andersson actually puts this number on the permanent inside neck label of her garments and it may not be a bad idea to put it on some inconspicuous place on the merchandise you send out. Make sure the phone number is available and serviced during business hours and that an answer phone takes a message after hours. Convenience makes sales and once your customer knows she can shop with you by lifting the telephone, she will do so more often, like her American counterpart.

We haven't yet really talked about the beginning—The business of starting a direct marketing business on your own.

The joy of direct response is that you can begin it from your kitchen table or you can run it as a department within a multinational organisation. Both can work well with very much the same set of rules.

The first thing to get right, and it is *always* the first thing to get right, even before the loan from the bank, is the product or service. Contrary to most thinking, I believe there is no shortage of products which can be promoted effectively in the direct marketing medium. In fact, it is difficult to think of a product or service that couldn't benefit from a direct response approach in their marketing mix—even coffins and funeral arrangements have been very successfully sold using direct marketing.

The problem isn't the product, it is the lack of knowledge about how to apply direct marketing skills and disciplines. This book is a small attempt to change this state of affairs. We've tried to address how to get the essentials correct, how to get products and services right, how to target the right audience and, finally, how to make the correct media choices. Now let us focus on the specifics of products in the world of direct marketing.

Start with a picture. The very first consideration of a product begins with its picture, the visual representation of the product to the customer. Is the product photogenic? Or does it diminish, or look over-complicated, or too simplistic, when reduced to a picture? Good products that take bad pictures are always difficult to sell. Remember, your customer will have only one visual method of judging the value of the product. This will take place in a brochure, print advertisement or on a television commercial. He or she can't feel it, judge its quality or even wind it up or display it somewhere. They can only see it in the picture you provide. In direct marketing, the picture is often the *thousand words*. We are not talking about trick photography, or a product which has been visually tarted up, we *are* talking about a Polaroid shot you take of the product and then lay down on a blank piece of paper **to see if it 'laughs' back at you.**

Sometimes, it is possible to enhance the picture of the product by changing the nature of the offer. This was brilliantly done by a company in South Africa, which was selling a water-proof watch by direct response. The problem was, of course, that a watch is a watch but how did the potential customer know the Barracuda Sports watch was all it claimed to be, a totally water-proof watch to a depth of 30 metres.

They solved the problem by packing the watch in a thick, flexible plastic cushion filled with water. Not only did the water protect the watch from being damaged in the mail, it conclusively proved the product claim—there it was in the brochure illustration floating in a clear plastic container filled with water. Needless to say the offer worked gangbusters, as the photograph did the work of a thousand words or more. We attempted to replicate this offer in Australia but despite conclusively proving our case to the Post Office, they remained afraid that the water would leak and denied us the opportunity for this unique mailing.

So that's the first reason for rejecting a product. Ask yourself how it looks in a one-dimensional picture? If it doesn't pass the picture test, then look for another product and leave that one to a normal retail outlet where the product can be handled and so overcome it's lack of photogenic qualities. If it doesn't picture well, it won't sell well in direct response—unless you can come up with something as dramatic as the watch floating in water.

Finding the right product is easy, all it requires is patience and determination. We have five people in our product development department whose sole job is to source products. They then visualise potential products by photographing them and placing them into a brochure or print environment. You can do the same from your kitchen table. Simply take a picture of the product, place it on a blank white page, draw a series of black lines under it and place it in the magazine you think would be the best environment for it to attract your target audience. If it does not laugh back at you, or at the very least smile charmingly, forget it.

Our product development team used to see around 1000 samples in a year, from which we select three to four hundred for a second look. Now that we are in the catalogue business as well the numbers are much greater. Our small catalogue carries around 200 products alone. We started getting serious after we've reduced the second-look items to around 120. After some discussion and serious picture taking, we go ahead with around 80. Remember, we selected the first 1000 because we thought they all had some potential. Of the 80 or so we finally selected, thought about, discussed, tested and photographed again, a further one-third will fail in the market. But the good news is that two-thirds will succeed and that's a terrific hit rate. But then, we've been doing it for 20 years!

If you're thinking about going into direct marketing, then you must understand clearly that the best failure rate you could hope for is around one third, even if you have most conscientiously done your homework. There are simply no guarantees that you will succeed. So don't get excited when someone brings you his cousin's invention and you get a feeling this will be the one to start your fortune. Photograph it first, as cousin's inventions have a bad habit of taking lousy pictures.

After you've looked at the picture and decided it's a pretty ordinary-looking product and hardly likely to visually excite, give the product a second chance. Ask yourself if it does something so remarkable that, despite the poor picture, you can find the words to make it work. Sometimes words become the best pictures in the mind.

Let me give you an example. We bought some very unimpressive grey square tin boxes with Twinlock hanging files inside them. The boxes were a home-filing system, somewhere to keep your most important papers. It was a useful sort of box. But no picture we could take of it would change the fact that it remained simply a tin box. It was difficult to explain how useful it could be in any household.

But a good copywriter can often change this perspective with words. You and I may see a tin box but a communicator sees, instead, a large benefit. The tin box, despite its lack of photogenic properties, was the ideal direct-marketing product because its benefits could be easily presented with words. The home-filing system worked very well for us when we carried a picture of it open showing the inside divisions neatly labelled. Under a label marked Birth Certificates, we had a woman's hand slipping a child's birth certificate into the appropriate slot. The simple though relevant headline read:

Never lose another important paper.

The copy went onto remind the reader of the feeling of frustration when the fridge blew up and you ransacked the house to find the guarantee. Or when you have to find your birth certificate, because you need a new passport and you know you put it 'somewhere safe' but you can't imagine where. It was precisely because all of us have been in this position that the home file sold its little head off with five simple little words in the headline. The same brochure, which is hardly a creative breakthrough, sold hundreds of thousands of home files and was translated into 15 different languages. The copy and not the picture had worked the trick of triggering a very familiar experience. And it developed a powerful promise.

Perception is vitally important in selling, as is illustrated by this example. People could immediately perceive the problem and recognise the solution. But perception can sometimes work against you as well.

In the '70s, the clever people at Union Carbide created Yatrillium Aluminium Garnets, in other words fake diamonds. They were known by the acronym YAGs. They looked and felt like the real thing and were absolutely 100 per cent flawless. Indeed, it was their perfect composition which gave them away. No diamond of any reasonable size is flawless and this is one of the major ways jewellers have of telling a real diamond from a fake. The YAG shone as beautifully, caught the light as radiantly and sparkled as brilliantly as real diamonds. So, we ordered several hundred stones to test and told ourselves we'd lucked-in on the world's best offer. There had been several very successful mail order YAG promotions in the U.S. so we even had a precedent.

We had no intention of trying to fool anyone and were happy to sell them as fake diamonds with a copy-line which we thought unbeatable. We told ourselves that tens of thousands of women would embrace the idea of owning a diamond ring as big and impressive as the one owned by Elizabeth Taylor (which only a real diamond expert could tell was faked). We even used her name and correctly pointed out that the diamonds she wore in public were in fact YAG, the real thing being too precious to wear. Our brochure boasted that if anyone could tell the difference between an actual one carat diamond, valued at $3000, and the 'diamond' they were buying from us, then we would gladly refund their money.

We test marketed the concept and, joyously, the offer worked like magic. Our orders were well above budget forecast. We hugged ourselves, we were onto a million-dollar promotion of the kind every direct marketer dreams will occur but secretly knows is impossible.

Then, during the free-trial period, something strange began to happen and the YAG rings started to come back, first a trickle and then by hundreds and, finally, just about all of them. We were stunned. There seemed no explanation; the 'diamonds' were as flawless as ever.

We hurried into the marketplace and started to ask women questions face-to-face, What is wrong with the 'diamonds', we wanted to know. 'They look like a piece of glass!' came the reply in chorus, 'a cheap, worthless piece of glass!'

We went back and showed them a *real* one-carat diamond and they looked disgusted. 'See, it looks like a useless piece of glass!' We were completely puzzled and totally mortified and, being men, couldn't accept this explanation until one of the packers in the despatch department said: 'It's simple, when you know it's a fake you can't turn it into the real thing!'

'Yes, well what about the *real* thing—when we showed them the real diamond?'

'It doesn't matter,' she said. 'Diamonds are glamour and all those lovely ads you see, soft lights, love, a handsome man, champagne, the twinkle of a diamond ring reflecting the candlelight. We don't see a diamond, we see romance!' She opened a box containing one of our YAG's. 'This isn't romantic, so it isn't a diamond, it's a fake! A diamond is something that happens in your heart.'

We were beaten, our YAG couldn't possibly happen in the heart and so, with some tremendous disappointment, we agreed we couldn't emulate the perception de Beers had spent several generations developing for their particular kind of glass, which they happened to have picked up in a dry river bed or dug up in a pipe of clay, and which weren't even as flawlessly perfect as our own laboratory grown product. We didn't proceed with the full launch simply because we didn't have the words which triggered the perceptions we needed. Besides, most of our customers had never seen a genuine one-carat diamond, so their perception was very different.

**One of the unchanging laws of marketing
is that perception is reality.**

At least we didn't lose our shirts on the great YAG rush, because
we had the good sense to test it first, even though we were 100
per cent positive that we'd discovered Eldorado. I'll say it again:
whatever you do, always test your offer—running a live test is the
key to keeping the direct marketing roof over your head. The
question is not: 'Can I afford to test?' The question is always: 'Can
I afford not to test?' And the answer is always the same: **'No, you
cannot afford not to test!'**

The great majority of direct marketing disasters come about
because the decision is made that testing is a waste of time and
money. Here is a general axiom for the direct marketing business:

*'The more certain you are that you have the perfect product or service for
your target audience, the more inclined you are to punt the farm on this
knowledge, the more likely you are to lose the lot.'*

Marketing, measurable marketing, is about conviction and belief.
It isn't about 'feeling something in your water'. Faith may well
move mountains, but it won't create mountains of mail at your
doorstep, or have the phone 'ringing off its head', or even convince someone to buy something they don't need, or want, or
which hasn't been explained carefully enough to them.

I find it curious that a marketer will convince himself that a test
is not affordable but that the failure of the campaign somehow
is. That's wacky thinking. In fact, very few direct marketers can
take too many failures, so we simply have to test our assumptions
and we are often surprised at the result. The one certain thing
you learn in our business is that there are no sure-fire direct marketing offers or solutions. Many traditional marketers coming into
direct marketing believe that half a dozen focus groups are a substitute for testing.

Focus groups versus a market test. A focus group consists of carefully picked people in your target audience, usually eight to a

group. They are divided into between four and eight groups and exposed to your direct marketing campaign to test their reactions to it.

While a focus group can be very useful to sniff out problems, it is by no means definitive and cannot deliver the breadth of experience you get from a live test. There is no substitute for testing your campaign and offer by literally exposing it to a small part of the market.

The differences are obvious. A focus group can only *speculate*. You are simply asking for people's opinions and when people carry no direct responsibility for their opinions, such as putting money down to confirm them, they are happy to give you their observations which, though useful, are by no means definitive.

A live test achieves a number of hugely important things. It determines whether people will buy in the first instance, and how many are likely to do so and, having done so, how many will, as in the YAG experience, return the merchandise. It sorts out details of despatch and demand and supply, and whether the production department or the suppliers can deliver the goods on time at the acceptable rate and, also, whether your warehouse and customer service is operating efficiently. In summary, you are actually **testing the three pivotal aspects of your campaign—the audience, the offer and the creative executions**, as well as many other mechanical details.

It is as well to remember that the focus group can only react to the creative offer. It doesn't actually receive the goods, or experience the service. The group can only, therefore, judge the piece of paper you put in front of them. While this is of some importance, the absence of actually handling the goods doesn't complete the transaction.

The real objection to focus groups is that they are not in a real buying environment in which they must make a decision. They are not real people going through a real process, they are invited people imagining how they would react to a given stimuli.

But focus groups are infinitely better than no testing at all. They at least give you an indication of attitudes which may come up in the market place. And they allow you to see weaknesses and priorities. Finally, you can often run a proper test more cheaply than you can conduct focus groups.

But, in putting together *affinity groups*, say of women doll collectors over 50-years-old, we have found focus groups, or discussion groups as they're sometimes known, to be great value. They significantly add to the level of knowledge about the target group—their likes, dislikes and attitudes to the world around them. If focus groups are not always great for testing, they are invaluable for understanding attitudes. And if you understand how and what your target audience thinks, you're already a fair way along the path to righteousness.

I must caution you to **never** test the reaction to a product by showing it around the office, or asking people to take it home to test, or by showing it around a focus group. This isn't objective data and it certainly isn't indicative of future response. All it can possibly tell you is two things. Firstly whether the product functions well (and if you haven't tested this exhaustively yourself beforehand then you are not a professional.) Secondly, what the returns are likely to be once it is in the customer's hands—that is, after the sale has been made.

Some difficulties with testing. It is worth saying a few words about the specifics of testing here in small markets, such as Australia, New Zealand and South Africa, because they do pose particular challenges. These three countries are not the easiest environments in which to put together an effective test programme, especially if you are dependant on the print media.

Reader's Digest is the only publication in which you can conduct an A/B split test. An A/B split test means that half the total circulation of the magazine carries the 'A' version of your offer and the other half the 'B' version. That is, every second magazine carries an alternative advertisement even if both magazines end up on the same news stand. This allows a totally fair and random evaluation of the creative message carried in an advertisement.

In a number of magazines you can buy a region and split your ads this way. But such a test isn't entirely satisfactory. **The single**

most important rule of testing is that you test only one thing at a time—otherwise, it becomes impossible to know from the text results which thing has succeeded or failed.

However, this is true in the best of all possible worlds, but a regional split is still better than trying to decide, without testing, which of two different creative solutions is likely to work best in the market.

If the Reader's Digest isn't your mark, there is still one way out of it, though it is somewhat more expensive. This is the insert drafted into either magazines or something already being mailed. Inserts generally pull two or three times better than a full page advertisement, though you may not be able to afford inserts in your over-all campaign and, so, using them in your test campaign can be fairly tricky. But if you're only using them to find out which of two creative approaches is likely to work better, you are measuring quality and not quantity and this can work nicely for you.

Inserts as a test medium. Inserts are effective as a test because you can mix them thoroughly into the test market in the same way as the A/B split test in the Reader's Digest described previously. That is, your printer can collate them in the boxes he delivers to the magazine printer so that they can be machine fed into the chosen magazine alternatively. Say, for instance, you have three different inserts. These can now be fed in as a 1, 2, 3—1, 2, 3 arrangement, rather than all the 'ones' together, then the 'twos' and finally, the 'threes'. In this way, you achieve a perfect random test procedure, with each pile of magazines having each of the inserts evenly distributed throughout the pile.

Some publications, mostly newspapers, in these three markets, can give you a *geographical insert.* You can get geographical variants if you desire. For instance, you may be selling matching covers for a set of golf clubs and one part of the country is hot and the other cold. So one set of covers might be chamois leather, and the other sheepskin. It's a silly example, but I'm sure you get the idea.

But, as a general caution, don't try to get too smart and test too many variations, the multi-variant test almost always leads to incorrect diagnosis. Keep it simple where you can.

If you have a sound database which corresponds with your offer, it is always best to use them for your initial test before you go into a media test. Testing new products in all of these environments is very risky and not the way to go about building a sound business base. Try the product on the people you know, your own database. They are your friends. If they don't like the product it is unlikely that people who don't know you, out there in the wild and wicked land of media, will respond favourably to it. But do be careful. It is not always absolutely conclusive to test with your database. Your own database has been educated to your way of doing things and can be so responsive that it doesn't accurately indicate what might happen in the media. But the reverse, not testing but going directly to the media, can put you out of business in a frighteningly short time. Take the safest route: test!

Testing one thing at a time. Another word of warning. If you choose a publication in which to test a product then you must make sure you know the likely direct market response of that magazine. Most importantly, check that it has a successful history of direct response products of the same kind as yours. Some perfectly good mass circulation publications, Australian Womens Weekly, for instance, are simply not mail order responsive. If you *don't* know the direct response characteristic, then you are not testing one thing, you are testing two—the product *and* the magazine. The product might be great and the magazine a lousy direct market vehicle, but how will you ever know which of the two it is?

Which brings me to another point. Do not test a product's responsiveness with an offer which is in itself experimental. Test it with an offer you know has worked in a particular magazine before. Use a **buy-one, get-one free** offer, or **an interest-free, three-months-to-pay** offer, or **an affinity gift**, or some such familiar proposition. Otherwise, if the offer is an unusual one, you end up testing two things again—the product and the offer in which it is presented. And you will never know which one has worked. You can only test one thing at a time.

The creative execution. At the risk of diminishing the importance of the creative execution we are less interested on a cost benefit test to bother with testing the creative content of a campaign. This is not to under-estimate its importance, but getting the product and the offer together with the right media is the real key to success. In any professional environment, the creative execution can be executed at a very high level of efficiency. If you keep it sensible, with good people pictures and make it always easy to understand, it is very hard to mess up the creative component. Far too many direct marketers are quick to give their agency creative department hell when a campaign doesn't work. We always look everywhere; often it is something else that has screwed up.

Testing and financial modelling. Bill Jayme is a direct marketer whom I admire greatly and, in his field, which is designing solicitation packages for subscription magazines, he is without peer in the U.S.A. I visit Bill and his partner Heikki Ratalahti nearly every year at their beautiful home in the Sonoma Hills in Northern California. Each time I am with these two very clever people, I marvel at their skill and wisdom. Both have been credited with some of the most successful subscription magazine launches in America.

Bill and those who pay him are always on the look-out for the opportunity to launch a new magazine which may capture the hearts and minds of an affinity group large enough to be financially viable. It's not putting a magazine together that is difficult, it is finding out what people want in the editorial enough to fork out a year in advance for the magazine. This is where Bill shows himself to be very clever, because he not only puts together a series of test packages which will help determine the content of a proposed magazine, but his test result data will project roll-out figures which the publisher can build into a successful financial model.

Let me give you an example. A publisher may come to Bill with a new publication dealing with say, interior design. He thinks it has a good chance of finding a large target audience or affinity group. He commissions Bill and Heikki to design a direct mail subscription package. In the U.S. lists are readily available for rental which will fit the readership profile at which the magazine is aiming. Bill and Heikki might then put three mailings together, each on interior design. But each would feature a different aspect of design so that if any one is preferred by a future reader, it will give the magazine its overall *personality*. Say, for example, he puts together packages which show:

● Homes of famous people
● Features on the great American designers and their recent work
● Features on design techniques, tips, furniture trends etc

Dummy Magazines are created for photography, so that when Bill and Heikki have completed the direct mail package these look as though the actual magazine is in existence. This is a rather expensive process, especially in photography, but it is still only a fraction of the cost of printing an entire magazine, while giving the effect of a complete magazine in the brochure illustrations.

This is no dummy run. The subscription offer actually asks the respondent to send in a cheque, or sign a credit card authority, for a full year's subscription, to all intents it is a 'live test' except that, at this stage, no design magazine exists.

When the subscriber responds, the cheques are returned as are the signed credit card authorities, together with a polite note and a free gift explaining that the magazine has been delayed. The gift would more than likely be a high quality book on some aspect of architectural design, probably a book which has been remaindered, with a retail price of $30, but bought by the publisher for less than $5. In the direct marketing industry this type of testing is known as, 'a dry run.' (i.e. without the product to ship.)

The packages are tested against a known database of magazine responders. Not only does Bill get directly to his target audience, but he also begins to gather the ingredients of a financial model. Most magazines require borrowed capital to start up, which is often a loan from the bank or some other financial source. When he gets the results of his test, and now knows what sort of personality the magazine will have, the promoter, or publisher, can project the roll-outs and also build a financial model for the bank or prospective financier. This includes the cost of setting up, the expected circulation, the anticipated break-even point, the rate of growth, the size of the market, the investment required to operate within it, and the advertising and promotion costs.

The only piece of information missing is what the renewal rate will be. As the subscriptions are sold for a full year it is going to take that long to know if the magazine will eventually stay in business.

The genius and extraordinary creativity of Bill and Heikki eliminates most of the considerable risks involved in launching a new magazine. Everything, with the exception of the renewal rate, has been measured through testing. The potential financier and the publisher have proof that the public needs a magazine which strongly features the homes of famous people. This is hard evidence in a world where finance people have to make decisions based on trust and past experience. This means that the potential source of finance is seeing something he or she can relate to—a model tested and not a blue sky idea based on an editor's hunch. At the same time, it means the magazine has a better than average chance of being a success. This is because the audience it will appeal to has decided what *they* would prefer in a magazine based on a choice of three possible editorial approaches.

Nine out of every 10 new magazines fail in the launch period. Almost the same number are born not after sound testing, but often on wildly enthusiastic and esoteric ideas of editors beguiled by their own good taste and interests. Bill and Heikki do not make this mistake and would-be publishers are lined up for their services. These two very clever people are the most successful creators of subscription mailings for magazines in North America. Among some of their notable achievements are New Yorker Magazine and Architectural Digest. They can only manage to do about six packages a year but, at their prices, this is more than sufficient to keep them living in a manner to which they have every right to become accustomed.

This dip-stick approach of taking a proposition to your most likely audience, and allowing the results to determine the specifications of the product, is a formula for success. The answer is to have your potential readers or customers putting their money up. In direct marketing, there are no absolute certainties. But you are unlikely to come much closer than having your future customers backing their preferences with money.

Just as importantly, it demonstrates the importance of the customer in selecting, from several choices, the product *they* want. Research, even good qualitative research and sampling, can never substitute for creating the actual selling environment, which includes the vitally important final action—the actual payment for the goods or services.

Sourcing a product. Conventional wisdom says that the best way to find a new product to trade is to look into the market and discover an unfulfilled need and then source or develop a product to satisfy that need. Like most conventional wisdom, this is a load of codswallop which, at best, involves years of research. Besides, deciding what people need is always a dangerous business.

In fact, it is far more cost effective to take something you already know people need, and which is available to them in some markets while not in others. The task then is to become a trader and to bring it into a new market for the first time, or in a new convenient way to an existing market. This works exceptionally well in the smaller markets like Australia.

This is an approach which requires some real discipline and research and, predictably, there are a series of steps you ought to know about. You might even call them rules to follow.

In looking for new consumer products to sell in Australia, New Zealand, the Asian region and South Africa, you should take your cue from a mature market such as North America and, to a lesser extent, Europe, particularly the UK. To make it easier for you here are a list of subscription magazines which, together, form a base of information for mail order merchandise. You will soon learn to find others that deal with your own particular speciality. The magazines are:

- Asian Sources
- Trade Winds Monthly (Hong Kong)

- Hong Kong Enterprise (The Hong Kong Development Council)
- Collectables Market Guide and Price index (US)
- Made in Europe (A general merchandise buyers guide)
- Collectors Mart Magazine (US)
- Australian Collectors Quarterly
- Australian Business Collectors Annual
- The Reid Report (U.S.)

The Reid Report, and there are similar services available in Australia at a price, tracks all the activity of all the mail order companies in any field you specify.

It is essential to find those direct marketing companies which seem to trade in much the same type of goods and services as you do. You should subscribe to all their product offers. This does three things: you don't duplicate a product; you learn what works and what doesn't; and you can often find a product ready-made with the right package in an overseas market—which can be easily tailored to your own.

We are a fairly large company by most Australian direct marketing standards and we maintain a clipping service in the U.S. and the UK by simply appointing one person to scan magazines for direct response product and offers. I employ a lovely lady in Dallas, who is a retiree from the Direct Marketing Association of America. It works beautifully and she soon learned what we particularly required.

Beware of market differences. There are two strings to the market differences bow. The first is that there can be marked differences from one market to another. The second is that you can often imagine a difference where none exists. Differences are less likely to be of product and more of media selection. Some markets have an entire direct marketing industry built around a single medium. The colour supplements in the UK are a major direct marketing medium whereas it hardly exists here in Australasia. Take an offer out of a UK supplement and put it into Australia's Good Weekend colour magazine and I absolutely guarantee it will bomb! The

MERCHANDISE SOURCES

market here is simply not yet attuned to the colour supplement as a medium for direct marketing sales. It is a matter of maturity.

However, if you are a marketer who is here to stay, as we are, every once in a while run an offer in a colour supplement. Because sooner or later this media should work well for direct marketing. Already the TV magazines inserted into the Sunday newspapers are beginning to be a reliable direct response media. It's always worth keeping a 'toe in the water' as a new media outlet that works is a very valuable acquisition.

The Wall Street Journal, in the U.S., is one of the great examples of a direct response media to reach business people. But if you tried to emulate its performance through the Australian Financial Review, you'd lose your shirt overnight. The Financial Review may well be beautifully targeted to business people, but they have simply not become accustomed to using it as a buying medium. Again, time and circumstance will tell whether this will change. So keep banging the odd advertisement in from time to time. You never know your luck in the big city.

Some prejudices do exist from market to market and, so, you wouldn't lift a product from one market and sell it in another without testing it. Our much beleaguered Australian Wool Market suffered a further blow when I decided that, with items of millions of automobiles in the U.S., there was an opportunity to sell many millions of wool car seat covers. The brochure we prepared worked well in Australia and I convinced Michael Harrison, of The Ziff Dog fame, to conduct a test in the U.S. He ran, what for him was a small test of 300,000 people who seemed likely prospects—and the final result was 11 orders! Holy Macaroni, you simply can't do much worse than that! You and I know that wool keeps you warm in winter and cool in summer, and is the world's best air-conditioner, but try telling that to the average American motorist. 'Wool! Cool? You crazy, man!' Most habits are awful hard to change and, for some, there just isn't enough money in the world to set about changing them.

I guess I'm getting to sound pretty one-eyed, but that's why you need to test everything—and also why you can't simply stay at home and source products by correspondence—if you want to be successful in the direct marketing business. You need to get out and about, sense what's going on, understand the climate of a happening or an offer. If you happen to be in Dallas and Willie Nelson is playing the Colosseum, and you see that 30,000 fans are all wearing the same Willie Nelson black Stetson, you might return to Australia and research to see if this item is also required headgear for Nelson fans here. How many such people exist and where are the hats sourced and for how much? You might find a market waiting for you when Willie Nelson tours Australia or New Zealand, or on the other hand, the hat may be solely an American thing. You need to get around, travel to trade fairs, pick up ideas, talk to people, walk through shops, read all the catalogues, get on the network and make friends. You'll be both surprised and gratified at how generous people can be in sharing ideas from country to country or market to market. It is, generally speaking, a nice industry.

However, people in this highly competitive business rarely tell the truth, or all of it anyway. Everyone wants to sell you something and so, instantly, everything becomes a bestseller! You need friends in the business you can trust, such as the redoubtable Michael Harrison, an industry giant. These will come if you play fair and honest as most Australians and New Zealanders do.

Things not to do. There are some things to do and some things not to do. Revolutionary new products are extremely dangerous, even if your cousin is an inventor. The business of product development is not the business of direct marketing. Direct marketing works because your customer already knows about the use and quality of the product. She hopes only to get her needs fulfilled in a configuration which is more unique or handsome or useful or convenient. Besides, there are more products available with a little searching than any of us could ever possibly handle in one lifetime. Why take a risk when it isn't necessary?

The new product development business requires specialist skills which direct marketers don't have. We are not manufacturers, we are traders and marketers. We shouldn't mix the two ideas.

Inventing and developing products is a very difficult and expensive task and the failure rate of such products is staggering. Just because you've got to the tooling and manufacturing stage, does not mean you have a product which will necessarily meet with the approval of your customers. The rule is: **Seek to acquire and not to invent**.

Just a word of caution about inventors. We all like the sound of inventors. They are the wacky, crazy people who persist through thick and thin and eventually change the world we live in. That's true. But, unfortunately, it's not true of the direct marketing business. We have always encouraged people to talk to us and sometimes our reception area looks like the foyer in the U.S. office of 'patents pending'. But I can honestly say that of the thousands of ideas I've had presented to me, only five seemed like workable ones—and only two of these succeeded in the market place to some degree!

It can be an interesting way to waste time, though. One inventor brought us a machine which pre-mixed eggs in the shell. You placed your eggs in the machine and an ultra-sonic wave mixed them to a perfect omelette consistency. If you are partial to scrambled eggs or omelettes for breakfast it could have been ideal, except that what you normally did in thirty seconds with a large fork now took four minutes in the ultra-sonic whirler at a cost of $199.

Running an absurd second, perhaps even first, in the invention stakes, was the automatic lobster killer. For a start, how many live lobsters have you been forced to kill in your kitchen? Anyway, this machine allowed that you would grab the lobster (very carefully) and strap its legs into the machine, a bit like the electric chair. Then you pressed a green button and very slowly the unfortunate lobster moved along a little rail and came to a halt under a deadly looking needle. You pressed a red button and zit! The needle pierced the crustacean through the head to kill it instantly and also presumably, painlessly. The entire procedure took 20 minutes from start to finish and the lobster liquidator cost a mere $3400. The lobster-killing machine arrived by courier, together with a hessian bag which contained three very large live lobsters, which were moving around like small contortionists. Laurel Jackson, of the A.M.P., our biggest client, was waiting in the foyer as the whole contraption and caboodle arrived. Unaware of what was in the bag, she was watching it with some fascination as I came out to greet her.

'Ian, I think one of your mail order customers is sending you back a very angry message!' she said.

What I find fascinating is that someone gets up one morning and says: 'Bingo! I know what the world needs—a painless lobster killing machine!' How do they convince themselves that every household is bound to want one, lobster only being $45 a kilo with 89 per cent of all Australians never having tasted one? In the fever of excitement surrounding the project, how do they come to think that a lobster liquidator is a necessity of life, is ecologically sound and will also greatly please the animal liberation lobby? The mind boggles!

Another invention that left me somewhat lost for words was the Diet Loafer. A tiny, sadistic and admittedly ingenious shoe-maker, who had a fat wife and an inventive streak, invented a pair of loafers fitted with a tiny weighing window which showed your correct weight at every step in both pounds and kilos. You simply programmed your shoes to the required weight, and if you exceeded this weight, presumably after having tucked into a couple of illicit hamburgers, when you rose to leave your shoes shrieked at you, with an ear-piercing alarm warning you that you'd exceeded your maximum allowable weight. To my amazement, he sold the idea to the Japanese who no doubt paid him enough money to invent another highly useful and politically correct item. Maybe a concealed water jet in your tie that was activated by an alarm to douse you down every time you saw a pretty woman and an improper thought passed through your head.

Finally, there was the man who came in and said that he had invented the ideal entertainment for long trips along endlessly boring roads, of which there are, admittedly, a great many in Australia.

This was in the form of a photographically illustrated booklet

titled, *The Official Roadside Dead Animal & Bird Spotter's Guide.*
Now, for the first time you could identify every flattened and
squashed furry bit you spied on the Australian outback roads.
The kids would act as spotters and every time you passed a
dead something you could squeal to a halt, reverse rapidly, get
to the flattened object, open the guide and photo-compare until
you found the perfect match, and learned both its common
and its Latin name. It was fun and at the same time educational
and made the long trip pass by effortlessly. This particular bloke
referred to himself on the cover as 'author, traveller & pho-
tographer' and claimed to have taken nearly 20 years to compile
the guide.

I appear to be cruel to inventors and so, not to end on a negative note, I agree they must have to go somewhere to talk about
their ideas, as most of their families have given up talking to them
years ago. If you are an inventor and you plan to call on a direct
marketing organisation, you should first team up with a good
product developer to bring your invention to at least, the proto-
type stage. Then the marketer has something to go on. Not very
much, but something.

If you want to get into direct marketing, first get onto the network.
Starting up in the direct marketing business in merchandise in
Australia or New Zealand, has two major advantages:

- You are on the very doorstep of the world's best manufacturers—the countries of South-East Asia.
- You are working in a relatively under-developed market in both
  countries and the competition, unlike the U.S. or UK, is not
  too fierce in many of the areas of direct marketing.

Furthermore, there is an international community of direct
marketers who talk to each other, trade information and do deals.
It is often quite possible to get a licensing deal for your country
for a product that is a proven success in a number of other countries. This gives it a high likelihood of success in your market. Not
only the product, but the know-how becomes available to you.
This can often be an enormously helpful step in starting up a

direct response business. Eliminating as many risks as possible is what you have to do while you gain experience.

However, when you approach an overseas direct marketer for licensing rights, a word of warning—question the success of the product very closely. When you walk in from Australia and say that you are interested in sourcing products, *everything* is successful! It is vital to sort out the truth from the exaggeration.

Direct marketers are, by nature, optimists and even the most reputable, tend to somewhat colour the accounts of their successes. Why not? Perhaps their biggest failure will *really* work in Australia or New Zealand, what the hell do they know? Take it from me, they usually know! Careful questioning will generally sort out the real successes from the also-rans. So, as they say in the American vernacular: 'Listen up good.'

Always ask for their detailed promotional information—the actual names of the promotional media, the magazines, TV stations, newspapers etc, and the number of orders or responses each delivered and the cost per order from the individual media and, of course, the overall cost per order.

In this manner, you will immediately eliminate half of the 'great successes'. This is *not* because you will be able to completely evaluate the information in a market in which you are unfamiliar, but by the very fact that the marketer won't make this information available to you. The other half you will carefully sort through and, usually, you will be able to pick the truly successful concepts with potential for your own market. Over time, you will build relationships you can trust in the same way as you do in any other business.

An interesting market, especially for someone starting up in the direct marketing business in Australia, New Zealand or South Africa, is *left-over merchandise*. This is the stuff you inevitably have left over at the end of a campaign, even a highly successful one. These are often collectable so they can't be sent to a discount house. Large overseas collectable companies often write them off and destroy them. Keep your eyes and ears open and you can often make a very rich haul.

It's always good news for both parties when you walk into a large

American direct marketing organisation and say: 'Hey, guys, show me what you've got left over. I'm from Australia so we're not going to damage your market!' The welcoming smiles when our buyer walks into a foreign direct marketing house are usually very genuine. The joy is, of course, that what amounts to a trickle of left-overs in America can service a regional market in Australia very well indeed. Also you can usually pick up the merchandise at a very competitive price. Though, don't forget to add the shipping costs, import duty and sales tax!

Here at Bond we have developed an excellent relationship with several U.S. and European collectable companies. This very profitable relationship began when I offered to purchase their end-of-range stock, which, for good commercial reasons, they didn't want to discount to their U.S. customers.

In the collectable business, as well as in many other product categories, you can never discount your stock. Your only option is to get it into another market where you don't sell. This almost always means another country. If we can't export our excess stock, we destroy it. It makes you wince when you see an exquisite piece smashed to smithereens. But if you are a collector, the last thing you want to see is a limited edition item, for which you paid $100, marked down to $30 on a junk table at the Saturday markets. Do so, do not even be tempted to discount remnants, your company's reputation is much more important than the few extra dollars you may make.

The way to acquire rights to various products is to agree to pay a royalty to the owner of the product or the company that owns the rights to it for Australia and New Zealand, or the country in which you want to conduct your business. This royalty would be for the rights to sell the product and to use the promotional material which has been successfully used elsewhere. However, you might adapt it, or even develop your own promo material. The accepted royalty is 5 per cent to 7 per cent of the nett paid sales. This we have found to be a very fair figure for everyone involved and seems to be acceptable internationally.

The temptation is huge to change the offer made in the host country where the product was first marketed. America is not

Australia. The argument is that we're different; we don't react or think the same and we have different needs. Usually, this is all nonsense. My advice to you is to only change the dates and places and an expression which may not be known in your market. **Change nothing else! A successful and tested promotion is money in the bank, even if it has been tested and successful elsewhere! People are people through other people**.

In 1985 we found the American Eagle Knife and never was there a more 'American' product. It was developed to commemorate the anniversary of the American eagle as the symbol for the United States. This was American-apple-pie-marketing down to the last, crumby slice. I was surprised when I picked it up and opened the blade that it didn't play 'Stars and Stripes Forever'.

'It won't work here, Ian,' the experts warned me, 'At least change the copy; it will make Australians want to throw up!'

Let me tell you a little more about the miracle of the American Eagle Knife. My brilliant partner Michael Harrison, with absolutely no inspiration from The Ziff Dog, discovered this whole new category of collectable in 1984. By simply adding an elaborate engraving of an American Eagle to the blade of a pretty standard pocket knife, to commemorate, his copy said, the great symbol of the U.S. of A., he turned a very mundane item into a huge bestseller.

His genius went even a step further and he numbered each blade with an individual number which gave it that extra touch of individualism. Of course, we didn't match the numbers with the purchaser's name. The Japanese manufacturer simply kept a register of the numbers at the factory.

I guess knives attract some of the wrong people and not infrequently we would get a call from the police in Australia telling us that knife number 46831 had been involved in a stabbing or a hold-up, in some suburb and could we please give them the name of the purchaser? Alas, we had to confess to the boys in blue the reality of the collectables business. They would get very upset and the sergeant would come onto the phone and abuse us. They loved the idea of solving a stabbing by numbers and were naturally upset that such a simple solution to a crime wasn't going to work.

Despite the urging from my associates to drop the idea of the American Eagle knife in Australia, I convinced myself that I had very little to lose in a test. The knife could be sold in this market at a very attractive $19.95 and I had the complete artwork intact, and in English, for pretty well the price of the paper it was printed on.

The American Eagle pocket knife had a response rate three times better here in Australia than it had in the U.S.A. We took it to 15 other countries, where it was just as successful. In South Africa, it was the most successful of all, nearly five times the spectacular response of the original U.S. result.

But there was one blip on the screen and it's an interesting one to note. The American Eagle knife offer did not work very well in New Zealand and for a noteworthy reason. In 1984, there was a ban on U.S. nuclear ships entering New Zealand harbours. A big fuss had been made about this by the Americans, who appeared to New Zealanders as over-assertive and aggressive and so things American were very unpopular. This included the American Eagle knife, which bombed. I guess the lesson here is to keep your ear to the ground, nothing, not even the American Eagle knife, is failure proof. Though it nearly was. In fact, the American Eagle knife eventually grossed $40,000,000 in sales without changing a word in the copy or re-arranging a single picture. The offer ran exactly as it was originally conceived in the USA.

The manufacturer in Japan was so gratified that he gave Michael and myself a solid gold version of the Great American Eagle knife to commemorate the single biggest knife order Japan has ever received. (see pic)

Sourcing product locally. Sourcing local product is always a difficult business. This is mainly because manufactures, especially in Australia, are not familiar with direct marketing requirements. It is always difficult to convince manufacturers to do things slightly differently to suit the needs of our industry. Even when you are selling traditional retail products, such as luggage or cashmere knits, the colours, design and detailing needs to be noticeably different. Furthermore, the special packaging requirements which are often needed, seldom interest the manufacturer, who sees only the short run involved and not the potential to sell more goods.

In the U.S. and the U.K., there is a quite different attitude. Direct marketing is simply seen as an additional way to sell and as a well established distribution method for goods and services. Manufacturers have happily and willingly embraced the medium. They have representatives who do nothing else but call on direct marketers. These men and woman are experts in the special requirements you may need in packaging and innovation. They also have a method called 'drop shipping,' which means they hold your order in their warehouse and as you generate sales you send the address label to the manufacturers' warehouse and they attach the label and dispatch it directly to your customer.

In Australia there is a tendency in manufacturing to think that by co-operating with a direct marketer, they are going to mess up the retail trade, which they regard as their bread and butter. This, by the way, is simply not true and there is a lot of evidence to disprove this notion. A direct marketing campaign, with price parity with retail outlets, will always help retail sales. Bell & Howell were the first people to actually document this discovery with their home movie products in the U.S. nearly 25 years ago.

Every time Bell and Howell mailed their big, colourful home movie promotions direct to consumers, the sales in their retail outlets (to which they sold wholesale) rose significantly. Many customers, preferring the contact and reassurance of their local camera shop, came in clutching the brochure even though it clearly stated: 'This special offer only available through mail order.' Bell and Howell quickly recognised that direct marketing was a very effective way of advertising and that every time a well-constructed, good-quality and highly-exciting mailing went out, it left behind a strong and impressive awareness of the brand.

The fact that some customers simply will not respond to a mail order offer, but will go looking for the same product in the shops, was well known to them. They exploited it with good point-of-sale promotions in their movie camera outlets.

Every direct marketer worries about the 98 per cent of people who don't respond to a direct marketing offer. When retail sales rise as a direct result of your direct marketing campaign, then you know that you are tapping into this non-responsive majority and doing the retailers' work for them. Lester Wunderman, the father of our business, is unable to explain why response rates have remained the same over the 30 years since he coined the phrase, 'Direct Marketing.' I guess that while the life of a direct marketer is in the fast lane, the traffic doesn't seem to get any heavier.

Properly-managed direct marketing and retail activity are complementary. When, one year, we became the biggest outlet for Onkaparinga blankets, all sold by direct response, the great Adelaide retail shop, John Martins, the home of Onkaparinga, would applaud every promotion we ran as they too would register record sales of that particular brand name during and immediately after the promotional period. Ironically, they did not stock the exact Onkaparinga blanket we were selling.

The point is, that many people actually enjoy shopping and the success of direct marketing, except in deeply rural areas, is not due to location. Shopping at home is a different experience to shopping in town and people demand and enjoy both shopping systems. Browsing can still be a lot of fun and is, in effect, building a catalogue in the heads of the customer, a list of things to note for future reference. A direct response mailing or advertisement is an individual consideration. Women will tell you they don't go shopping for a single item; they go shopping for an experience. In direct marketing catalogues are more of an experience than single item offers and these days retail shopping is not always a nice experience. Late night shopping isn't simply a convenience, it's an opportunity to take the family for a good look around and end up at McDonalds for a special treat for the kids. The two methods of acquiring goods and services should never be confused and while, in certain product categories, they may compete for the same dollar, they never compete for the same experience.

There are also some products which make people feel uncomfortable in a retail shopping environment and which suit direct marketing ideally. Collectables are just such a market. People who buy collectables are, in effect, amateur collectors. They are novice enthusiasts who will often go onto possess a surprising expertise in their product areas. Such a person is often intimidated by 'expert' salespersons who start throwing dates and periods around.

This is similarly true of the wine collector, who is new to the mystique of the grape. I can remember how surprised I was to learn that the name of the variety of grape told you precisely what to expect in the bottle. That a chardonnay was a white grape with a taste that wasn't sweet, but crisp and light. We all have to acquire our knowledge from somewhere, or someone, but preferably not from a snotty-nosed salesperson who pauses too long and coughs into his fist when you ask a basic question which clearly indicates to him your amateur status and pathetic ignorance. Like Dud asking for milk when he'd ordered black coffee, or once, when I was having lunch with a noted gourmet, he suggested gazpacho as an entree. As it was a cold, blustery day of the kind you occasionally get in Sydney in mid-summer, I said: 'That will be great, nothing like a bowl of hot soup to warm one up on a miserable day like this!'

There are **two great qualities** *of direct marketing that greatly help this situation. These are:* **privacy and branding**. In the privacy of her own home, without any embarrassment or pressure, your cardholder, customer or collector can read about the winsome ceramic doll, the china plate, or the exquisite burgundy, or special offer. With a well-known brand name and lots of credentials in the brochure, she or he feels reassured that they are making a wise choice.

Direct marketing has forged a strong alliance with some of the world's great manufacturers so that, in some instances, they market a particular product only through direct response. We used to market with the manufacturers of the world famous Waterford Wedgwood glass and china. Two impeccable brand names personalised in Australia by the wonderful relationship I enjoyed with a true professional and great Welshman, John Thomas, from Wedgwood. This joint venture between Bond and Wedgwood was living proof of the synergy between direct marketing and retailing.

Wedgwood produce an exclusive direct marketing collector's

range which we made available in Australia in an affinity group called, The Wedgwood Collectors Society, which boasted more than 35,000 members at its peak. This direct marketing activity creates image and awareness among people who may not previously have known the brand name. They look out for it in retail outlets and so confirm the validity of the brand name. Over a period of 15 years, we have run a great many full-page advertisements for items not available in retail stores and Wedgwood have received only one complaint from a retailer.

This is good for our industry, good for Waterford Wedgwood, good news for retailers and, of course, highly reassuring and good for customers. Everyone wins.

Protecting your marketing exclusivity—don't bother! If you were a new direct marketer and came to me, rather than to a lawyer, for advice about protecting your patent or marketing exclusivity, I'd tell you not to bother. This kind of angst you do not need, even though your lawyer does and will advise you to sue the living daylights out of the intruder into your product's private rights. One of the hard facts of life to remember is that if you are successful, someone, some unscrupulous operator, will copy what you are doing. Companies , mostly in America, make commercial decisions daily, based on what it will cost them to break a patent and copy an idea. You won't stop this happening. It happens to Coca-Cola, Toyota, to IBM and it will happen to you.

Australia is full of people who have bought the 'exclusive rights' to all sorts of rubbish. Certain kinds of Asian companies will give you the exclusive rights to anything as they simply have no intention of keeping this promise, whether legal or otherwise. You need to be very careful and very cynical, and have an understanding of international trade before you make a move. And even then, don't make book on being safely protected.

A friend of mine, an orthopaedic surgeon, in the anything goes entrepreneurial market of the high-flying 80s, bought a container-load of plastic prawn peelers from Asia with a watertight guarantee of market exclusivity. The agreement leaked so much that the supermarkets were flooded with the prawn peelers before his container had actually landed in Australia.

Wedgwood's first trip to China resulted in them commissioning an exclusive pattern, which turned up in K-Mart even before their merchandise arrived in Australia.

On one occasion, we had a Korean ship's captain steal a whole ship full of merchandise after he had signed the bills of lading. Also quite often the shipment doesn't match your product sample from the manufacturer, and it is absolutely essential to get the right to approve the pre-production sample in the letter of credit.

Let me tell you about the 'Busts of American Presidents'. In one early venture, Michael 'Ziff Dog' Harrison and I came up with the idea that we would commission from Hong Kong busts of all the Presidents of America, the perfect collectable for every God-fearing and loyal American home. If it had worked in America, I thought I might try it in Australia with all of the past Prime Ministers. Good ideas like this don't come along every day—and this was even before the American Eagle knife. It had all the feelings you get for a great, great promotion. We were inexperienced, but not so inexperienced as not to test the offer. We decided to test a small run in America, a mailing of around 300,000 households. We ordered sufficient busts to supply the expected response and because we wanted to do the promotion in a hurry, we didn't ask for pre-production samples.

I recall the day they arrived. The production department brought through the first small packing case and Michael and I, conscious that this was our very first truly big idea, opened it together. I know I was shaking with anticipation as he lifted out the first beautifully-made ceramic bust. It was absolutely perfect, except for one small detail. It had oriental eyes and every one, all 27 American Presidents, had oriental eyes! You haven't lived until you've seen Abraham Lincoln with oriental eyes!

The best way to get any kind of exclusivity is to be first and fast. Your strongest weapon is your speed and your customer base. As an instance of this, we are still the biggest supplier in the collector doll market in Australia and we are determined to hold this position against increasing competition from the big multi-nationals, who are now very active in the market. But our database is very precious to us, collected with care and consideration and with much of it long turned from prospects to advocates. It isn't going to be easy to catch us! Furthermore, because we are a highly innovative company, unlike our competition, we are developing dolls with an Australian theme. When you make the running there is far less chance of someone catching up and passing you—provided you do not grow complacent.

How to price a new product. Let me begin this section with the last little story from my past. Michael Harrison and I were out walking The Ziff Dog in New York's Central Park one sunny Sunday afternoon when a quite attractive prostitute stopped us. She started to chat to us about The Ziff Dog. As we chatted, I noticed that she was wearing a very unusual pair of sunglasses. My then wife Suzi, whose father was one of the original founders of OPSM, Australia's best known optical company, must possess one of the world's largest collection of spectacles. But these, worn by the street lady chatting to us, were special. I knew Suzi would simply love to own them. As such conversations are always slanted in one direction, the prostitute finally suggested that Michael and I, together with The Ziff Dog, come up to her room for a combined good time. While The Ziff Dog seemed willing, having quite taken to the lady, Michael and I politely declined. But her glasses still fascinated me.

'Will you sell your sunglasses to me?' I asked.

She removed the glasses and looked at me with large and pretty brown eyes: 'You don't want no trick with you and the dawg, that cost hunnerd dollars: You want these glasses? Man, that also gonna cost you hunnerd dollars!'

While it was probably an outrageous price for the glasses, I knew they would amuse Suzi and so I paid her the $100 for her glasses. I must confess, I never told Suzi where they came from and every time she wore them at a party, I would wonder what Michael, The Ziff Dog and I had missed by buying the glasses instead of the original proposition.

I guess the point here is that the way you price an item is rated by the demand for it and, of course, its exclusivity. There is also the Sheinberg system which I mentioned earlier in this book— some items look expensive and can therefore command a higher price, as demonstrated by the way he made us price a handbag without knowing its manufacturing price.

However, there are certain psychological barriers to take into consideration, The magic mass market price point in Australia and New Zealand is still $19.95, the price of this book. This is a kind of discretionary limit. When I started in business in 1972, it was $9.95—that was how far people were prepared to go before they got serious about a buying decision. In the near future, it will become $29.95.

It is a curious thing, proved too often to dispute, that while logic tells us that $29.95 and $30 are too close to bother about, our eye settles on the number $29. We don't seem to bother with the 95 cents. We decide the offer is affordable and, at the same time, we reject the $30 item, which we decide isn't. People are people all over.

Don't make the mistake of thinking you'll clean up by pricing something in between $19.95 and $29.95—say $24.95. This will simply not work. It is a curious fact that in direct reponse there doesn't seem to be any half-price points between the two acknowl-edged price points of $19.95 and $29.95. If you were to price some-thing at $24.95, the loss in sales can be very large. It will almost never be made up by the extra $5 you earn with the in-between price. If you are faced with the decision to price between $19.95 and $24.95, it is no decision at all, simply go for the first. The real decision will lie between charging $19.95 and $29.95 and the only way you will resolve this is to price test in two separate markets.

By the way, this 'no half-point price theory' also works over $100. The three price points are $98.00 then $148.00 then $198.00. The same principles apply to the price points of monthly payments, which are just as critical as price points of goods and services. A very up-to-the-moment example is that the price point for pay television is less than $50 and will probably come in at $12 per week, or $48.00 per month, to keep it under the dreaded $50 price barrier.

Similarly, while there is a great sensitivity between price and response in direct marketing, there is hardly any price comparison between direct market prices and outside retail prices. You can ask a premium price on a direct response item which is available in retail for less. The reasons for this seem to be the absence of direct comparison, which leaves the customer to value the article or service on their own perception of what it is worth.

It's always a good idea to use the Sheinberg method—ask people around the office what they think the article is worth without letting them know the wholesale or cost price. Remember, your customer only sees perceived value and you must learn to price accordingly. A badly-designed product which functions brilliantly will not sell in direct marketing, no matter how cheap or expensive. It *must* be seen as good value and the eye is almost exclusively the decider—unless you have a brand name which is famous and the right words to back it up.

May your life in Direct Marketing
be filled with American Eagle knives,
and contain no
'Dead Roadside Animals
and Bird Spotter's Guides.'

The Last Word

'Who knows? Tomorrow in comes something
and you forget already to be clever!'
Albert Sheinberg.

★ ★ ★

One of the great joys of direct marketing is that when the boffins have hung up their thinking caps, and the theorists have told you just how things ought to be, and the analysts have predicted every possible outcome, and the computer has tracked and collected and collated all the information since the beginning of the world, it is still a business that works well on commonsense. Direct marketing is about getting the basics right, about using your intelligence.

Like every business discipline, there seems to be a great need for the technocrats to complicate things. For a start, it sells textbooks and computer programs and hardware and software and research and all the dinky little add-ons that make simple things difficult. But if you know and care about people, and have had a little experience of buying and selling to them, talking with them, and trying to understand their needs, then there is every chance that you are ideally equipped for a career in direct marketing.

Here then, is the final round-up, the commonsense things that drive the direct marketing business. If your kids decide to have a garage sale this Saturday, or you are the chief executive or marketing director in the throes of planning a multi-million dollar advertising campaign, there are six simple fundamentals you will have to observe if you are going to be successful. Together they form the logic and commonsense you will need.

1. The Power of One to One. The first fundamental has been the theme of this book. People. All good marketing is about individuals. The very first lesson I learned, is that all response marketing is one person to one other person. Me to you. Every marketing and advertising proposal must end up talking to one person at a time if it is going to work.

The Body Shop founder, Anita Roddick, says: 'Don't sell to everyone; sell to someone'. The most important thing people in business ought to understand is that marketing observes the same rules as those of a personal relationship. Whenever you are looking at a marketing or a selling proposition, try to sit down and think about it in terms of you putting a proposition to one person.

I often put someone from the office in a chair at my desk and sit down and talk to them about what I am trying to do. I don't try and sell them an idea, I talk to them about it.

'We have come across this great idea, I'd love to know what you think about it.' That's the start-off sentence. Notice that I haven't said, 'I have this great idea!' The ownership, the possession of the idea, is not immediately challenging the listener. It is not interfering with the proposition while the most important point is established—that the listener is the most important aspect of the entire proposition. 'He wants my opinion; he values what I might think. Good things may happen because I have made an input.' That's what the listener takes out of your introduction.

From the very first sentence, the listener is made a part of the discussion: the one to one relationship is working. Do this often enough and you will start using different words and different thoughts, because one of the great truths in marketing, advertising and business is that individuals make decisions. Companies don't make decisions, audiences don't make decisions, companies don't write letters—individuals do. The one-to-one relationship is the only possible working partnership a successful direct marketing business can adopt. Nothing else works.

Good relationship marketers are amateur behavioural psychologists. You have to try to predict how someone is going to behave, and to do this, you have to see their desires from the inside out. To get inside their heads and their hearts, you are forced to focus on their needs and not yours. The result you are trying to achieve is one which will ultimately be of advantage to you—a sale made, or an influence achieved, or a decision reversed. You will only achieve this by convincing the person to whom you are talking that there is something in it for them. The person listening to you isn't doing so because they feel duty bound to be polite. 'What's in this for me?' is the question they ask themselves as you talk. If you can't answer this question to their satisfaction, you are a dead fish in the water.'

You will recall the story of how we achieved the licence to market the Ralph Lauren Polo brand in Australia. I had a half an hour to convince the Polo people that I should have the licence for Australia and I wasn't even in the clothing business. But that this was an advantage. So, to say the least, it was going to be a challenging half hour.

I had to ask myself what the objectives, the needs, of Mr Edwin Lewis of Ralph Lauren were? When you pause to think about it, the answer was simple: His objective was to get rid of me as quickly as possible. I could satisfy that very easily. I didn't need half an hour, 10 minutes was sufficient. When I thought about it, later, I decided three minutes would have been enough.

What was his second objective? That too wasn't so difficult: 'Get these Australians off my back permanently.'

I could do that, too. All he had to do was give me the file and the right to review anyone who wanted the Polo franchise in Australia.

I've told you the story of how, in a matter of only a few minutes, I was able to meet both *his* objectives and at the same time I achieved my own.

If I hadn't adopted the technique of getting into his head, of solving his problems, I would have said something like: 'I'm the best person in Australia to do this for you. I'm going to put together a syndicate of people … .etc, etc'. He, like most people, didn't want to hear my self-importance. He wanted to get rid of me. He wanted to get rid of the file. He'd had enough. I solved both problems quickly and, in the process, started a relationship that has led to a profitable and amicable partnership which has lasted for years.

Here is an example of how to reduce a complicated marketing problem to a one-to-one proposal.

I am on the Advisory Board of The Sydney Food Bank, a charity organisation which distributes food to needy families. Food companies give us food that they no longer need for various reasons. They may have produced too many of something, or something else didn't sell well in retail or was left over from a special promotion, or was wrongly-labelled, or any of a host of things. The Food Bank stores it and transports it to welfare agencies who, in turn, distribute it to families in need.

Like most charities we have a fund-raising problem, and like most charities we decided to 'stick out our hands' and ask people to give. We would explain what the Sydney Food Bank did, how it got its food, how it distributed it and how it needed money to run the warehouse, the trucks, the staff and all the other administration. And then we'd wait for the cheques to arrive. When we'd received all the donations, we would run a full page in one of the newspapers and print all the names of all the companies who gave more than $10,000. You've seen this sort of thing before and, of course, it breaks every known rule in relationship marketing. It is possibly the most common and certainly the worst fund-raising idea ever devised.

Fortunately, commonsense prevailed and, ultimately, we built our campaign around the idea of good management. We showed that because of the extreme care we take with the funds given to us we are able to feed one hungry person three meals for $1 a day. For one year it costs $365, and to keep an average Australian family the cost is just $4 a day. We then asked each company to feed one or more families with three meals a day for a year at a cost of $1,500 per family. And, of course, it worked very well.

What we gave them was an easy decision, a reason to act with a generous spirit. They knew where their money was going—to seven families who were battling to make ends meet—at least the kids would eat properly. They felt that as business people they had acted not only decently but prudently by having supported a charity that stretches every dollar and spends it wisely. Finally, they felt like real heroes and their staff felt good about the company. They have all done something tangible for seven real families who were having a rough time. They could easily visualise the families as not very different from their own. What we gave them was the opportunity to solve a problem on a one-to-one basis. There are a lot of rewards in there for the donor.

World Vision is the most successful charity in the world. The reason is simple. They put the donor directly in touch with the child. The donors feel they have a relationship with that child and that they can really make a difference.

I know in my work with the Starlight Foundation that one of the reasons this charity has been so enormously successful is because we managed to introduce a sponsorship scheme where people can actually grant the wish of a particular child. And that's one of the reasons why the money comes into Starlight at a time when all the charities are having difficulty. Individual donors both corporate and private feel they can make a difference to the quality of life of a seriously-ill child.

Never has the power of one-to-one had more meaning for me than with the work I do with other people on the Starlight Foundation. It's a charity that soon gets you hooked because it brings so much joy to so many families. Before I joined I felt, as I think most people do, that charities are overburdened with top-heavy bureaucracies and filled with people more interested in social status than in helping the disadvantaged. The Starlight Foundation has a strictly business attitude when it comes to spending a dollar in infrastructure.

The Starlight Foundation ensures that hundreds of Australian families benefit to the maximum extent. The idea with the Starlight Foundation is to grant a critically, chronically or terminally ill child a wish. It may be arranging for him or her to meet a famous celebrity, or a visit to Disneyland, or a holiday for the family or a computer or just food for the family for a year. In fact, it is seldom that a child will make a wish we cannot find a way to grant through the ingenuity and generosity of the people who donate, manage, market, persuade or simply contribute on behalf of the foundation. Ordinary people by their thousands want to come onto our database and their contribution surpasses any loyalty program I've ever encountered in commerce. People are people through other people.

2. Marketing relationships parallel personal relationships. When you first meet somebody in a business environment, the situation is exactly the same as if you had met them in a personal environment. The way in which you react to them, and the speed with which you contact them the second time, significantly affects the quality of the relationship from that moment on. You meet someone at a cocktail party or a dinner party at a mutual friend's place, you enjoy their company and the evening goes well. Finally, the time comes to go home. You shake hands and say your good-byes. 'We must meet again soon, dinner perhaps? I'll call you.' They agree this would be nice.

If you're fostering relationships and you meet somebody and they are enthusiastic about you, and you express interest in them and you have a great conversation, and then you never hear from them again it is disappointing. It takes ages to claw your way back to the situation you had at the first contact. It is no different in business. If you want to build quality relationships, personally or commercially, get in touch with them as quickly as you possibly can after the very first contact.

In fact, in a direct marketing campaign, get in touch with them within two days from the moment they send in the coupon, or make some sort of affirmative response to your offer. That's all the time you've got. Two days or, if there is a weekend in the middle, four days. Get the personalised letter out, or get on the phone and call them. If you take longer than two days, you are seriously damaging the potential of the relationship.

How often should you contact them thereafter? Well, again, it's like a personal relationship, it has to be maintained. In the case of direct marketing, four times a year is the minimum to keep in touch, to have somebody welcome the prospect of doing business with you again.

If you can afford it, six times a year is even better. Once every couple of months. By direct mail or via the telephone are still the two best ways to maintain contact in Australia, and both are still very cost effective.

When you don't maintain regular contacts with your prospects you insidiously, though relentlessly, destroy the goodwill of your business without even knowing you are doing so. What's more, your customers won't know the relationship is dying: they will simply forget you exist, because you are no longer meaningful to them. In direct marketing, not making regular contact I call *the silent destroyer*. That's because your prospect or your customer friend doesn't ring you up and dismiss you officially, or even complain, they simply forget you. They silently destroy the relationship.

Some mail order companies still believe that their customers are prepared to wait 21 days for delivery. You will recall when it was more or less standard for mail order companies to say: 'Please allow 21 days delivery'. Those days, if they ever existed, are well and truly gone. Your customer, like your new friendship, will only blossom with fast initial follow-up and regular further contact.

Good direct marketing companies have proved that, whenever possible, the expense of maintaining extra inventory to enable them to deliver customers faster is more cost effective than the damage that late delivery does to the goodwill of their business.

Micro Warehouse in the United States, a $600 million business selling hardware and software direct, delivers by midday the next day providing you order before midnight. They deliver every day of the week in 92 per cent of the United States in this time. If you do not deliver promptly, the next time you try to sell your customer something, they will simply say: '*Ah, thanks but no thanks, I waited to long for my order to come last time. I wanted it for the holidays and it arrived the day after I returned to work.*' The silent destroyer has silently destroyed once again.

And as for the old adage: 'If you are not entirely satisfied your money will be cheerfully refunded,' the hoary old money-back guarantee which indolent direct marketers for so long thought got them off the hook for everything, is now just a routine part of consumerism in the 90's. In fact, the money-back guarantee today is among the dinosaurs of direct marketing.

People who make a decision to buy something don't want their money back, they want the something they used their money to get, and they want it to come fast and they want it too be good. They didn't fork out money to be disappointed. The money you sent back to them is an admission, from both parties, that the transaction, has failed.

You have to have a money-back guarantee, if for no other reason than that the law demands it. But in the bad old days direct marketers used to say: 'Oh, give them their money back! That'll make them happy and take care of our obligation to them.'

It should be painfully obvious that it is no longer sufficient to do this. It probably never was. Your prospect will still drop you like a hot potato, even with the money safely back in his pocket or her purse unless all the other requirements have been met for a long term relationship.

3. Like personal relationships, successful marketing relationships are built on trust. The very same trust that you have with friends, family and close business associates, is the sort of trust that you now have to build with your customers. The breaking of this trust will always greatly affect any relationship. It is no different than it is with a friend. Let a friend down when he or she has implicitly trusted you to deliver, and you place your friendship in real jeopardy.

In today's environment, people are naturally anxious. They are mistrustful and cautious and the traditional routines and disciplines of assumed trust between two parties have diminished. Trust is not automatically given and you should not assume that you have it by implication.

However, this very lack of trust in today's business and personal environment presents you with an enormous business opportunity to be the exception. There has never been a better time to build a relationship based on trust. If you can do so in today's environment, more than ever, this will be the major prerequisite for your success.

In the mistrustful 90s, it is no longer enough to ask people to keep buying your goods or services. That is, simply presenting the opportunity to buy. Increasingly, consumers are asking whether or not *they* want to keep doing business with *you?* You are not presenting your services as a personal favour to them; your customers are using your services because they enjoy the process of dealing with you. Those companies and individuals who understand that the customer is making the rules, and not the supplier, are enjoying wonderful success in direct marketing and, indeed, in every other type of business.

How do you go about making your customer want to buy from you, even when the merchandise you sell is available elsewhere, and sometimes at slightly less cost?

Once again it amounts to putting what your customer's need ahead of your own. Ask yourself what the values are of the people with whom you are doing business? If you know their beliefs and values, you can reflect those values as your own corporate or personal ones. Their values become your values. That's how you build trust. That's how you build relationships that last. You stand for something, beyond doing business, with which your customer can readily identify.

McDonalds sold their hamburgers in styro-foam containers and their customers objected because they were a product of the petro-chemical industry and not ecologically sound. So McDonalds changed their containers to conform with the values of their customers. The styro-foam containers were undoubtedly cheaper than their replacement. But in the long term, they would have alienated McDonald's traditional base of young people who care about the environment. So they assumed the values of their customers. For very sound commercial reasons, McDonalds became ecologically involved.

The Body Shop turned this strategy into an art form. The Body Shop is a modern-day commercial phenomenon. Based on profits per square foot of shop space, they are the most successful retail trading organisation in the world.

When you walk into The Body Shop, there is simply no mistaking the values they espouse. Not only do their customers get the most beautiful skin and body care in the world, they also get the safest, the purest, the most chemical-free and the most natural and ecologically-sound products possible.

This is a very compelling promise when you are young and care about such things. Increasingly, people are making stands on issues, using their wallets and purses as the major weapon. The Body Shop knows all about reflecting the values of its customers.

Who wouldn't want to do business with a company which plants twice as many trees as the paper it uses in its daily corporate life. That's exactly what Optus Communications is now doing in Australia and what Hanna Andersson, one of the most successful children's catalogue companies in the U.S., is doing.

Howard Draft, the President of Kobbs & Draft Worldwide, evolved this strategy and called it *The Value of Values*. It should be one of the major strategies for all marketers in the 90s. Esprit, the Melbourne-based clothing company largely involved in clothes for young adults, understands the value of values very well. Esprit has built a help organisation called Esprit de Cause, where they take kids off the street with no skills and not much of a future, and re-train them to be skilled and responsible for themselves. The late John Bell, the Esprit Australian chief executive, started Esprit de Cause and now that company has adopted his value-of-values strategy world-wide.

The value of values is also the reason why Levi Strauss, the jeans manufacturer, pulled out of China over the human rights issue. They won't do business in any country where they are forced to pay bribes, or where human rights are neglected. These two onslaughts against humanity seem always to pair. This means about half the countries in the world are no longer available to the famous jeans name. The cost to them in lost sales will be high, but they have kept faith with the intrinsic values of their customers and their own principals. I hope the rewards for doing so will more than compensate them in the markets where they are loved and respected for their corporate integrity.

4. Understand that Relationship Marketing is data driven. The starting point for everything is the database. It becomes at once fairly obvious that if you want to become involved on a one-to-one basis with your customer, that the more you know about him or her the more likely you are to succeed.

Many marketers are deterred by the cost of building the database. It requires a major commitment and a major change in thinking, particularly in Australia and New Zealand.

However, today many intelligent marketers realise it's not just a marketing cost. Their financial people now acknowledge that when you build a sound database, you are building a major company asset. A hotel which has a database and uses it to re-book last year's functions or accommodation is worth at lot more on resale than the hotel whose planning executives are flying by the seat of their pants. The database has increased the capital value of the hotel. I am told by the Sheraton Hotel marketing department that in a business hotel, such as theirs, at any one time 30 per cent of their rooms are occupied by their own loyalty card holders. In building the database, you are actually creating an asset which can be valued and written into the books.

If all this is so simple and straightforward and these are the fundamentals, why do marketers consistently get them wrong? Because they constantly undervalue the importance of gathering meaningful data on their customers.

In direct marketing, everybody loves putting the offer together, and even more, doing the creative work. It's great fun to sit around and argue about what the brochure should look like and what the pictures should be. If you are a creative director, and are lucky enough to have a Porsche, and a pony tail with no grey hair streaking it, you get a hell of a lot of dinner invitations from all the right sorts of people. But, in the short back 'n sides of a database consultant's life, there are a great many lonely take-away meals eaten at your desk late at night.

5. Understand the limitations of mass media in direct marketing. Mass media is not ideally suitable for one-to-one marketing, and so you have to learn how to turn it to your advantage and make it work for you.

The print mass media, newspapers and magazines, are a total anachronism and mass broadcast media, television in particular, is rapidly becoming so. Newspapers are basically the same as they were 50 years ago. This is one of the reasons there has been a huge growth in small specialty magazines and niche publications. The mass media has let the individual down. Many direct marketers have become so disenchanted with the failure of mass media to deliver, that they have come to rely on their database used together with a newsletter, because they can personalise their marketing and create the conditions for a one-to-one relationship.

But the good news is the Information Super Highway. The advent very soon of interactive TV, video on demand, and other new broadcast technology, means that narrowcasting (the opposite to *broad*casting and mass media), is the medium of the future. This change is occurring very, very rapidly.

There are 20 million people world-wide now who are on the *Internet.* Twenty million people! Just a scratch on the surface, but all in less than three years. So there is already a large number of your customers who come home and switch on a PC instead of the TV. This will expand by millions each month as the technological revolution starts to bite.

There are 300,000 CD Rom installations in Australia alone and we expect them to keep growing strongly. We already have the same number of installations as the U.K. Someone recently described the Information Super Highway as a bit like teenage sex—everyone is talking about it, and is very excited about it. But hardly anyone understands it. Practically nobody is doing it, and those people who are, are doing it well and keeping very quiet about it.

There will be a big strategic change when the media breaks down from big to small, from general to particular, from impersonal to personal.

What is and will continue to increasingly happen from a strategic point of view, is that the media will move from intrusion to invitation. Or to put it into non marketing terms—from ambush to romance.

We will have to change the way we market and sell so that we get prospects to invite us to make contact instead of smashing down the front door. And, of course, that is what multi-channel and multi-cable TV will do. The consumer will be given such a huge choice that the challenge will become how you get them to choose you. The subtle-as-a-meat-axe school of hard-sell advertising will finally disappear. The blatant and uninvited intrusion into your living room is about to end.

Think about your database as a media in its own right. Think about it as a magazine you own, which has the capacity to compete with other media. But, because you own it, you have total control over it. You can control what goes into it, you can control its circulation and, best of all, you can control its tone of voice.

If you think about your database as a media, it will give you a new and correct perspective. So, the first important lesson to learn, is not to leave the database to a consultant or technician. They do not know how to arrange your customer information into a user-friendly system. They only know how to do the technical part. *Only* the marketing people understand the solution to a workable database. They are the only people who can ask the fundamental questions, which are: How did people behave? When did they buy? When did they last buy and for how much? What did they say at the last sales course? Did they come to the cocktail party? Did they respond to the newsletter? Behaviour is the most important criteria for organising the database and if you don't organise it along behavioural lines, it will never work as a relational database. If you think you can survive without a database in the direct marketing of the 90s you can forget it. But, remember, a good database doesn't always have to be a bank of computers. If you're working off the kitchen table, a well-constructed card index system will work. The next huge extension, a PC (personal computer) with CD ROM can carry all the names in the Yellow Pages on a single disk. The database has become available to all if you want to build one and it will fit in the corner of your desk or on the kitchen dresser.

6. It is essential to understand that the consumer is gaining

control and calling the shots. This is the most exciting time that I've ever seen in relationship marketing. It's not being driven by us any more, it's being driven by the customer. Not only does she or he decide with whom to do business, but your customers will also tell you how to modify the goods or services they want to suit their individual needs.

Your potential customers are demanding, in a business sense, intimate relationships. Before the Industrial Revolution, if you wanted a pair of shoes, or a coat, you went to the bootmaker or the tailor and you had them made to your personal fitting. Then came the Industrial Revolution with the invention of the factory. Things were made in bulk and on an impersonal basis and stored in warehouses to be shipped out to wholesalers and retailers to advertise and sell to a look-alike and act-alike industrialised society. Now the whole cycle is starting to come around again and we are getting back to the bootmaker and the tailor, who will make things precisely the way you want them to be. Levi announced recently in the U.S. they will tailor jeans individually for women.

Dell Computers sells $3 billion worth of computers direct. That means no wholesaler or retailer. This would have been regarded as a fantasy just 5 years ago. If you had predicted this outcome to anyone in the computer industry, that is, that without a salesman or a wholesaler or a retail outlet, $3 billion worth of computers could be sold, they would have had you certified.

Ninety-two per cent of Dell Computers are configured individually and delivered within 72 hours in the United States. Configured and delivered within 72 hours? Just extraordinary!

The Motorola Pager in the United States is available in 3000 different versions. The Salesman takes your order, puts it on the modem, pumps it down the line to the factory, and 17 minutes later your pager drops off the end of the assembly line. One-to-one marketing is changing the way we make things.

We are changing the way we look at goods and services. The National Bicycle Company in Japan makes 11 million variations of bikes, and commands 10 per cent higher pricing than the rest of the bicycle suppliers because you can buy a bicycle which precisely meets your needs.

Consumers will always pay for personalisation simply because the ownership of the item becomes emotional. Consumers are also prepared to pay for trust in a relationship. Hooray! The customer is finally back in control. Multi-channel broadcast media in Australia (is exports), and with an index finger you will be able to select from 40 different channels. The revolution has begun.

So there it is. I have tried to give you most of what I know and I hope it has been helpful. With the stuff I've talked about, we have managed in 25 years to build the only Australian-founded, direct-marketing organisation that has operated successfully in many other countries and achieved some small international reputation. You can do the same thing in an age where almost anything is becoming possible in the direct marketing business.

In that 25 years, direct marketing, or relationship marketing, as it is now called, has grown from being a dirty word into a buzz word. Direct Marketing has become an accepted way of doing business and more than that, in the last few years there has been a staggering amount of change which is driven by business itself.

Never before have I seen so many clients demanding direct marketing. We've always had to push it. Not any more. Never before have I seen new business pitches for advertising accounts contain, as one did recently, an absolute condition that only agencies which have combined general advertising and direct marketing need submit.

Much more than this, all of the technology is moving in favour of direct marketing. Fibre optics is doing for the direct marketing industry what postcodes did more than 30 years ago. It is making possible in broadcast media, the true advent of one-to-one marketing. Direct Marketing is sitting on the edge of the biggest boom imaginable. There is no advertising agency, or marketing consultancy, in the world that can afford to any longer ignore it. It will become part of the armoury of every single person in the marketplace. There never was a better time to incorporate it into your business, your advertising agency, or your kitchen table operation.

The advertising agency of the future will not be a creator of mass media communications, but a business that provides marketing solutions. If you look at some of the very successful agencies in the U.S. you will see they are moving along this path. Not only do they embrace direct marketing, but also sales promotion, public relations, as well as general advertising.

Many of them have attached to the agency system, units that specialise in database management, and management systems, to measure the loyalty and relationship marketing achieved by their clients. As well, they have developed research units that specialise in the sort of direct testing and quantitative research needed by direct marketing. In reality, this is the development of seamless advertising—that is, you can't tell where one discipline begins and the other one stops. This marketing discipline, already inherent in some agencies, will become the norm. The latest buzz word is that there will be no distinction made in the importance of *above* the line and *below* the line. All the disciplines will simply be *through* the line. Clients should have no perception as to where the advertising ends and the direct marketing begins. And nor should there be a different method of charging for direct marketing, which has always been a problem because it is so labour intensive. There will be, as a matter of course, a direct marketing expert in every agency-planning meeting with the client.

We have reached the end of this book and, like any journey, getting to the destination has been the best part. When we started Bryce Courtenay said to me:

'Ian, I'm not going to write another bloody text book, the world is filled with information too dry, too smart-arse, too serious, too obtuse and too boring to take seriously into one's life. To add yet another such book should be declared a mortal sin.'

What we have tried to do instead, is to write a book you will not only find (instructional) but also one which represents the sum of a man's life experiences in business. We so often forget that business is part of life and is in no way different to any other path our lives may take.

Business isn't simply the means to have another life. It is what most of us do for most of the time we are alive and not asleep.

I have spent the larger part of my life in pursuit of one or another business end. Business, for me anyway, has been a completely full life with all the thrills and spills, the highs and lows. Several times, I've been a millionaire and as many time I've been totally broke. Sometimes, I've been both of these things in the same year, even the same month.

I have never, for one moment, believed that anything in life is free and I have always expected to work for the food on my table.

Having said all that, I have gambled on the outcome of my judgement and I have often stretched my luck to breaking point and sometimes beyond, when a million dollar gain has snapped from the strain and turned to a million dollar-plus loss.

But, always, because I thought of business as a grand adventure, as a chance to pit my skill and brains and guts against someone or something else, it was worth daring my particular genius, small though it was, to take the wildest unknown way.

When I found direct marketing, I realised that I had died and gone to heaven. It had all the ingredients of a grand and on-going adventure and one of which I have never for a moment grown weary.

This book has tried to outline that adventure for you as well as supply you with a good road map of Direct Marketing. Should you not care for the anecdotes at the beginning of each chapter, then simply skip them and read The Power of One to One as a book of instruction, which you will find every bit as detailed as most text books on the subject.

Don't be misled by the easy going nature of the book, as a text book it is as hard a task master as any you will ever be given in some pompous study program. In it is contained all the truth I know how to tell about a business that is, in business terms, the new frontier.

Direct Marketing is one of the few remaining businesses where you can still start at your kitchen table baking cookies, or mixing face cream, and have your small beginnings lead onto outrageous fortune. It is also a business which you can organise on a global scale with millions of dollars of technology and know-how and still be under-spent and not fully informed. But, mostly, it is a business about people, knowing and liking people. And ideas, knowing how to have them and how to take risks with them. Both the secrets, big and small are in this book, and they are as available to the office cleaner as they are to the chief executive of the company. Reach in and take what you need.

If you are a purist, you may see this book as neither fish nor flesh, not quite autobiographical and not quite a tome dedicated to instruction. But that's business for you—a bit of everything thrown in and, when you think about it, God is a generalist, anyway.

Direct Marketing is the business of throwing yourself into the thick of things. It is about taking a chance with your life, confident that if you plan well, think well, imagine well and work well, you will do well. And, mostly, you will. But that's the beauty of it— sometimes you won't. And, sometimes, you'll come across something so wonderful, so brilliant and so meaningful, that you will forget all the lessons and as Albert Sheinberg would say:

'Who knows? Tomorrow comes something , and you forget already to be clever!'

That something can make you a millionaire overnight or render you destitute. That something is the business of Direct Marketing, the most exciting business in the world and probably better even than sex. Come to think of it, at my age, definitely better than sex!

Thank you.

The End.

Ian Kennedy

Ian Kennedy. A direct marketing visionary. A man whose extraordinary insight into the business earned him the honour of Australian Direct Marketer of the Year.

Ian was one of the pioneers of direct marketing in Australia and in 1972 he founded Bond International—a company that's now at the forefront of Australian mail order.

With a direct marketing career spanning an incredible 25 years, Ian's 'guru' status in marketing circles is well deserved. In fact, he is often referred to as the father of Direct Marketing.

For over ten years, he was a member of the International Advisory Board of the Direct Marketing Association of America. He's given keynote and workshop presentations in over 15 countries, and was inducted into the Australian Direct Marketing Hall of Fame.

Ian's world-renowned one-day seminars in Australasia and South East Asia attract thousands of people and his unique business acumen saw him bring Polo Ralph Lauren to Australia in 1990.

But it's his involvement with The Starlight Foundation that sets him apart. Ian is the Chairman for this charity recognised for granting the wish of a seriously ill Australian child nearly every day.

A man of many talents and achievements, Ian is currently Chairman of K&D Bond Direct, one of the biggest direct marketing agencies in Australasia. Under his direction, this agency's clientele includes Australia's largest corporations.

There is little doubt, that Ian Kennedy is one of the world's leading direct marketers. His passion, his affinity for the industry and his unparalleled know-how comes to life on every page of this book.

Bryce Courtenay

Bryce Courtenay was born in 1933 in South Africa. He came to Australia in 1958 and a year later became an Australian citizen. He is married to Benita and with her raised three sons.

Courtenay began his advertising career with McCann Erickson at the age of 26 and was Australia's youngest creative director and a director of that company.

He remained with McCann for ten years whereupon he joined J. Walter Thompson as its creative director and he remained for a further five years before leaving to start his own agency which he sold to the international BBDO group. In 1987 Bryce joined George Patterson Advertising as a creative director. He retired at the end of 1993 to write full-time.

His first novel, *The Power of One*, is an international bestseller which has been translated into eleven languages, the latest being Japanese. It has now sold over two million copies. The movie of the book has been an international success. *The Power of One* is also the largest selling book by a living Australian author within Australia with over half a million copies sold locally. When compared with the next best selling *The Thorn Birds*, 170,000 copies sold locally over a period of thirteen years, this, in just four years, is a phenomenal record.

Bryce's second novel, *Tandia* has also been an international bestseller, and is now the second largest selling book by a living Australian author in his own country.

Courtenay's latest book, *April Fool's Day*, is a departure from fiction and is a biography of his youngest son who died in 1991 of medically acquired AIDS. It is already being described as his best work to date.

Bryce Courtenay has also been a columnist in a national newspaper, *The Australian*.

Bryce's new novel, the first book of a trilogy titled 'The Potato Factory' will be published in late 1995.